CRUSADER ONE

OTHER TITLES BY BRIAN ANDREWS AND JEFFREY WILSON

Tier One Thriller Series

Tier One
War Shadows

WRITING AS ALEX RYAN

Nick Foley Thriller Series

Beijing Red
Hong Kong Black

OTHER TITLES BY BRIAN ANDREWS

The Calypso Directive
The Infiltration Game

OTHER TITLES BY JEFFREY WILSON

The Traiteur's Ring
The Donors
Fade to Black

CRUSADER ONE

A TIER ONE THRILLER

ANDREWS & WILSON

THOMAS & MERCER

Published by Thomas & Mercer, Seattle

www.apub.com

Amazon, the Amazon logo, and Thomas & Mercer are trademarks of Amazon.com, Inc., or its affiliates.

ISBN-13: 9781477809051
ISBN-10: 1477809058

Cover design by Mike Heath | Magnus Creative

Printed in the United States of America

For Jim and Buz, men of action, honor, and character.
Terrific fathers who first taught us the value of service
and made us into the men we are. We love you.

PROLOGUE

Mediterranean Sea
October 23, 1995
0140 Local Time

Lieutenant Commander Kelso Jarvis ignored the burn—the burn in his quadriceps from this marathon finning session, the burn in his eyes from the salt water, and the burn in his lungs from exertion. He was a SEAL, and his capacity to overcome pain, fatigue, and injury with willpower was what separated him from the rest . . . the rest being pretty much everyone else. For men like him, it wasn't the desire to win—it was the refusal to lose. Under fire, under pressure, and under inhumane conditions, that refusal was the difference between victory and death. The outcomes of missions like the one he was leading were binary.

Bullets simply don't negotiate.

As he kicked, he arched his spine into an airfoil shape to minimize the drag of his pack through the water. He had precious little body fat left and was anything but buoyant, but with speed and body position, he could compensate. Choppy waves buffeted his torso, trying to roll him, but he used his hands like the ailerons on an airplane to counter the surface action and maintain stability. Despite the speed he was making through the water, the downward-curving fins he wore over ultra-low-profile combat boots never broke the surface, thereby ensuring a silent approach to the target.

Behind him, four members of the Israeli Defense Force's Shayetet 13—the IDF's equivalent of the US Navy SEALs—followed in a tight *V* formation. Under normal circumstances, these men would not fall under his chain of command. He was seven and a half weeks into a six-month Defense Personnel Exchange Program to facilitate cross-training between US and Israeli Special Operations. Until tonight, the program had tried his patience, leaving him languishing in a purgatory of inaction as an "observer" of field ops. This afternoon, after his request to join tonight's operation had already been rejected, something mysteriously changed. Not only had he been placed on the mission, but he was given command of a squad.

He had chosen not to question this divine providence, because this was where he belonged, leading from the tip of the spear. Like most SEALs, Jarvis had a visceral need to be in the action, but unlike most, he knew that he had been born for something more than just door kicking. This tour was about learning and teaching, but more important, it was about making connections. He had a destiny beyond the Teams, a destiny that would permit him to use *all* his gifts for the good of his nation.

And her allies.

Tonight's target, the *Muharram*, meaning *Forbidden* in Arabic, was a medium-size freighter anchored off the coast of Limassol, Cyprus. The Israeli Intelligence Corps had confirmed that the ship was carrying Iranian-supplied rockets destined for Gaza and the Palestinian Liberation Organization. For the IDF, a mission like this served two purposes: first, to intercept enemy rockets before they could rain down on Israel's civilian population, and second, to expose and stymie Muslim nations like Iran that supplied arms to terrorists bent on destroying the Jewish state. The implications of the Oslo Accord—a supposed declaration of peace between Israel and the PLO—being signed in Washington, DC, probably helped explain his host unit's reluctance to involve their American *guest* in this operation. Hopefully the person responsible for reversing the policy and letting him get wet would be revealed to him after the op.

Tonight, Jarvis and his four Shayetet 13 commandos—call sign Mercury—comprised the boarding party. Phase one of their mission objective was to board the *Muharram*, quietly and invisibly, and then provide eyes and fire support for the helicopter INFIL of an additional dozen operators—call sign Neptune. During the chaos of the assault, Mercury would then transition to phase two, securing the bridge and taking control of the vessel. It was a classic Tier One SEAL mission, the type of operation he'd conducted with his American unit many times. And even though he was a transplant tonight, he trusted the four operators with him implicitly. They were well-trained professionals with as much, if not more, operational experience as his own unit back home. *For us, the drive for perfection is born from necessity,* one of the Shayetet 13 operators had explained to him. *We sacrifice our lives so that Israel may persevere.*

They reached the stern of *Muharram* without detection. Jarvis looked up. From the water, the anchored vessel towered overhead, the freeboard at the stern equivalent to a three-story building. A fingernail crescent moon hung high in the hazy night sky. He decided that the moon, along with the ambient glow from the vessel's anchor lights, would provide just enough light that NVGs would not be necessary for the op. He finned to maintain a static hover, his head barely above the water, while his Israeli teammates moved in beside him. He slipped his goggles into a pouch on his vest, then checked his Suunto watch—they were ninety seconds early. During the brief hold, the team scanned the deck rails overhead for threats and indications they were being watched.

On the mark, Jarvis signaled to the operator beside him. The Israeli unstrapped a cylinder that looked like a tiny bazooka and aimed it upward. With a dull, quiet *whump*, a grappling projectile sailed skyward, arcing up and over the side of the ship, trailing a flexible assault ladder behind it. The hook landed on the deck with a soft thud, and then the Israeli commando slowly and methodically reeled in the nylon webbing until the rubber-coated tines of the hook snagged the rail. The operator tested the connection using his body weight. A beat later, he gave Jarvis a thumbs-up. Jarvis nodded and signaled to the others to commence boarding.

After securing his fins to his pack, Jarvis pulled himself up and onto the ladder. Constructed from black nylon strapping, the ladder had stiffeners woven inside the rungs to keep its rails from collapsing inward and regularly spaced, black rubber bumpers to minimize the noise against the side of the ship. Yet despite all its genius, the narrow, twisting ladder was a bitch to climb, and it took all his core strength to keep it from spinning and swaying as he ascended. Hand over hand he worked his way up, all the while fighting to keep his M4 assault rifle from clanging against the steel hull.

He reached the top and slid quietly over the rail onto the deck. Dropping into a combat kneel, he scanned his assigned sector for threats. The first two Shayetet assaulters had already cleared the immediate vicinity. Moments later, the remaining two commandos were up and on the deck beside him. The bridge tower of the *Muharram* was located aft of midships, creating an approximate sixty-forty split of the vessel's main deck, with two cranes forward and one crane aft. The ship's aft deck was flat to the stern, punctuated by two large cargo holds with removable covers to facilitate loading cargo below deck. The main deck was free of stacked cargo, thereby providing excellent sight lines in every direction. The five-man team quickly cleared the aft deck from the boarding point all the way to the stern without resistance or detection.

With the stern secure, Jarvis pointed at two of his men and chopped his hand left, right, and then forward. Then, he pointed to himself and gestured to a generator box located on the starboard side, approximately fifteen meters from the stern. Acknowledgment came via four silent nods, and then his team spread out as directed, with Mercury Four and Five remaining aft and Two and Three dashing forward to take up covered port and starboard positions along the outboard. Jarvis hunched beside the three-foot-tall metal generator box, covering his advancing teammates and scanning the bridge tower for movement and silhouettes.

Nothing.

He checked his watch and keyed his radio. "Neptune, Mercury One. In position," he whispered into the mike boom resting beside the right corner of his mouth. "Fantail is clear."

"Roger, Mercury One," came the reply in English from the lead Israeli chopper pilot. "Leaving orbit. Six minutes out."

Any minute now, two Israeli Yanshuf S-70A helicopters would materialize on the horizon. The helos would scream in low, hover over the deck just long enough for the Neptune assaulters to fast-rope in, and then bug out. Behind Neptune, two fast boats carrying additional QRF assaulters—call sign Jupiter—were standing by to help in the event things went to hell. Neptune's arrival would be the most dangerous part of the mission. When the birds showed up, the noise would alert the ship's crew to their presence. They'd lose their stealth, and during the drop, both the helos and the fast-roping assaulters would be vulnerable.

But Jarvis had a plan for this.

When two minutes had ticked by, he spoke into the mike again.

"Two and Three—forward with me. Four and Five, hold and cover."

The two forward operators popped up into combat crouches from hides where they had been completely invisible. They advanced swiftly and silently along the port and starboard rails, while Jarvis followed, drifting left to stay in the shadows. In a few seconds, Two and Three had reached the corners of the ship's main superstructure and cleared the narrow walkways that reached forward on either side. Two oval hatchways, both of which appeared to be shut, provided port and starboard side access to the bridge tower. The Israeli commandos took mirror-image positions, sighting around the corners toward the bow along the walkways. Jarvis dropped to a knee behind the base of a static crane and scanned again for human figures on the catwalks and in porthole windows on the superstructure. In his mind, a countdown timer silently ticked off the seconds in the background, an uncanny skill he'd first realized he possessed at the Naval Academy. At the two-minute mark, he keyed his mike. "Two, Three, reposition inboard."

He watched the two commandos check the side rails one last time and then move away from the corners, both taking a knee inboard of the hatches with their weapons at the ready.

He shifted his radio to VOX. "One minute."

The unmistakable thrum of helicopters on approach rumbled like a storm in the night. It wouldn't be long until the noise reverberated loud enough that it was audible inside the superstructure, and when that happened their enemy would finally wake up. A beat later, night turned to day on the main deck as *Muharram's* floodlights kicked on. An alarm wailed overhead, ear-piercing and angry. Jarvis spied movement on a catwalk high above him; a hatch swung open, and two men emerged holding assault rifles. Jarvis put the dot of his holosite on the forehead of the first shooter and squeezed the trigger, dropping the man. He shifted his aim to the second sniper and this time sent two rounds into the torso of the figure, who dropped his weapon and crumpled in a heap against the railing.

On the main deck, the port and starboard superstructure hatches flung open, and enemy sailors began pouring out onto the cargo deck with AK-47s at the ready.

"Two, Three—stand by. Shooters coming at you," he whispered. "Engage at will." Gunfire and muzzle flash erupted from his two commandos. In seconds, all thirteen AK-47-armed terrorists were bleeding on the deck, having gotten off only a few stray shots in the confusion.

Jarvis scanned the catwalks and bridge wings for more snipers. Seeing none, he said, "Two and Three . . . Commence phase two."

Behind him, the helos had arrived, and Neptune assaulters were executing their fast-rope drops. Jarvis sprinted toward the bridge tower as Two and Three breached the port and starboard hatches, disappearing out of sight. He anticipated a second wave of enemy shooters topside any moment. When he reached the bridge tower, he angled his weapon around the corner and fired several bursts along the port walkway, before popping his head around for a quick look.

Clear.

As he moved toward the hatch, gunfire erupted and bullets ricocheted and sparked around him. He glanced up and saw a shooter on a catwalk two levels up firing at him through the grating. A round from an unseen Israeli teammate took care of the problem, and he dashed through the open hatch into the superstructure unscathed. Scanning over his rifle, he had three choices: take a passage leading forward, take a passage leading athwartships, or take the ladder up. Schematics had shown the bridge on the 0-4 level, so he needed to go up. Two was nowhere in sight, which meant the Israeli operator had already advanced up to the 0-2 or possibly 0-3 level.

Jarvis climbed the ladder, sighting over his M4. Before he'd made it halfway up, gunfire erupted somewhere above. He paused a beat, and then, leading with his muzzle, he broke the plane to the next level. He cleared the passage left and right, only his torso sticking out of the ladder well. A door swung open and a bearded figure stepped out into the passage, still securing the sling to his rifle. When he saw Jarvis, the enemy crewman spun on a heel and ran. Jarvis's 5.56 round plowed through the back of the man's head and sent him pitching forward down the passage.

"One, Two. Set on level four," came a voice in his ear.

"Check," he said. "Coming to you."

More gunfire echoed above, heavier this time. "One, Three. Engaging."

Jarvis climbed a couple more ladders to the 0-4 level and joined Two, who was in a combat kneel sighting down the narrow port-side passageway leading to the bridge. The intensity of gunfire coming from the starboard side was picking up.

"Looks like we picked the easy side," Jarvis said with a wry grin.

"He's unlucky that way," the Shayetet commando said with a heavy Israeli accent, referring to Three. "Just ask his last several girlfriends."

"Poor bastard. I think we should give him a hand." Then into his mike boom, Jarvis said, "Three, One. Coming to you."

"Roger, One. I'm caught in a cross fire in the middle of the passage. I have a shooter forward, and a shooter aft."

"Copy, Three." Then, turning to Two, Jarvis chopped a hand forward. Next, he pointed to himself and chopped his hand toward the crossing passageway. "Let's flank them."

The Israeli nodded and they split—Two advancing and Jarvis crossing via the rearmost passage to the other side of the ship. He moved in a combat crouch, scanning over his weapon and pausing at a shut hatch in the middle of the passage. With Three caught in a cross fire, taking time to clear the room was problematic, but so was leaving himself open for an ambush from behind. With his left hand he pulled a tactical mirror from a pocket on his kit and angled it for view inside the porthole. The room appeared empty, so he checked that the hatch was dogged shut hard into its stop and then ducked to cross beneath the porthole. He advanced the remainder of the passage to the intersection, where he stopped and used the mirror for a glimpse around the corner. He saw Three pressed into an alcove on the port bulkhead, ducking behind a water fountain and taking fire from both sides.

Muzzle flares flashed at the forward end of the passage.

There's the forward shooter . . .

A beat later, he watched a torso angle out from a nearby doorway, fire a burst up the passage at Three, and then disappear behind a door frame.

And that's the aft shooter.

Jarvis commenced a silent count: *One, two, three . . .*

AK-47 gunfire—*forward shooter.*

Four, five . . .

Return fire—*that's Three.*

Six, seven.

AK-47 gunfire—*and the aft shooter.*

Jarvis dropped to a knee, exhaled, and started the count anew. On the three count, AK-47 rounds ripped down the passage, starting the pattern over again.

Four, five . . .

Jarvis leaned out into the passageway, sighting at the spot where he'd just seen the aft gunman. He waited, tension on the trigger . . .

A head full of shaggy hair emerged.

Jarvis squeezed off a round.

The top of the head exploded in a red cloud, and the man slid down the door frame to the floor. Jarvis pulled back around the corner and checked his six, verifying the hatch behind him was still shut. A beat later, gunfire popped toward the front of the long passage.

"One, Two," came the report over the wireless. "Forward shooter is dead."

With both enemy shooters down, Jarvis moved swiftly around the corner and up the passageway to Three, scanning over his rifle. "You okay?" he asked, crouching beside the Israeli operator, who was still dug in next to the water fountain.

The commando nodded tightly but pointed to where a red stain was growing on the thigh of his gray tactical pants.

"Artery or bone?" Jarvis asked.

The operator shook his head. "Just a graze. I'm operational."

"Two, One. I'm going to breach with Three on starboard. You go port."

"Copy. Repositioning to port."

Taking the lead, Jarvis and Three moved forward along the passage toward the bridge, clearing two crossing passages en route. When they reached the hatch to the bridge, Jarvis pressed his back to the bulkhead and used his tactical mirror to survey the bridge through the porthole window in the hatch.

"Two shooters in the forward port corner and one in the forward starboard corner. One crewman at the helm, another on a radio with a rifle beside him, and then a man seated between them—probably the captain," he reported softly into his mike. "Can't see the rear corners."

A double-click in his ear told him that Two copied the report.

Jarvis watched and waited as Three prepped a breacher charge beside the hinges on the hatch. In his mind, Jarvis pictured Two performing the exact same operation in mirror image. Once the charge was set, Three glanced at Jarvis. Wordlessly, they both repositioned clear of the blast arc.

"Set," Two reported a beat later.

Jarvis lowered his head, looked away, and said, "On my mark—three . . . two . . . one . . ."

The breacher detonation roared in the narrow metal passageway, the concussive shock wave hitting Jarvis in the chest like a club. He turned in time to see the hatch tumble into the bridge, blown completely off its hinges. Without missing a beat, he was up and moving into the bridge. He spun right first, killing the shooter he'd seen in the forward starboard corner. Next, he swung his M4 left and used a headshot to down one of two shooters in the forward port corner, at the same time as Two took out the other. In his peripheral vision, he saw Three clearing the rear starboard corner. He crouched low and continued to spin toward the helm. An AK-47 barked and a 7.62 round smacked the steel bulkhead just over his head. The higher-pitched double crack of an

M4 discharging behind him ended that threat, but a different bearded crewman lunged and grabbed the barrel of Jarvis's M4 midswing. At the same time, the bearded fighter drew a revolver from a thigh holster. Jarvis stepped in and smashed his helmet into the man's nose and followed with a knee strike to the groin. The pistol discharged, sending a round into the floor. Jarvis stepped left, crashed his forearm down on the back of the man's wrist, breaking the bone and freeing his weapon. He dropped his shoulder and took a knee, then squeezed off two rounds with upward trajectories, the first blowing out the crewman's jaw and the second exiting the crown of the head.

The Captain barked surrender in Arabic, and both he and the helmsman threw their hands up in defeat. The crewman manning the radio, however, was too slow and took a bullet in the temple from Three.

"Bridge is secure," Jarvis said as his teammates forced the remaining two men onto their faces.

"Fantail secure," came the reply from a voice he recognized as Four.

"Mercury, this is Neptune. We have confirmed Ophelia in the cargo hold," a new voice added, using the code word for the illegal Iranian arms shipment.

"Check," Jarvis said. "Any CASEVAC?"

"Negative, Mercury," said Neptune. "Just a minor ankle injury."

"Roger. We have a non-urgent flesh wound here," Jarvis said. "Ready for EXFIL."

"Copy. We have a helo en route, nine mikes out, with a proxy crew to take control of the ship. We'll EXFIL the two wounded on that bird and everyone else will EXFIL as briefed."

"Roger that, Neptune. Nice work," Jarvis said.

"You, too, Mercury. Not bad for a Yank."

Jarvis lowered the barrel of his M4 until it pointed at the floor. He checked his watch and then let himself smile. They'd conducted a flawless ship takedown in less than ten minutes from initial boarding.

The Israeli proxy crew would be here soon to sail the ship to Haifa and confiscate the rockets that had been intended for terrorists. Tonight, millions of Israelis were sleeping a little easier, but none of them would ever know the reason why.

The next six hours passed in a blur as the survivors were taken off the ship, the command of the vessel passed to the Israeli Navy, and endless checks were conducted by the security detail. Jarvis felt a new sense of camaraderie and respect from the rest of the Shayetet 13 commandos as they flew together by helicopter back to base. Not only did he feel like part of the team now; he felt like a brother. After stowing their gear and debriefing with the Head Shed, they were free until the 2000 briefing. After checking in on the Israeli operator designated as Three to make sure the man's thigh wound had been patched up okay, Jarvis stepped out into the light of day. But before wandering back to his very dark and very cold air-conditioned room to grab some well-deserved rack time, he needed to work out the knots from the tension of combat. Some guys hit the weights, others put on their running shoes, but Jarvis's preferred means of decompression was an open-water three-mile swim. And so with goggles and fins in hand, he made his way to the beach in front of the base.

As he stripped off his shirt, a voice behind him said, "There's a wonderful gym on the base, I'm told."

Jarvis didn't look over at the thin, middle-aged Israeli smoking a cigarette and sitting on a nearby rock. He'd already decided that the man's presence was of no immediate concern—especially here, on a beach secured by the Shayetet 13. Nevertheless, the man had garnered Jarvis's attention, because he was the only person on the beach dressed in slacks and a starched shirt. He was no Shayetet commando, this man, but Jarvis had assigned him an 85 percent probability of being a spook.

"I imagine that most of the Shayetet maritime commandos are probably there now, if you're looking for company," the man continued.

"I'm not," Jarvis said, looking over, and set his brain to work trying to match this man's face with everyone he'd met, seen in pictures, or surveilled. A beat later he had it; this guy had been in the TOC during last night's pre-mission brief, standing quietly by the back door, chain-smoking.

The Israeli stood and flicked the filterless cigarette toward the rolling surf. It landed on the wet sand, rolled a half foot, and then lay smoldering until a wave took it.

"Those things will kill you," Jarvis said.

"So they tell me," the man said with a wry smile. "But in my line of work, to live long enough to die from cancer would mean only one thing."

"And what's that?"

"That I was a miserable failure."

Jarvis laughed and decided he liked this spook.

The Israeli took a step toward him and extended his hand. "Levi Harel."

Jarvis clasped the other man's hand. "Kelso Jarvis."

"Nice to meet you, Commander. Shayetet 13 has much they can learn from one of JSOC's Tier One SEALs. I hope they are taking advantage of the opportunity."

Jarvis scanned Harel's face, probing for subtext or insincerity, but found none, and so he worded his reply accordingly. "I think there's much we can learn from each other."

Harel nodded. "Indeed, indeed . . . Learning from each other is exactly the reason you are here as opposed to one of a half-dozen other Tier One operators who applied for the exchange program. I must confess, I've had my eye on you for some time—congratulations on selecting for O-5, incidentally."

Apparently, this *chance* encounter was clearly anything but. "It seems you've caught me at a disadvantage, Mr. Harel," Jarvis replied.

"You've clearly done your homework on me, but I wasn't afforded the same opportunity."

"I'm sorry," Harel said. "It's a terrible habit. My staff tells me I'm always playing games, but I say life is too short not to play games. Besides, how we play says more about us than how we fight."

"If that's your philosophy, then maybe for your next exchange program billet you should request someone from Navy Morale Welfare and Recreation instead of from the Tier One. MWR is all about fun and games."

"See, there you go," Harel said with a chuckle. "I knew you had a sense of humor hiding in that commando body of yours."

Jarvis sighed. "As fun as trading jokes with you is, I've got a three-mile swim to do. So, if you'll excuse me . . ."

"Not a problem. Go enjoy your swim. We can talk about your future another time," Harel said. "When you're not *busy*."

"Are you always like this?" Jarvis said, shaking his head.

Harel shrugged. "Yes."

"In that case, what about my future is Mossad so interested in?"

"Not Mossad, just me. In our current positions, we are instruments of policy. But down the road, men like us must transition or we become irrelevant."

Jarvis narrowed his eyes, intrigued. "And by transition you're speaking of command?"

"I was going to say that we must transition from being instruments of policy to the architects of policy, but command works, too," Harel said, fishing another cigarette from his pack. "Very American construct, command."

"So you're out here on the beach this morning to recruit me to be your—what? Your American mole in JSOC?"

Harel screwed up his face at this and made an angry *pffttt* sound. "There's no reason to insult me. I'm not looking for a mole. I'm here because I was hoping to forge an alliance. The day will come when we'll both need a friend on the other side. I believe our countries share something much more intimate than defense contracts and Hanukkah."

"And what's that?"

"We share enemies, my friend. Enemies everywhere."

Jarvis met Harel's gaze, and in the other man's eyes he saw integrity, wisdom, and hope. "It was you, wasn't it?" he asked. "You're the reason they put me on last night's stick."

The spook flashed him a sly grin. "What's the point of the exchange program if Shayetet is going to keep you locked up in the TOC? Like I said, there is much we can learn from each other. Allies work together. Allies fight together."

Jarvis flashed Harel a smile of his own. "You ever heard of Texas Hold'em?"

Harel shook his head. "No."

"It's a poker game. Maybe after the 2000 brief, if there's nothing going on, we could grab a beer and I'll teach you. After all, you like playing games."

Harel nudged a new cigarette from the pack. "I accept, under one condition."

"What's that?"

"Beers are on me," Harel said, turned, and walked away.

He watched the man head up the beach toward Chateau Pelerin—the castle that rose like a fortress from the center of Atlit Naval Base. As the Mossad spy disappeared from view, Jarvis replayed in his mind the most profound snippet of their conversation.

We share enemies, my friend. Enemies everywhere.

PART I

Never underestimate the power of murder.

—*Arkady Zhukov*

CHAPTER 1

Present Day
Key West, Florida
April 8
0830 Local Time

Dempsey squinted against the glare of the morning sun.

Despite it being April, and despite it being early, he could already tell that today was going to be a hot one. A bead of sweat ran down his back between his shoulder blades.

Hot *and* muggy.

Things could be worse, he told himself. *I could be in Iraq.*

Key West was a ghost town this time of day. The streets were deserted, the town's all-night revelers having long since found a bed to pass out in—their own, or that of a willing stranger. On the horizon, beyond where Greene Street dead-ended at Front Street, he could make out the marina and its docks stretching like fingers into the blue. The Keys formed the boundary line separating the warm waters of the Gulf of Mexico from the Atlantic, and the mixing of currents helped support a vibrant marine ecology. But he wasn't here on vacation. No snorkeling or deep-sea fishing for him today. He was in Key West on business. Ember business.

His target was inside Captain Tony's Saloon. As he scanned the area, the cool metal of the Sig Sauer 229 against the small of his back reminded him not to take anything for granted. It was extremely unlikely that either he or his target was being surveilled, but the events of the past few months had proven that simply being on American soil did not guarantee his safety.

He slipped on his wraparound sunglasses and turned right, walking down Greene Street toward the corner and adding a tired stumble to his gait for anyone who might be watching from behind a window or inside a parked car. He pulled out his phone as he approached the corner and made a show of rotating and repositioning the screen for optimal viewing in the sunlight, when in fact his real objective was to scan the street and check his six. Satisfied, he walked to the corner of Telegraph Lane, where he stopped and leaned against the newspaper box, this time pretending to make a call while checking the next block. He spied a single car pulled in tight to the curb, facing him on the one-way street, and despite the tinted windows, he saw motion inside.

He crossed the street, heading south on Telegraph and pretending to talk on the phone, all the while keeping his eyes fixed on the car. As he approached, he could hear that the engine was running. And the driver, a twentysomething male, was watching him.

Dempsey lowered the phone from his ear and reached around to slip it in a back pocket—putting his hand inches from his pistol. Suddenly, the rear driver-side door popped open. Dempsey's hand went immediately to grip his Sig and his body came alive with adrenaline. He squared his shoulders to the vehicle, readying himself for whatever threat climbed out.

A bare foot with brightly painted toenails appeared below the doorsill, followed a beat later by another.

"You are such an asshole, Doug," a young woman hollered as she stumbled out of the car onto the sidewalk.

She slammed the door, and when she saw Dempsey looking at her, she smiled and attempted to straighten her tangled hair. With blushing cheeks, she crossed the street and headed north on Telegraph as the car pulled away from the curb. The driver beeped twice at the girl, who waved and then turned left on Greene Street and disappeared.

Dempsey released his grip on the pistol and let his arm fall to his side. With no other cars, and no suspicious characters loitering in the vicinity of Captain Tony's Saloon, he decided it was time to head inside. There was absolutely no telling how this encounter was going to go, so he readied himself for the worst.

As he stepped inside, he expected to be hit by a blast of cool AC, but the bar wasn't running any air-conditioning. He slipped off his sunglasses, pausing a beat to let his eyes adjust to the dim ambient light. He quickly checked the exits, having scouted the place in advance yesterday. Three middle-aged women occupied a booth to his left. They looked sunburned, haggard from lack of sleep, and hungover. The only other patron in the joint sat on a stool at the bar, his hunched back callously turned to the entry. Overhead, hundreds of bras—donated over the years by inebriated female patrons—swayed gently in the breeze.

"Sit anywhere youz like," the overweight barkeep said without looking up.

Dempsey nodded and feigned indecision about where to sit. Meanwhile, the bartender shifted his attention to the hunched figure on the stool.

"Rough night, Doc?" the bartender asked.

"Yeah," the man groaned. "Coffee, Mike."

"Sure thing." The barkeep laughed, filling a mug with coffee. "I hope last night ended with you landing a hot-bodied chick in your bed for once."

The man grumbled something inaudible in reply, and Captain Tony waddled into the kitchen. Dempsey walked to the bar, not happy that the initial approach would require him to place his back to the door. With a final glance at the entrance, he took the stool beside his target, keeping one foot on the ground, ready to move and react if needed. His gaze fell to the small tattoo on the man's left wrist—a SEAL trident with six stars underneath.

Dan Munn looked older than Dempsey remembered. And thinner by at least twenty pounds. The last time he'd seen his friend was in the hospital, when the former SEAL turned Special Warfare Surgeon was overseeing Jack Kemper's recovery from spine surgery after he'd broken his back on a mission with his old unit. That was only a year ago, but it felt like a lifetime. So much change. So much pain and regret. Dempsey swallowed. Munn hadn't met John Dempsey yet, and he wondered what would happen when his former teammate looked at him. Would recognition flash in his friend's eyes? Would Munn's eyes fall to the serpentine scar on Dempsey's left forearm, an un-erasable mark of the SEAL he'd once been? Would their bond, forged in the kilns of violence and brotherhood, allow Munn to see past the modifications made to his face by the plastic surgeon's scalpel?

He blew air through his teeth; he was about to find out.

Dempsey placed a gentle hand on his broken friend's shoulder. "You look like shit, Munn," he said. "Too many margaritas last night?"

Munn's eyes sprung open, but he didn't look over; his face was frozen, as if he'd just heard the voice of a ghost.

"Jack?" he whispered, keeping his gaze straight ahead.

"Yeah, Dan. It's me."

Munn turned his head slowly, his eyes wide with what looked more like terror than surprise. "Jack?" he said again, this time with a trembling voice. He blinked hard several times, and looked confused when Dempsey didn't disappear. "But you're dead. I saw your coffin in the hangar. I went to the funeral. Kate and Jacob were there . . ."

"Jack Kemper is dead, my friend, dead and buried," he said as gently as possible. "You can call me Dempsey now—John Dempsey."

Munn's face turned red, and for a moment, Dempsey thought the man might be having a heart attack. But Munn spun off the stool with speed that took Dempsey by surprise—as did the force with which his fist flew toward the side of Dempsey's face. He parried the blow with his right forearm, rotated his grip, and clutched Munn's wrist. He pulled the last of his surviving Tier One SEAL brothers close.

"Stop it," he ordered as the surgeon stumbled from the bar stool. "It's me. Dan, it's me; I swear to God."

Munn shifted into a tactical stance they'd learned in the Teams and glared at him, his glazed and drunken eyes now alive and full of fire.

"You sick son of a bitch," Munn said, spittle flying from his lips and his drunken slur now barely noticeable. The surgeon swung again. This time, Dempsey chose not to block the punch; instead, he turned his head just before impact to lessen the blow. Still, he tasted coppery blood as the inside of his cheek split against his teeth. He dropped to a knee, both for effect and also hoping to preempt another blow. Munn needed to get a swing in, but Dempsey wasn't keen on taking another punch.

"How could you fucking do that to me, Jack? How could you let me think you were dead? How could you fuckin' . . ." Munn choked on the words and tears streamed down his cheeks. "I died that day. I died with you and everyone else. I died with Thiel and Spaz and Pablo. My marriage died. You fucking asshole. How could you not tell me you survived?"

Munn's fists were balled at his sides, but Dempsey had the sense Munn was done throwing punches for now.

"What the hell is going on here?" a voice boomed from behind the bar. "Everything okay, Doc?"

"It's okay," Dempsey said, his hands raised to Munn in surrender. He watched as Captain Tony reached under the bar—presumably for the loaded handgun he concealed there. "I'm a friend of Doc Munn's. Isn't that right, Dan?" Dempsey asked, rising back to his feet.

Munn stared back, his eyes full of rage, but said nothing.

"He don't look like any friend of yours, mister. So why don't you get the hell out of here before I call the cops."

Munn's shoulders sagged. Then he dropped to the floor, landing cross-legged before Dempsey. "It's okay, Tony," he mumbled to the barkeep. "I know him." There was a pause, and then Munn looked up, red-eyed. "This man was my friend, but he sure as hell ain't my friend anymore."

Dempsey reached a hand down to the former frogman. "Let's go grab some breakfast and talk."

"I've got nothing to say to you."

"I know, but I've got plenty to say to you, and it starts with an apology. I'm sorry for what I just put you through, and I'm sorry for bringing back all the pain. I know how you feel, because I lost everyone, too. And I had to suffer alone, just like you. But now I'm here, and regardless of what you might think, we're still brothers."

"How?" Munn asked. "How'd you pull it off?"

Dempsey answered the complicated question in a single word. "Jarvis."

Munn reached up and let Dempsey pull him to his feet, but then shook his hand free.

"I'd like to pay his tab," Dempsey said, turning to the bar owner.

Captain Tony snorted. "Today's or the whole thing?"

Dempsey laughed and looked at Munn, but the man was staring at the floor.

"The whole thing," he said and handed over a credit card.

"Well, you're sure as shit a friend now," the big man said with a chuckle, taking the card. "Sorry, Doc," he added.

Munn waved his hand over his shoulder but didn't turn around.

Dempsey signed the receipt for the $500 tab and added an absurdly generous tip.

"Shit, make that my new *best* friend," Tony said, taking the receipt and handing back his card. "See you tomorrow, Doc."

"I doubt it," Dempsey said with a smile. "Thanks for being a friend to him."

"You taking him somewhere?" the bartender asked.

Dempsey put his arm around Munn's hunched shoulders, and as he led him out of the bar, he looked over his shoulder and said, "Yeah, I'm taking him home."

Munn hissed like some creature of the night and shielded his eyes as they stepped outside into the light of day. Dempsey led the doc to a restaurant across the street and selected a table in the back, seating Munn between him and the door so he could keep his friend's six clear. The waitress stopped by a beat later, and Dempsey ordered two black coffees and two breakfast scrambles.

"So, I hear you're working in a VD clinic," Dempsey said, breaking the silence.

"It's not a fucking VD clinic," Munn grumbled. "It's an urgent care center. I take care of all kinds of shit."

"Sure, on paper," Dempsey said, defaulting to the ribbing that had carried them through many a tough mission on the Teams. "But the word on Duvall Street is that if you have the clap, then you go see Doc Munn on the night shift."

"Or if you need stitches," Munn countered, with more than a little irritation.

"Or have a foreign object wedged in an incompatible orifice."

"Or are having a heart attack," Munn said.

The coffees arrived, and Munn greedily took a long swallow. Then he looked down, and Dempsey watched him start picking at the gusset stitching along the knee of his Ridgeline pant. The doc was either planning his next zinger or drifting back to his dark place; Dempsey couldn't tell which.

"I'm not accusing you of *having* VD, Dan, just taking care of people with it," Dempsey said, grinning.

"Yeah, well, no different than taking care of Spaz back in the day, right?" Munn chuckled before catching himself. Dempsey watched his face cloud over again.

"Yeah," Dempsey said and let the silence that followed hang in the air while Munn wrestled his demons. With the massacre of the Tier One SEALs during Operation Crusader, they'd both lost their brotherhood. "It's okay to remember them," he said at last. "You just can't let yourself get sucked down the vortex every time you do."

Munn looked up at him, the fog in his eyes now burned completely away by emotional and chemical sobriety. "How did you survive, Jack?" Munn whispered, watching the bartender putting away glasses and restocking her beer fridge for the next onslaught in a few hours. "You were in the TOC in Djibouti. It was hit right after the ambush in Yemen. Everyone was killed. Everyone. How did you manage to get out?" Then, something like an epiphany washed over his face. "Or . . . were you never actually there?"

"Oh, I was there, all right . . ." Dempsey said, his voice trailing off while he decided what to say next. Certain questions needed to be answered for Munn to be of any value to Ember. The taste of that was bitter—doling out just enough information to ensure his lifelong friend became an asset of *value*. He swallowed down the revulsion at the cold spook he was becoming and reminded himself that there was a methodology to the madness. The same methodology Shane Smith had used on him. Right now, Munn needed purpose. Right now, Munn needed tough love. It was okay to throw the headshrinker handbook at his friend. If he failed, Munn would end up hunched over on some other bar stool, in some other bar, by some other beach. Dempsey couldn't let that happen.

He leaned in, his elbows on the table, and held Munn's gaze. "I know you have questions, and I'm gonna answer them as best I can, but first," he said, and it hurt to have to say it, "I need you to call me Dempsey. I know that's hard. It's even harder for me." He realized as he spoke that it wasn't as hard as it used to be. In some ways, he barely remembered Jack Kemper, the man he'd been when Munn last saw him. "Call me John, or Dempsey, or JD—but Jack Kemper is dead."

"So, you're a full-fledged fucking Jones now, is that it?" Munn asked.

The words stung. As SEALs they had both shared a disdain for the spooks who breezed in with their fake names and half-truths and jacked up their Tier One operations. But then Jarvis had pulled back the curtains and let him look at the big picture that had been obscured from him his entire career as an operator.

Dempsey shrugged. "Yeah, I guess I am," he said. "But John Dempsey knows things that Jack Kemper never did. The world don't work the way we thought it did in the Teams."

"Ah, fuck that bullshit. They got you brainwashed, Kemp."

"It's Dempsey, and no, Dan, they don't. We both felt it before, but we chose to ignore it. Life is easier in black and white. Gray is fucking hard. Besides, do you really think that the people pulling the strings are morons? They're not. That's the lie we tell ourselves; it makes us feel better about our notch on the totem pole. At Ember, we can accomplish more in one week to neutralize a threat than we could have accomplished with a whole deployment back in the day."

"And you work for Jarvis?" Munn asked, his tone finally taking on a conciliatory note.

Dempsey leaned back and crossed his legs. "Yep."

That would go a long way with Munn. It had with him. Hell, it would with anyone who had ever served under Captain Kelso Jarvis, the legendary SEAL officer and Tier One operator.

Munn shook his head. "I knew Jarvis wasn't just saying hi that day in the hospital in Tampa when you were recovering from spine surgery. He was recruiting you even then, huh?"

The conversation stopped as the waitress walked up carrying their breakfast. As she set the two steaming egg scrambles down in front of them and left, Dempsey let his mind drift back to that day in the hospital. The memory was foggy now, like a fading dream. Had Jarvis been recruiting him? The Skipper *had* given him a card that day, but he'd been on pain meds, and the nuance of the exchange was probably lost on him. "I don't know," he said. "I suppose he might have been—recruiting me for the future. At that time, Ember didn't even exist. It rose from the ashes of Yemen and Djibouti—the tragedy that was Operation Crusader. I was the only one left alive from our unit to recruit."

"So, what do you—what does this Ember—need from me?" Munn asked.

"I think . . . we need each other, Dan," Dempsey said. Munn raised an eyebrow but said nothing. "I need you to help grow and develop my team. I need you to round out what is becoming the best frontline defense against the universe of threats trying to bring our country to its knees. Mostly I need you to help me finish what I started—to help me bury the last of the assholes who murdered our brothers."

He could tell that his words resonated with Munn, who nodded and straightened a bit in his chair.

"And what is it that I supposedly need from you?"

"A reason to get out of bed in the morning," Dempsey replied.

Munn nodded; he didn't even try to argue this time. "So, I would be the medical support for your operational unit in this, this Ember thing?"

"No," Dempsey said, shaking his head. "Your surgical skills and trauma experience will be invaluable, obviously. As will your scientific mind. Baldwin will love you, by the way," he said with a chuckle.

"Who's Baldwin?"

"We'll get to that if you decide to move forward," Dempsey said, holding up a hand. "We are an insanely small task force and don't have the luxury of having anyone just hanging out in case someone gets hurt. So no, I'm recruiting you for something above and beyond med support. We need your skills as an operator and your mind as a tactician every bit as much as we need your surgical skills."

Munn took that in as Dempsey's thoughts drifted back to the terrorist attack in the Old Town Market in Omaha six months ago. Dan Munn the combat surgeon would have been the perfect teammate at his side that day. Yes, the future held an unlimited number of prospects for a man like Munn.

"Wait . . . I would function as an operator?"

Dempsey nodded. "Operator, field medic, tech guru, intelligence analyst, spy—everyone on the team cross-trains to wear multiple hats."

"I don't know, dude," Munn said with a sigh. "In case you've forgotten, it's been a while since I kitted up. This body ain't the same one I took down range back in the day. I'm fucking old, bro."

"Naaaah, old is a state of mind. Look at me."

"Yeah, *look* at you," Munn said and laughed. "You're forty, right?"

"Thirty-fucking-nine, thank you very much," Dempsey growled. "And I'm in peak physical condition . . . for a man my age."

They both were laughing hard now.

The waitress returned, tossing her hair and smiling. "Can I get you beautiful men something harder to drink? A Bloody Mary maybe?"

Dempsey smiled up at her. "Just more coffee," he said, glancing at Munn to gauge just how strong the pull for alcohol may have become. Munn just nodded, lost in thought. She filled their mugs and left the brown plastic pot behind this time.

"What about oversight?" Munn asked, leaning in, his voice enthusiastic and conspiratorial now.

"We work directly for Jarvis."

"And what paper-pushing pogue does he report to?"

"Direct line to the Director of National Intelligence," Dempsey said. "No red tape. No bullshit. Ember is off the grid. It's far more secret than even the Tier One. There's no glass prison. No information blackout. We have the autonomy and the budget to get shit done—on time, on target."

"And you guys are hunting down the assholes who wiped out our brothers?"

Dempsey nodded. "Among other things, yes." If it were up to him, they would do nothing else but hunt down the enemy who had killed their brothers. But that was not how it worked.

"Have you gotten any of them?"

Dempsey smiled broadly. "Oh yeah. And we recently bagged a blast from the past who killed another buddy of ours."

"Who?"

"Romeo."

Munn's eyes widened. "You killed Mahmood Bin Jabbar?" he said, clearly astonished. "After all these years?"

"When we found him, he was using a different name and fighting under the ISIS flag, but we bagged him and his friends, disrupting a massive terror attack here in the States."

"That shit in Nebraska and Atlanta? That was you guys? They said it was an FBI task force."

"That's our MO," he said. "It's just like the old days in the Tier One. We can't take credit for shit we do since Ember doesn't exist. Right?"

"Right," Munn said, nodding. He locked eyes with Dempsey. "Okay, count me in. What now?"

Dempsey took a deep breath and then said, "Before we get on the plane, I need you to be sure. There's no going back from Task Force Ember. I can't *read* you in, unless you're *all* in."

"I work at a VD clinic, remember? There's nothing here to go back to." The SEAL-turned-surgeon held out his hand and Dempsey grasped it. "You're sure?"

"One hundred percent," Munn said. "I'm in, Mr. Dempsey. All in."

CHAPTER 2

Never underestimate the power of murder. It is the ultimate tool, but one rife with contradiction. For those with political agendas, it can be used as either a catalyst or as a suffocant. For those seeking power, it can be used to destroy the status quo or to preserve it. And for men like us to survive, our quarries must die. Fail to understand the nature of murder and you will never achieve mastery of our craft.

That was what the Russian had said to him after confiscating his gun and mobile phone and kicking him out of the Renault hatchback miles from the park where his final assignment awaited. Dispatch the target and his training was over. Fail, and he wasn't sure what would happen to him. This was not a business of second chances, and back in Tehran, his uncle was growing impatient.

He wasn't surprised that Arkady had taken his gun and his phone. The Russian spymaster was a product of the Cold War and a devout disciple of the *old ways. Reliance on technology and firepower makes for a lazy, stupid spy,* the old bear liked to say. At the moment, Cyrus Modiri was inclined to agree, because he desperately wished he had both items back in his possession. He'd spent the last three weeks being drilled and tested on how to dispatch an enemy with weapons of opportunity. It only made sense that this mission would test his cunning and creativity rather than the rote application of firearms, knives, and explosives. Arkady had given him no choice but to embrace the impotency of his circumstances and figure out how to use it to his advantage. It was up to him to find strength in weakness, and over the past hour he had seized an ironic opportunity the universe offered him to do just that.

He glanced down at the toy poodle tethered to him via an eye-rolling, gaudy leash—white patent leather studded with faux jewels. The dog was walking in fits and starts, always stopping and looking back, insecure and uncertain in the relationship with its new master. The dog looked up at him now, open mouthed, and wagged its furry white tail expectantly. Cyrus tossed the creature a treat, which it snatched in midflight. The dog, whose name he did not know, had stopped barking and pulling thirty minutes ago. Its allegiance and obedience had been obtained easily with a single silencing blow to establish dominance, followed by measured affection and periodic food rewards. The animal was his now, despite how initially upset it had been watching its previous owner murdered in front of it.

The instant Cyrus had spotted the blatantly gay man walking on the opposite side of the street, a plan had formulated in his head. *Strength in weakness.* Since the forced Russian annexation, there was no place for gays in Petrov's Crimea. In the aftermath of the coup, Serge Askinov, Crimea's self-proclaimed leader, used his pro-Russian "self-defense" squads to drive the homosexual community out of the peninsula. Gays who chose to stay had been forced underground or risked a beating . . . and yet here this man was, strutting the streets of Simferopol and spitting in the face of suppression. This man was impossible not to notice, and therefore the perfect cover persona for the assignment. Cyrus figured his target would be on the lookout for dark, lurking figures. So instead of hiding in the shadows, he had decided to hide in plain sight.

Cyrus had followed the young man back to his apartment and murdered him at the threshold—severing his spinal cord with a sharp twist of the head as the youth knelt to kiss the dog. Cyrus had then dragged the body inside, stripped it naked, and arranged it under a running shower. A decent medical examiner would determine that the man had not slipped in his shower and broken his neck, but that would be days from now, and besides . . . who in the Simferopol Police would care about some dead sodomizer? By the time anyone connected the dots—*if* they connected the dots—he would be safely back in Tehran.

The dead man's clothes—a blue leather jacket and black jeans—were uncomfortably tight. But Cyrus forced himself to embrace the feeling because it served the caricature he was trying to portray. He sashayed his hips, just as he had observed the gay man doing while walking down the sidewalk. He talked to the little dog in French, because despite his time with Arkady, his Russian was dreadful. He spoke French nearly as well as Farsi. Besides, French was appropriate in this circumstance, an effeminate language for an effeminate man with an effeminate dog. He couldn't help but smile at the cleverness of it all as he walked through the park to meet his imaginary lover under the cover of darkness—a forbidden relationship, but one he'd risk a beating for. He wasn't going to stop being gay just because some Russian megalomaniac stole his beloved Crimea. And when he felt a surge of angry indignation at this thought, he knew he was fully in character and he could move on his mark.

He found a bench near the meeting site and took a seat. This would be his first assassination, though not his first murder. His initial teacher, VEVAK's wet-work specialist Behrouz Rostami, had insisted that Cyrus demonstrate the resolve to kill on his first day of training in Tehran. Back then he had been hesitant—tentative.

What has this man done? he'd asked, staring at the hooded prisoner who was bound to a chair in the corner of a dark and dirty cell. *That is not your concern,* Rostami had replied. *It matters only that your orders are to kill him. This is your new life. This is how it will be. What you do now, you do for Persia and for Allah. What you do now, you do for your mother.*

It was the latter that had compelled him.

He remembered raising the pistol and aiming it at the bulge under the black hood. He remembered hesitating. He remembered feeling sick. And he remembered squeezing the trigger anyway. He'd fired once, and then as thoughts of his murdered father and the brother he'd lost to the Navy SEALs during a mission to provide arms to Iran's allies flooded his mind, he'd unloaded more bullets into the faceless hood. With tears streaming down his cheeks, he'd squeezed the trigger until the magazine was empty. And then, he'd kept on squeezing, until Rostami took the gun away from him.

His thoughts drifted to his dead doppelganger, lying naked with a broken neck in the shower. Ten months ago, in that prison cell in Iran, Cyrus had felt remorse. Now, he felt nothing. How far he had come. Rostami's training had been ripe with passion and emotion, fueled by purpose, and driven by commitment to God and country. Arkady Zhukov's had been cold, clinical, and detached. For the Russian, murder was a tool, used methodically and without passion or ethos; killing was a craft, not a calling. Arkady had completed the evolution that Rostami had set in motion.

Cyrus suddenly felt a swell of gratitude toward his uncle for shipping him off to Russia these last six months. In short order, he would be a better operator than Rostami, if he wasn't already. Tonight, he would assassinate a covert American agent and, in doing so, begin the process of avenging his family.

He heard hushed voices to his left. With an exaggerated head turn, he looked, sighed, and then forced himself to appear disappointed. He turned his attention to the dog while he parsed the mental snapshot he'd just taken: Caucasian man, medium height, medium build, dark hair, both hands in his pockets; Caucasian woman, short and lean, blonde hair, hands also in her pockets; both dressed in rain jackets and dark pants.

He waited a beat and made an exaggerated *tsk* sound, rolled his eyes, and then pulled out the mobile phone he had taken from the dead man. Pretending to make a call, he lifted the phone to his ear. "Are you coming or not?" he said with a subtle lisp, finding it easy to sound gay speaking French. "I know, I know, but it's cold, and I can't wait all night. Okay, then hurry up and get that tight ass of yours over here so you can warm me up . . ."

He paused as if listening to his lover's reply, while in reality he was straining to hear bits of the hushed conversation between the two approaching Americans.

"I don't care, Jason. My gut tells me he'll spook. Stay at the edge of the park and run some counter for me."

"It's a big fucking park. I don't like leaving you alone and unprotected like that."

"Well, that's the job. I'm perfectly capable of handling a sixty-five-year-old academic, I assure you."

"He's not just some random professor, Anne. That's the point of this."

"Just meet me at . . ."

As they passed out of earshot, her last words were impossible to make out.

It didn't matter. It would have been useful to know where the American partners were supposed to rendezvous after the meet, but this information was secondary. The essential takeaway was that the female agent was his target, and her colleague was running countersurveillance.

"*Ça va, ça va, à bientôt,*" he said into the mobile and pretended to end the call. He set an alarm timer with a ringtone then slipped the mobile phone back into his pocket. The toy poodle, which was huddling on his lap, licked his hand. He gave it another treat and affectionately rubbed its head until the Americans were out of sight around the corner. Then, he set the dog on the ground and set off in trail. After a few steps, he remembered to put some sway back in his hips as he scanned the park around him. Other than the two Americans, it appeared to be deserted.

Cyrus wondered if Arkady had known that the target would be a woman. *Of course the old bear did.* This was all part of making his final exam a true test. During their time together, the Russian spymaster had quickly discovered all his weaknesses, including his devotion to his mother and a predisposition for chivalry toward women instilled in him by his father. But he was a Persian millennial, and like his Western counterparts, he thought and viewed the world differently from the generation in power. Despite the Supreme Leader's concerted efforts to keep Persian women as second-class citizens, Cyrus viewed them as intellectual equals deserving of the same opportunities. And he didn't care what the Quran said on the matter, either. To lead one's life according to the archaic scrivenings of men whose worldview was centuries out of date was lunacy. Of course, he would never verbalize his true opinions on such things in Persian company; doing so in front of his uncle would have disastrous consequences.

As he rounded the bend, the target came into view. She was seated on a bench recessed into a small arc of gravel that dipped a few feet into the tree line. She was alone and loitering, her colleague running counterdetection surveillance as she had instructed. Any minute now, the Belarusian informant would arrive and greet her and, in doing so, seal her fate.

The timer went off on his phone and the ringtone sounded. He retrieved it, swiped, and pretended to answer an incoming call. As he passed the American agent, speaking in French, he smiled at the woman. She was quite young, much younger than he'd expected. Not much older than he was, in fact, midtwenties perhaps. And she was pretty—very Slavic, with high, slanted cheekbones; a hard, angular nose and jaw; and deep-set, almond-shaped eyes. He continued to babble in French, tugging gently on the bejeweled leash as he passed. He could feel her eyes on his back as he strutted around the corner.

He felt a twinge of hesitation. *Why does Arkady want this girl dead?* But no sooner had the thought crossed his mind than he heard Arkady's voice in his head, as clear as if the Russian were walking next to him: *Never ask this question. It is not a matter of what I want. It is not a matter of what you want. You are a weapon of the state. Today, you are an instrument of foreign policy, tomorrow a stratagem, and the next day maybe you are settling a personal grudge on the whim of the President. It does not matter. These things are not your concern. Does a precision-guided missile contemplate the implications of its payload on its target? Nyet! You do not think; you only do. If your orders were to kill me tonight, instead of this girl, could you do it?* Could you do it?

"*Dah,*" he heard himself say.

Under Arkady's tutelage, he had come to view himself as a computer program—executing line after line of code without emotion or contemplation until the instructions were completed. This was how the mind of the perfect assassin was supposed to operate. Just yesterday, the Russian had embraced him like a father while confessing how proud he was of Cyrus's progress. Then, a beat later, Arkady drew his blade and aimed the point at his own heart. *Could you drive this blade into my chest if ordered to do so?* his teacher had asked.

Yes, he'd replied.

Then do it. Kill me. This is your final test. Take my life and take my place.

Robotically, Cyrus took the knife and plunged it into the Russian's chest. Arkady had grunted and stumbled backward from the blow, but the blade failed to penetrate. *Very good, my son,* the old Russian said with a laugh, lifting his sweater to reveal a puncture-resistant ballistic vest. *Very, very good.*

If he could kill Arkady, he could kill this woman. He felt nothing for her. She was not a woman; she was a weapon of the state . . . of the American state, the same intelligence machine that had left him brotherless. Left him fatherless. Left him motherless . . .

He twisted the leash in his hands. He was ready.

He stopped on the path, cocking a hip to the side and talking more animatedly on his phone while scanning the path behind him as well as in all three other directions. He saw nothing. The American agent conducting countersurveillance was either well hidden or out of range. He would learn which soon enough. Cyrus swept the small dog up into his arms and slipped quietly over the low black chain that marked the edge of the path, then disappeared into the dark of the woods. He looked down at the white-haired dog in his arms, its tongue out and tail wagging—expecting yet another treat. He patted the dog's head, hesitating for only a moment before doing the deed.

Unencumbered now, he stripped off the blue leather jacket and print shirt he'd been wearing, exposing the skintight, black tactical shirt beneath. He rolled the sleeves down and pulled tactical gloves from his back pocket and slipped them on over his hands. He had only a few more minutes before the Belarusian arrived, giving him just enough time to conduct his own countersurveillance sweep.

As he moved silently through the trees and underbrush, Arkady's tutelage echoed in his mind: *On the hunt, forget your technology. Embrace your senses. You are an animal—a predator. Rely on your ears. Use your sense of smell. Your nose might be your only means of detecting danger. If you do not do this, then you are no longer the hunter—you become the prey.*

After successfully clearing the woods, he approached the park bench where his target sat waiting. He took a knee and scanned in all directions. Then, he closed his eyes and inhaled deeply through his nose. To his surprise, he was able to detect a feminine scent—perfume or maybe a floral soap. A beat later another scent registered. The Belarusian must have arrived, because the air now carried the musky tang of sweat and cigarettes. He crept forward until he could just barely make out snippets of the conversation taking place in Russian.

Although Arkady had not shared with him any of the background precipitating this meeting of spies, Cyrus had his own working hypothesis. During the past six months, he had immersed himself in Eastern European politics and become a student of Russian clandestine strategy at work in the region. According to the file, the informant was a professor at Belarusian State University in Minsk. However, Cyrus suspected this was his official cover—and that the old man had *siloviki* roots. It was no secret that Belarusian President Lukachenko maintained a cooperative relationship with Russian President Petrov and that the Belarusian Security Service worked closely with its Russian counterparts. Men like this Belarusian "professor" had proven to be much more effective at gathering intelligence inside the Baltic states than Russian operatives. It made sense to Cyrus. A government official in one of the Baltic states would certainly be less suspicious if approached by a Belarusian academic than by a Russian. Knowing this, the FSB made use of partner agency operatives. If Americans were aware of the FSB's tactics, then it made sense the CIA would try to find informants to turn inside the "retired" Belarusian siloviki network.

From his back pocket, Cyrus retrieved the paring knife he'd taken from the gay Crimean's apartment. He quietly slipped off the plastic sheath and slid it into his pocket. Clutching the blade in his right hand, he listened as the Belarusian spoke about some operation in the Ukraine. Cyrus shelved the names in his head should they be demanded during post-op debriefing with Arkady. The American asked why a history professor should have such knowledge. Answers came. Finally, the Belarusian's nerves seemed to get the better of him, and he said, "I need to go."

"I would like to meet again," the woman said.

"Perhaps," the professor answered and then coughed. "I have much more information. This is but a taste—a small amount so you will know I am of value. But it comes with a price. Get me out of Belarus. Get me out of the service. I want to spend the rest of my days somewhere warm. Like Antigua."

"I'll speak with my superiors. How will I get in touch with you?"

Cyrus heard the shuffling of the older man getting to his feet. He peered through the brush and saw the Belarusian standing beside the bench. The woman was up now, too.

"Don't contact me. I'll signal you when I'm ready—just as before," he said, looking around nervously. Cyrus wondered if the performance was an act for his benefit or if the Belarusian man was exactly what he'd portrayed—a tired old spy wishing to check out of the game for good.

The American woman handed him a scrap of paper.

"Memorize this. It's my personal number. I can be ready to get you at a moment's notice."

They shook hands and the old man turned and headed north along the path. The American spy turned and walked south. Cyrus moved with the stealth and speed of a tiger through the trees, keeping low and staying parallel to the woman, the blade clutched in his right hand. Their vectors were converging at the point where the sidewalk bent left, nearly touching the tree line before it changed direction to arc around a lily pond. His preference was to take her there because he could remain hidden until the very last second, but if she attempted to make contact with her colleague before that, he would strike early.

As it were, the two triggers merged into one, with the American spy pulling her phone from her coat pocket just as she approached the bend. Cyrus caught himself panting, not with fear or fatigue, but with excitement. Any hesitation he had felt at killing the woman was gone. There was now only predator and prey. He shifted the blade to his left hand and readied himself. As she walked past his hide, he stepped silently onto the path behind her. He snaked his left arm around her torso and simultaneously clamped his free right hand onto her windpipe.

She made a soft *nuhhh* sound as he lifted her completely off the ground and disappeared with her into the trees. He twisted at the waist and threw her hard onto the ground. Before she had time to recover her wits and breath, before her self-defense training kicked in, he drove the paring knife into her neck at the base of her skull. The woman's body instantly went slack, and the stench of excrement hit him a beat later as her bladder and bowels let go.

Cyrus withdrew the blade and crouched beside her, scanning and listening for her partner. The night was still—not a sound, not a shadow. He grabbed the woman by the collar of her jacket and dragged his quarry deeper into the woods. Ten meters in, he rolled the body over. Looking at her pretty Slavic face, her painted lips frozen open in surprise, a strange compulsion washed over him, and he kissed her. She tasted of lip balm, stale coffee, and fear. "You are my first," he whispered and gently brushed her blonde hair off her forehead. "Thank you."

Bring me proof—physical proof—that it's her and she's dead, said Arkady's voice in his head.

He gripped her ear and positioned the paring knife to take it but, before making the cut, realized that an ear was not positive identification, something the Russian would probably demand. So instead, he sliced off her right thumb at the end of the first metacarpal. Dark blood dribbled—did not spray—from the wound, confirming her heart had stopped beating and she was finally dead. He wrapped the severed thumb in his handkerchief and shoved it into his pocket. He quickly found her identification, powered off her mobile phone, and stuffed both items into his other pocket.

Then, without regret or afterthought, he walked away and disappeared into the night.

CHAPTER 3

Tehran, Iran
April 10

He is standing in a dark, dirty prison cell. In the corner sits a man, hooded and bound. His teacher hands him a semiautomatic pistol.

"What has this man done?" Cyrus asks, taking the weapon.

"That is not your concern," the teacher answers. "All that matters is that I am ordering you to kill him."

He squeezes the trigger. The bullet finds its mark and the hooded man shudders. Blood pools on the floor, expanding and expanding until he is standing in it. How can so much blood come from one man? Someone is screaming, with rage and pain the likes of which he's never heard before. At first he thinks it is the hooded man . . . but he is the one screaming. The scream fades, and his teacher takes the pistol from him, flashing him a malevolent smile.

"Who was he?" Cyrus asks.

"It doesn't matter."

"I need to know," he says and walks toward the slumped figure. He swallows . . . reaches out . . . and lifts the hood.

The dead man's eyes flick open. The face is his own.

"You did this to me," his doppelganger hisses. And then with astounding speed, it grabs him by the throat and screams, "You did this to me!"

Choking and gagging, Cyrus leaped out of bed. He scanned the room for threats, sweat pouring from his brow. *"Gde ya?"* he muttered, in Russian, not remembering where the hell he was. A beat later, adrenaline burned off the fog of sleep and his wits returned. He was in Tehran, at his uncle's house. Exhaling through pursed lips, he sat down on the edge of the mattress. Having completed his training with Arkady in Crimea, today was his official indoctrination into VEVAK. Beginning today, Cyrus Modiri was no more. Beginning today, he would be whoever his uncle told him to be.

The anemic hue around the drawn curtains told him it was still early. He checked his wrist, and the digital display on his watch read 05:25. Not enough time to go back to sleep and yet not enough time to do anything productive. He rolled off the bed and banged out a set of fifty push-ups. When he finished, he flipped onto his back and did one hundred crunches. He followed that with planks and squats and then repeated the body-weight circuit three more times. After that, he showered, shaved, and dressed. With a growling stomach, he made his way to the kitchen, where he found his aunt Maheen making coffee.

"Good morning, Cyrus," she said, keeping her back to him while she filled two porcelain cups with steaming brew.

"Good morning, Aunt Maheen," he replied, studying her from behind. To his uncle's great disappointment, she had been unable to conceive children. This had undoubtedly contributed to his aunt keeping—what looked to Cyrus like—the body of a teenager.

She turned, greeted him with a warm smile, and handed him a coffee. "And how did you sleep?"

"I slept fine," he said, and then accepting the cup, added, "Thank you for this."

He was not a coffee drinker, but this morning he would make an exception. Despite being twenty-five years his senior, his aunt's beauty was distracting. In her presence, he reverted back to his awkward twelve-year-old self. Little boys were not supposed to have crushes on their aunts, but Maheen was impossible not to covet. On more than one occasion while making love to some girl, he'd closed his eyes and imagined his aunt was the one beneath him. It was wrong. So wrong, and yet—

"Nightmares already?" she asked, her nonchalant tenor at odds with her steely, penetrating gaze.

He felt his cheeks flush with confirmation, which angered him and made them flush all the more.

"I know it's difficult, Cyrus, but you need to find a coping strategy."

He stared at her. Was this another twisted dream? Was he still asleep? Or was this yet another test . . . something his uncle had put his aunt up to in order to validate Cyrus's ability to compartmentalize and keep secrets, even from trusted family members? Had Amir told her that he'd recruited Cyrus to work for VEVAK? How much did she know about her husband's professional life? Did the wife of VEVAK's Director of Foreign Operations get read into the program out of necessity? These were questions he had not contemplated before and unfortunately had not had an opportunity to discuss with his uncle.

"I don't understand what you're talking about, Aunt Maheen."

"I think you do," she said, taking another sip of coffee. "And so let me offer you a little advice, favorite aunt to favorite nephew. When you're forced to sleep with demons, it's best to keep your wits about you at all times. Just don't become too reliant on sleeping pills. It's the coward's antidote."

Suddenly, he understood. She wasn't talking about VEVAK and wet work. She was afraid he was going to end up like his mother, who met her end with a bottle of sleeping pills in her hand.

"This is the first time I've been back home since she—" He choked on the words and couldn't finish the sentence.

"I know," she said and reached out as if to touch his cheek but stopped short. "We all miss her very much."

He dropped his gaze into the brown abyss inside his coffee cup.

"So," she said, her voice suddenly upbeat, "how was your semester abroad at Lomonosov? I want to hear all about it. Amir tells me you've fallen in love with Moscow."

He looked up at her, and her face was transformed, suddenly aglow with enthusiasm. This was the Aunt Maheen he remembered. This was the Aunt Maheen he'd expected to meet this morning. As he fumbled for words, he heard footsteps behind him. "Moscow is—"

"Cold as hell," his uncle interrupted, his face all smiles. "I don't know why any warm-blooded Persian would want to go there."

Cyrus forced a polite chuckle.

Maheen poured Amir a cup of coffee. She sidled up next to him and wrapped an arm around Amir's waist. In that instant, he saw his aunt and uncle as a duo of demigods—a charming, beautiful, brilliant power couple virtually unrivaled in Tehran. With Amir's rank and wit, and Maheen's wealth and beauty, they were practically Persian royalty—untouchables plugged in to the highest circles of power and influence.

"Come on, Cyrus, you must have at least one story to tell," Maheen coaxed with an easy smile.

In his mind, Arkady spoke to him: *At its core, a proper legend is nothing more than a life story. And what is a life story but a patchwork of short stories stitched together? These stories are your parachute when you're falling, a life preserver when you're drowning, and a fire extinguisher when you're burning. Use unbalanced dichotomy—humor to mask vulnerability, accomplishment despite pain—to make yourself relatable, admirable, and interesting. Master this and you will pass every social test.*

And so Cyrus told her one of seven scripted narratives he had crafted under Arkady's tutelage. The story was about a wild night out in Moscow with two crazy Russian boys he befriended despite being a Persian Muslim. By the end, he had both his aunt and his uncle laughing and seemingly enraptured in the tale.

"Well, that is quite a story," Maheen said.

"It certainly is," Amir added. "I've never been to Moscow, but after hearing that, maybe I should take a semester abroad at Moscow State."

Maheen playfully wagged a finger at her husband. "Over my dead body," she said and chuckled. "Not with all those tall Russian fashion models walking around."

"I'm joking, I'm joking," Amir said and then leaned over to kiss his wife. "I've always had, and always will have, eyes for only one woman in this life, and that woman is you."

"Ah, so sweet," she said, put a hand on his cheek, and kissed him back. But as she did, she snuck a glance at Cyrus.

After the kiss, Amir looked down at his watch. "Well, it's time for me to go to work," he said. Then, as if an afterthought, he added, "You're welcome to stay here at the house, Cyrus, or if there is somewhere you'd like me to drop you in town, then you can ride along."

"I think I'll take you up on that offer," he replied. Then, turning to his aunt, he said, "Thank you for the coffee, Aunt Maheen. I'm normally not a coffee drinker, but this was very good."

"It was nothing," she said. "Will you be joining us for dinner tonight, or do you have plans?"

He glanced at his uncle, looking for nonverbal instruction.

"Of course he will join us," Amir said. "He can catch up with friends another day."

"Then it's settled. Dinner will be at seven thirty. Don't be late, boys."

Five minutes later, Cyrus was sitting in the passenger seat of his uncle's Mercedes Benz en route to the VEVAK complex in Tehran. His uncle had canceled his driver this morning, claiming he wished to practice his driving skills lest he forget them. Privacy, however, was the real objective.

"You seem very nervous this morning," Amir said, kicking off the conversation.

"I am, or at least I was."

"Does my beautiful wife still make you uncomfortable? Since you were a little boy, you've always been shy around her."

Cyrus decided honesty was prudent; he was not a skilled enough liar yet to fool his uncle, and besides, what was the point? "Very uncomfortable," he said. "Does she know about me? I mean, does she know that you recruited me for VEVAK? Does she know why I was in Russia?"

"If you're asking me if I told her these things, the answer is no. If you're asking me if that matters, the answer is also no," he said with a chuckle. "Maheen sees all."

Cyrus exhaled with relief, which made Amir laugh out loud.

"Maheen is the best training I can possibly give you for developing your social skills. Fool her, and you can fool anyone."

Cyrus hesitated. His next question was critical, but he was afraid to ask it.

"Go on. Ask. It's okay," his uncle said.

He swallowed. "Is she . . . one of us?"

"No." His uncle's reply came quick and hard, but there was something, some undercurrent in his tone, that made Cyrus wonder if the answer was not that simple.

"But she is read into what you do?"

"No, she's not."

"Then I don't understand. How does it work between you?"

Amir smiled. "You have to understand, Cyrus, before VEVAK there was Maheen. Since the moment I first saw her, it has always been Maheen. There is no me without her. She's all that matters. I would do anything for her. Make any sacrifice. Rise to any challenge. Slaughter any foe who tried to hurt her . . ."

"I understand that, Uncle, but isn't it dangerous for her to know too much? Arkady taught me that the best Russian spies are able to lead two, three, sometimes four different lives simultaneously, often with different wives and children while maintaining their legends."

Amir snorted. "Yes, maybe, but these men are not married to Maheen. She is like . . . she is like an X-ray machine. She sees under the skin; she sees you to your bones. To pretend otherwise would be self-delusion and irresponsible tradecraft."

"So how do you do it? How do you keep our secrets?"

"I don't sing the lyrics to our songs."

Cyrus considered this for a moment. "But she hears the music nonetheless?"

Amir nodded. "The music, I can't turn off. So we waltz to the melody, and the words I keep to myself."

Cyrus nodded. He'd asked Arkady if he was married, and the Russian had said wistfully, *Once,* his answer a thousand words crammed into one.

"Speaking of our mutual friend, Arkady and I spoke yesterday. He wanted to give me his assessment. You are the first Persian and first Muslim he's trained."

"And?"

"He said if I have any more like you in the pipeline, he would be willing to train them, too. I would say that is the ultimate praise, coming from this particular Russian."

"So are you going to send him more students?"

His uncle shook his head. "No."

"Oh," Cyrus said, a little surprised. "Why is that? I assure you he is a very good instructor."

"Because," Amir said, laughing ruefully, "I don't have anyone else in the pipeline like you."

"I find that hard to believe, Uncle. There must be dozens of candidates out there with credentials superior to mine."

"On paper, maybe. But this is not a paper business. I know your mind. I know your heart. We are bound by the same God, the same blood, the same pain. Most importantly, we are bound by the same debt of vengeance. Do you remember the conversation we had in the courtyard of your father's house almost one year ago?"

"Yes."

"Then you understand the Modiri family blood debt must be settled."

"Yes."

"I sent you to Arkady because I needed you to be trained for an operation that no one in the ranks of VEVAK could possibly execute."

"Not even Rostami?"

Amir frowned. "Rostami has grown to be more of a liability than an asset these days. No, I would not trust Rostami to do this alone. I conceived this mission with another in mind, and according to Arkady, you're ready."

"What is it?" Cyrus asked, his heart rate amping up with anticipation and pride.

"In three weeks, the Zionists and the Americans are holding an intelligence summit in Washington, DC. The new Israeli head of the Mossad will be meeting the US Director of National Intelligence face-to-face for the first time. We've gained intelligence that the DNI will be hosting a private party at his estate. Security will be tight, but you will work on a plan to gain access. This is a once-in-a-lifetime opportunity, Cyrus. Never again will we have an opportunity such as this to decapitate two serpents with a single stroke of the blade."

"You're trusting me to lead this operation?"

"Are you prepared to give your life in the service of Persia?"

"Yes, Uncle," Cyrus said, nodding.

"Then the honor and the privilege will be yours."

CHAPTER 4

Galway Bay Irish Bar
Annapolis, Maryland
May 3
1745 Local Time

"How many fried oysters can one SEAL eat?" Shane Smith asked as the server set another half-dozen in front of Dempsey.

Dempsey grinned and stared down at the steaming plate of heaven. "What's this make?"

"Two dozen," said Elizabeth Grimes. "Give or take," she added with a sly grin as she poached an oyster and popped it into her mouth.

Dempsey shot her a sour look.

Smith took advantage of the moment and swiped a golden breaded nugget from the opposite side of the plate. "Make that twenty-two," the Ember Operations Officer said.

"Twenty-one," Richard Wang chimed in, his right hand shooting in and out like a serpent strike and swiping a third.

"Correction, it's actually twenty," said former CIA agent Simon Adamo.

"Make that nineteen," Dan Munn said, his voice low and gruff as he reached over and took the larger of the two remaining oysters.

"What the hell is this?" Dempsey grumbled with a playful scowl.

"It's called teamwork, JD," Smith said, taking a swig of his beer. "We're helping you complete your mission objective."

"I don't see the logic. How does your filching my oysters help me fill my belly?"

Smith laughed. "No, see, that's the problem right there. You don't understand the mission objective. Operation Cholesterol is not about you breaking the pub's single sitting fried oyster record; it's about us trying to prevent you from going into cardiac arrest tonight."

"Is that so?" Dempsey said, shaking his head.

"Yeah, John. Why else would we have invited your doctor to come along?" Grimes said, winking at Munn.

"Man, get a few beers in this crew and you're all comedians," he said, picking up the last oyster between his thumb and index finger and holding it up for inspection. Then, instead of tossing it in his mouth, he offered it to Jarvis, who was sitting across the table from him. "I think this one has your name on it, Skipper."

The former SEAL Captain and now Director of Ember shook his head. "I wouldn't want to spoil my appetite. Gotta save room for caviar and goose liver pâté at tonight's soirée."

Groans of disapproval reverberated around the wooden table.

"Wouldn't you rather hang with us, boss?" Wang said, his speech beginning to slur. "You don't want to hang out with those Israeli dudes. They're way too uptight."

Dempsey watched Jarvis's eyes narrow at the IT genius.

"I wonder if perhaps you could learn something from their discipline, Mr. Wang?"

Wang's smile disappeared and the younger man blushed. "I just meant—"

Jarvis held up a hand. "I know, you were just talking smack. The joint training we just conducted at the Farm was as much for you as for them. Try to remember that."

Wang nodded, sufficiently cowed in front of the group.

"You gonna eat that last oyster, JD?" Smith asked after an awkward beat, trying to revive the withering party atmosphere before it died.

Dempsey popped the golden nugget into his mouth. Then, with a grin on his face, he snapped his fingers in the air. "Waiter, waiter, another plate of fried oysters for *me* and a glass of Chabliss for my friend."

Everyone laughed, even Jarvis, but Grimes cracked up most of all.

"It wasn't that funny, Lizzy," Dempsey said, looking at her.

"I know," she said. "I'm laughing because you're a total redneck and you don't even know it."

"What'd I say?"

"It's *Chablis*, not Chabliss. You don't pronounce the *s*."

"Really?" he said, looking at Smith.

Smith nodded.

"Did you know that?" he asked, turning to Munn.

Munn nodded, doing his best to suppress a grin.

"Wang?" he said, searching for an ally.

"Sorry, Dempsey. Everybody knows that," the techno kid-wonder said with a snicker.

"Ah, damn," he said, grabbing his beer. "So, I'm the dumbest guy at the table?"

Smiles and nods all around.

"Well, I guess I can drink to that." He raised his glass for a toast.

"To the dumbest guy at the table," Grimes said, but then leaned in and gave him a kiss on the cheek. "What would we do without you?"

"Hear, hear!" the crew cried in unison, clinked glasses, and took pulls from their respective mugs.

"To Baldwin and his twins, Chip and Dale," Grimes said, laughing, "who are manning the TOC back home so we can eat oysters and drink beer."

"Hear, hear!"

"And to our newest team member," Dempsey said, fixing his gaze on Munn. "Welcome aboard, Doc."

"To Doc!" came the cheer.

Munn's cheeks flushed with pride, just enough for Dempsey to notice. The draining of their beer glasses drew their waiter's attention like a bee to nectar. A beat later, the server was tableside, eyeing fluid levels and empty plates. "Getcha another round? How 'bout some more appetizers?"

"Keep those oysters coming, and bring another round of Smithwick's for me and all my friends," Smith said, setting his empty glass down hard on the table with a broad, tipsy smile.

"Oysters and another round, coming right up," the young man said.

From the corner of his eye, Dempsey saw Munn discreetly wave off the server. Dempsey had been logging mental observations of Munn's behavior and sobriety all evening. Since his indoctrination into Ember, this was Doc's first night out drinking with the team. When it came to Ember, drinking in public was a rarity. Inebriation was generally reserved for only one of two scenarios: a quiet celebration of a victory, or a somber toasting of the dead—both of which were best suited to a private venue.

When Dempsey found Munn in Key West, he'd been worried that his friend had surrendered to the bottle. Given the demands of serving in Special Warfare, and especially the covert Tier One unit, Dempsey well understood alcohol's siren song. "Novocain for the soul," Aaron Thiel, his now dead best friend, had once called it. Dempsey had witnessed alcoholism in his unit. He was relieved to think that in Munn's case, the bottle had simply been a surrogate for the thing in his life he had lost—the one thing that mattered above all others. Purpose. Give a man like Dan Munn his purpose back, and suddenly drunkenness becomes an unsatisfactory state of being. In that way, he and Munn were kindred spirits. Which is why even on a night like tonight—a night when it was okay to cut loose and party—both of them were still nursing their second beers.

Dempsey realized he was a bit envious of his inebriated teammates. The thought of surrendering to a state of complete well-being—no matter how artificial—was tempting. But he had learned long ago that once there, he found that state horribly uncomfortable. Years of honing his psyche to be ready did more than just leave him with an inability to put both legs under the table in case he needed to spring into action; it left him with a powerful need to be in complete control of not just his environment, but himself, at all times. Always be ready . . . that was the unspoken, personal mantra for guys like him and Munn. *Evil never takes a day off,* Munn had once said to him down range, *and neither do I.*

"How are you feeling about the training?" Jarvis asked, watching Munn. It had been more than a few years since they had served together in the Teams, but Jarvis knew the former SEAL officer very well. The bonds formed in combat were almost unbreakable.

"Feeling sore," Munn said, smiling at his former—and current—boss. "And maybe a little old."

"Training at the Farm will do that, especially when that training includes the Israelis," Smith said with a laugh, checking around casually to make sure no one was in earshot. At the CIA's secret training facility, the Ember team was allowed to train as "contractors" for an unspecified DoD entity. Even from the CIA, Ember NOCs were always protected.

"He's doing great," Dempsey added, feeling a little protective of Munn. "He's fully operational as far as I'm concerned."

"Which means you are just under halfway there, Dan," Jarvis said softly. "The skills you are relearning from being an operator are actually a pretty small part of the skill set you will need. The real challenges are coming."

"I'm ready, sir," Munn said, and Dempsey was happy to see more than a glimmer of the badass SEAL Munn had been when they were at the Tier One. "And I'm honored to be part of the team you've built here."

"To the team!" Wang chimed loud enough to confirm his own rising state of inebriation.

"We're lucky to have you, Dan," Jarvis said more softly. Then he glanced at his watch and stood. "As much as I'd love to stay and party with you yahoos, I should probably hit the road."

"Ahh, you've got time for one more," Smith said, looking up at his boss. "This round's on me."

"Thanks, Shane, but I'm already late as it is," Jarvis said. "Tell you what, put everything on the company tab tonight. This one's on me."

"Be sure to tell Director Philips we said hello," Grimes said. "And even though he ran out of invitations for the rest of us, make sure he knows there's no hard feelings."

Dempsey smiled at her sarcasm and the warm little slur in Grimes's voice. Tonight, she was having fun. Tonight, she felt comfortable enough to let her guard down. Over the past year, the bond between them had deepened, and not just because they shared the loss of her brother, Spaz—one of Dempsey's teammates who had died during Operation Crusader. Her fiery personality and natural disposition to play devil's advocate had put them at odds from their very first encounter. Since then, he'd ridden a roller-coaster ride with her: from finding her presence on the team a nuisance, to recognizing her tactical and strategic prowess, to viewing her as an indispensable teammate. Grimes was like a sister to him now, but there was also something else between them— something he couldn't quite articulate. And as long as they were both working at Ember, romance was categorically off the table. He'd seen entire commands undermined by secret affairs between personnel when he was in the Navy; he would never let that happen here.

"Tell the DNI he's welcome to join us for the after-party," Wang added. "I have a feeling we'll still be here."

"Don't worry; I'll be sure to convey the team's warm regards," Jarvis replied with a wry smile. His eyes then found Dempsey's, and a silent message passed between them: *You're in charge . . . Don't let them do anything I wouldn't do.*

Dempsey gave the Ember Skipper a nod and then watched him disappear. A beat later, Dempsey stood and scanned the pub.

"Ah, don't tell me you're bailing on us, too," Smith said.

"No, no. I'm just looking for the pisser."

"I'll show you," Grimes said, getting up from her chair. "I gotta go, too."

As they left the table, Dempsey heard Wang make some wisecrack about which of them would win the pissing-for-distance contest, to which he couldn't help but chuckle. *For having never been a sailor, that kid has the filthiest mind.*

"I've been watching you with him the last couple of weeks," Grimes said, taking him by the arm.

"Who?"

"Munn, of course," she said, fixing her pale baby blues on him. "You've done a good job bringing him back from the edge. I'm impressed."

Dempsey shrugged. "I happen to have personal experience with the matter . . . That's all."

"Don't sell yourself short, John. Dan needed a rock, and you've been that for him. Hell, after we lost Mendez, you've been that rock for all of us—including me."

She stopped in the middle of the short hallway leading to the restrooms and turned to face him.

"You've been there for me, too," he said, looking down at her.

Her hands found his waist and she stepped into him.

"You're drunk, Elizabeth," he said quietly.

"I know," she said through her breath. "And I don't care. Kiss me."

"Uh . . . I don't think that's such a good—" But he wasn't able to finish the sentence because her lips found his.

He didn't kiss her back, but he didn't pull away. A relationship with him was not what sober Elizabeth wanted. Her heart was confusing fraternal intimacy with physical intimacy.

When she stepped back from him, her cheeks were crimson. "Apparently that was a mistake."

"It's okay," he said. "It happens."

"Not to me it doesn't," she snapped. Then, with an about-face, she retreated into the women's restroom.

"Elizabeth, c'mon. I'm sorry," he called after her. As he spoke the words, he felt someone else's gaze on him. He turned left to see Smith standing at the end of the corridor, eyes narrowed in condemnation. No, not condemnation . . . something else.

Envy?

"Women," he said, holding up his hands and shrugging at Smith.

Smith shook his head and strode toward the men's lavatory. When he walked past Dempsey, he muttered, "I can't believe you did that."

"What I did?" Dempsey said in disbelief. Surely Smith must have seen that Grimes was the one who kissed *him*. He had been a gentleman and a friend, minimizing what could be a devastating mistake for the team. "Oh, c'mon. *She* kissed *me*," he called after Smith, but the men's-room door was already swinging closed. He loitered there in the hall for a minute, unsure what to do, until the awkward prospect of simultaneously confronting his two closest colleagues drove him to flee the little hallway. Fists clenched, he walked past the Ember table without making eye contact with anyone.

"Where you going, Dempsey?" Wang called after him.

"To get some fresh air," he growled, and then under his breath added, "and to take a piss in private."

CHAPTER 5

US Highway 50
Annapolis, Maryland
May 3
1915 Local Time

Inflammation.

Inflammation was the bane of Kelso Jarvis's existence. Chronic and omnipresent—inflammation was breaking him down. For years, his philosophy toward this internal enemy had been that the best defense was a strong offense. Problem: Achy joints? Solution: Navy SEAL willpower, exercise, and a shitload of ibuprofen. But that wasn't working anymore. Something else was happening inside him.

Something insidious.

Something systemic.

The first warning sign had been subtle: a coffee mug had slipped out of his grasp and shattered on the floor. He'd written it off as an accident, but then he began to notice episodic weakness and a tingling numbness in his hands, along with bouts of vertigo when he was tired. When he dropped a mug for the second time, he immediately went online and began researching. His symptoms correlated most closely to four different degenerative neurological diseases, none of which had a favorable prognosis.

He gripped the steering wheel of his GMC Yukon, alternately clenching his right and left hands. Tonight, he felt fine. Strong. Like himself. *Whatever this is,* he told himself, *I'll defeat it.* Fighting disease was no different from counterterrorism operations. The body was the battleground, disease the terrorists, and his immune system—Special Forces. He would tackle this problem like any other search-and-destroy mission. He would identify the target, plan the offensive, deliver the payload, and annihilate. Simple, efficient, effective.

He spied the sign for Exit 32 ahead, braked, and exited US 50 East onto Oceanic Drive. He took a quick right onto Skidmore, then a left onto Holly Beach Farm Road, which led to the private residence of the Director of National Intelligence. This was his second invitation to the Philips estate. During his first visit, the DNI had given him a personal tour of the house and the grounds while sharing the story of the property and his early married years. The twenty-five-acre estate on the Chesapeake belonged to Philips's wife, Jackie—the property having passed to her upon her mother's death in 2013. Jackie hailed from a wealthy Maryland family. The fact that Philips had married into money was something the man neither took pleasure boasting about nor tried to hide, Jarvis had observed. Philips had met Jackie while enrolled as a midshipman at the Naval Academy. Jackie's father, although having never served himself, was a staunch supporter of the Navy and a decent sailboat skipper. Oliver had treated his future son-in-law like family from the first day they'd met and on multiple occasions had tried to woo Philips away from the Navy to join his real estate business. But as Philips explained, he'd had only one career aspiration, and that was to become Chief of Naval Operations. Neither Jackie's father nor her mother lived to see the day that he eclipsed that goal—the day he'd been sworn in as Director of National Intelligence.

Jarvis piloted his big black SUV slowly along Holly Beach Farm Road. The private driveway to the estate was not well marked, and he'd driven past it on his last visit. This time, however, the security detail at the gate made the turn impossible to miss. He stopped at the gate and handed his ID to an armed sentry. A second guard inspected the undercarriage of the Yukon with an angled mirror attached to the end of a five-foot pole. Without having to be told, Jarvis popped the hood and opened the tailgate for inspection. Two minutes later, they waved him through the gate.

The long asphalt driveway snaked through a grove of trees, dog-legged right to run along the bay for about a quarter mile, and finally turned back toward the house. The ten-thousand-square-foot redbrick Georgian Colonial stood majestic in the glow of the setting sun. He looped around the circle drive and was directed to park his Yukon along a row of other government-issue vehicles in the grass. He backed into the spot, leaving extra space on the driver's side for easy access. Stepping out of the Yukon, the first thing that hit him was the aroma of meat being grilled. He was surprised the caterers would be running grills, but it was a beautiful evening, and Philips definitely wasn't a caviar and champagne kind of guy. He had expected that the menu choices would be highbrow nonetheless, with Philips tending to defer on such things to his charming and sophisticated wife. Now that he could smell the grills, however, Jarvis grinned. Hell, he wouldn't be surprised if the DNI was out there tending short ribs on the barbecue personally.

As he walked toward the house, he scanned the area, looking for any gaps in the security. When he reached the entry, he stopped before two men in black suits who flanked the door. He flashed the right-hand guard his ID and asked, "How are the appetizers tonight?" which was a scripted statement conveying he had a concealed carry.

The older of the two guards validated his ID while the younger gave him a pat-down, passing over the pistol in the small of his back without stopping. The pat-down was just a show for anyone else watching—the password game verified he was one of only a handful of guests authorized to carry a weapon on the property.

A beat later the older guard said, "Enjoy the party, Director Jarvis, but I recommend you steer clear of the egg rolls."

Jarvis nodded and walked inside. Five steps into the vestibule, he paused to marvel. The Philips mansion looked like it had been ripped from the pages of *Architectural Digest*. The French provincial style—with its ornate moldings, white marble floors, and luxurious appointments—occupied the niche opposite his own clean, contemporary taste, but he could appreciate it nonetheless. His eyes were tracing the soaring spiral staircase when a familiar female face slipped into his field of vision.

"Kelso!" Jackie Philips exclaimed. "So sorry to leave you stranded in the parlor—come in, come in."

He leaned in to embrace the hostess, both giving and receiving a polite peck on the cheek.

"You look beautiful tonight," he said, making a show of admiring her summer dress, which he imagined rivaled the cost of most monthly mortgage payments. Jackie Philips was tall, with a handsome face and lithe frame. His compliment was not a hollow one.

"Oh, you're sweet," she said with a dismissive wave of her hand.

"Where is everyone?" he said, glancing past her and the empty parlor to the living room beyond. He could hear the din of voices, but they were very much alone.

"Some are in the dining room, most are in the kitchen, but the Israeli contingent has laid claim to the sunroom, and despite being packed in there like sardines, they refuse to relocate."

"Sounds very Israeli, if you ask me." He chuckled. "Sharott will probably demand you relocate your bartender in there, too."

Jackie laughed. "How did you know?"

Jarvis shrugged. "It's a gift."

He followed her to the kitchen, where the DNI was talking to a circle of guests who were hanging on his every word. When Philips saw them, he smiled and gave a little nod, but didn't miss a beat. When he finished, everyone laughed, and he got a pat on the shoulder from an Air Force General that Jarvis didn't recognize. The DNI excused himself and made his way over.

"Kelso," the DNI said, extending his hand. "I see it didn't take you long to find the most beautiful woman at the party to keep you company."

Jarvis shook Philips's hand. "Well, sir, I tried my best to steal her away, but she seems hell-bent on sticking with you. I guess she's got a thing for fighter jocks—or else something against frogmen."

The DNI laughed. "Glad you could make it. Although you do realize the party started an hour ago."

"I'm terrible at these things. It's usually best if I don't start making small talk until the important folks already have a couple of drinks in them. Otherwise I'm liable to create an international incident."

"Oh, Kelso, don't you know? Small talk is what wives are for," Jackie said with a coy smile. "And when are we going to get to meet Mrs. Jarvis?"

"As soon as I meet her," he said, then made a show of scanning the room for women. "Any recommendations?"

They all three laughed at this, and he felt his mood begin to lighten.

"Have you ever met Mossad Director Rami Sharott?" Philips asked.

"No, sir. But his reputation I'm quite familiar with."

"And I understand you're close with his predecessor, Levi Harel."

Jarvis nodded, though he knew the DNI's comment was a statement, not a question. Philips made a point of knowing everything about those who served below him—just as when he'd commanded a fighter squadron, then a wing, then a carrier battle group. "Harel and I have a long working relationship," Jarvis said, choosing his words carefully.

"Good. Well, it's definitely time you got to know Rami. Smart as hell and tough as nails. I have a feeling the two of you will get on like brothers."

"Lead the way," Jarvis said and followed Philips to the four-seasons sunroom.

Despite having never met Rami Sharott, Jarvis felt like he knew the man. He'd ordered his Ember analysts to prepare a dossier on the Mossad Chief, and he'd memorized every word of it. Sharott was the exact same age as Jarvis—fifty-two—and, aside from their different haircuts, could have passed as his Israeli doppelganger. They were cut from the same mold, having both served as operators before running their respective clandestine operations. While Jarvis was leading a Tier One SEAL team, Sharott was running a Sayeret Matkal unit. Tasked with intelligence collection inside denied areas, counterterrorism operations, the prosecution of enemy HVTs, and hostage rescue, Sayeret Matkal was the IDF's Tier One equivalent of the Army's Delta Force. Unlike his friend Levi Harel, who had spent his entire career working as a spy, handling spies, and hunting spies for the Mossad, Sharott had been an operator his entire career, rising to the rank of General two years ago. When Harel announced his retirement a few years ago, Sharott was one of three candidates considered to fill the role of top spy in Tel Aviv. Initially considered by most to be a long shot for the post, Sharott made a quick impression on the Prime Minister and won the job. Since its founding, the Mossad had been led by eleven different Chiefs—six career spies and five former IDF Generals. Just like presidential politics in America, the two-party system of governance kept Israeli's preeminent clandestine service from homogenizing its ranks and falling victim to groupthink biases. Periodic changing of the guard was essential to the success of any organization, even when the man in charge was as capable and competent as Levi Harel. Jarvis wondered how much, if anything, Harel had shared with his successor about Jarvis over the last few years. Did Sharott know that Ember was a secret sister unit nearly identical in form and function to the one that Harel ran from "retirement"? Did he know that Harel's "little contracting office" in Tel Aviv had been instrumental in helping Ember on more than one occasion in the clandestine war raging between Ember and VEVAK? Had Philips and Sharott compared notes and agreed to share best practices and lessons learned from their respective black ops task forces?

Jarvis accompanied the DNI into the sunroom where the Israelis had, as Jackie had said, set up shop. The atmosphere in here was completely different from the kitchen, the word *raucous* coming to mind, but the good kind of raucous. It was immediately evident to Jarvis that the Israeli contingent in attendance was a tight, collegial group. And with the Prime Minister dining with the President at the White House tonight, they were partying like kids without parental supervision. No surprise, Sharott was in the middle of the crowd, drinking red wine and in the company of three women. Two of the women Jarvis did not recognize, but the third he knew—Catherine Morgan, the Principal Deputy DNI. Jarvis felt her gaze on him, and he chose not to make eye contact with her.

"Director Philips," Sharott called as they approached. "This is a wonderful party, but we have a small problem."

"What's that, Rami?"

"This sunroom is too small. We have too many Jews and not enough space," he said. "We've decided we're going to expand our settlement to the west. That wall over there is going to have to go."

This garnered a round of laughter, and even the DNI couldn't help but chuckle at the double entendre.

"I'll have to bring your proposal to my governance council," Philips said, glancing over his shoulder at his wife, who had stopped to talk with one of Sharott's deputies. "Her vote will determine whether the resolution passes."

A second round of laughter ensued, and Jarvis sighed inaudibly with relief. This good-natured, friendly banter mattered. It meant that

Philips and Sharott had established a cooperative and friendly working relationship during the year since Philips had taken the reins as the DNI. As far as Jarvis was concerned, Israel was America's most important and strategic ally in the world. And continued cooperation with their clandestine service was essential to staying one step ahead of Tehran, ISIS, Al Qaeda, Hamas, Hezbollah, Boko Haram, and every other radical faction with aspirations of building the next Islamic caliphate and sowing seeds of fear, instability, and violence in the West. Yet with all the damage that had been done to the West, it nowhere near approached the damage the extremists had meted out on peace-loving Muslims worldwide. The extremists had killed more Muslims than any other group.

"Rami," Philips said, stealing the beat, "I'd like to introduce you to a good friend of mine, Captain Kelso Jarvis. Captain Jarvis retired from the SEALs and now he works in the private sector as one of our key security contractors."

Sharott smiled broadly and extended a hand to Jarvis. "A pleasure to meet you, Captain Jarvis. Any friend of Director Philips is a friend of mine."

"The honor is all mine, General," Jarvis said, shaking hands with Sharott, noting the other man's rock-solid grip. His own grip, however, seemed to falter during the exchange from a sudden flare of weakness in his fingers. He resisted the urge to frown at this, keeping his smile up and genuine. "I had the privilege of working with the 269 during several occasions when I was down range. In fact, I had the great honor of serving as an exchange officer with Shayetet 13 earlier in my career and learned more than I can say."

Sharott's gaze sharpened, and he looked at Jarvis with a shared appreciation. "I am sure they learned much from you as well."

"Maybe," Jarvis said. "But I can tell you I have great respect for both S13 and the 269. Earlier in the Iraq War we worked very closely together. Hell, I might not be standing here if it wasn't for you and your brothers."

The left corner of Sharott's mouth curled up. "You are referring to 2003?"

"That's the one."

"I heard stories," Sharott said. "Wish I could have been there."

"No—you don't," Jarvis said, and both men laughed.

"I'd be interested in learning more about the company you work for," Sharott said. "Contract security operations, is it?"

Jarvis nodded. "I have a small team, but we stay busy."

"No doubt . . . I'm not sure if Director Philips has told you, but the Mossad sometimes utilizes the services of private contractors. There is a small Israeli security company that does work for us from time to time. Maybe there could be some synergies all around. I could put you in touch with their Director if you're interested."

"Thank you. I would like that," Jarvis said, studying the Mossad Chief's face for information beyond the words. He would confirm his conclusion with the DNI later, but this exchange seemed to indicate that Sharott did not know about Ember, nor did he know about Jarvis's history with Harel.

"Excellent. When can you come to Tel Aviv?" Sharott said.

"Hey, hey, hey—don't think I don't see where this is going," the DNI interjected. "I invite you to DC, throw you a party at my house, open a case of wine from my private collection, and you're already trying to steal my talent."

"Never," Sharott said with a sly chuckle.

"Don't worry, Director Philips," Catherine Morgan said, slipping her arm inside Jarvis's elbow to link arms. "I'll keep him on a tight leash."

Jarvis turned to her, meeting her gaze for the first time since joining the circle. She was staging a little coup, extracting him from the budding conversation at the worst possible time.

"See that you do," Philips said.

"If you'll please excuse us," she said, shifting her attention to Sharott. "I have a few pressing matters to discuss with Captain Jarvis."

"Of course," the Mossad Chief said with a nod. "It was an honor to meet you, Kelso. I look forward to continuing our dialogue in the future."

"The honor is all mine, sir."

Morgan escorted him wordlessly out of the sunroom. When they reached a door leading to the backyard, she released his arm and gestured for him to step outside. The hair on the back of his neck bristled, but he complied. Outside, the aroma of barbecue hit him once again, making his mouth instantly salivate, but he knew better than to think she'd led him here to lay claim to a slab of ribs on the grill.

"Did I say something wrong?" he asked, knowing full well he had not.

"No," she said, shaking her feathered silver bangs at him. "But I didn't want Ed to give Rami the wrong impression about you."

"And what impression is that?" he asked, silently noting how she referred to the two most powerful men in the global clandestine war on terror by their first names.

"The impression that you and your organization are important," she said without a hint of humor.

Multiple acerbic retorts to this unprompted slap to the face populated his mind, but he simply said, "Excuse me?"

"Walk with me," she replied and set off across the lawn toward the swimming pool. "Of all the troubling reports that filter across my desk," she continued, her voice oozing with bureaucratic superiority, "the ones that trouble me most always seem to concern the activities of a particular entity operating right in our own backyard down in Newport News."

Resisting the urge to roll his eyes at the hyperbole, he simply said, "Oh really? I would have thought as the Principal Deputy Director you would find the reports concerning terrorist activity aimed at slaughtering Americans the most troubling . . . not my little group, which devotes all of its resources to *counter*terrorism operations."

"You might think that, but you'd be wrong," she said, stepping off the lawn onto the wide concrete pool deck. "Would you like to know why that is, Kelso?"

"Yes, Catherine," he said, matching her tone. "I'm dying to know."

"There is a multibillion-dollar apparatus powered by thousands of highly skilled people using highly developed technology and carefully harvested human intelligence to prosecute the terrorist threat. And all of that activity is reported to and managed by us—all activity, that is, except for yours."

"I'm sure you are aware that my organization is tasked directly by the DNI," Jarvis said, his eyes narrowing.

"Perhaps," Morgan said. "But he allows you an unprecedented—and in my opinion, dangerous—degree of autonomy."

Jarvis felt anger rising and swallowed it down. His lips curled into a wry smile. "You yanked me out of a conversation with the Mossad Chief and the DNI, your boss, to talk about oversight?"

Her face hardened. "Yes, Captain Jarvis, I did, and it does not appear you appreciate the gravity of the situation."

"With all due respect, I understand the gravity of the situation all too well. The multibillion-dollar intelligence and clandestine apparatus you're touting is the reason that Ember exists. The old expression 'Necessity is the mother of invention' applies in this case. Ember was born from necessity, and we—" He stopped midsentence, his gaze fixed on the back of the house.

"What is it?" she asked, turning to see where his attention had relocated.

"Why is that vehicle backed up to the house?" he asked, eying a catering van that was parked right next to the back patio, a mere ten feet from the kitchen.

"That's the caterers'. It's a full-on mobile kitchen. They even have a grill inside," she answered. "Apparently, it's the newest catering meme—keep the caterers and the mess out of the kitchen so the guests can mingle there. If you've ever thrown a party, you know that everyone gravitates to the kitchen whether you want them in there or not. Why fight the inevitable?"

His pulse picked up. "Yeah, but that vehicle is violating the safety setback. Just like out front, all vehicles should be parked outside a fifty-foot radius of the house."

"Every vehicle was inspected at the gate," she replied.

"I don't care. It shouldn't be there," he huffed. "If you'll excuse me, Catherine, we can continue our conversation after I get it moved."

He turned his back on her, not giving her an opportunity to rebut, and set off toward the house. He only managed two strides before the explosion drove him backward. Muscle memory took over. He spun in midair and dove on top of the Deputy DNI, shielding her body with his as a fireball four stories high engulfed the house. Pieces of slate roof tile, glass shards, and chunks of wood and brick rained down over a four-hundred-foot radius, pelting him on his back and legs. Jarvis absorbed the shock and the pain with the expertise from years in the field and far too many explosions. He kept his chin tucked, protecting his head as best he could—the only body part that could not recover from a direct blow from a brick. He felt something heavy hit him in the back of the right thigh with the impact of a sledgehammer, and he raised his shoulders beside his head even more. Finally, he felt only the pelting of the smaller particles and then only dust. He rolled off the woman beneath him.

"Are you okay, ma'am?" he said, the SEAL in him now in complete control.

"I think so," she said, wiping her right cheek and then inspecting the blood smear on her fingertips.

"It's just a scratch," he said. He quickly inspected her head, neck, and torso for any legitimate impalements. Finding none, he said, "Do you see that grove of trees over there?"

She followed his eyes to a stand of birch trees behind the pool house. "Yes," she said, her voice quavering on the brink of panic. The Deputy DNI was *not* a former field agent, and he guessed this was much closer than she had ever come to dying before. But despite surviving the blast, they weren't safe yet. In theater, explosions were inevitably followed by sniper fire. Relocating her to safe cover was imperative.

"Go there, stay low, and get small," he said, pulling the Sig Sauer 226 from the holster at the small of his back. "I'll come back for you."

"Where are you going?" she asked, wiping her face again and looking at the back of her hand.

"This might not be over," he said.

"Okay," she said. Then, struggling for control, she swallowed hard and closed her eyes tightly for a beat. When she reopened them, her face became stone. "But first, I'm going to call this in."

"Do it," he said, scanning around them over his Sig Sauer.

Three hundred feet away, what had been Jackie Philips's one-hundred-year-old family estate was now a raging inferno. The devastation was simply tremendous. There would be few, if any, survivors. *Was this terror, or was it a hit?* He retrieved a wireless earbud from a pocket inside his suit coat and pressed it into his right ear canal. The earbud automatically synced with the mobile phone in his pocket. He tapped the end of the earbud three times, a preset that triggered the phone to dial the Tactical Operations Center at the Ember hangar in Newport News, Virginia.

In a low crouch, he moved in an arc around the rear perimeter of the house, first scanning the grounds between the pool house and the main house and then surveying the property's southwestern-facing shoreline.

The call connected.

"Zero—how's the party, sir?" The voice in his ear belonged to Ian Baldwin, Ember's signals guru and head of data analytics.

"The DNI's house just got nuked. From the looks of things, no one inside survived. Mobilize everyone, get eyes on my location, and scan for comms."

"Yes, sir," Baldwin answered. "But first I have to inquire, are you injured?"

"No, don't worry about me. Just find me a trail to follow."

"Roger that. I'll try to hijack some time on the satellite. Maybe I can task a drone. And of course we'll start looking at cellular traffic. Who am I looking for exactly?"

"Just do it, Ian," he barked. Baldwin, as usual, was just thinking out loud. Jarvis moved toward the east end of the house. If the attack had been perpetrated by operators rather than martyrs, then a water egress across the bay to the adjacent peninsula was tactically superior for their getaway.

Sirens wailed in the distance as Jarvis scanned over his weapon left and right, moving toward the tree line in a low tactical crouch. He entered the woods, wishing for both younger eyes and night vision goggles. The sliver of moonlight and the glow from the raging fire were stolen by the foliage around him. His body was a weapon now, all thoughts of aging and aches and pains a distant memory as the SEAL that would never die inside him took over. He moved quickly but quietly through the woods, acutely cognizant of the terrain and each footfall. He glimpsed movement ahead, a shadow skirting along the shoreline. He squeezed both eyes shut to sharpen his night accommodation and then looked again. He tightened his grip on his weapon and trained the muzzle toward what looked like a hunched figure on the beach. Before squeezing the trigger, he needed to be sure he wasn't stalking a roving security guard who, like him, was searching for attackers. He didn't dare call out and forfeit his tactical advantage, which meant he needed visual confirmation.

The low rumble of a gasoline engine, barely audible, pricked his ears. He pivoted left, toward the sound, and scanned the dark waters of the Chesapeake to the horizon. Twenty-five meters offshore, a small wake bubbled white in the moonlight. *A RIB*, his mind told him, from the way it displaced the water—and it was moving toward the shore. This had to be the pickup team, the EXFIL for the attacker or attackers.

He tapped his earpiece again, his voice a soft whisper.

"Zero, we have a watercraft approaching the east end of the property. Get eyes on it now."

"Working on it, sir," came Baldwin's response.

Where was the fucking perimeter security team? Was this the water patrol? Surely the DNI's protection detail had arranged for that. Jarvis advanced, growing more and more convinced with each passing second that these were *not* the good guys. His mind drew the approach vector for where the RIB would intersect the shore and he shifted his gaze there. A cloud drifted in front of the moon. He squinted and scanned the beach, having lost the hunched figure in the darkness. He held, statue still, and waited.

The sky began to brighten.

Movement on the shoreline . . .

He squeezed the trigger.

A figure stumbled, but didn't fall. It turned, and then a muzzle flash lit up the night, wrecking his night vision. Reflexively, Jarvis juked right, and a bullet that had been on a trajectory to hit him square in the face whizzed past his ear. He ducked, took cover behind a stump, squeezed his eyes tight for a three count to restore his night vision, and then scanned the beach. The shadow was on the move, heading toward the RIB. Jarvis shifted to one knee and fired five rounds, but none hit their mark as the shadow rolled into the RIB. Cursing, Jarvis popped to his feet and sprinted through the trees, darting and dodging low-hanging branches and tree roots. By the time he reached the water's edge, the RIB was screaming away.

He skidded to a stop, took a bent-knee firing position, and emptied his magazine—firing at the craft as it sped away, spraying a rooster tail and leaving white wake trailing behind. He swapped magazines and sent another volley of rounds into the night . . . powerless to do anything else but watch as the boat sped away into the black.

"Zero, where the hell are my eyes?" he demanded.

"I'm coming up real time on the satellite now and have a drone en route."

"Ping on me."

"Just another forty-five seconds," Baldwin said softly, a professor speaking to his class.

"Hurry, they're getting away."

"We'll get them."

Jarvis could no longer see the RIB or its wake. A beat later the night went quiet. Clutching his pistol, he contemplated the attack. Clean. Fast. Efficient. This was no half-baked homegrown terrorist event.

"What's taking so long?" Jarvis barked, staring out into the night.

"Coming up now," Baldwin said in his ear.

"Their escape vector was north-northeast from my position."

"I'm looking . . . I don't see a boat. Is it possible that they—"

"Fuck," Jarvis seethed, cutting Baldwin off. "Look across the inlet. Scan the shoreline. It's a short hop by water but a long haul by car. These guys were professionals, Ian, which means they would have planned for satellite and drone coverage. If this was my op, I'd ditch the boat, egress on foot under tree cover to a vehicle, and then get lost in Annapolis or DC."

"Copy that, sir. We'll keep looking."

"Spin up the team and get them heading north."

"Yes, sir."

"And Baldwin," he said, as a color-coded probability matrix began to take shape on the whiteboard in his mind.

"Sir?"

"This feels like a false-flag terrorist attack. It was too well planned and executed to be ISIS or some other extremist terror outfit. Work with our friends at Fort Meade and start mining facial recognition for all known VEVAK assets and contractors. Low threshold. Fifty-one percent match or better."

"Already in progress," came Baldwin's reply.

"This has Modiri's signature all over it," Jarvis said, talking more to himself than Baldwin now. "VEVAK is here, and we're going to find them."

"Roger that, sir."

"I'm going back to the house to look for survivors. Update me immediately with any new information."

"Copy. Zero out."

Jarvis checked his watch. More than eight minutes had passed since the explosion and now three minutes since the RIB had escaped, but there was still time. Whoever the attackers were, they were good. But he had something they didn't . . .

He had John Dempsey.

CHAPTER 6

Galway Bay Irish Bar
Annapolis, Maryland
May 3
2030 Local Time

Dempsey sipped at his ginger ale and sighed.

A year running operations at a breakneck pace had earned the team this night of revelry, but somebody had to play parent, and when he saw things begin to digress, he'd naturally slid into the job. Thank God Jarvis had thought to book everyone a room at the Flag House Inn Hotel just a few blocks away. Corralling these guys and flying home in this sloppy, sorry state would have been a complete pain in the ass.

Jarvis had arranged for Ember's Special Activities Division to meet and share strategy with a tactical contingent from Mossad. After joint training with the Israelis at the Farm for two days, they had concluded with a best-practices swap summit of their own in Annapolis today. His team had been professional, and their Israeli guests had seemed impressed—although maybe a little more interested in gaining than sharing information. Now, as he watched his teammates bust up with sophomoric banter, he couldn't help but feel a little jealous.

"Are they always like this?" Munn asked, his gray eyes sharp and clear. The doc took a sip of his drink and then smiled. "Tonic sans gin."

After two beers each, they'd both switched to the light stuff.

"Actually, no," Dempsey said, shaking his head with a smile. "This is the first time in months the entire gang has been out together. Everyone's been burning the candle at both ends since, well, since I got here."

"Then it's all good," Munn said. "Apparently they needed to blow off some steam."

Wang suddenly snorted loudly, and Grimes, who was still giving him the cold shoulder, giggled along and elbowed Smith—who actually fell out of his chair onto the floor with a howl. The one-time CIA agent, Adamo, had his forehead on the table and was either asleep or passed out. Either way, the spook was dead to the world.

A double-chirp from his left cargo pocket gave Dempsey a start and his pulse quickened. He looked at the drunken rabble that was his team and shook his head.

Not a great night for a call on the secure phone.

He popped his tactical earbud into his left ear canal.

"JD," he said, loud enough to be heard over the din in the bar.

"We have a serious problem, John," came Baldwin's voice.

Dempsey's throat tightened, despite the calm, almost hypnotic voice of Ember's analytics guru. *Serious problem* from Baldwin translated to *fucking crisis*. He got to his feet, motioned for Munn to follow, and headed for the exit.

"Talk to me," he said.

"I tried Shane's phone, but he didn't answer," Baldwin began.

"I know. Just give me the SITREP," Dempsey said, his jaw tightening with worry.

"There's been an attack," Baldwin said. "The boss made it out, but the DNI and the Israeli contingent are gone . . . completely wiped off the face of the earth."

"The DNI is dead?" Dempsey asked, shock settling in. Then he glanced quickly around, glad that only Munn was in earshot, and switched into operational mode. Using Philips's Ember call sign, he asked, "Do you have *positive* confirmation that Condor is an angel?"

"No, but—" There was a pause and then a sigh. "The estate is in ruins, John, razed to the ground by an explosion. It seems unlikely there could be any survivors at all. The boss was on scene . . ."

"Is Eagle hurt?"

"No. He was a safe distance. He and the Deputy DNI, Catherine Morgan, are trying to coordinate the casualty response on the ground."

Dempsey glanced around, the hair on the back of his neck standing up.

"Are we secure?"

"Completely," Baldwin said.

"Get me on with Eagle."

"Until Annapolis Fire and Rescue arrive, Jarvis is OIC on-site. He's unavailable at present," Baldwin said. "His instructions were to spool the team and prosecute. How long until you can be ready to move?"

Dempsey glanced back at the bar where he could still hear the howling of his drunken teammates inside. "I'm one hundred percent operational," he said. "Unfortunately, I can't say the same for the rest of the team."

There was a short pause and then, "You're the only one sober, John?"

"Me and Munn."

"Okay. We don't have a target yet, but we need to get you two moving north as we shrink the uncertainty radius."

"What about the rest of the team? We need to get them clear."

"I'll send a car service to pick them up and take them back to the plane."

"Roger that." He clicked off with a tap on his earpiece but left the device in his ear. Then he turned to Munn, who was staring at him expectantly.

"What happened?"

Dempsey shook his head and started jogging toward the Tahoe. "I'll brief you en route. But Dan . . ."

"Yeah?"

"It's bad," he said solemnly.

"Time to kit up?" Munn asked.

Dempsey nodded. "Looks like it's you and me tonight."

CHAPTER 7

West Bank of the Whitehall Estate
Less Than a Mile North, across the Inlet from the DNI Estate
May 3
2020 Local Time

Cyrus grunted as he strained and heaved the heavy inflatable boat out of the water. His two accomplices—Lebanese jihadis with a thirst for blood and money, but not for martyrdom—helped him drag the boat up the embankment toward the tree line. Air hissed from the bullet holes along the port side of the RIB. He leaned hard, using all his weight and strength to help move the boat nearly fifteen meters from the water to the base of a large oak tree. Here, beneath the tree's stately canopy, the boat would be hidden from the satellites and drones that would be—if they hadn't been already—tasked to scour the waters and coastline of the Chesapeake for them. The boat would ultimately be located by the Americans, but the how and the when were the variables he needed to dictate, which was why his exfiltration from the DNI's residence had been little more than a quick jaunt up the peninsula.

Evade, distract, evade—that was the plan.

"This is good enough," he huffed and let go of the boat.

The two men followed his lead and squatted next to the RIB, panting.

Cyrus pushed his eyeglasses—thick, gray frames with heavy, clear glass—back up on his nose and resisted the urge to scratch at his face. The glue holding the fake beard he wore was itching like mad. He scanned left and then right for threats, the long fake ponytail tapping him on each shoulder as he did. He prayed the disguise—engineered to obscure the bone structure of his face and make his eyes appear closer set—would defeat any facial recognition they might run post facto on the security feeds from the DNI's home. While working as one of the catering staff, he'd actively managed his exposure to the house's visible surveillance net, but cameras were small and easy to conceal. It was impossible to know how many he'd missed.

"Praise Allah!" the younger of the two men said, having fully recovered his breath. Then, clamping a congratulatory hand on Cyrus's shoulder, added, "We did it. We actually did it."

Cyrus pulled away, recoiling from the man's touch. He'd noticed, over recent months, that he'd come to find unsanctioned human touch repulsive. A side effect of Arkady's training, he surmised.

"How many rich American capitalists do you think we killed tonight?" the other mercenary asked.

"Enough and more," Cyrus whispered. "Now, be quiet."

He wondered if they knew they'd killed as many—if not more—high-ranking Jews as Americans tonight. In a single attack, they'd wiped out the Mossad's leadership echelon, crippling the Zionists' famed intelligence and clandestine operations entity. The irony was, the Jews had no one to blame but themselves—undone by their own hubris and unbridled faith in the Americans. This was the brilliance of his uncle's plan; it achieved multiple goals simultaneously. Not only would it send both the American and Zionist intelligence communities into tailspins; it would undermine Israeli-American trust and confidence.

Cyrus would scrub any and all signatures overtly linking the operation to Iran, leaving behind only a single clue—one that *only* the ultrasecret American counterterrorism unit responsible for killing his father could pick up. The trap had been baited; now all they had to do was wait. If his uncle was right, this would draw the American ghost team to Israel and eventually into Iran itself. He would avenge both his father and his brother and, in the process, put an end to the deadliest threat to Persia's covert operations.

"Both of you, help me scuttle the boat," Cyrus said. "No trace can be left behind."

The older of the two men mumbled something in Arabic, making no effort to hide his annoyance at being bossed around by Cyrus, a Muslim ten years his junior. He stepped into the boat and began rigging the gas tanks to blow while the other man gathered their gear. While they busied themselves, Cyrus reached into his satchel and palmed the suppressed Strizh 9 mm pistol. In one fluid motion, he raised the weapon, took careful aim, squeezed, resighted, and squeezed again. The pistol burped twice, and the two men slumped dead, one on top of the other—blood, brains, and bits of bone spattered all over the inside of the boat.

Cyrus tucked the pistol in his waistband and returned his attention to his satchel. From the bag, he pulled an unsophisticated but effective IED—constructed of three grenades fixed in place by a strand of soldering wire triple-wrapped around the circumference, holding the handles in place. He pulled the three pins and hit "Start" on a timer device clipped to the wire. When the timer clicked to zero—fifteen minutes from now—a magnesium charge would ignite and burn quickly through the solder, thereby releasing the grenades. The grenades would explode, igniting the RIB's fuel tanks, resulting in a fireball that would be visible for miles. If the investigators managed to obtain salvageable DNA from the burned corpses, his uncle assured him they would not find a match in any American or Zionist database.

He pressed the "Start" button again, and the numbers on the counter began to count down. Then, he zipped the satchel closed and placed the bag between the RIB's twin gas tanks, careful not to step in the blood now pooling at the stern. He removed his wig, fake beard, eyeglasses, and black waiter's shirt and tossed them into the boat. If the Americans had somehow recorded an image of his disguised face at the DNI's estate, facial-recognition software wouldn't be able to match it to his real face were he to be picked up on surveillance video in the days to come.

He took a deep breath and checked his watch—*two minutes behind schedule*. At a brisk clip, he set off north through the woods. In a hundred yards, he would drift east and make his way to the bend in Whitehall Drive, where he'd hidden a bicycle in a ditch along the road. A quick pedal north to recover the BMW motorcycle he'd stashed, then he would head west on 50.

He pushed a tiny earbud into his ear and tapped it twice.

"This is Alpha; it's done," he whispered.

"Well done. Go black, Alpha. See you on the other side. Omega out," said Rostami's voice in his ear.

Cyrus felt a sudden surge of anxiety as he reached the roadside ditch and began searching for the bicycle. The element of surprise was gone, and so soon would be his head-start advantage. The next hour would be the most dangerous of his young career. He needed to get to Route 301 before they shut down the highway. Where he was heading next, they would never suspect.

CHAPTER 8

Ember SUV
Route 301
Annapolis, Maryland
May 3
2050 Local Time

"Dagger, this is Zero," Baldwin's voice said through the Chevy Tahoe's speakers as Dempsey and Munn sped east across the Severn River Bridge. Dempsey loved his call sign tonight. With any luck, he'd be afforded the opportunity to sink his own dagger deep into the heart of the asshole responsible for blowing up the DNI and fifty other innocents.

"One—Dagger, go ahead," Dempsey said, his phone synced to the Tahoe's infotainment system.

"Comms are now secure."

"Understood. Please tell me you have something?"

"Yes. I'm diverting you to the scene of an explosion that just occurred across the inlet north of the Philips estate. The location is inside the escape radius the attackers could have traveled by boat before I got eyes in the sky."

"Give me coordinates or an address."

"Syncing with your nav system . . . I have you coming off the Severn River Bridge now. Take the Whitehall Road exit in three and a half clicks."

The console screen refreshed and a magenta line appeared on the map, highlighting the route Baldwin wanted them to follow.

"Copy."

"After you exit, head east on Whitehall Road. There's a confusing intersection where Whitehall runs into Skidmore—just past a Motel 6. Skidmore continues east in a straight line, but Whitehall doglegs south. You want to stay on Whitehall Road and head south toward Whitehall Manor. Do you see the route highlighted in magenta?"

"We know how GPS works, Zero," Dempsey said, laying the sarcasm on thick. "No need for the play-by-play."

"At Whitehall Manor, I will be routing you off road," Baldwin continued, unfazed. "No time for confusion or wrong turns, John."

Dempsey glanced at the nav screen and saw that their track would indeed diverge from the paved road and take them across the grounds of an estate property. "Copy all, Zero."

A beat later they reached the exit, and Dempsey piloted the Tahoe down the ramp and onto Whitehall Road eastbound. With the clock ticking, Dempsey pressed the accelerator to the floor. As they zoomed past the entrance to a strip mall, Munn shouted, "Look out!"

Dempsey hammered the brake and swerved to avoid rear-ending a turning Lexus that had abruptly stopped in the middle of the street. In his peripheral vision, he saw a figure on a bicycle pedaling furiously across the road at the mall entrance.

"Jesus Christ," Dempsey barked over squealing tires as he wrangled the big Chevy back under control. "Fucking idiot."

Then something occurred to him.

"Baldwin, do you have eyes on me?"

"No, John," Ian replied. "I am working to get more eyes on, but I am focused on the target site. What can I do for you?"

Dempsey looked in his rearview mirror, but the cyclist was gone.

"Saw a guy on a bike heading north. Check him out if you can."

"Understood," Baldwin answered, "but I have only one drone with eyes on the explosion and I'm using the satellite to scan shoreline everywhere a boat could have made landfall in the time allotted. Do you want me to retask?"

"Negative," he said. "You're doing all the right things."

At the next intersection, Dempsey whipped the steering wheel around and made a hard right turn to keep on Whitehall, heading south just as Baldwin had advised.

After a beat, Baldwin asked, "Do you see smoke on the horizon yet?"

"Negative, too dark," Dempsey said. "What about you?"

"Any first responders on-site we need to worry about?" Munn asked.

"Negative. I'm monitoring the response. Annapolis Fire Department sent all their units to the DNI estate. Anne Arundel County is sending two engines to your six, but they're at least fifteen minutes out. The state police tactical unit will arrive next, but they are still at least thirty minutes out. Local police are busy assisting at DNI estate and setting up roadblocks . . . you're at the turn, John."

"I know, I know," Dempsey growled and braked before maneuvering off road. The Chevy jarred violently as he traversed a shallow drainage ditch at a forty-five-degree angle, each wheel taking the culvert in staggered sequence. The rear differential bottomed out as he crawled up the other side. The headlight beams danced as the SUV rocked and rolled over the field and Dempsey weaved between trees trying to maintain a southwest vector.

"Here," Munn said, handing him a helmet with NVGs already glowing green on their bracket up top. "No sense in making our arrival too public."

"Thanks," Dempsey said, switching off the headlights. With his free hand, he donned the helmet and clicked the binocular night optics down in front of his eyes. The world switched from black to gray-green, and his field of vision instantly deepened in all directions. He weaved around a large oak and then accelerated across a clearing toward a cluster of trees. Straight ahead, a fire raged bright white, flames licking skyward.

"Shit, dude," Munn said, his face glowing green behind his own NVGs. "That's a fire."

"Target site dead ahead," Dempsey reported to Baldwin. "We're going in, full tactical."

In silent reply, Munn reached behind his seat and pulled a large duffel into his lap. Dempsey kept his concentration focused on the approach, scanning for tree stumps or deep fissures that could wreck the Tahoe and leave them stranded. To his right, he heard Munn load magazines into two short-barrel Sig Sauer tactical rifles and click PEQ-4 IR targeting lights on each. Munn laid one of the rifles in Dempsey's lap and then fished out two Sig 229 9 mm pistols, again checking the rounds and magazines.

The pungent odor of burning leaves was seeping inside the cabin now. Dempsey eased the SUV to a stop and killed the engine.

"You good?" he asked, turning to Munn.

Munn flashed him a SEAL's grin. "Hooyah, brother."

"Zero, Dagger. Do you hold any thermals that could be tangos?"

"Negative, John," came Baldwin's reply. "But the heat from the fire bleeds into a pretty large radius. If the bad guys are dug in close, I might not see them."

"Check," Dempsey said. "We're moving in."

"Roger, I see you," Baldwin said.

Dempsey and Munn fanned out, putting ten yards between them, their movements driven by muscle memory, habit, and operational familiarity. Two-man assaults, something they'd drilled thousands of times, came as natural as breathing. As they closed on the site, Munn drifted farther left, opening the gap between them and flanking the target site. Scanning over his assault rifle, Dempsey searched the green-gray woods for movement. After a dozen closing paces, the light from the fire was bright enough to wash out his night vision. He flipped his NVGs up and took a knee, giving his eyes a second to adjust.

"Hold," he whispered into his Bluetooth mike.

Angry red-orange flames climbed the trees—licking at the canopy branches and bathing a forty-yard diameter with a golden glow.

"Two—One—anything?"

"No movement," Munn reported. "Hard to see with the damn fire."

"Check," Dempsey said. "I'm circling around."

In a combat crouch, he crept toward the northeast, knowing Munn was completing his circle and would come around from the other side. As he slowly circled a large, stately oak tree in the very middle of the blaze, the charred remains of what appeared to be a boat came into view. "We may have a RIB," Dempsey said.

His heart rate picked up, and he flipped down his NVGs and turned back to the dark woods behind him. Scanning over his rifle, he methodically searched a 180-degree arc, but nothing caught his attention. No movement. No crouching figures. Turning back toward the light, he flipped up his night vision and said, "Clear."

A beat later, Munn's voice in his ear: "Clear."

"What about you, Zero? Anything?"

"I hold no heat signatures outside ten meters."

"Check," Dempsey said and lowered his assault rifle to a combat carry. Staring into the inferno, he approached the charred remains of the boat. The gas from the fuel tanks was long consumed, leaving the twisted, melted mess in the center of a twenty-five-foot circle of scorched earth. The fire was moving into the canopy above now, but patches of bark on the giant oak's trunk were still sizzling and popping, sending blue tendrils of smoke skyward.

A gust of wind blew embers into his face. A beat later, the smell hit him—the nauseating fetor of cooked flesh. This was not the first time he'd encountered charred human remains.

"Looks like two bodies," Munn said, crouching down beside the smoldering remains of the boat.

Dempsey squinted at the outline of two or maybe three smoking piles of flesh. Just past Munn, he saw a charred boot with a hunk of burned leg sticking out the top. Dozens of other unidentifiable body parts, he realized, littered the area around them.

"Not gonna get much out of this," Dempsey said, screwing up his face at the gruesome scene.

"Well, I don't think this is all of them," Munn said. "Be pretty shitty luck to pull off the worst attack on the US since 9/11 and then get killed in a freak explosion *after* you pull your boat outta the water."

"These guys were loose ends," Dempsey said, nodding in agreement. "Blowing up the boat is a good diversion, too—slows down the search and ties up assets here while the lead guy works his EXFIL plan."

"Dagger, this is Eagle. Do you see anything there? Anything at all?" It was Jarvis's no-bullshit voice in his ear now. As he suspected, the Skipper had been monitoring the op the entire time.

"Nothing *we* can use," Dempsey said.

"What about forensics?" Munn asked, clearing his throat and spitting.

"FBI forensics will find whatever the terrorists meant for them to find," Jarvis growled, his tone implying he was thinking exactly what Dempsey was.

"Roger that, Skipper," he said. "You want us to bug out?"

"Yes," Jarvis said. "Zero, find us another target."

"Roger, Eagle. We're working on it."

"Work faster, Zero. The team leader is still out there, and we need to find him before anybody else does. I want this bastard all to ourselves. No red tape. No paperwork."

Dempsey met Munn's gaze and nodded in the direction of the Tahoe.

"I'm ready," Munn said. "Let's get the hell out of here."

They huffed it back to the Tahoe, and Dempsey retraced their path to Whitehall Road. They hadn't even made it back to 301 before Baldwin was on the line again: "I might have something."

"Talk to me," Jarvis said, beating Dempsey to the punch.

"With the help of our friends at Fort Meade, we've been searching camera data from all accessible sources in Annapolis, but also inside the beltway," Baldwin said. "It's a tremendous amount of data."

"Get to the point," Jarvis snapped.

"You told me to search for known VEVAK operatives and affiliates with a fifty-one percent confidence level. We did just that, and we have a sixty-seven percent match on Behrouz Rostami."

For a moment, Dempsey couldn't speak, his foot easing off the accelerator and the SUV slowing in the middle of the road. Rostami . . . in DC? How had that bastard gotten into the country undetected again?

What the hell is wrong with security in this country?

"You have him entering?"

"No, better. I have him in the DC metro. A traffic-light camera got a decent image of him through the windshield of a car, believe it or not."

"Today?"

"Yesterday," Baldwin said.

"So do we head toward DC?" Dempsey asked, turning to Munn. "It's certainly possible that Rostami was running command and control from the city for the shitheads in the field."

"Or he could have staged there last night and led the op himself. This is all guesswork unless your signals guru can find us something real time, or at least close to real time."

"God, I want to catch this bastard," Dempsey said through gritted teeth.

"I may have something else . . ." Baldwin said.

Painful second after painful second ticked by, and Dempsey pictured Baldwin hunched over a computer screen flanked by his twin prodigies, junior analysts Chip and Dale, looking at facial-rec images annotated with colored dots and zigzagging lines.

"We're waiting, Zero," came Jarvis's voice, ripe with the same impatience and irritation Dempsey was feeling.

"Well, isn't this interesting," Baldwin commented, as if browsing for a dinner reservation on OpenTable. "Convenient, too."

"What's interesting?" Jarvis said, his temper clearly at the ragged edge of control.

"Rostami's in Cleveland Park."

"Now?"

"I have him in a car at a traffic light at 1612 hours this afternoon."

Dempsey punched the accelerator and screamed toward the 301.

"Anything after that?" Jarvis asked.

"Not yet. We have a lot of raw data to run, but this will narrow it. No sign of the car leaving the area," Baldwin said. "Now if I can just get a hit of him on foot . . ."

"What's special about Cleveland Park?" Munn asked as Dempsey accelerated up the ramp onto westbound route 301. A new magenta line had already appeared on his map display, showing the route from Annapolis into the upscale residential district.

"Sorry," Baldwin said. "I should have explained before. Cleveland Park is home to a number of international embassies."

"But I thought Iran didn't have an embassy in the US," Dempsey said.

"They don't," Jarvis chimed in. "But the Pakistani embassy maintains an Interests Section for the Islamic Republic of Iran, where they process visas and the like."

"And where is the Pakistani embassy?" Dempsey asked, but he was looking over at Munn, tight-lipped. Munn arched his eyebrows as they waited for the answer they knew was coming.

"In Cleveland Park," Baldwin said.

"Motherfucker," Dempsey hissed at Munn. "Running a terrorist op out of the fucking Pakistani embassy right under our noses."

"Hold on a second," Munn said. "We're not gonna hit the Pakistani embassy, are we?"

"If Behrouz fucking Rostami is hiding inside, we sure as hell are."

"You can't be serious."

"Everybody settle down," Jarvis chimed in, his voice having regained its operational composure. "I'm en route now, ten minutes behind Dagger. If you see him, you prosecute; otherwise we do this together. Understood?"

"Roger that," Dempsey said.

"We don't even know if he's still there," Munn cautioned.

"I'm working on that," Baldwin said. "Just need a little more time."

Dempsey's heart quickened at the thought of putting his red targeting dot on the Iranian operator's forehead. Four times he'd been within yards of nailing the bastard, and four times the slippery snake had slipped away. Frankfurt, Geneva, New York, and Omaha . . . he would not let it happen a fifth time here on his home turf of all places.

"Dude, if he's in the embassy . . ." Munn said, just soft enough not to resonate over the open channel.

"Then we take him," Dempsey said tersely.

"That's like attacking Pakistan."

"It wouldn't be the first time I've violated Pakistan's sovereign territory to take down an enemy of the United States. I don't see how this is any different."

Munn shook his head but didn't say anything.

Dempsey glanced over at his friend. "Rostami was the key operator on the attack at the UN, and we're certain he played a role in facilitating the massacre of our brothers during Operation Crusader. The *only* way this bastard is getting away this time is over my dead body."

CHAPTER 9

West Parking Lot of University of DC near the Pakistani Embassy
Cleveland Park Neighborhood of Northwest Washington, DC
May 3
2155 Local Time

Cyrus sat in the driver's seat of the gray Infiniti and tapped his thumb on the leather steering wheel. *This is not doubt,* he told himself. *This is preparation.*

He needed to be ready for anything and everything. He needed to have a plan for any, and all, deviations from the script he'd prepared in his mind. Meticulous scenario planning was a technique taught to him by his Russian tutor, but also by the Persian he was going to rendez-vous with. He was parked in a commuter lot at the rear of the campus and knew he had only a few minutes to complete the exercise before a campus security officer drove by and noticed him loitering. The sight lines around the embassy were poor from most angles, including his current position. He had hoped to observe Rostami, to see him pacing in front of a window, or talking on the phone. Just a single glance at the man's face before the encounter would tell him much. One could learn volumes by watching someone who did not know they were being watched. If Rostami suspected what Cyrus planned to do next, his face would betray that.

He raised the Nightforce NXS scope from his lap and quickly scanned the brick courtyard beyond the closed iron gate at the front of the Pakistani embassy. The courtyard was deserted. Despite the hour, lights were on inside the embassy, but he saw no movement. The administrative and security building to the right of the gate was also well lit, and inside he could see two uniformed men, chatting while a TV played in the background. He scanned up and down the street for signs he'd been followed, but traffic was nonexistent. No loitering pedestrians. No patrolling police vehicles. No idling black SUVs.

Cyrus lowered the scope.

Rostami was not expecting him, but even so, Cyrus would not be able to use the element of surprise to his advantage. Rostami was safe inside a citadel, while he was in the position of needing to storm the castle. Thankfully, there were protocols in place he could leverage. The last radio call with Rostami was supposed to be his final communication with VEVAK personnel until his safe return to Tehran, but meeting here was an authorized contingency plan in the event something interfered with Cyrus's ability to exfiltrate the United States. Exfiltration was supposed to be his own responsibility—his uncle had made that clear. Arkady had once explained that veteran operators rely heavily on a personal network of trusted underground contacts to leverage in times of need. A robust and reliable network, the Russian had said, takes decades to develop. But Cyrus was only a few months into this new life, and for now he had no one he could count on other than himself. Rostami understood this, and it was this lone vulnerability that Cyrus intended to exploit.

He removed the ceramic blade from the sheath strapped to his calf and shifted it to a secondary sheath sewed inside the left sleeve of his jacket. He was about to get out of the car when the feeling of impending doom washed over him. He scanned the street in front of the embassy again. Something suddenly felt wrong, like a dark force closing in on him. As a civilian, he'd dismissed the notion of a sixth sense, but Arkady had insisted that sharply honed instincts were the difference between life and death in their profession.

He tried to articulate the emotion. *Either I'm being watched by the Americans, or I'm afraid that Rostami will see through me.*

It was hard to imagine that Rostami would risk killing his boss's nephew, but Rostami had been playing this game much longer than Cyrus had. It was only the two of them left now. If Rostami detected even the slightest threat, he might be inclined to draw first blood. Afterward, Rostami could simply lie to Amir and say that Cyrus had martyred himself in the explosion. His uncle would not be able to prove otherwise. He doubted the American intelligence community would let the details of the explosion reach the media, but even if that were to happen, the reporting outlets would spin conflicting tales. The only reliable aspect of the media was its unreliability.

I will have to act quickly, he told himself.

He tucked the scope under the driver seat and grabbed his backpack from the passenger seat. After four deep, cleansing breaths, he slipped the pack over his shoulder and climbed out of the Infiniti. He crossed the lawn at the back of the campus, angling north, before making his way across the street to the west side of International Drive. From there, he passed the Nigerian embassy, heading south, all the while scanning the street, sidewalks, and adjacent buildings' windows for surveillance threats. It was then that he noticed the lights and heavily fortified perimeter of the Israeli embassy on the other side of Van Ness Street. The irony of this made him smile as he circled around. He jumped the iron fence and cut across the lawn between the Malaysian and Pakistani embassies. When he reached the main gate, he pressed the buzzer on the call box. Set back from the gate by about one hundred feet was a small administrative wing, connected to the main building and extending out at a ninety-degree angle, where he presumed the security staff had an office. A blue light came on in the right upper corner of the call box.

"State your business?" a voice said.

"I am Hamza Samak, from Quaid-i-Azam University. I'm supposed to meet Mr. Nasir, who is in residence here. He's expecting me, but I'm late in arriving. Please inform him that I have important news from my visit to Amsterdam."

The message contained coded information that only Rostami would understand. Had Cyrus declared a European city other than Amsterdam, it would have meant he was under surveillance. Had he said Dubai, it would have meant he was under duress and needed help. This protocol had been established during the planning stage of the operation and was known only to the two of them.

"Wait there while I call him," the guard said, and the speaker went silent.

Cyrus felt naked and vulnerable standing under the white light at the gate. He shifted his posture to appear confident and casual, but inside he was counting off the seconds. After what felt like an eternity, he heard a double-beep, and the heavy iron gate rolled to the right, slipping behind the fence line. Cyrus stepped onto the grounds and was met by an approaching guard.

"Good evening," he said in Urdu.

"Good evening," the guard answered in heavily accented English, his eyes going straight to Cyrus's backpack. "What is in the bag?"

"Just a change of clothes and some personal items."

"Come with me," the guard said, making a U-turn and leading Cyrus to the small administrative wing at the front of the embassy. The guard led him inside to the security checkpoint and gestured to the bag. "Open it."

Cyrus unzipped the main compartment and tilted the mouth toward the man. The guard made a cursory check, rummaging through the contents and saying nothing about the oversize, empty plastic bag inside. Then, the guard pulled out a handheld metal detector. Cyrus stepped his legs apart and held out his arms for scanning. The guard ran the wand quickly but expertly over his body.

"Okay," the guard said, stowing the wand and gesturing to a paper log. "Sign here."

Cyrus signed in to the access log under his assumed name, after which the guard escorted him past the administrative building to the lobby of the embassy proper, where he was greeted by a middle-aged Pakistani wearing a finely tailored suit.

"Welcome, Mr. Samak," the man said, greeting him with a wide plastic smile. "Mr. Nasir asked that I meet you here in the lobby." They shook hands and then the smiling Pakistani said, "You must be exhausted from your trip. Do you require any refreshment? Water or tea perhaps?"

Cyrus immediately recognized this for what it was—secondary vetting now that he was inside the safety of the embassy walls.

"I'm feeling rested and require no refreshments, thank you," Cyrus said, indicating that he was neither injured nor in need of urgent assistance.

"Wonderful," the Pakistani said, but this time his smile was genuine. He gave a curt nod to the guard. Officially dismissed now, the guard promptly turned and left.

"Follow me, please. Mr. Nasir is ready to receive you."

They walked briskly to a set of marble stairs, and Cyrus trailed his escort by a body length up to the third floor. The Pakistani had neglected to provide Cyrus with his name or title, but Cyrus knew exactly what role this handsome, well-dressed attendant fulfilled for the embassy; he was a human German shepherd, trained to greet, impress, and if circumstances demanded, intimidate. Cyrus was 100 percent certain that none of the staff at the Pakistani embassy or the Iranian "cultural mission" had been read into either their operation or their legends. Which made what was about to happen all the more diabolical.

Cyrus followed his escort through the embassy to another wing of the building secured with its own guard station. A tired-looking Persian in a gray security uniform sat behind a built-in desk. A banner hung across the front with print in Arabic and English: "Interests Section of the Islamic Republic of Iran."

"Sign in. Mr. Nasir is waiting for you," the guard said and rubbed the corner of his left eye.

"Thank you," Cyrus said with a young man's eager smile. He signed the open book with "H. Samak" and noted the time of 10:05 p.m. on his watch.

"This is where I leave you," said the Pakistani in the suit.

Cyrus thanked him, then turned and walked toward a heavy wooden door in the hallway beyond, but it swung open before he could reach for the knob. Rostami greeted him, smiling broadly. "Hamza, my friend. Come in, come in. I can't wait to hear all about your trip."

Despite the playacting, Rostami appeared relaxed. Cyrus knew better than to read a seasoned agent's body language as scripture. If his former mentor meant to turn the tables on Cyrus, the privacy and security afforded to Rostami in this facility were second to none. If his uncle no longer trusted Rostami, then for certain he should be careful, too.

Time is my enemy. I must act first, Cyrus reminded himself.

Rostami nodded to the guard and then closed the door behind them. The instant the heavy wooden door shut, Rostami's warm smile disappeared. "You're not supposed to be here unless something has gone terribly wrong. You coming here puts both of us at risk."

"I know, but I was not followed."

"In our final communication, I was very clear," Rostami said, wagging a finger at him. "No contact until after exfiltration."

"No," Cyrus said, shaking his head. "In our last communication, you ordered me to 'go black' and then severed the circuit before I had a chance to finish my report. I have a problem, and it's something I have to deal with before exfiltration."

Rostami sighed. "And what is the problem?"

"The problem, my friend," Cyrus said, shrugging off his backpack as a diversion while he slipped his blade from its sheath, "is you."

CHAPTER 10

Ember SUV
University Parking Lot Adjacent to the Pakistani Embassy
Washington, DC
May 3
2345 Local Time

Dempsey put the Tahoe's transmission into park and killed the SUV's engine. His own motor, however, was revved up to redline, and he was ready to go. "We're here, Baldwin. No time for fucking around. Is Rostami in the embassy or not?" he said on the open circuit.

"We have a seventy-five percent confidence match on a local security camera aimed at the embassy's main gate. At 1655, Rostami arrived on foot, cleared security, and entered the building via the main lobby." In the background, Dempsey heard what sounded like multiple hands typing furiously on multiple keyboards.

"That was nearly five hours ago," Munn said. "He could be anywhere now."

"No, I don't think so," Baldwin replied. "I don't have him leaving."

"What about secret exits? He could have left through an underground tunnel," Munn countered.

"This is the Pakistani embassy," Baldwin replied with a hint of sarcasm. "Not the White House."

Dempsey cocked a *c'mon, bro* eyebrow at Munn.

"What?" Munn said.

"Munn has a valid point," Jarvis said on the line. "We need to entertain all scenarios. What about internal camera footage, Ian? Surely the embassy has a network security-camera system you can hack?"

"They do have a system. It's a terribly old legacy system, however, which paradoxically makes penetrating it harder rather than easier, but we're online with a colleague at the NSA trying to gain access as we speak," Baldwin said.

"What's your position, Skipper?" Dempsey asked, imagining that Jarvis couldn't be that far out.

"I'm parallel parked on International Court between the Pakistani and Nigerian embassies," Jarvis said.

"Perfect," Dempsey said. "We EXFIL in your vehicle?"

"That's the plan."

"So we're really going to do this?" Munn asked, looking at Dempsey with incredulous eyes. "We're going to hit the Pakistani embassy?"

Dempsey wanted to answer, but this call was above his pay grade. "Skipper?" he said. "What's the call?"

"We're going in," came the Ember Director's reply. "Can you give us some night, Ian?"

"Yes, but it's complicated," Baldwin said. "Just the embassy or everywhere?"

"Total night," Jarvis said. "For several blocks. I don't want to make it blatantly obvious the Pakistani embassy was targeted, or even Embassy Row for that matter. I want some bleed on the blackout."

"Okay, but people are going to notice. Phone calls are going to be made," Baldwin said. "I cannot guarantee how long before the power company figures out the exploit we're going to use."

"I understand. Your best guess—how long?" Jarvis asked. In the background, Dempsey heard the familiar sound of a pistol slide release and a round being chambered. Jarvis was kitting up.

"Ten minutes, plus or minus two," came the reply. "Also, I should make you aware that the embassy is equipped with standby electric power generators—" Baldwin abruptly stopped talking, and Dempsey heard one of Ember's junior analysts, Chip or Dale, interrupt him. After a frustratingly long delay during which the two tech geniuses argued, Baldwin said, "We're into the embassy's control system now. Dale says the generator has a wireless monitoring system. The genny will start automatically on loss of grid power, but we can shut it down immediately thereafter on low oil pressure."

"Just make it happen," Jarvis said. "Do I have eyes in the air?"

"Yes, we have an RQ-7B in orbit that Shane, despite inebriation, launched successfully from the airport when the rest of the team got back to the jet."

"Can you pull up the thermal on the drone? We need to know where the warm bodies are."

The infotainment screen on Dempsey's console refreshed and the drone feed from orbit appeared.

"This building is a problem. Lots of structure, and do you see those dishes on the roof? Those are active jammers; it's wreaking havoc with the drone feed, forcing me to keep a long-distance setback to prevent interference with our control of the bird."

"Shit," Jarvis grumbled.

"It's okay. For obvious reasons this building has always been of particular interest to our spooky friends. We've managed to cobble together a pretty comprehensive floor plan for you from prior collection activities. I'm uploading a file to your console displays and mobile devices as we speak," Baldwin said. "Notwithstanding recent internal modifications, of course, the layout should be accurate. As soon as we get access to internal security feeds, which I hope to have any minute, we'll compare video images against the plans to give you a heads-up on any discrepancies . . ."

While Baldwin prattled on, Dempsey looked over at Munn. "Time to kit up, Dan. Big-boy rules, so if you're not game—"

"I'm all in," Munn said, cutting him off. "I was just pointing shit out and making sure we know what we're getting into before we go."

"All right," Dempsey said, watching Munn's face as he grabbed the duffel bag from the back seat. He pulled out the long guns and slipped a sling over his head. "Somewhere inside that building is the asshole who has led five attacks on US soil in the past year." He paused while he checked a round in the chamber of his assault rifle and then did the same for his Sig, which he slipped into a drop holster on his right thigh. Then he pulled out three extra magazines for the rifle and two for his pistol. "Behrouz Rostami is one slippery, tricky bastard, Dan. The information about VEVAK's operations in that fucker's brain is gold. Shoot to wound. We cannot let him die, and we cannot let him get away."

"I understand," Munn said, passing Dempsey his vest.

Dempsey slipped the vest over his head and secured it around his waist with the large Velcro panels while Munn did the same. Next, the doc grabbed their helmets, with NVGs still intact from their tromp through the woods. Both men checked the batteries and then they were ready. Dempsey looked at the building plans for the embassy on his console display. He used the touchscreen to scroll through all three levels, committing the layout to memory.

"Just to be clear, the Iranian cultural mission is on the third floor, southwest corner, correct?" Dempsey asked.

"That is correct, John," Baldwin said.

"Call signs?"

"Dempsey is One, Munn Two, and I'm Three," Jarvis replied. "Baldwin stays Zero."

"Roger that, Three," Dempsey said.

"We're split now," Jarvis said, "but we'll merge during the western approach after you cross International Court behind the embassy. We go in as a three-man team. Dempsey is point with a standard fan. Zero, you need to get that front gate open before you cut power. Otherwise it will fail in a locked-shut setting."

"Understood," Baldwin replied. "Also, I should point out the embassy is likely using fail-secure magnetic locks. However, by code, emergency egresses must use 'fail-safe' models that unlock in the event of a power outage. You will be safe to use any doors designated as emergency exits for INFIL and EXFIL, but the others I cannot guarantee."

"Roger. Thank you, Ian," Jarvis said. "The secure entrance is located in the admin wing, which juts out from the main building on the southwest corner of the property about thirty yards away from the iron gate at the street. We're going to attempt to avoid that entrance and make a covert pass across the north side of the courtyard and down the ramp into the underground parking garage. We will enter on the basement level via emergency exit. Once inside, we take the north fire-escape stairwell to the third level. I don't expect interference or resistance until we reach the third level, but navigating the third floor to the Iranian mission could get hairy. Lots of opportunities for civilian interference en route, and I anticipate we'll encounter security at the Iranian mission. Stay nonlethal if possible, but lethal force is authorized inside the Iranian spaces. Anyone with Rostami is likely a lethal hostile and so we operate accordingly, but we must take Rostami alive. EXFIL is a retrace—down the fire-escape stairwell to the garage, up the ramp, sweep north, down the hill, and back to my vehicle on International Court. Any questions?"

"No sir. One and Two are set," Dempsey said, not giving Munn a chance to lob another "what if" grenade.

"Zero, call the approach," Jarvis said.

"You're clear. Not a soul out and about," Baldwin said.

"One is set," Dempsey said.

"Zero, open the gate and give us the night," Jarvis said.

Dempsey was out of the car now, adjusting his rifle across his chest in a tactical carry. As if there were a giant light switch somewhere, the entire world went dark. Baldwin had, as promised, cut power across a swath of city blocks. Dempsey flipped down the NVGs on his helmet and entered the familiar green-gray world of night vision. They crossed the commuter parking lot, hopped a fence, and bolted across International Court into the shadowy pass between the Pakistani and Nigerian embassies. With expert precision, Jarvis fell into formation, and now they were a three-man team moving up the hill and toward the embassy's main gate.

"I have you on IR and thermal from the drone," Baldwin said. "The gate is open. The courtyard is clear. You're good to cross."

A beat later, they swept south and were crouched outside the gate, scanning for threats. Dempsey trusted Baldwin's eyes in the sky, but he trusted his own more. After quickly confirming the approach was clear, Dempsey pushed the gate open on its rollers just enough for them to squeeze through in single file. Weapon up, Dempsey dashed through the opening then twisted right to scan the administrative building for emerging security personnel. He chopped a hand at the ramp leading to the underground garage fifty feet ahead.

"Movement at the admin building," Baldwin reported. "Someone is stepping out."

Dempsey picked up the pace as Jarvis and Munn followed behind him. Twenty more feet and they would be clear, obscured from view by the concrete wall on the south side of the ramp. He looked right as he moved and saw two guards emerge from the admin building. He noted they were not wearing NVGs, and their native night eyes were probably still adjusting to the dark after the power cut.

Almost there—just ten more feet.

Dempsey's left foot hit the downward-sloping concrete of the ramp just as one of the guards clicked on a flashlight. He crouched lower and ducked behind the sloping wall of the ramp. Munn and Jarvis fell in behind him, all whirling and taking knees behind the wall. The wall blocked Dempsey's view of the guards to the south, but he could see the flash beam moving along the iron spindles of the front gate. When the beam reached the gap at the end, it stopped.

Shit.

He glanced at Jarvis, who shook his head; Dempsey got the implied message: *We'll deal with the gate on the way out.*

"One, Zero, both guards are walking to the gate," said Baldwin's voice in his ear. "They'll be able to see you in six . . . five . . ."

Dempsey double-clicked acknowledgment, chopped a hand toward the garage, and set off down the ramp. They moved swiftly and silently into the pitch-black subterranean parking structure, which without night vision would have been impossible to navigate. Dempsey led Munn and Jarvis between a row of parked cars toward an elevator bank on the far wall. Beside the elevator, he spied a steel door, which he figured must lead to a stairwell. As he reached for the handle, he prayed Baldwin was right about fail-safe locks on emergency exits. They had breacher charges, but using breachers on this op was an option of last resort. Tonight they needed to be ghosts, not leaving a single trace of their presence behind. He depressed the lever and, to his great relief, pulled the door open easily.

Munn held the door open while Dempsey stepped into the stairwell, clearing the bottom landing first and then sighting up. Seeing no one, he paused a beat and listened, but the three-story stairwell was dead quiet. Dempsey waved Munn and Jarvis in behind him and moved toward the first flight of stairs. His first footfall on the metal steps echoed in the cavernous cement stair tower, making Dempsey cringe. A perfect stealth ascent to the top would be impossible; on the plus side, the instant anyone else entered or moved in the stairwell, they'd know. His next step was more deliberate and quieter, but time was their nemesis. He glanced back at Jarvis, who gave him a *shit happens* shrug. Jaw clenched, Dempsey led the controlled ascent as quietly and expeditiously as possible—the metal staircase thrumming and echoing to the cadence of three pairs of footfalls all the way up.

When they reached the level-three landing, Dempsey took a knee by the door. Baldwin must have still been having problems getting imaging from the drone because normally they'd be getting a warm-body report before entering the hall. Dempsey had become spoiled enough running ops with Ember's superior tech that now he felt entitled to the information before turning every corner. He glanced at Jarvis and Munn, saw they were set, and grabbed the lever. He raised three fingers: *Three . . . two . . .*

The lights went on.

Blinded, Dempsey released the door lever, knocked his NVGs up, and squeezed his eyes shut. "What the fuck is going on, Zero?"

"The standby generator just came on," Baldwin replied. "It failed to start immediately after the outage and just came on now."

"Turn it off!"

"Working on it, John . . . patience."

He had a tactical decision to make: light-adjust his eyes, or hope Baldwin worked quickly and try to keep his night vision. He listened for the sound of boots converging in the stairwell from below or the hallway outside the door . . . Nothing at the moment, but that could change. There was no way he was going to lead the team into the hallway with lights bright, but they couldn't remain in the fire-escape stairwell indefinitely, either.

"Baldwin, get that fucking genny shut down, ASAP," Jarvis commanded over the comms channel.

After a beat, the lights in the emergency stairwell flickered twice and then went dark.

"Don't let that happen again, Zero," Jarvis said.

"No guarantees, Three," came Baldwin's reply. "But we're primed and ready for the next restart."

Dempsey dropped his NVGs back down into place and assessed the quality of his vision. *Just a few more seconds.* "Two, Three—ready to go?"

"Check."

"Check."

Dempsey reached for the door lever, and this time the lights did not go on when he opened it. Munn and Jarvis slipped past him into the hallway, the doc clearing left and Skipper clearing right.

"Clear," both operators said in unison.

With the immediate vicinity clear, Dempsey chopped his hand south and took point. They moved like ghosts, three seasoned SEALs in perfect combat crouches sighting over their weapons.

"Zero, report," Dempsey said, hoping for something, anything, useful from their eyes in the sky.

Baldwin's voice chimed over the comms channel, "One, Zero, now that you're out of the stairwell, I have you on intermittent thermal. With the jammers powered down, drone performance is much better, but even with XIR, the system is still having trouble with structural interference."

"Need data, Zero, not exposition," Dempsey growled.

"Your hallway is clear ahead and behind. I have three bodies in a room fifteen meters down the hall on your left. Must be living quarters, because I hold a man, a woman, and what can only be a child."

Dempsey kept advancing and soon made out a dim light dancing along a doorsill.

That's a flashlight . . . Stay in your room, people. Please stay in your room, he chanted silently to himself, his finger on the trigger guard as he glided past the occupied space.

"Right turn at the next intersection, then forty feet, and then a left turn onto the hallway leading to the Iranian mission," Baldwin said.

"Be advised, you have one body, definitely male, moving away from you toward the mission."

Could it be Rostami?

There was no way Baldwin could possibly know the man's identity from an XIR signature, but Dempsey couldn't help but hope this was it. At the corner, Dempsey glanced back over his shoulder and saw Jarvis clearing their six.

"Lost thermal," Baldwin said. "We've only got good coverage in a fifty-five-degree sector. Bringing the drone back around."

Dempsey's mental operational alarm clock was beeping at him. This was taking too damn long, and they needed to pick up the pace. Rostami would have evacuation and contingency plans in place. The man was an experienced VEVAK operator and terrorist—the instant the embassy went dark, he would have taken action to protect or exfiltrate himself. Dempsey took the corner, cleared left while Munn cleared right. The hallway ahead was clear; the figure that Baldwin had seen moments ago had either already rounded the corner or disappeared into a room. Dempsey's heart rate picked up. He put the odds of a Rostami ambush at fifty-fifty.

Fuck it . . . Dempsey lengthened his stride, pushing forward. *May the operator with the best reflexes win.*

"Multiple bodies on the first floor, generally moving southwest toward the admin building," Baldwin reported. "I have two bodies below you heading north, possibly toward the fire-escape stairwell you used. Be alert on EXFIL."

With the power out all over Cleveland Park, the resident staff would not have reason to be suspicious, but the duration of the blackout was now stretching long enough to induce anxiety and even panic for those without flashlights. Realistically, a chance encounter with a panicked civilian was their greatest counterdetection threat, but as Jarvis had warned, they had no choice but to treat every encounter inside the Iranian mission as potentially hostile.

Dempsey paused at the corner and waited for Munn and Jarvis to get set.

"Zero, report contacts," he whispered.

"No coverage at your six," Baldwin said, his voice apologetic. "I don't know where the male contact went."

Scowling, Dempsey raised three fingers and counted them down: *Three, two, one . . .* He rounded the corner, every nerve in his body primed and ready for bullets to come flying at him, but the hallway was empty. At the end of the hall sat an abandoned security desk with a sign: "Interests Section of the Islamic Republic of Iran." On the right and left sides of the hall were two doorways. Dempsey chopped a hand at each, Munn taking the right side and Jarvis taking the left as Dempsey slowed his advance and kept his holographic sight fixed on the wooden door behind the desk.

"Clear" and "Clear" came the nearly simultaneous reports from Munn and Jarvis clearing their respective doorways. Together, they advanced until Dempsey reached the heavy door behind the security desk. He placed a gloved hand on the large brass knob and slowly checked it. To his surprise, the knob turned easily.

This was it. Finally.

He reminded himself that it was imperative to take Rostami alive. Not shooting this terrorist motherfucker in the face would take all the self-control he'd developed as a Navy SEAL over the past two decades. With a final, definitive exhale, he pushed the door open and moved left. He quickly cleared the left corner then swiveled right to scan the small foyer. With Munn and Jarvis in matching tactical crouches beside him, they crossed the marble tile floor in perfect synchronicity toward a cased opening on the facing wall. Dempsey held up a closed fist, and in unison the team halted. His weapon trained on the archway, he listened. The room was silent except for the sound of his own breath and that of his teammates—no fleeing footfalls, no rustling of clothing, no weapons clatter. He chopped a hand forward and they moved swiftly to the archway. At the threshold, they paused again, and Dempsey tapped out a three-count cadence by nodding his head. They rounded the corner and stepped into a sitting room that was outfitted with old-school decor, complete with leather club chairs flanking a fireplace nestled between bookshelves. Dempsey's blood pressure ticked up a couple of notches in aggravation, but he checked the emotion so as not to lose his tactical edge. They cleared the empty room and advanced on the set of double doors on the wall opposite the fireplace. Dempsey took up a position next to the left door, while Jarvis took a crouched position on the right. In his peripheral vision, he saw Munn check their six then take a tactical knee and sight on the middle of the double doors. Another three count and Dempsey pushed the door in, but it stopped abruptly on contact halfway through the swing arc. Heart pounding, he swept around the door and into the room, scanning left then forward. He instantly registered the two motionless bodies on the floor, but he focused his active attention on sweeping the office for upright threats.

"Clear," he whispered.

"Clear," echoed Jarvis as he advanced on another door on the right wall. Munn fell in beside Jarvis, and they cleared the next room while Dempsey trained his rifle on the closer of the two bodies, the one behind the door he'd hit on the in-swing.

Jarvis was back a beat later. "Kitchenette," he reported. "Clear."

"Looks like a security guard here," Dempsey said, poking the dead body with the muzzle of his rifle.

Munn drifted over and took a knee beside the fallen guard, downed with what appeared to be a single round to the forehead. "Dead."

"So's the other guy," said Jarvis, who had moved to a position behind the room's massive executive desk. "No need to check this one for a pulse."

Dempsey walked over to where Jarvis was standing and was greeted by the stuff of nightmares—a headless corpse sprawled in a lake of blood. He couldn't tell if the body lay prone or supine because the hands had been expertly amputated at the wrists. Twin ovals of blood, black in his NVGs, stained the Persian carpet at the ends of the outstretched arms.

"Zero, One—where's the warm body we were trailing?"

"After I lost him, I never regained contact on level three," Baldwin answered. "It's very possible he took the south stairwell down to the ground floor and out with the others."

"Shit," Dempsey growled and checked his watch. Seven minutes had elapsed. He looked at Jarvis. "We need to go, Skipper."

Jarvis was scanning the headless corpse with a light he had clicked on from the Picatinny rails of his rifle. Dempsey could see now that the corpse was lying facedown.

"Zero, Three—we have a body we will be taking with us," Jarvis said over the radio.

Dempsey flipped up his NVGs and scanned the body with his own light. "It's him—it's Rostami," he said, both rage and joy competing for dominance of his emotions.

"Maybe," Jarvis said. "Or maybe it's the lead bomber from the DNI attack."

Dempsey took in the size, the shape, the curve of the spine below the ragged stump of bleeding neck. He thought back to the figure moving through the tunnels beneath the UN a year ago. "It's him," he said again. "I'm positive."

Munn had taken up a position by the office door, still scanning over his rifle. "I guess fingerprints and dental records are out of the question," he said.

Jarvis turned back to Munn. "Dan, you are on corpse detail. You'll carry the body and stay between us on the EXFIL."

"*Fuuuck,*" Munn grumbled while double-timing it over to Jarvis. "Gonna leave one helluva trail behind me with all the blood leaking out of that sack o' meat."

"We'll be long gone by the time they put it together," Jarvis said. "Now let's get 'em up."

Munn grunted as he heaved the headless corpse up and into a fireman's carry across his broad, powerful shoulders.

"Zero, status report on external security?"

"Security is actively sweeping the embassy grounds now," Baldwin said. "Three guards, but they've been staying together in a bunch."

"Where are they now?" Dempsey asked.

"Walking the front perimeter between the gate and the admin building."

"Shit," Dempsey huffed. "We gonna need a distraction if we want to retrace our INFIL route."

"Or we could go over the east fence behind the building," Munn suggested. "It's a pretty big drop, but doable."

"What about the north side?" Jarvis said. "Is there an emergency exit from the north stairwell at level one?"

"I remember seeing a door," Dempsey said.

"Perfect," Jarvis said, looking at Dempsey, his SAD Chief. "You good with a north side level-one exit, John?"

"Yeah," Dempsey said. "Zero, guide us out of here."

"Drone is in position. I have good eyes everywhere except inside the north stairwell, just too much steel and concrete even for augmented thermals," Baldwin said.

Dempsey nodded to his teammates and lowered his NVGs. Settling into a tactical crouch, he led them out of the Iranian mission and back into the hallways of the Pakistani embassy's third floor.

"Ah jeez. What a mess," Munn grumbled as they retraced their steps toward the north stairwell. Dempsey knew exactly what Munn was complaining about; he'd seen the bloody neck and wrist stumps start leaking blood all over Munn the instant he'd picked up the corpse.

"That family still holed up in their room?" Dempsey asked as they approached the final turn.

"Hold," Baldwin said.

They all took a knee, Munn grunting under the deadweight and Jarvis and Dempsey taking up security postures, scanning the hall behind and ahead.

"The family is still in the room, but we have another problem . . . Two tangos just entered the north stairwell on level one . . . Hold in place . . ."

Dempsey gritted his teeth, feeling the crushing weight of time running out. Baldwin had said they'd get ten minutes of night, plus or minus two. They'd been here nine fucking minutes already.

"Zero, status?" Dempsey whispered but just got static from Baldwin.

Finally, after an eternity, Baldwin said, "Okay, they're on the second floor now, moving south . . . You're clear."

Dempsey nodded and he and Jarvis cleared the corner. They rushed past the occupied room to the stairwell. At the stairwell door, Dempsey paused again for a three count: *Three . . . two . . . one . . .*

He pushed the door open and advanced into the stairwell with Jarvis right behind him. The stairwell was dark, even for NVGs, but he trusted his ears and waved Munn in. As Jarvis eased the door shut behind them, Baldwin's voice crackled over the radio.

"One, Zero, you need to move. The two tangos are coming back. I repeat, two tangos heading toward the stairwell on level two."

Dempsey didn't bother responding, just double-timed it down the stairs—trying to be as quiet as possible but erring on the side of speed. The metal staircase began to thrum and vibrate as their combined weight and cadence seemed to set the entire structure into some sort of harmonic resonance.

"Ten seconds," Baldwin reported. "Hurry!"

Dempsey glanced at the level-two door as he passed, looking for some way to jam the handle, but saw nothing expedient and just kept moving. His mind automatically began a silent count from Baldwin's last report: *Eight . . . seven . . .*

Ten more steps.

Six . . . five . . .

His boots hit the level-one landing, but Munn was still half a flight behind, doing a damn fine job considering the weight of the corpse on his back, but lagging nonetheless.

Four . . . three . . .

Dempsey pressed the push bar on the emergency exit door and opened it. A blast of wind buffeted his cheeks and howled through the gap in the door. Jarvis ducked outside and Munn followed right behind him.

Two . . .

Fighting the wind, Dempsey eased the door shut silently into its frame.

One.

"Holy hell that was close, John," said Baldwin's voice on the wireless, with what was probably the most emotion he'd ever heard from the Professor.

"We're not out of the woods yet," Dempsey said and chopped a hand toward the fence along the north perimeter. The three former SEALs moved swiftly toward the six-foot-tall fence that ran along the top of a stone retaining wall that sloped from west to east. Dempsey peered down through the bars. From their location, it was approximately a seven-foot-drop from the top of the wall to the ground.

"What you want me to do with him?" Munn said.

"Chuck him," Dempsey said.

"You fucking serious?"

"Yeah, dude, we gotta motor."

Dempsey took a step in to help, but to his astonishment, Munn military-pressed the headless corpse into the air and lobbed it over the fence. The body tumbled about its axis as it fell and hit the ground on the other side of the wall with a resounding thud.

"You're a beast, you know that?" Dempsey said with a crooked grin as he hoisted himself up and over the fence.

"Zero, Three," Jarvis called in while sighting west along the side of the embassy toward the gate. "Report threats."

"You're clear—wait, one of the roving guards at the gate just turned your direction."

Dempsey dropped from the stone wall and hit the dirt beside the body. He looked up and saw Munn going over the fence, with Jarvis following a beat later. Dempsey sighted up the sloping grounds between the Pakistani and Nigerian embassies.

Munn dropped next, stumbling on the steeply sloping ground, but quickly regained his footing. A flashlight beam arced overhead as Jarvis dropped next. Munn wasted no time slinging his rifle and hoisting the bloody corpse back up onto his shoulders.

"Did he see you?" Dempsey asked Jarvis.

"Don't know, but let's move," the Ember Director said, turning east toward International Drive.

"One, Zero—hold," said Baldwin's voice in his ear. "You've got a southbound vehicle on International Court."

To the west behind them, somewhere above the retaining wall but out of view, Dempsey heard shouting. "I think the guard saw you. Sounds like he's calling for reinforcements."

"That's correct. I see two more guards closing on your position," Baldwin confirmed.

"We move to the bottom corner of the retaining wall," Dempsey said. "I'll watch our six; you guys load the body."

He got simultaneous nods from Munn and Jarvis.

"How long on that car, Zero?" Dempsey whispered, sighting over his rifle up the hill as he backpedaled.

"Five more seconds."

"We don't have five seconds," Dempsey said, watching more flashlight beams scanning the north side of the building overhead and hearing Arabic voices getting louder.

"I'll try to buy you some time," Baldwin said. A beat later, Dempsey heard the high-pitched whine of the RQ-7B's pusher prop in overspeed as Baldwin dove the drone behind the guards. The flashlight beams changed directions and the shouting stopped.

The sound of car tires on pavement echoed behind Dempsey as the southbound vehicle on International Court drove by.

"Now," Jarvis said, and he was up sprinting toward their parked SUV in a combat crouch.

Dempsey whirled and followed Munn, running a body length behind and scanning over his rifle for threats. Jarvis's Suburban beeped, and the tailgate opened under electric servo power. Munn flung the corpse into the cargo area with a wet thud, leaped in beside their head-less cargo, and pulled the tailgate shut manually. Jarvis was already in the driver's seat, helmet off, engine running, and transmission in gear when Dempsey leaped into the back seat. They were under way before Dempsey got his door shut, dashing toward the intersection at Van Ness. Dempsey took his own helmet off and looked back at a crouching Munn and saw the doc's neck, hands, and clothes were smeared with blood.

"Got a towel?" Munn said with a tight smile.

Dempsey stuck out a fist; his friend and teammate slammed his knuckles hard into it—the Tier One equivalent of a fist bump.

"Zero, Three—get us the hell out of here."

"Roger," Baldwin said. "Sending optimal routing to your GPS now."

"What about the other vehicle?" Munn asked.

"We leave it," Jarvis said. "The priority now is EXFIL. We can send a recovery asset later."

"Shane, are you up and listening?" Jarvis asked over the still active comms channel as he followed Baldwin's route out of the dark Cleveland Park neighborhood.

"Of course, sir," a sheepish Smith answered. "Been eavesdropping the whole time."

"Get back to the airport and prep the yacht," Jarvis said, referring to Ember's full-size Boeing 787 executive jet. "We're leaving."

"We're in the plane already," Smith reminded him. "When and where?"

"I've gotta phone an old friend first before we can set the itinerary," the Ember Director said. "Just have her ready to go."

"Roger that, sir."

Dempsey swiveled in his seat and looked back at Munn. "You gonna ride in the trunk the whole way back?"

Munn grinned, wiping his bloody neck with a towel he'd found. "It's that or I get blood all over the Skipper's truck."

"Wouldn't be the first time," Dempsey said and then shifted his gaze to the headless corpse.

"You really think it's him?" Munn said.

Dempsey nodded. Maybe he was being obdurate, or maybe it was just wishful thinking, but he could feel it in his bones. The corpse was Rostami.

"Well, whoever this hunk of meat turns out to be, as a doctor I can promise you only one thing."

"What's that?"

"He ain't gonna be doing much talking."

Dempsey sighed, deflating with post-op decompression and disappointment. It wasn't supposed to have gone down like this. Justice was supposed to have been his to mete out. A wave of painful imagery—the faces of his dead SEAL brothers—indexed through his mind. Tonight, he'd let them down. He felt Munn's eyes on him, but this time he didn't meet his friend's gaze.

"Well, maybe this was for the best," he said, turning in his seat to stare out the window as they left DC behind.

"Why's that?"

"Because if we'd had the chance to take him alive, I don't know if I would have had the willpower to resist pulling the trigger."

CHAPTER 11

Northbound on I-95
Approaching the Churchville Road Exit near Aberdeen Proving
Ground
May 4
0020 Local Time

Cyrus took his time as he drove, following all the rules and posted speed limits. It would not serve to get stopped by a Maryland state trooper; the contents of the backpack in the passenger's seat, wobbling back and forth, would be impossible to explain.

He smiled at the black humor of it all.

He took no satisfaction in what he'd done. He did not relish killing a fellow Persian, even one as vile as Rostami, but he felt no remorse, either. It had been a necessary and strategic part of this operation. Yes, the American DNI and the Israeli Mossad Chief had been eliminated, but the mission had a second component as well—to draw the American devils who had killed his father and brother into action. To activate this covert cell, Iran needed plausible deniability on the public stage regarding the attack on the DNI. His uncle had been explicit on this point. They had been careful to leave no concrete evidence—even the burned corpses, if identified, had no relationship with Iran's covert operations. Without proof, the White House would not be able to justify overt military retaliation. To punish Iran, the American President would have no choice but to task his elite black ops unit to find the responsible party and deliver justice. This was the genius of his uncle's plan. The American spies needed to think Iran was responsible, while lacking the necessary proof to broadcast it to the world. Killing Rostami and leaving the body inside the Iranian mission meant that tomorrow morning, the Iranian diplomatic proxy would arrive at work to find a naked, dead body in his office. Proxy Hadid would phone Tehran immediately, and the call would be routed to Amir Modiri. Since the Pakistani embassy was sovereign soil, the American police had no jurisdiction on the premises.

As for him, Cyrus would continue north on I-95 to a safe house in Perryville, just outside the fishing village turned yuppie suburb of Havre de Grace. He would rest there for the night. The backpack and its gruesome contents he would store in an ice chest in the garage should a contingency occur in the coming weeks that would necessitate its recovery by VEVAK. That responsibility would fall to others, a member of his uncle's Suren Circle sleeper cell most likely. Cyrus's tasking was to travel to Amsterdam, then begin the long trek south back to Persia, where his fate—God willing—would intersect with the American assassin whom he held responsible for the murder of his entire family.

He took a long, deep cleansing breath and said a short prayer—asking for stealth, patience, and most of all, for vengeance.

CHAPTER 12

Office of the Director of Ember Corporation
Ember Hangar, Newport News International Airport
Newport News, Virginia
May 4
0630 Local Time

It happened again.

Jarvis had no sooner finished filling his coffee tumbler than the damn thing slipped out of his hand. *At least stainless steel doesn't shatter,* he thought, looking down at the mess on the floor. Time to say good-bye to ceramic mugs. Time to say good-bye to glasses. He picked up a wad of napkins from the counter by the coffee mess and dropped them on top of the puddle.

"Let me get that for you, sir," a voice said beside him.

He looked over and saw Munn taking a knee. Ember's newest recruit handed Jarvis his tumbler off the floor and then proceeded to blot up the liquid with the napkins.

"What are you doing?" Jarvis growled. "You've known me long enough to know I'm the kinda guy who cleans up his own damn messes."

"I do," Munn said. "But I also know that you're the Director of this dog 'n' pony show and you'd be better off leaving the grunt work to the grunts."

"It's been a while since you rated the rank of *grunt* . . . Commander."

Munn shrugged. "The way I see it, as the new guy here, I'm at the bottom of the totem pole."

Jarvis shook his head. Munn was already starting to look like his old self. The lumberjack was back—a two-week beard, untucked plaid shirt, and hiking boots completing the look. It was going to be nice having med on the team. Dempsey had made a good call.

"How close were you to the DNI's house when it blew?" Munn asked, standing and tossing the soggy mess of brown napkin into the trash. "Any ringing in the ears? Lingering vertigo? Headache?"

Jarvis reached out and gave the combat doc a squeeze on the shoulder. "It's good to have you on the team, Dan." Acutely aware of Munn's scrutinizing gaze, he set his coffee tumbler down on the counter with a definitive thud. "You saw me on the op. I'm fine, so instead of trying to diagnose me, if you really want to make yourself useful, you can refill my damn coffee tumbler."

Munn studied him for a beat. Then, he flashed a crooked smile, grabbed the coffeepot off the warmer, and refilled the tumbler to the three-quarter mark.

"Thanks, Doc," Jarvis said and this time held the damn thing down on the counter while he screwed on the lid. "I'll be in my office if anybody needs me."

Munn hesitated, clearly something on his mind.

"What is it, Dan?"

"With all due respect, sir, I know I'm new here, but everybody's wound up pretty tight from last night. A debrief from you might go a long way to settling nerves."

Jarvis ran his fingers through his hair, which recently seemed to be going silver on him at an alarming rate. "I appreciate the feedback, Dan, but I've got some calls to make before I'm ready to do that. Everybody's just gonna have to percolate in hot standby until then. This is a delicate situation, and until we get an ID on our tangos, there's not much to be accomplished by bullshitting at the round table. Why don't you go find Baldwin and the boys and familiarize yourself with the type of work they do? Whoever hit the DNI left electronic fingerprints, and our Signals department won't stop until they find them all."

"Roger that, Skipper," Munn said and went about pouring a mug of joe for himself.

Jarvis walked back to his office and shut the door. He sat down in his task chair, set the tumbler on his desk, and stared at it. *Looks like I'll be drinking coffee out of adult sippy cups for the foreseeable future.* He balled the fingers of his right hand into a fist and squeezed. After pumping his grip several times, he flexed his fingers straight, but the weakness and tingling did not abate. Jarvis repeated the exercise with his left hand, which he quickly assessed as normal. Only the right hand was giving him trouble at the moment.

I don't have time for this shit.

He took a deep breath. The two most powerful intelligence Chiefs in the world were dead, assassinated on American soil. Yes, technically the attack was terrorism, but unlike other recent terror events, this had incendiary geopolitical implications. Both Israel and the United States would retaliate. If the perpetrator was aided by a state actor—which Jarvis fully suspected was the case—then both governments would likely classify the attack as an act of war. The conclusion was premature, but this had Amir Modiri's fingerprints all over it. Persian-Israeli conflict scenarios played out in his head:

David's Sword: Upon confirmation that Iran has possession of nuclear warheads, Israel launches preemptive first strike with nuclear EMP detonated in the atmosphere over Tehran. IDF conducts air strikes on key Persian military bases and hard target munition (HTM) bombardment of nuclear facilities. With its military crippled, Tehran responds by tasking regional allies to retaliate. Hezbollah and Hamas launch rocket barrages across Israel. Iron Dome underperforms, leading to significant civilian casualties. Israel launches retaliatory cruise missile strikes against Gaza and Lebanon. Ultimate outcome: neighboring Arab nations pulled into a protracted war with Israel, destabilizing the Middle East and leaving hundreds of thousands of dead.

Jaffa Scenario: Hezbollah and Hamas launch full-scale rocket offensive against Israel. Hezbollah uses precision-guided munitions obtained from Iran to strike IDF and government targets. Iron Dome is overwhelmed by a barrage in excess of fifty thousand rockets. Israel attacks Lebanon and invades Gaza. Iran declares war on Israel and responds with missile attack and mobilizes the Persian Army. IRGC leads full ground invasion of Israel . . . Ultimate outcome: occupation of Israel, Jewish genocide.

Son of Saladin: Iran declares Tehran the head of a new Islamic caliphate upon declaration of the imminent return of the Twelfth Imam. Supreme Leader declares Iran's intention to conquer and eliminate the Jewish state. With its regional partners, Iran launches full-scale first strike, overwhelming Israeli defenses and crippling IDF air assets. United States mobilizes to defend Israel and launches operation Blue Crush against Iran. The attack on Iran prompts the formation of an Arab state coalition, which engages American military assets, leading to escalation and eventual Russian intervention. Ultimate outcome: World War Three and global thermonuclear war.

Persian Noose, Rogue Wave, Trojan Horse . . . The list went on. Probabilities for every what-if scenario populated the white space in his head. His mind's eye traced the colored lines and logic gates for a myriad of US, Israeli, and Iranian moves and countermoves. *Strike, retaliate, escalate. Strike, retaliate, escalate.* Every path was different, but the river of falling dominos always led to the same ultimate outcome: catastrophe. Early intervention was the key to preventing everything from spiraling out of control. Israel, not the United States, was the linchpin in this grenade. And whoever would replace Sharott as Director of Mossad was a critical unknown who would have tremendous influence on the timetable and manner of Israeli retaliation. He needed to talk with Levi Harel, and it was a conversation he was not looking forward to having.

He reached for the receiver just as the secure line rang. There were only three people in the world with knowledge of this number. One of them was dead, one was sitting in the TOC, which left only one other possibility.

He took a deep breath and answered the call. "Kelso Jarvis."

"Director Jarvis, this is the White House. Please hold for the President," a voice said.

The line clicked three times, and then he was greeted by President Warner. "Kelso, this is President Warner. I understand from Catherine Morgan you were at the DNI's house when it got hit."

"Yes, sir. I was."

"She also indicated that you left to pursue the bastards that hit us."

"That is also true, sir."

"And?"

"We have three dead suspects. The first two were taken out with headshots and then burned to a crisp near the scene, but not by my people. We believe this was a result of the operation lead cleaning house after the hit."

"And the third?"

"A corpse we recovered," he said, hesitating a beat, "at another location with his head and hands chopped off. This last guy we believe was running command and control."

"Any positive IDs?" Warner asked.

Jarvis exhaled, dodging the Pakistani embassy bullet for now. "CIA forensics is working on it. Hopefully we can get a positive ID on one or more from DNA because that's all we've got to work with."

"Did you lose anyone on your team?"

"No, sir."

"Good, good. Who else knows about the bodies you recovered?"

Jarvis paused. He suspected he and the President were in agreement on keeping this circle tight—incredibly tight. That's why they had taken the last body with them. The only people who knew anything had been handpicked by Jarvis within the other agencies. Still, the President had clearly spoken with Catherine Morgan—and he knew how she felt about Ember, didn't he?

"The circle is tight, sir," he said. "I am controlling the access to information myself and involving only critically necessary people—like the forensics experts that are running this in the black for me at CIA."

"Look, Kelso," the President said with a heavy sigh, "the Israeli PM just left the Oval Office. He's not taking this well. Christ, none of us are. The audacity of this attack boggles the mind. We kept the incident on lockdown for as long as possible, but the press is all over it now. The entire world now knows that we lost our Intelligence Director to a terrorist attack at his private residence mere miles from the capital. What message does that send our adversaries and our allies about our security? What message does that send our foes about our readiness? What message does that send the American people about our ability to protect them if we couldn't even protect the DNI?"

"Yes, sir, I understand—"

"I'm not finished," Warner barked. "Whoever did this will be held accountable. Prime Minister Shamone and I have agreed that our two governments will share any and all intelligence and cooperate fully to hunt down and capture the bastards responsible. Now I know your theory on the matter; you don't have to remind me. If this was a false-flag operation, masked as an act of terror, I will consider it an act of war and respond accordingly. But I cannot act without proof."

"Understood," Jarvis said, wondering how he should interpret *respond accordingly*.

"Catherine Morgan has assumed the mantle of acting DNI until we can get Philips's successor confirmed."

"Have you made a decision on who that will be, sir?" Jarvis felt his jaw tighten. The wrong person at the helm as DNI could mean the end of Ember, or worse, its emasculation to just another bureaucratic, ineffective tool for the politicians.

"I have a short list—a very short list—and both you and Ms. Morgan are on it."

The President's words took him by surprise. He couldn't possibly be the DNI. Who would lead Ember? Smith wasn't ready for the chair, and Dempsey wasn't ready to be Ops O yet. The team needed him at the helm. Besides, he didn't *want* to be the DNI. The position represented everything he loathed in their line of work: bureaucracy and red tape, politics and gamesmanship. As DNI, he would be batted and buffeted a million different directions, never able to focus on seeing any single operation through to completion. As DNI, he'd constantly be fending off efforts to undermine his authority, denigrate his effectiveness, and diminish his reputation. But worst of all, as DNI, he would be forced to delegate work he was best qualified to do to lesser men who would achieve lesser results. In Jarvis's mind, becoming the DNI was a *demotion*, not a promotion. He simply could not afford to accept such an offer. And neither could the country.

"I'm flattered, Mr. President, but—"

"Let me stop you right there, Kelso. The job is not yours to refuse. I'm simply informing you that your name is being considered."

"Yes, sir."

"But, that being said, I would expect that if the time comes that you are called upon to do your duty for your country, you will shoulder that ox yoke and pull the damn cart no matter what your personal feelings might be on the matter. Is that understood?"

"Yes, sir."

"In the meantime, I expect you and Ms. Morgan to find me the person responsible for this disaster. Do you hear me, Kelso? I want a name."

"Yes, Mr. President. If it's the last thing I do on this earth, I will find you that name."

"Oh, and one last thing."

"Sir?"

"Remember that you and Director Morgan are on the same team. Try and act like it."

He opened his mouth to reply, but the line was already dead. Without setting down the receiver, Jarvis dialed Levi Harel's encrypted mobile phone from memory. The line rang, and rang, and instead of going to voice mail, continued to ring. Only when he was just about to end the call did the legendary Israeli spymaster pick up.

"This should go without saying, but I'm kind of busy right now," Harel said with his trademark sarcasm and rapid-fire cadence.

"We need to talk, my friend," Jarvis said, cutting right to the point.

"Yes, we do, but I can't leave. You'll have to come to me."

"Where are you?"

"Tel Aviv, of course."

"What's the mood there?"

"Fucking terrible. What do you think?"

"I just got off the phone with the President."

"What a coincidence; I just got off the phone with the Prime Minister."

"What did he say?" Jarvis asked.

"He offered me my old job back."

"What did you say?"

"I said the only thing I could say . . . yes."

"Congratulations," Jarvis said, and they both knew he didn't mean it. Harel undoubtedly felt the same as Jarvis about such a "promotion."

"Fuck you," Harel growled.

Jarvis chuckled and heard a rustling and then a match strike as Harel lit himself a cigarette. Then, the once and future Chief of the

Mossad said, "Don't keep me in suspense. What did Warner say to you?"

"He told me I'm on the short list to replace Philips."

Now it was Harel's turn to laugh. "Now that is funny. And I suppose you were stubborn and self-righteous enough to turn him down?"

"I tried, but he cut me off."

Harel started to laugh again, but this time it morphed into a coughing fit. The cough was dry, deep, and unproductive. Jarvis could practically hear the old man's ribs rattling in his chest.

"You all right, Levi?"

"I'm fine," Harel barked, his voice taking on a hoarse timbre now. "We don't have much time, Kelso."

Jarvis looked down at his tingling right fingers and sighed. "I know."

"Shamone tasked me with finding the responsible party so Israel can retaliate. The bombings, the stabbings, the constant incursions by our enemies—I'm telling you, Kelso, he's had enough. And so have I. We all have, for that matter. Israel is not going to be used for target practice anymore."

"So, what are you saying?"

"I'm saying that a policy shift is coming. Israel is switching from playing defense to offense."

"Well, it is the fifty-year anniversary," Jarvis said, referring to the famed 1967 Israeli offensive—the Six Days War—in which Israel surprised its Arab neighbors with preemptive strikes, laying claim to the Sinai Peninsula, the West Bank, and the Gaza Strip.

"It's not a joke, Kelso."

"I know," Jarvis said. "Believe me, I know."

"How is the investigation going on the attack? Any progress?"

"We have a body."

"Who?"

"It's headless," Jarvis said with a snort. "We're still trying for a positive ID."

"Did you run DNA?"

"Of course. Nothing popped in our database, but my team is convinced it is Behrouz Rostami."

"Oh my God."

"Which brings me to one of the reasons for my call. I assume you guys collected DNA samples on Rostami in Frankfurt when you were running Effie Vogel?"

"Of course. Send me a sample and we'll run it."

"I might do one better and just bring the body with me. If my suspicions are right and this attack was VEVAK, then we have much to discuss."

Silence hung in the air between them for a long minute. Finally, Harel said, "When can you leave?"

"Today."

"Very good."

"Also, Levi, I'm going to bring my team along," Jarvis said.

"Why?"

"I'll explain everything when I see you in person."

"Fine, fine. Bring them."

"One last thing. The acting DNI, Catherine Morgan, well, let's just say she isn't a supporter of Ember. Which means this visit is off the books."

"No problem. We'll keep it low profile. You can stay with the Seventh Order."

"Thank you. I knew I could count on you."

"All right, my friend. Be safe and Godspeed."

CHAPTER 13

Dempsey twisted his shoulders right and then left, cracking his spine. Then he rolled his neck and wrists and straightened each elbow, getting satisfying pops and clicks from all.

"Jesus, dude," Munn said, standing in the doorway holding a cardboard carrier with four coffees. "You sound like a bowl of fucking Rice Krispies."

"Snap, crackle, pop. Hooyah."

Munn walked over and collapsed in the chair next to him. "Jarvis finally gonna debrief this thing?"

Dempsey nodded. "You think forensics found anything?"

"If they did, I suspect we'd know by now." Munn sighed and handed Dempsey one of the coffees.

"Doesn't matter. The headless fucker is Rostami," Dempsey said.

"How can you be so sure?"

"I just know it," he grumbled. "I can feel it in my bones. This is Modiri, and we know Rostami worked for him. Nobody else has the balls and the resources to pull something like this off."

"That's the same guy behind the massacre that killed our brothers in Yemen and Djibouti?"

Dempsey nodded. "And the same bastard behind the ISIS attacks six months ago in Seattle, Omaha, and Atlanta. He's the prince of global false-flag terrorism—getting others to do his killing and achieve Iran's goals, with all evidence pointing away from Iran. It's his MO, and he's fucking good at it."

"So what's next on his list?"

Dempsey gritted his teeth. "God only knows, but I'll tell you one thing, I have no intention of waiting around to find out. I don't know what Jarvis is thinking, but as far as I'm concerned it's time we take this sick bastard out. And if that means I have to go to Tehran and do it my fucking self, then that's what I'm going to do."

The door opened and a grim Shane Smith walked through, with Grimes and Adamo in tow. Smith stopped and asked the former CIA agent a hushed question, and Adamo leaned in to answer him. While Dempsey strained to figure out what they were whispering about, Grimes dropped in the chair beside him, looked at her lap, and sighed.

"Look, JD," she began. "About last night . . ."

He held up a hand, stopping her. "I have no idea what you're talking about," he said with a warm smile.

She smiled back, all the angst in her face gone. "Thanks. And I'm sorry."

"Still don't know what you're talking about," he said, taking the lid off his coffee and breathing in the pleasant, burned aroma.

She nodded and her shoulders dropped down to a more comfortable position. "Wish I could have been there with you guys last night."

"Yeah," he said, "but I'm not sure the forensics guys would have appreciated you puking tequila all over the scene—contaminates the samples, I hear."

She flipped him the bird while Smith and Adamo took their seats. A beat later, Baldwin strolled in with Chip and Dale, carrying open laptops with them. They stopped at the workstation beside the door and began plugging in their devices. Just as conversations renewed around the room, the door burst open and Jarvis strode to the podium. The lights dimmed, and a collage of photos of dead bodies filled the screens behind him—two burned beyond recognition and one headless corpse with missing hands.

"I just got off the phone with forensics," Jarvis said, grim-faced, "and I'm sorry to report they didn't get a hit. On any of these guys."

In the corner of his eye, Dempsey saw Grimes slam her fist down on the table in anger.

"I feel your frustration, believe me," Jarvis said. "Which is why we are not going to take a 'wait and see' tack. Everyone here is thinking it, so let's just address the elephant in the room right now. There is only one man brazen and motivated enough to hit the DNI and Mossad Director on American soil, and that man is Amir Modiri."

Dempsey silently exhaled with relief. This was exactly the speech he'd prayed the boss would deliver. He couldn't help but flash a tight and satisfied grin at Smith, who acknowledged the mutual sentiment with a nod. Dempsey would follow Jarvis to the gates of hell if the man asked—now, he simply had to ask.

"But we still need proof," Jarvis continued. "I've spoken with the President. It is his position that false-flag terrorism perpetrated against the United States by a nation-state will be considered an act of war. The Israelis are taking the same position, with one key difference. What constitutes proof for the Israeli PM and what constitutes proof for the White House could be very different animals. It's no secret that Prime Minister Shamone has been waiting for any excuse to hit Iranian nuclear sites. He believes the Iranian nuclear treaty is feckless and President Esfahani is using smoke and mirrors to dupe the world—feigning compliance while doubling down on their R&D efforts in secret. Everyone in this room knows firsthand the duplicitousness of the Iranian regime and the clear and present danger that a nuclear-armed Iran poses to both Israel and the United States."

"An IDF first strike against Iran could have disastrous consequences," Adamo said, using an index finger to push his glasses back up his thin nose. "The tactical picture today is not the same as it was ten, or even five, years ago. Iran has already received its first shipment of Russian S-300 missiles—fully integrated interceptors with capabilities on par with the Patriot missile system. They can target incoming missiles, fighters, and high-altitude bombers. They also have developed their own indigenous S-300 clone. The new base in Abadeh is operational now, giving the Artesh a fully integrated command and control over all their air-defense assets and facilities. An IDF air strike against Iran is not the walk in the park it once was. Israel *will* suffer casualties and that's a cold fact."

Dempsey nodded and smiled. This was just the kind of thing the former CIA man was brought to the team for. He was an encyclopedia of intelligence information with the analysis built right in.

"On top of that," Smith added, "Tehran has been steadily arming Hezbollah and Hamas with rockets, and not just the little stuff anymore. The agency estimates that Hezbollah and Hamas could possess upward of one hundred thousand rockets. Israel's Iron Dome is good, but it was never designed to protect against thousands of rockets fired simultaneously. If Iran is attacked, you can bet that they will engage their proxies to retaliate. The civilian casualties could be significant."

"Agreed," Jarvis replied. "Escalation is my primary concern. Assuming our theory is correct, then Amir Modiri has given Israel justification to go to war with Iran—a war that could rapidly spiral out of control and engulf the entire Middle East. If America and Russia are both drawn in—God help us; we could be looking at World War Three." Jarvis paused, momentarily closed his eyes, and took a deep breath before continuing. "Until now, our focus has been finding a way to stop Modiri and hold VEVAK accountable for the Operation Crusader massacre. But the stakes have just gone up, and the clock is ticking. As of today, our charter has expanded. Not only are we going to take out Modiri, but we're going to find a way to stop this war before it starts. Are you with me?"

A flood of emotions washed over Dempsey. On the one hand, he wasn't sure how taking out Modiri could possibly stop a war, but on the other hand, Jarvis had just given them the green light he'd been waiting for since the day he joined Ember. They were finally going after the man responsible for wiping out his brothers and wrecking the life he once cherished. Dempsey met Jarvis's eyes and saw both fire and ice—the heat of ire and the cool dispassion of calculation. Jarvis had a plan, a plan that he would reveal to them when he was ready. He did not know what god Jarvis communed with, or how all the puzzle pieces fit together, but what he did know was that he trusted the algorithms running in the computer Jarvis called a brain.

"Get packed," Jarvis said. "We're leaving in an hour."

"Where are we going?" Dempsey asked, unable to contain himself.

"Tel Aviv," Jarvis said. "What we're about to do, we can't do alone. Our fate and Israel's fate are joined."

"And the President is okay with this?" Smith asked with an incredulous look on his face.

Jarvis flashed his second-in-command an ironic smile. "The President has instructed us to deliver him proof of the party responsible for the DNI's murder," Jarvis said, his voice suddenly taking on the swagger of the SEAL commander from days of old. "And that is exactly what I plan to do. He did not ask for details, Shane, just results."

Translation: Ember was, as usual, on its own, giving the White House plausible deniability if things didn't work out the way they were supposed to.

"And what about the acting DNI?" Smith asked, ever the mother hen.

"I have decided not to inform Catherine Morgan of our plans at this time. I don't believe that Ms. Morgan's oversight will facilitate our success in this operation. What do you think, Ops O?"

Dempsey immediately recognized the question for what it was—a test of leadership. The message was clear: Jarvis intended to keep the new DNI in the dark and assume all risks and consequences of side-stepping the chain of command. Ember had always been black, but Director Philips had functioned as a backstop as well as a champion for the organization's charter. With Philips dead and Morgan at the helm, Jarvis was betting everything that—if forced to choose—President Warner would back him over Morgan. Unlike Jarvis, Smith was more consensus builder than lone ranger. Were Smith the Director of Ember, Dempsey suspected that the former Delta operator would have tried to build a bulletproof case for the operation and then argued for permission to act. Unfortunately, things like consensus, permission, and bridge building took time, and time was not something Ember had in unlimited supply.

All eyes went to Smith, who met his boss's steel-gray gaze. After a long beat, the corner of Smith's mouth curled up. "I think that's a question best left to worry about when we get back."

CHAPTER 14

Ministry of Intelligence (VEVAK)
Tehran, Iran
May 5
1130 Local Time

Esfahani swept into the briefing theater like a thunderstorm, electric and full of bluster.

Amir Modiri checked his watch, noting that the President's motorcade must have made the trip from Sa'dabad to the Ministry of Intelligence complex in record time because not even all the principals had arrived yet. They sure as hell were scrambling now.

"Are the reports true?" the President barked before he'd even made it around the table to his seat.

"Yes, it's true," answered Mahmoud Safavid, Minister of Intelligence and Modiri's boss. "An attack was carried out against the American intelligence Chief at his private residence during a dinner party with senior Israeli officials in attendance."

Esfahani cursed under his breath, making no effort to conceal his anxiety. Modiri had never seen the President like this before. The

Esfahani he knew, both through interaction and by reputation, was unflappable. From a self-preservation perspective, Modiri took this to be a good sign. The President was still trying to get his bearings and make sense of the situation. The likelihood that Esfahani had learned anything tying the bombing to VEVAK was slim to none.

"Who is responsible for this?" the President said, staring at the satellite imagery on the flat-screen monitors—where the charred remains of what was once DNI Philips's estate lay smoldering on the bank of the Chesapeake.

Safavid shook his head. "We're working on that, sir."

Behind his glasses, Esfahani narrowed his eyes. "Please assure me that we had nothing to do with this."

"I assure you, Mr. President, that VEVAK was not responsible," said the Minister.

"And what about our affiliates? From what I understand you've been actively and aggressively facilitating operations with our affiliates against both the United States and the Zionists," Esfahani said, but instead of looking at Safavid, this time he shifted his gaze squarely to Modiri.

The hair on the back of Modiri's neck stood up, but his expression did not waver when he said, "Against the Zionists, yes, but even the most brazen of our regional partners would never dream of doing something like this without first getting our buy-in."

"Has the Islamic State claimed credit?"

"No, sir, not yet."

"Even if they do, it was not them," said Esfahani.

"How can you be certain?" Safavid asked.

"It doesn't fit their modus operandi. This was no lone-wolf attack against a civilian target. An operation like this requires prior intelligence collection and a level of operational sophistication the Islamic State simply does not possess," the President said.

"If not ISIS, then who?" asked Safavid.

"That is what I want you to find out, Minister."

"Yes, sir. I will make it the top priority."

Esfahani's expression darkened, and he let his gaze arc across all the faces in the room.

"I want to make something perfectly clear. The American President will not view this as an act of terror. He will pronounce this an act of war and respond accordingly. The American response will be brutal. And don't fool yourselves into thinking our innocence will shield us from retribution. Innocence did not shield Iraq; innocence did not protect Saddam Hussein. The Americans have been waiting for an excuse to invade Persia since the fall of the Shah. The CIA's charter is to manufacture evidence and spread falsehoods to advance American hegemony. If the Warner Administration desires to turn global opinion against us, then we can expect to soon find our fingerprints on this attack."

Heads nodded in agreement around the room, but no one dared speak. It was clear from his body language that Esfahani was not finished.

"However, despite everything I just said, the Americans are *not* my first concern. We have enough allies and assets in the West that any move against us by Washington will be telegraphed. We will have time to pursue a diplomatic solution. No, my immediate concern is Israel. The Zionists will seek retribution, and they will do it swiftly. I expect condemnation out of Tel Aviv by the end of the day, and rest assured, brothers, they *will* blame us. I've already met with the Supreme Leader and the Joint Staff, and we agreed to raise the defense condition and put the Artesh on alert. Khatam al-Anbia Air Defense Base has been placed on high alert, and I've instructed the Air Force to begin flying security sorties around Tehran. Chief of Staff Major General Bagherdi briefed me on what he considers to be the top five scenarios for Zionist aggression and the targets he believes they would strike. In addition to preparing our conventional military defenses, I met with Major Generals Jafi and Solemnani—of the IRGC and Quds Force respectively—to ready a counteroffensive *inside* Israel. If the Zionists hit us, we will hit them back within the hour."

Modiri's stomach went into knots. He had not anticipated that Esfahani would take such dramatic action without incriminating evidence or overt accusation and condemnation from the United States or Israel. Esfahani was preemptively mobilizing for war, a decision that, while tactically advantageous, was strategically imprudent. Of all people, Esfahani knew better. Like Ahmadinejad before him, Esfahani's road to the Iranian presidency had taken a detour through VEVAK. As the former Minister of Intelligence, he was known to possess foresight that bordered on prescience, and unlike Ahmadinejad, his decisions were not guided by prideful obduracy or paranoia. He was a clever fox with a serpent's tongue and a venomous bite. He knew the mind of the Zionist better than anyone. How could Esfahani not know that Prime Minister Shamone would interpret the change in the Persian defense condition as an admission of guilt?

Modiri felt a cold bead of sweat roll from his armpit down across his ribs. He had dreadfully miscalculated the probability of his operation leading to conventional war between Persia and her enemies. The dialogue around him faded to background noise. It didn't matter that the bombing was the most brilliant, brazen, effective strike against their enemy's leadership in the history of VEVAK. If Esfahani discovered what he'd done, Modiri would either find himself in Section 209 of Evin Prison with a car battery hooked up to his scrotum or hanging from his neck in a public square.

Fortunately, he had taken great care to compartmentalize the operation and eliminate loose ends. The only person in the world who knew he was behind the attack was his nephew, Cyrus. The operation's success was all the proof Modiri needed to assure himself of Cyrus's capabilities. Safavid did not possess the resources to identify Cyrus as his black operator and tie him to the attack. But the Americans did . . .

His nephew's fate, as well as his own, was in Allah's hands now.

". . . we are in an extremely delicate position right now," Esfahani continued. "Western sanctions have been lifted. Persian oil is once again trading on the open market. The oil refinery optimization project in

Esfahan is well under way with the South Koreans. We recently closed a monthly export agreement with the Philippines, and we have a commercial jet contract with Boeing. A prosperous Iran is a strong Iran, and we can ill afford to jeopardize everything we have accomplished over the past two years. I refuse to turn back the clock. I refuse to go back! While our military prepares for war, it is up to VEVAK to prevent it. The party responsible for this bombing in America must be found and revealed to the world. Succeed, and Iran will continue to flourish. Fail, and the Persian caliphate will go up in flames. We are not ready yet. This is not a war we can win, but it is a war I will fight down to every last able-bodied Persian if I must. And know this, gentlemen—if Persia burns, then I will raze Israel to the ground."

Esfahani stood, signaling that the meeting was over. There would be no debate. There would be no further discussion. The message was simple and clear: find him a sacrificial lamb to offer the Americans and redirect the Israelis, and do it now. Right now.

Modiri disconnected the cable from the display port on the side of his laptop, closed the screen, and got up to leave with the others. He did not make it five paces.

"Director Modiri," the President said, "a word before you go."

He stopped and turned. "Yes, sir."

Esfahani then looked at Safavid with eyes that said, *You, too.* Safavid would not have dreamed of leaving him alone with Esfahani, so it mattered not, but Safavid nodded piously and approached the President.

Esfahani began with a sigh—a sigh that said everything: *The timing of this debacle could not be worse. Why hasn't VEVAK identified the responsible actor already?* When he finally did speak, what he actually said was, "Don't forget, I've been in your shoes. And it was not so long ago that I've forgotten what it is like to walk in them. Is there something either of you are not telling me? I've dismissed the room. It's only us now."

"I can assure you, sir," Safavid replied, "that the Ministry will do everything in its power to identify the party responsible for the attack.

You have my grave and humblest apologies that we don't have answers for you already."

Esfahani nodded dismissively at the Minister of Intelligence. Modiri knew that Safavid had not been Esfahani's first choice for his successor, but in Iran, even the President didn't always get his way. "What about you, Director Modiri—is there something you're holding back?" Esfahani asked.

"No, sir," Modiri said, resisting the impulse to scratch his nose. "I have nothing else to report."

Esfahani eyed him from behind his trademark silver-rimmed glasses. After a long beat, the President said, "You seem nervous, Amir."

"I am nervous," Modiri said. "You've just raised the defense condition and mobilized our military. The Jews will perceive this as an admission of guilt, and so too might the Americans."

"What other choice do I have? Do your job and find me the people responsible for this attack so I can stop this war before it's too late. You're dismissed," Esfahani shouted. Then, turning to Safavid, he said, "Not you, Minister. I want a word in private."

Modiri nodded with deference at Esfahani, tucked his laptop under his arm, and walked out of the briefing theater. As he strode through the halls of the Ministry back to his office, he had no regrets. He'd assassinated the American DNI and the Head of Mossad in a swift, single blow, and only two people in the entire world knew—except deep down in the pit of his stomach, he knew there was another. His mind went to the grainy color photograph he kept in his top desk drawer of the American operator who had single-handedly foiled his previous two operations on American soil. His nameless nemesis, the devil's Lieutenant with the serpentine scar around his forearm, also knew. That was the nature of blood feuds; that was the nature of spiritual adversaries. A blow such as this would not go unpunished. This time, the American assassin would come for him personally, and when he did, Modiri would be ready.

PART II

The problem with revenge is that when adversaries seek parity, escalation is inescapable—even when it leads to their mutual undoing.

—Levi Harel

CHAPTER 15

Tehran, Iran
May 6
0615 Local Time

Cyrus sat cross-legged at the base of his mother's tombstone, his eyes closed. To a passerby, he might have appeared to be asleep, but nothing could be further from the truth. His mind was active, contemplating both past—the events that had led him to this purgatory he now resided in—and future—the events that he intended to manifest. If Arkady could see him now, his Russian teacher would be angry.

And disappointed.

"A clandestine operator must live in the present and only the present. A spy must be mindful. Do you know the meaning of this word, mindful?"

"To think and reflect?" Cyrus had replied.

"No, that is wrong. To be mindful is to be an observer—an observer without prejudice or preconception. The mindful spy does not pass judgment. The mindful spy does not wallow in regret or preoccupy himself with revenge for past wrongs. The mindful spy resides only in the present. The present is the only thing that matters, because it is the only place where a spy can collect

information and exert influence. Forget the past. Worry not about events unsung. Only by conquering the present can you reach your true potential."

Maybe the meditative philosophy worked for the old Russian because he was old and jaded, or maybe it was that the fire in his soul had long since been extinguished, or maybe it was because the man had never loved or been loved . . . Whatever the reason, Cyrus didn't care. He would never forget the sacrifices of his family, nor would he deprive himself of the joy of plotting his enemy's demise. Without the past, without the future, he was nothing.

He inhaled deeply through his nose and then blew the air out of pursed lips. The waiting was difficult for him. He was like a loaded weapon, ready to be fired, ready to roar and unleash murder on his adversaries, but cruelly holstered, waiting on the whim of his master. His uncle had promised that he would have new tasking soon, but for now there was nothing to do but wait.

He let his mind wander, until an approaching presence jerked him from his fugue. His eyes snapped open, and to his surprise, he spied his aunt several meters away. He moved to get up, but she waved at him to stay seated.

"How did you know I was here?" he asked.

"I didn't," she said, taking a seat cross-legged beside him.

"You came here on your own?"

She nodded. "Why? Does that surprise you?"

"To be honest, yes, it does."

She smiled at him without judgment and said, "Coming here keeps me grounded; it reminds me of what is important in life."

"And what is that?"

She didn't answer for a beat, and when she did, her answer was not what he'd expected. "Relationships."

"Interesting," he said, considering her response.

"You disagree?"

"No, actually not. I just thought you were going to say *family*."

She nodded, her gaze going to the middle distance. "In my opinion, family is only meaningful in terms of the relationships we keep. Your mother and I were not sisters, but I loved her as sisters should love. The relationship we nurtured over the years was stronger and closer than the one I have with my own flesh-and-blood sister. I miss not having Fatemeh in my life."

"So do I."

She turned to look at him. "There's still time."

"Still time for what?" he asked, confused by the non sequitur.

"To change paths. I know that you think what you're doing is noble and strong, and that if you spill enough American blood it will ease your grief and fill the void in your heart, but take it from someone who knows that the only true salve for a vengeful heart is forgiveness."

He narrowed his eyes at her. "You should not be saying such things, Aunt Maheen."

"Amir drafted you into his order of spies," she continued, unperturbed. "But it is not a world for souls like ours. It is a dark place, one where you will quickly lose your way and find yourself alone with only shadows to keep you company."

"What do you know of it?" he growled.

"More than you might think," she said, placing her hand on his knee.

He hesitated. "Are you . . . one of us?"

"Yes."

"But then, why did Uncle Amir say . . ." He let the rest of the question go unsaid.

"First of all, because it is not his place to speak for me, and second, because I specifically asked him not to tell you."

A knot formed in Cyrus's stomach. The revelation that his aunt—the aunt whom he had adored his entire life—worked for VEVAK upset him in a way he could not articulate. It made him angry. It made him feel foolish. It made him feel naive. "Don't tell me he works for you?"

"No, no, no," she said with a wan smile. "Amir is the Director of Foreign Operations, whereas my department, let's just say, focuses on domestic affairs."

"But there are no female department heads in VEVAK," he stammered, suddenly wondering if this was some sort of operational security drill his uncle had put her up to.

"Is that so? And how do you know this? Have you met all thirty-nine thousand of us during your indoctrination and training?"

"Of course not."

"Then you think the Ministry recruits only men?"

"No."

"Oh, I see," she continued, her voice ripe with sarcasm. "You think all the women in VEVAK work in secretarial roles."

"No, I didn't say that."

Suddenly, her face returned to the mischievous visage he was accustomed to. "I'm just playing with you, Cyrus. Relax."

"So, you don't actually work for VEVAK?"

"No, I do work at VEVAK. I was just having a little fun at your expense playing the wounded feminist. Believe me when I say this is not a business for a woman with thin skin. I know the names they call me behind my back. Maheen Bee, the Queen Mother, Bitch in Heels— none of it bothers me anymore."

"And for as long as I've known you, you've worked for VEVAK?" he asked, incredulous.

She nodded. "They recruited us as a couple before we were married for a special clandestine program that is above your clearance level, but Amir and I had grander aspirations and grander talents. Our place is in Tehran—in the melee of politics and propaganda, espionage and indoctrination. We have no children of our own, but we have fathered and mothered hundreds."

Cyrus stared at her. She was not trying to speak in riddles, but he contemplated her words as such. Perhaps his aunt was a talent spotter, a recruiter, or a handler—or possibly all three rolled into one. Given what he calculated to be at least twenty years of agency service, she probably started in one of those roles and had worked her way up to become a department head overseeing a small army of people doing what she had once done. She was not a field agent; she was Uncle Amir's analog on the domestic side.

"I see I've left you speechless," she said with a wry grin. "Well, it wouldn't be the first time with a younger man." She then leaned in and gave him a kiss on the forehead. "Think about what I said. There's still time. I can get you out."

He glared at her, angered by her misplaced maternal counsel. "I don't want out. What I want is vengeance."

She got to her feet and looked down at him. "The game you're playing, Cyrus, is very, very dangerous. Take it from someone who knows—some choices cannot be undone; some paths cannot be retraced. Be careful, or you might find yourself standing on a chair with a noose around your neck of your own making."

"I could say the same to you," he said, fixing her with a cold stare. "What would Uncle think about this conversation? I can't imagine he'd be too pleased to know you're meeting with me behind his back and counseling me to quit."

She met his gaze with unbridled confidence, completely unfazed by his thinly veiled threat.

"Oh, my dear, dear nephew, there is so much your male tutors failed to teach you. Your competence as an agent is not a function of how well you can threaten, blackmail, and murder—it is a function of how well you develop and manage relationships. In life, in all things professional and personal, the only thing that matters is relationships. My relationship with Amir is a citadel. Feel free to test it by throwing as many stones as you wish, but I warn you, don't be surprised when the wrath you imagined he would rain down on me is directed at you instead. Amir has killed for me, and he would die for me. Never underestimate the power of true love."

CHAPTER 16

Ember's Executive Boeing 787-9, N103XL
Government Hangar #3
Sde Dov Airport, Tel Aviv, Israel
May 6
0620 Local Time

Dempsey sat on the edge of his bunk, elbows pressed into his thighs, and massaged his aching temples. He hadn't slept on the flight from Newport News to Tel Aviv, and now he'd squandered his first full night in Israel, too. Sleep was a valuable weapon, but his inner monologue simply wouldn't shut up.

He'd done it to himself, of course, by checking Facebook when no one had been looking. He'd promised Smith and Jarvis after the terror attack in Atlanta, when his personal connection with his ex-wife and son had hurt his objectivity, that he would stay off social media, and he'd kept that promise . . . for two months. But then one night, after drinking a couple of lonely beers at home, he'd given in to the tempta-tion. Kate and Jake were his family, damn it, and it was his right to know how they were doing. He might be dead on paper, but the heart pounding in his chest proved he was still very much alive. Smith and Jarvis had never married. Hell, if either one of them had fathered a child, they'd understand—they would empathize instead of judging him. But right now, he wished he'd listened to them. Right now, his heart was bleeding and his soul was smoldering . . .

Kate had found someone.

On the surface, her Facebook post was innocent enough. A picture of her sitting next to a guy at a restaurant, saying that she'd had a "great night" out with Steve at their favorite local Italian joint. To the untrained observer, the scene might even appear platonic, but he knew Kate; he knew her better than anyone. Kate looked relaxed. Not just her face, which seemed capable of selling a state of ease no matter the tension raging underneath. Kate carried discomfort in her shoulders. It was a subtle sign, visible only to him—or had once been, he supposed. In the picture, her shoulders, and her upper arms, were relaxed and at ease. This was happy Kate—a content Kate he had not seen in the several years leading up to their separation. This alone was enough evidence to prove this wasn't her first date with *Steve*. Also, by calling it "their favorite" Italian place, she communicated they had a history of dinners out. Third and most important, Kate was not an impulsive woman, especially when it came to intimacy. For her to post this picture meant that *Steve* had passed the vetting period. This Facebook post was her subtle and yet self-assured way of presenting her new beau to the world. She had never posted about Steve before, not once.

Fuuuuuck.

He wanted to rip Steve's arms from his "I play golf for exercise" body. Without any arms, this poser couldn't hold Kate's hand, or wrap her in a hug, or caress her in bed . . .

God, arrrrhhhh!

He leaned over and retrieved the bottle of ibuprofen from the nightstand bolted to the deck beside his bed. He shook out four tablets and then tossed them to the back of his mouth, chasing them with nasty warm water from the half-empty bottle on the table.

"I shouldn't have looked," he mumbled, staring down at his feet. "I shouldn't have fucking looked."

The sound of knuckles on the bulkhead jerked him back to the here and now.

"You awake?" said a familiar voice.

Dempsey looked up at Smith, who was standing in the doorway already dressed in his cargo pants and short-sleeve shirt. Dempsey shot him a *what the hell does it look like?* scowl and gestured to his half-naked self sitting on the bed.

"You okay?" Smith pressed. "You look pissed off."

Dempsey sighed, then stood and stretched, his back cracking as he twisted left and right. "Nah, I'm good," he said, boxing Jack Kemper's demons and letting John Dempsey retake control. "Just getting fucking old. I used to be able to sleep like a baby inside a hollowed-out log or under a helicopter in the friggin' dirt; you'd think I could catch some Zs in the master suite on the whale."

Smith laughed. "Yeah, well if these accommodations don't work for you, I'm happy to trade bunks with you. Hell, I'm even willing to find you a nice piece of real estate in the cargo hold. I'm sure we've got a foam roll and a sleeping bag around here somewhere."

"You know, I might just take you up on that," he said with a smile.

"I'll grab you a coffee and meet you in the TOC," Smith said, turning to go.

"Dude, I don't want any of that foo-foo shit that you and Grimes drink," he called after him.

"Uh huh, yeah, sure."

"I'm serious, Smith . . ."

With Smith gone, Dempsey reached for the handle of the tall wooden locker built into the bulkhead beside the bed. He retrieved and donned a pair of 5.11 TACLITE Pro cargo pants and a black sports shirt and then slipped into a pair of socks and ankle boots. He twisted left and right, trying for that one last pop still hung up in his battered spine, but instead of relief, he was rewarded with a stinger that shot down his left leg. *Wonderful.* He winced as he gingerly straightened out. The last thing he needed right now was to aggravate the spot where Munn and the spine surgeon had knitted his vertebrae back together after he'd taken a sniper round against his SAPI plate. This was a reminder that some old wounds never fully healed.

He pushed through the door and it swung into Grimes—the door catching her in the hip.

"Shit—sorry, Lizzie," he said, steadying her by the arm.

She shrugged off his hand. "No worries," she said, avoiding eye contact. The tension was back.

Oh Jesus, not this again, he thought, wondering what was going on now. That silly shit at the bar was just silly shit in a bar. He thought they'd moved past that. There was no way they could let it affect them as friends, or especially as teammates.

Just make a joke. It'll go away.

"What—no kiss?" he teased.

"Screw you, JD," she said and walked away.

"I was just kidding," he called and chased after her. When he caught up to her in the short hall leading to the TOC, he said, "I thought we were good? It was just a drunken kiss—just alcohol, impulse, and camaraderie—nothing to be upset or embarrassed about."

"Yeah, well, trying to kiss the ugliest guy in the bar ain't the reason I'm upset," she quipped, all Elizabeth Grimes now. She turned to him. "I fucked up the operational response to the attack," she said, grim-faced. "This is a twenty-four-seven job. That can never happen again."

She held his eyes, looking for . . . something.

"And I'm sure it never will," he said.

"It can't," she said tightly. "I signed on to this job for a reason. You know what I want. I need to see this through—to see those responsible for my brother's death erased from the earth. When I worked at the Office of Science and Technology Policy at the White House, I was literally in the heart of government, and yet I felt completely disconnected. I was effecting real policy change, but every victory felt entirely academic. At Ember, it's the opposite. Every mission, every operation, every victory—they're all immediate, tangible, real. And there are no second chances. I have to get it right, every time."

"Look, I get it. But that's not the only reason you're here."

She nodded. "You know that. I'm here for Spaz. And if I'd been on the job the other night, maybe we would have gotten Rostami ourselves."

Dempsey's stomach tightened at the mention of Grimes's brother, his lost SEAL teammate. He did get it. More than most, perhaps. Her soul was raw and bleeding, and the only way it would heal was by meting out justice to the bastards responsible for her brother's murder.

"Don't kick yourself for being human," he said. "One slip-up doesn't mean you failed your brother. The operational tempo this past year has been insane. You guys earned a night of decompression. It was just Murphy's Law kicking in, nothing more."

Her expression, which had softened, turned angry again. *"You guys,"* she parroted back. She glared at him, and he wasn't sure what he saw in her eyes. "But not you, right? You don't need any decompression because—what?—you're a superhero? A steely-eyed frogman who never lets his guard down? The comic book superhero version of a SEAL my brother was trying to be?"

He stood frozen, not sure what to do. "Clearly you're upset with me . . ." he started.

"Forget it, John," she said, opening the door to the TOC and turning away. "It's all good. We're cool."

He paused a beat before following her in. *What the hell is going on? I don't get women. I don't fucking understand them at all . . .*

When he stepped into the TOC, he saw Munn tipped back in his chair, his Oakley boots on the long conference table, sipping his usual black coffee.

"There you are," Munn said to him. "Smith has your whipped-cream sundae here," he said, gesturing with a thumb at the tall ceramic cup beside his, thick foamed milk floating on top.

Dempsey laughed and flipped Smith the middle finger, then took his seat between them. Grimes grabbed a seat on the other side of Munn.

"Ooh, the band is all here," Richard Wang announced as he entered from the door that led back into the lounge and the bunkrooms. As usual the kid had the look of a college fraternity pledge—just one not likely to make the frat. He ran a hand through his thick and unkempt black hair, pushing it out of his face; then he dropped into a seat at the end of the table. The perfect seat, Dempsey mused, straddling the operators on this side of the table and the analysts who would normally fill the other side. Wang was a cybergenius, and while they had cross-trained him to work as a field asset, he was not and never would be an operator.

"Don't get comfortable, folks," Jarvis announced a beat later as he entered, immediately commanding the room. He was carrying the handled stainless-steel tumbler he had lately been sporting his coffee around in and was dressed in dark jeans and a sports coat over an oxford shirt, left open at the collar.

"Our friends are finally ready for us," Jarvis continued. "We're heading out; bring your coffee if you want."

"Are we taking the SUVs?" Smith asked.

"No. We have a ride coming. They should be here any minute."

"Weapons?" Dempsey asked.

Jarvis nodded. "We're guests with permission to carry, but be discreet."

They all stood and moved around the table to follow the boss out, Dempsey conspicuously leaving his cup of foo-foo coffee untouched on the table. He walked in the single-file line through the narrow hall and exited two mahogany doors that looked like they belonged in an uptown law office rather than a mobile operations center inside a Boeing jet. On the other side, he stepped into a transverse bulkhead stretching port to starboard and perpendicular to the long axis of the aircraft, with ladder wells in both outboards. The one on the left was wider; beyond stretched a narrow hall with forward access to the cockpit and flight-crew quarters. The team split, descending both ladder wells to the cargo hold below.

The ceiling was low but just tall enough for Dempsey to stand. On either side were four metal cages full of tactical gear. Past that was a door that led into the IT and comms suite. The tech suite ended in a chain-link gate with access to the aft portion of the aircraft, where the cabin above came to an abrupt end, and the cargo hold extended floor to ceiling to allow room for the vehicles and drones they carried—including a rather tall flat-black MRAP vehicle that needed a lot of headroom. For this trip, only two black Yukon SUVs were in the aft hold—and a handful of drones of various sizes and shapes, from dragonfly-looking things that would fit in your hand and operate from a smartphone app to the twelve-foot, thirteen-hundred-pound RQ-7B, which could fly to altitudes of eighteen thousand feet with a loiter time over six hours. That drone had been specially modified to launch from a catapult system straight out the rear cargo door of the jet. They also had several of the smaller and much slower RQ-11B DDL drones—a hand-launched drone that could be broken down to fit in a backpack and controlled by the team from a laptop for up to three hours thanks to a new battery system.

Dempsey and Munn entered the first cage, and Dempsey opened the gun cabinet. He selected a Sig Sauer 229 for his primary and a Glock 43 as a backup. Then, he stepped aside for Munn to make his selections. Dempsey checked both pistols, making sure they had rounds chambered. Then, he slid the larger 229 into a leather waist holster he wore at the small of his back and the Glock into a compact ankle holster concealed by his left pant leg. He stuffed two extra mags for his primary into a covert magazine pocket on his upper-left thigh and two more for his ankle gun into the mirror-image pocket on the right side. He looked over and saw Munn smiling at him.

"What?"

"If you strap on a fanny pack you could probably carry another dozen magazines . . . you know, just in case."

Dempsey laughed. "What are you packing?"

"Just a Glock and a spare mag."

"Well, not everybody shoots like you, *Dead-Eye Dan*," Dempsey said, slapping the doc on the back. "You ready?"

"Yeah, man. Let's do it."

They joined the others outside the cage, where Jarvis stood like a Roman centurion, his hands clasped behind his back.

"So what's the plan, Skipper?" Dempsey asked.

"To meet your Israeli counterparts," Jarvis said simply, and then under his breath added, "and fate willing, stop a war."

Dempsey nodded, but Jarvis had essentially told him nothing. What about the DNA results on the corpse? Surely the lab results were back by now. Was the boss keeping something from them? Then a terrible thought occurred to Dempsey—was the silent treatment something else altogether? What if Jarvis was just as much in the dark as they were? What if Jarvis didn't have a plan?

Ridiculous. Kelso Jarvis always *has a plan.*

Dempsey followed his teammates to the door—an oval egress hatch with a pneumatic staircase. Grimes hit the button, invisible mechanisms hissed, and the steps lowered to the ground. Dempsey ducked his head and stepped out into the blinding glare. The morning air was crisp and comfortable, and Dempsey inhaled deeply. Beside the aircraft, three gray Lexus SUVs idled, parked in a semicircle. The vehicles didn't have the "government agent" look of the black GMCs the Ember team had brought. On the side of each, in dark block letters, was written, Musa Eretz Israel Museum Research Team.

"Time to go see what the Israeli version of Ember looks like," Smith whispered to Dempsey as they walked to the waiting vehicles. "What do you think their facility will be like?"

"Don't care," Dempsey said. "The only question that matters is, will they help us kick some ass, or are we going to have to do it by ourselves?"

CHAPTER 17

Acquisitions and Research Center
Nechushtan Pavilion, Eretz Israel Museum
Ramat Aviv Neighborhood, Tel Aviv, Israel
May 6
0800 Local Time

If Ember had been located in Tel Aviv, Dempsey imagined this was precisely how Jarvis would have done it—hidden in a basement vault on the grounds of the Eretz Israel Museum, perfectly camouflaged in the heart of the City That Never Sleeps. Hell, Dempsey halfway expected Ian Baldwin to emerge from a frosted glass door with Chip and Dale in tow and greet him with a paternal smile and an understated "Good morning, John."

So eerie.

The Nechushtan Pavilion, with its ancient artifact exhibits, reconstructed Bronze Age mine, and smelting furnace, was a helluva lot more interesting than Ember's biz jet hangar at the Newport News airport. Dempsey wasn't a "museum guy," but even a door kicker like him could appreciate what the museum curators had accomplished here in showcasing the dawn of mining and metallurgy. The room they were passing through presently appeared to be an artifact cataloguing and restoration suite. A young woman sat on a bench, gloved and white coated, intently scrutinizing what looked to Dempsey like a dingy copper pot. She worked without even a sideways glance in their direction. That was probably all part of the arrangement—*you work here, we work here, but we don't interact*—like two realities occupying the same dimension but offset in frequency so as not to interfere with each other.

Double eerie.

At the end of the room, a beautifully exotic and yet familiar-looking woman stood in front of a steel door with her arms crossed over her chest. She wore a dark-gray flannel shirt, unbuttoned and over a light-gray T-shirt, with black jeans and black boots. He searched his memory banks for her name and the place they'd met, but came up with nothing but fog. *Too many damn concussions,* he grumbled silently to himself. She was flanked by two men, both younger than him, who *sorta* looked like operators.

In his former life, Dempsey had worked often and intimately with his Israeli counterparts in Shayetet 13, Israel's equivalent to the US Navy SEALs. The Israeli commando unit had not only trained with his Tier One unit but also deployed with them on more than one occasion. At the end of one such deployment, an Israeli operator he'd befriended had gifted him a pair of brown canvas IDF jump boots, boots Dempsey had worn for two years until the soles were gone. He'd also worked with Sayeret Matkal—Israel's principal Special Operations unit—on a joint hostage-rescue operation in the dense jungle of Ethiopia. Success on that mission had been more about Sayeret Matkal's effectiveness than anything he'd contributed, he remembered reluctantly.

"As a courtesy, you may retain and carry your weapons, but please understand this is our home, and we ask that you follow our rules— especially those pertaining to operational security," the Israeli woman said without introducing herself. She did not seem pleased to be greeting them, nor pleased to extend the "courtesy" of letting them retain their weapons. Undoubtedly this had been Jarvis's handiwork, leveraging his relationship with Harel.

"Wouldn't want you to overextend yourselves," Munn said under his breath.

Dempsey elbowed the doc and then flashed the woman his best cool-guy smile. "We appreciate the hospitality, thank you," he said. "It's your house and your rules. We'll do our best to stay out of the way and not step on any fingers and toes."

The Israeli woman stared at him without smiling or blinking, and then turned away, shielding the touch panel beside the door with her body before punching in a code.

Strange rhythms this morning . . .

Dempsey glanced back over his shoulder at Jarvis for wordless affirmation, but the Ember Director was lost in thought. The magnetic lock clicked open, and one of the two Israeli operators held the door for them. Dempsey led the Ember contingent—Smith, Munn, Adamo, Grimes, Wang, and finally Jarvis—through the door. He trotted to catch up with the Israeli woman and said, "I'm John, by the way."

"Yes," she answered simply. "John Dempsey. Former Tier One Navy SEAL and now Special Activities Director at Ember. We've met."

He felt his cheeks flush. *Fuck, I knew it,* he thought, silently chastising himself.

"I thought you looked familiar," he said.

"You don't remember, do you?" The corners of her lips curled up just a smidgen, her first show of real emotion. She was toying with him and enjoying it.

He narrowed his eyes at her and studied her face. A beat later, it clicked.

"Brussels," he said. "That brasserie with the fire engine–red facade on the cobblestone street."

She nodded. *"Les Brassins sur la Rue Keyenveld,"* she said in perfect French.

"Now you're just showing off," he said, smiling.

"Not really. When that happens, you'll know it."

He chuckled politely, while cursing himself for not remembering her name. On that night six months ago, they'd only exchanged a cursory greeting before he and Harel had gone walking by themselves. If memory served, she'd stayed behind and talked with Grimes. Funny, he'd never thought to ask Grimes about their interaction. He'd assumed, obviously erroneously, that the woman had been a local Mossad asset in Belgium playing Harel's sidekick for the evening for the sake of their cover. Clearly, she was much, much more than that.

Her name started with an E, he realized. *Was it Estelle . . . Evelyn? Shit, I can't remember . . . Ah, probably just as well. I doubt she's still using the same NOC.*

The woman led them down a hallway to another, much heavier metal door. Again, she punched a code into a keypad, but this time a panel opened higher on the wall, revealing a flat, greenish glass square. She placed her hand on the glass and leaned in toward the opening in the wall above it. The glass lit up as her handprint was scanned while, he assumed, the other device performed a retinal scan.

Both panels slid shut with a loud click. A hiss signaled the opening of the final door—which turned out to be nearly a foot thick—and they entered the home of Israel's Seventh Order. They passed through a short foyer, flanked by walls on both sides displaying black-and-white photographs of small groups of commandos, posing after what he assumed were successful and secret missions. The number of people in the world who had seen these pictures, Dempsey guessed, numbered fewer than a hundred. Next, his gaze was drawn to an emblem in the center of the mosaic tile floor depicting a human silhouette, head bowed and arms holding up two crumbling pillars, with angelic wings outstretched in the background. Beneath the image was a line of text written in Hebrew, which Dempsey assumed translated to *Seventh Order*.

He strode across the emblem toward a pair of double doors that opened automatically on approach, revealing a Tactical Operations Center very much in keeping with the style and layout of the Ember TOC. The primary and marked difference was the fit and finish. The Seventh Order's TOC looked like an architecture firm had had a hand in the interior design. The color palette, the materials, the lighting, all worked in harmony. The long table held pop-up screens in front of each chair, much like at home at Ember. A short podium stood alone at the far end of the table, and a bank of large flat-screen monitors hung on the facing wall. The center monitor held a six-way split screen with live security feeds of various parts of the museum and the grounds above, and the others were tuned to a variety of international news channels, with all sound muted.

"Please make yourselves comfortable," she said, gesturing to the empty task chairs around the table. "There's coffee in the break room, as well as packaged snacks in the cabinet and fruit and water in the refrigerator. Our home is your home, for now. I'll be back in a few moments." And with that, she disappeared out a door on the far side of the room. Jarvis, who had not taken a seat, followed her without a word or glance at the team. The two other Israeli operators also wordlessly departed, but they headed for the break room instead.

No introductions. No brief. What the hell?

Dempsey looked at Smith, his eyes saying it all.

Smith shrugged. "No idea, bro."

Irritated, Dempsey took a seat at the table, and the rest of the team fell in around him, all subconsciously taking seats in the places they routinely occupied at the conference table back at home . . . all except for Munn.

"Well, I don't say no to free coffee," the doc announced.

"You don't say no to free anything," Dempsey said with a chuckle. But then what Navy SEAL did?

"I'm buying, so who needs one?" Munn asked, clearly enjoying himself.

Four hands shot up.

"Aw, come on, guys. I know I'm junior bitch, but seriously?"

"And you best remember how we like them," Wang fired back.

"I'll give you a hand," Adamo said, getting to his feet.

"Thanks, shipmate," Munn said and clapped a hand on Adamo's shoulder. Dempsey saw the much smaller former CIA man grimace awkwardly, which made Dempsey chuckle as the duo headed off toward the break room.

"I remember that chick," Grimes muttered, her eyes ticking to the door that Jarvis and the Israeli female agent had just exited through.

"Brussels," Dempsey said.

Grimes nodded.

"Out of curiosity, what did the two of you talk about that night?" Dempsey asked.

"Absolutely nothing. She wouldn't slip her NOC at all. Pretended she was Harel's daughter the whole time, acting like she'd never been to Brussels before. Talking about the food and sights they'd seen. I don't know . . . a little too hardcore if you ask me. I mean, clearly, we both were read into the meet."

"She's all business, huh?" Smith asked.

"Yeah," Elizabeth replied. "Must be a unit thing. They didn't exactly roll out the red carpet for us. Coffee and snacks in the break room and have a seat. Pretty cold welcome."

"I think it's fair for us to expect this," Smith said. "Imagine the Brits sent a shit-hot unit to our home base, ready to kick some ass and take names. Imagine that same unit is operating out of Ember headquarters and we were supposed to be their hosts and provide support for an operation in our sandbox that we knew Ember was better suited to conduct. It would totally chafe. So maybe we should try to put ourselves in their shoes and cut our hosts a little slack."

"There's only three of them, Shane," she pressed.

"And they sure as hell don't look like Tier One operators," Wang chimed in.

Smith shot the cyber whiz kid a *look who's talking* stare and then said, "Which is probably by design. IDF has commandos assigned to units across the Oz Brigade—the parent command for Israeli Special Forces. In my experience working with IDF, there's a smoother and more seamless integration of clandestine tasking and operators across the board than what we have at home. You're probably right that the team here at the Seventh Order are not door kickers. But that doesn't mean they don't kick ass in the field."

"You think so?" Wang said with swagger out of proportion for his stature, not to mention his role in the team.

Dempsey smiled. He was pretty sure even a Seventh Order agent could kick Wang's ass without breaking a sweat. In the dark web, Wang was a god, but in the field, the kid was meat. He followed Smith's lead. "I hear ya, Wang, but Smith is right. This is their turf, so no point getting in a pissing match. We need to show them we're team players. The time will come soon enough when we desperately need their support and expertise to pull off our operation. The Skipper wouldn't have us here otherwise."

"And just what is our *operation*?" Grimes asked. "How long are we expected to sit on our hands and wait? For Christ's sake, yesterday was a complete waste and today isn't shaping up much better."

Dempsey sighed. She was right. It wasn't like the boss to leave them in the dark this long, and he was wondering what the hell was going on just like everyone else. "I'm sure we'll find out any minute," he said with hollow conviction.

Adamo and Munn returned with the coffees, passed them out, and then took their seats. A beat later, everyone else returned, too, with

Jarvis stepping up to the low podium. Instead of the monitors flickering to life with satellite images, maps, or grainy photos, the news and security feeds continued to stream silently behind him.

"All right, guys, let's get started. First, I'd like to acknowledge our host, Elinor Jordan," Jarvis said, gesturing to the female Israeli agent. "Elinor is the acting Director of the Seventh Order. She's going to introduce her team and brief us on how she sees us working together on this operation."

Dempsey forced himself not to gawk. *Acting Director?*

Smith apparently couldn't resist and raised his hand like a schoolboy, but spoke at the same time. "What, exactly, is the operation, boss?" he asked.

Jarvis looked hard at his Director of Operations and said, "We'll have more details soon." Then, without segue, he stepped away from the podium and disappeared through the door at the back of the room.

"As Director Jarvis said, my name is Elinor. My colleagues to my right, Daniel and Rouvin, would like to welcome you to the Seventh Order. We're glad for your arrival and look forward to training together to achieve our mutual goals. I'd like to start by sharing some history about our organization. The Seventh Order is the evolution of what was originally the Shimshon Unit. Shimshon is Hebrew for Samson, a fierce warrior from the Torah. Like Samson, Shimshon Unit was a powerful tool against those who would destroy Israel. In the case of Samson, it was the Philistines; for Shimshon Unit, it was the militants in Palestine. The unit conducted undercover operations against the Palestinian terrorists in Gaza until it was ordered disbanded in 1995 by the Oslo Accords . . ."

Dempsey felt Munn's gaze on him but refused to look at his former SEAL teammate. He was no more interested in the history lesson than Munn was, but if they paid attention to the charter and capabilities of the Seventh Order, it might shed some light on the nature of their impending mission and how the Israelis planned to support them.

"The unit was officially disbanded but functionally folded into a sister unit known as 217, or Duvdevan."

"The Assassination Unit?" Grimes asked. There was no judgment in her voice, Dempsey noted. Just an honest question.

"The unit specializes in covert and undercover actions against our enemies. They infiltrate terrorist organizations, disrupt operations, and gather tremendous amounts of actionable intelligence to keep our nation safe. When the mission requires, they kill, but that is not the charter. These brave soldiers regularly and routinely sacrifice their lives in the service of Israel. Service in the unit is considered one of the most hazardous duties within the IDF."

The men beside her were nodding somberly. Perhaps thinking, as Dempsey was, of brothers and sisters they had lost. Elinor's eyes, however, did not betray emotion like her teammates'. She was a machine at the podium, simply stating facts.

"Like America," she continued, "Israel sometimes finds itself paralyzed by bureaucracy. The Seventh Order was founded by Director Harel as a highly black operation—known only to a handful of people within our government. In America, Ember exists to keep your citizenry safe. In Israel, the Seventh Order exists to safeguard the very survival of a Jewish state."

Beneath her stoicism, Dempsey at last detected a spark of passion. He thought back to his first encounter with Elizabeth Grimes almost a year ago, and the supersize chip she wore on her shoulder then. Where Grimes was overt with her emotions, Elinor's presentation was more guarded. She'd kept her brief clinical and academic. But a person did not make it to the table, especially at this level, without surviving some serious battle damage. Dempsey knew how to recognize a wounded kindred spirit. There was more to Elinor Jordan than met the eye, and maybe with time he'd catch a glimpse behind the curtain.

She continued talking, elaborating on the relationships that the Seventh Order covertly maintained with other organizations within

Oz Brigade, but Dempsey didn't care about the details. He wanted to know the mission. He wanted to know how Seventh Order was going to help Ember. He wanted to know the DNA test results from the headless motherfucker they'd delivered over twenty-four hours ago. What was the holdup? Why were they still in the dark?

Then, as if God himself were tuned in to Dempsey's internal monologue, Elinor paused and checked her mobile phone. "Excuse me," she said, glancing up at them. "I believe this is the call we've all been waiting for." She turned and exited the room, answering the call as she did.

Dempsey resisted the urge to sigh with exasperation. He took the lid off his still untouched coffee to check for foo-foo contamination and thankfully found the liquid inside to be a perfectly beautiful chestnut color. He raised the cup to his mouth, inhaled, and took a sip.

Even their damn coffee is better than ours, he grumbled to himself.

They didn't have to wait long. A beat later, Elinor returned with Jarvis at her side. She gestured to the podium, giving him the proverbial honor of breaking the news.

"I know it's been painful waiting, but we just got the DNA results back on our headless tango. We have a match with ninety-nine percent confidence the body is Behrouz Rostami," Jarvis said, gripping the sides of the podium.

"I knew it," Dempsey blurted. "I fucking knew it."

Anger welled up inside him, and he was suddenly furious that he had not been the one to kill Rostami. Ever since Frankfurt, when Rostami had corrupted, violated, and then gutted the German girl Effie Vogel, Dempsey had wanted to end that VEVAK bastard. God, it was stupid and selfish, he knew, but it gnawed at him that someone else had taken his prize.

Wait a second, he thought, silently arguing with himself now. *Rostami was murdered in the Iranian mission, which means it had to be an inside job.*

But why would Modiri order a hit on his Lieutenant?

Maybe once Rostami pulled off coordinating the attack on the DNI he had become a loose end. But if that was the case, why whack the guy in DC? Why not wait until he was safely back in Iran to take care of business? Unless Modiri wanted Rostami's body to be found . . . but then why work so hard to make the corpse unidentifiable? Dempsey rubbed his temples. This was exactly the sort of twisted spook shit that gave him a migraine. The John Dempsey of a year ago wouldn't have even bothered trying to connect the dots, but thanks to Jarvis and Smith, his mind worked differently now. He looked at Jarvis, who was still standing at the podium. The boss looked tired and—if Dempsey didn't know the man better, he'd be tempted to say—demoralized. Probably because Jarvis had already been thinking ten steps ahead. And now, with confirmation of Rostami's identity, he was wrestling with scenarios Dempsey had not even begun to contemplate. That's why they were here, after all, wasn't it? So Jarvis and Harel could plan their covert retaliation. The Americans weren't the only ones with a score to settle. The Israelis had lost their Mossad Chief in the attack. Over the past year, the Israeli Prime Minister had not been shy about condemning the nuclear treaty with Iran as both feckless and dangerous. Shamone had been waiting for an excuse to strike Iran's nuclear facilities, and now, with the evidence that a known Iranian assassin had been nearby when the bombing occurred, he finally had one.

"All right, people, enough," Jarvis said, his voice a megaphone silencing the din of heated conversation that had erupted in the room. "I know it's going to be difficult, but I need your patience while we process this information and contemplate our response."

"What does that mean?" Munn asked. "Contemplate our response—I thought our response was already contemplated and that's why we're here. We got hit by VEVAK; now we need to hit them back."

"It's not that simple," Elinor replied, beating Jarvis to the punch. "There are serious geopolitical implications for any action we take."

"I disagree. It *is* simple," Munn growled. "Eye for an eye. They took out our intelligence Chiefs; we need to return the favor."

"That's easy for you to say," the male Israeli operator called Rouvin interjected, "because your country is ten thousand kilometers away. You don't have thousands of enemy rockets and missiles trained on your capital. You hit VEVAK, then you retreat back to America and watch the aftermath on the TV from the safety of your living room. But not us—our lives, our families are at stake if this escalates into war."

Elinor held a stern finger up to the man beside her, silencing him, but not until after the point had been made. *Rouvin is right,* Dempsey thought. Jarvis had undoubtedly played out all the "what if" scenarios in his mind, which was why they were here. But if the plan involved Israeli support, then it meant that Israel was in the driver's seat. Which begged the question, why did they even need the Seventh Order? Why did they need Levi Harel's support? *Because our DNI is dead, you moron,* he thought to himself. The nuclear treaty with Iran had been brokered under President Warner's watch. There was no way Catherine Morgan would jeopardize her ascent to the throne of the US intelligence community by authorizing a covert action mission in Tehran that implied Warner had made a mistake. Dempsey shook his head at the sour taste that had developed in his mouth.

God, he hated the political shit.

"So what do we do in the interim?" Munn asked, not backing down.

"We train," Elinor said simply. "Together."

"How, if we don't even know what the hell we're training for?" Grimes fired back.

"I understand everyone's frustration," Elinor said. "But we need to trust the process. We are not the policy makers; we are the instruments of policy. So, while the bosses decide the response, we can go to the Kirya range and begin drilling. It will give us a chance to get to know each other and refine our methods."

"Our methods are battle tested," said Grimes. "I can promise you that."

Elinor smiled. "Well, as we like to say in the Seventh Order, first we practice, then we promise."

Grimes rolled her eyes at this, but otherwise chose not to escalate.

"When will we meet the rest of your team?" Wang asked.

Elinor glanced at the two men beside her. "You're looking at it," she said, gesturing to herself, Daniel, and Rouvin.

"Three of you?" Smith said. "That's it?"

"Seventh Order is a clandestine field unit, and as such, the majority of our members are embedded. We have a small support staff for analysis, cyber, and communications, but seventy percent of our members live behind enemy lines, some occupying NOCs for years. Our operations are not the kind that can be turned on and off. When the time comes, we will have people positioned to help us, no matter the mission, but until then, we are your team."

She looked at Jarvis with the weary eyes of a babysitter exhausted from a night of corralling a gang of unruly children.

"All right, folks," he said, taking the hint. "You heard the lady. Pack your gear and go play at the range. When the tactical picture comes into focus, I promise you, you'll be the first ones to know."

CHAPTER 18

Seventh Order Break Room
"The City That Never Sleeps"
Tel Aviv, Israel
May 6
2338 Local Time

The stink of cigarette smoke roused him.

Jarvis opened his eyes to find the former and current head of Mossad sitting in the chair across from him. He didn't remember falling asleep. Harel's expression was reminiscent of a parent gazing wryly at his toddler passed out from playing too long and hard on the living room floor.

"Sorry," Jarvis said as the blurry figure came into focus. "Must have dozed off."

Harel tilted his head back and blew a stream of smoke up at the ceiling. "When was the last time you got some sleep?"

"Apparently, just now," Jarvis said, straightening up in his chair.

"Before that?"

Jarvis shook his head. "I don't know . . . couple of days."

"I know the feeling, my friend. Believe me."

"How long have you known about Rostami?" Jarvis asked, shifting gears.

"Since yesterday," the Israeli spymaster said. "I could lie, but what would be the point?"

Jarvis shook his head and sighed. "You could have told us."

"The PM instructed me not to. He wanted time to think. Don't be mad, Kelso."

"I'm not mad. Just frustrated."

"I know, and so am I. We are men of action. There is nothing more aggravating for men like us than idle hands. But again, sometimes that's the game."

"Modiri needs to pay," Jarvis said, meeting the Israeli's gaze. "You realize that."

"He's a menace, Kelso, and so is the rest of VEVAK," Harel said, his expression darkening. "But if your government is so certain that VEVAK is responsible for this attack, then why has your President's big mouth suddenly gone mute? Why are your jets not dropping precision weapons? Where are the cruise missiles that you so readily fired at Syria? Where is the American response?" Harel's voice was tight with condemnation, and Jarvis understood his friend's frustration.

"Yes, we share common enemies, as you've preached for years, but our nations are fundamentally different. The President would never commit to a course of action that might lead to World War Three on intuition alone. While Rostami's body is an undeniable fingerprint of VEVAK's guilt to you and me, one headless corpse is not sufficient evidence for the American government to justify military intervention on the world stage. Don't pretend like you don't know this. Rostami was a loose end that was severed by Modiri, one he assumed he could discreetly dispose of by staging his execution inside the Pakistani embassy—sovereign territory on which US law enforcement has no jurisdiction."

"You think I don't know these things. But unlike Warner, Shamone doesn't give a shit about the circus you call the world stage. What he cares about is a future where Iran—emboldened by the brazen execution of Mossad leadership without consequence—escalates its agenda of terrorism, regional destabilization, and anti-Semitism. If we let this stand, if we do nothing, more Jewish blood will flow."

"I understand, but Persia's punishment must equal the crime. It is up to us to ensure the men we work for don't antagonize each other to action driven by pride and desperation rather than prudence."

"Contrary to what you might think, old friend, Israel is not interested in starting World War Three."

"I know," Jarvis said, leaning forward and placing his elbows on his knees. "Which is why I've come. I have a plan."

"Of course you do," Harel said, putting out his Noblest in an ashtray and shaking a new one from a pack he pulled from his inside jacket breast pocket. "Well, don't keep me in suspense."

"It's a joint operation, Ember and the Seventh Order. We send a team into Tehran and we disappear Modiri. Capture/kill. If fate smiles on us, we EXFIL him to a black site and harvest everything we can. If not, then Davy Jones's locker. Either way, life for Amir Modiri is over."

"That's your plan?" Harel said, the corner of his mouth curling into something resembling a smile. Then came the sarcasm, laid on thick and ironic like only a self-proclaimed "cranky old Jew from Tel Aviv" could manage. "It's brilliant, Kelso. Why haven't we thought of this before? Whose credit card do you want to use to buy the airline tickets? I hear the Hilton in Tehran is running a great special: fifty percent off room rates for Zionist and American operators." He paused for dramatic effect and then, shaking his head, said, "I think you need to go back to sleep. We can talk about this tomorrow."

"I'm serious, Levi. It's time we take this bastard out of the game."

"It's not so easy as that," Harel said with a snort. "Even before Crusader happened, I've been dreaming up ways to take out Amir

Modiri. But in five years, he's only left Tehran twice. Both times, he went to Switzerland. He's paranoid. He's smart. He knows he's a marked man and he behaves accordingly."

"That's why we have to take him in Tehran."

Harel laughed and scratched the two days' worth of stubble on his neck. "Do you hear what you're saying? Do you know how many agents and assets I've lost in that fucking country chasing much smaller fish than Modiri? For a Jewish spy, Tehran is quite simply the most dangerous place on Earth. If there was a way to get at Modiri, I would have done it already. In Tehran, Modiri is untouchable."

Jarvis stood and began to pace. "And two days ago, I would have said the same about the DNI at his home in Annapolis. But VEVAK somehow managed to pull off the impossible. Now it's our turn."

Harel took a long drag from his cigarette and exhaled slowly. "First of all, let me make something clear. Your tactical team is good, maybe the best in the world right now, but they wouldn't survive the mission. Maybe we get them in. Maybe they'd even get Modiri. But we wouldn't get them out. We've run all the scenarios. In my opinion, there's only one viable operation."

"Which is?"

"Single operative supported by my existing illegals network. Modiri is assassinated in his home. No guarantee of extraction."

Jarvis nodded. He'd run the scenarios, too, and he knew Harel was right. "Okay, we do it your way."

"You sound like you've already decided who you want to send."

"I have," Jarvis said. "John Dempsey."

Harel laughed, which triggered a coughing fit. When he finally caught his breath, he said, "I did not know this was comedy hour. You should have warned me."

"I'm serious."

"You want to send your bullheaded American SEAL into Iran?"

"Yes."

"Okay, we're done here," Harel said, getting to his feet. "You really do need to get some sleep, my friend. We can talk tomorrow."

Jarvis grabbed Harel by the arm. "He's ready. He can do this."

"Don't be ridiculous. He does not speak Farsi. His Arabic is dreadful. He knows nothing about Persian culture and politics. His spycraft is a work in progress. Don't get me wrong; as an operator Dempsey has no equal, but Iran is no place for a man like him. He wouldn't last a day."

"Then he needs a partner. We pair him up with one of your people. Who is your best? Who on your team could pull this off?"

"There's only one person I would trust, but I would never force a mission like this on her."

"Elinor?" Jarvis said.

Harel nodded. "She understands the proud, conflicted Iranian psyche better than anyone. Sometimes, I think she knows them better than they know themselves."

"Okay, perfect. She'll be the brains and he'll be the brawn. Let's call them in and tell them the good news."

"Kelso, even if I agreed with this ludicrous plan, which I haven't, but even if I did, the timing is terrible. Do you know why I'm late meeting you? Do you know what I did all day?"

"No, but I have a pretty good idea," Jarvis said, making his way back to his armchair.

"I sat in a briefing theater with the Prime Minister and a bunch of IDF Generals planning our retaliatory strike. We're going to hit Iran, and we're going to hit them hard."

"When?"

"Seventy-two hours."

"You can't do it, Levi," Jarvis said, shaking his head.

"The laundry list of reasons for hitting Iran has been building for over a decade. Unlike America, we do not have the luxury of waiting for incontrovertible evidence. The military buildup on Iran's border right now is alone sufficient provocation. My people are at risk long before Persia would ever turn their weapons on you. We must act—at a very minimum conduct strikes against strategic Persian nuclear targets. The pundits and the politicians will squawk and shout, but the world will have no choice but to accept our right to defend ourselves, just as the world gave the United States a free pass after 9/11 to invade Afghanistan and Iraq. Israel simply cannot afford to let this provocation pass unrequited."

"That's where you're wrong. The world is done with free passes. The pundits and politicians will rebrand your retaliatory strike as a first strike. Which will morph into an offensive. Which will in turn morph into an act of war, at which point Iran will play the victim and rally regional Arab support. Then, the counterattacks will begin, kicking off a war of escalation that will result in the US being dragged into the conflict."

Harel mashed his cigarette into the ashtray with a scowl, but he did not argue.

"You once gave me advice I'll never forget, but it seems you've forgotten your own counsel," Jarvis said.

"What did I say?"

"You said, 'The problem with revenge is that when adversaries seek parity, escalation is inescapable—even when it leads to their mutual undoing.' Is Israel ready to go down that road? Are you ready to launch a military campaign that in all likelihood could lead to World War Three?"

"It's not my call, Kelso. I'm the Chief of the Mossad, not the PM, remember?"

"But as the head of Mossad, your job is to give the PM covert action alternatives to conventional war. What I'm suggesting is such an alternative."

"How does disappearing Modiri address Iran's nuclear weapons program? Hmmm? Because that's what this is really all about. While the world has been lauding Tehran for opening their borders to IAEA inspectors, Esfahani has been funneling millions of dollars—dollars unlocked because of easing of sanctions—into secret programs to reinvigorate the nuclear weapons program. Esfahani is the ultimate sleight-of-hand magician, distracting you with a bouquet of flowers in his left hand while the right hand is pointing a pistol at your chest."

"How much do you really know about the current state of Tehran's nuclear program? We have the same concerns as you, but so far we've been unable to find any definitive proof that what we suspect is happening is really happening."

Harel made a *pffft* sound. "You sound like the rest of them."

"Taking Modiri could change that," Jarvis continued without missing a beat. "Don't get me wrong; he needs to die, but imagine if we were able to take him alive. Break his mind, and imagine the treasure trove of information we'll have access to."

Harel laughed and collapsed back into the armchair across from Jarvis. "What is the expression you use—never bullshit a bullshitter. Did I get it right?"

Jarvis nodded.

"You don't have to sell me on the merits of grabbing Modiri, Kelso. I want that bastard, too. But it's impossible. And Israel is going to hit Iranian nuclear targets regardless of whether we go after Modiri. It is not an either-or scenario."

Jarvis looked down at his hands, which at the moment felt completely normal. Maybe Harel was right, but maybe he wasn't. If he could get the old spymaster's help, maybe he could pull off the impossible and kidnap VEVAK's Foreign Operations Director. With Modiri alive, he could use the man as both a bargaining chip and scapegoat. "By making Modiri the fall guy for the DNI bombing, Esfahani can save face, and Warner and Shamone get their pound of flesh."

Harel snorted. "You have more faith in Esfahani's judgment than I have the luxury of presuming."

Jarvis nodded. "I understand, Levi, but do not underestimate the power of self-preservation. Even a blind man will eventually find a way out of a burning house. We have to give Esfahani a way out of *his* burning house. This plan might be the only thing that saves us from world war, and if not, we lose nothing by trying."

"I'm sorry, Kelso, but preparations for the strike are already under way."

"Okay," Jarvis said after a long beat.

"Okay what?"

"Okay, I accept that I can't stop Israel from attacking Iran, but it still benefits both of us if we disappear Modiri. Will you support the mission?"

"Not until after the attack."

"No," Jarvis snapped. "It has to be before."

"Impossible," Harel said. "First of all, there's not enough time to prep. Second, we might be walking into a trap: covert retaliation is exactly what Modiri will be anticipating. It's what I would expect in his shoes. And third, the mission will have a much greater chance of success *after* the strike, because Tehran will be in chaos."

Jarvis's heart sank; he shook his head but said nothing.

"I'm sorry, Kelso, but this is the way it has to be."

"Then I'm afraid you're putting the fate of the world in Israel's hands."

"It's better than the opposite—putting Israel's fate in the hands of the world. That is something we are simply no longer willing to do."

CHAPTER 19

West Wing of the White House
May 6
1535 Local Time

Catherine Morgan rotated an ink pen between her thumb and index finger and tried not to fidget. She had met the President before, briefing him on three separate occasions, but she'd always been with Admiral Philips. In those engagements, she had really just been delivering talking points on plans the DNI would assume ultimate responsibility for. Now, however, she felt the pressure of being the last link in the chain carrying the full burden and weight of national security. The safety net she had unconsciously enjoyed was gone. She was the boss now, and along with Philips's title, she also inherited the portfolio of assets and liabilities he had accumulated during his tenure.

The most beguiling of which was Task Force Ember.

Was Ember an asset, or was it a liability? She saw them as the latter for a number of reasons, but she had no idea how President Warner felt on the matter. Regardless, she planned to make the case that Ember was a loose cannon. Philips had been close to Kelso Jarvis, too close for

reasonable oversight, she would argue, the repercussion of this arrangement being the Wild West culture that Philips had tolerated, possibly even encouraged, in Ember. Were he alive, Philips would certainly
maintain that Ember's structure was by design—a semi-autonomous
off-the-books entity that provided the President with plausible deniability in case some operation went sideways. In such a scenario, Philips had
been prepared to fall on his sword to protect the President from fallout.

*Well, I'm not falling on someone else's sword to protect the President
from a bunch of door-kicking, tobacco-chewing good ole boys who think
they can make up the rules as they go along.*

"Ms. Morgan, the President will see you now," said the woman
behind the oak desk, a stale smile plastered across her face. She dropped
a hand out of sight and released a magnetic lock with a button press
beneath her desk.

"Thank you," Morgan said and pushed through the door into the
Oval Office.

Warner rose from his desk and strode toward her, leaving the two
younger staffers beside his desk talking in hushed tones. He met her
by the door, always the gentleman—or maybe just always campaigning
for more votes. He extended an athletic hand and she shook it firmly,
but his face was grim.

"Thanks for your patience, Catherine."

"Of course, Mr. President," she said. "I know there is a lot going on."

The President snorted and shook his head. "You have no idea."

She stiffened, wondering if this was just a euphemism or if he
meant it as a slight to her competence as acting DNI.

Warner gestured to the two sofas facing each other in the center
of the room.

"Please, have a seat," he said, indicating one while taking a seat on
the other. "I'm afraid I'm pressed for time, but you said this was urgent."

"Yes, sir," she said, her stomach tightening. Suddenly, she wondered
if calling this meeting had been a mistake. *Too late for second thoughts*

now, she decided, and so she dove right in. "I want to talk to you about Task Force Ember, Mr. President."

Warner screwed up his face and raised a palm, cutting her off and irritating her immensely. He turned and called out to his staffers over his shoulder, "Peter . . . Claire . . . Give us the room." The two staffers disappeared quickly through a door at the far side of the room.

With the office to themselves, the President leaned forward. His gaze hardened, all courtesy and chivalry noticeably gone. "I just want to make sure I heard you correctly, Catherine," he said. "Did you say you called this meeting to discuss Task Force Ember?"

Morgan shifted uncomfortably on the sofa. "Yes, sir. My predecessor—"

"With the shit storm we have brewing in Iran, you're really here to talk about Ember?" he said.

She hesitated a beat. "Yes, sir," she said, this time without trying to elaborate.

He shook his head and sighed with exasperation. "This better be good . . . Go on. I'm listening."

"As I was saying, sir, under my predecessor's watch, Task Force Ember has been permitted to evolve into something larger and more dangerous than I believe was intended."

"Dangerous to who?" Warner said.

"To you, sir. To this Administration. This task force operates with no oversight whatsoever. Captain Jarvis and his men run roughshod over the other agencies they are tasked to work with and then share almost nothing with them in return."

Warner abruptly stood. "You weren't present when Ember was formed, were you, Catherine?"

"No, sir, but—"

"You were not; that's correct. I was. I remember. Ember was born out of the ashes of an attack that decimated the Tier One Navy SEALs—the most lethal and reliable weapon I had in my arsenal in this never-ending war on terror. Ember's charter, a charter dictated by *me*, by the way, was to prosecute this new threat to our counterterrorism operations and function in parallel with the intelligence community. This arrangement was by design, unshackling Captain Jarvis from the chains of bureaucracy that presently paralyze the CIA. As the *acting* DNI, I assume you are now read into Ember's past successes?"

"Yes, sir."

"Then I ask you, Ms. Morgan, how are victories such as these *dangerous* to my Administration?"

The fact that he had just dropped the more intimate *Catherine* was not lost on her. She swallowed and said, "Sir, with all due respect, Ember is a loose cannon. It is only a matter of—"

"I don't have time for this," the President said, cutting her off yet again. "Despite the immediate denial of responsibility from Iran, Persian military forces are massing along Iran's borders. Their Air Force is flying patrol sorties and they're repositioning mobile missile launchers around the country. In my mind, and in the minds of the Joint Chiefs, this uptick in activity is an overt admission of guilt for the attack on DNI Philips and the Israeli contingent three days ago—the hell with their denials. I just gave the Secretary of the Navy permission to move one of our SSGNs into the Persian Gulf and reposition the Fifth Fleet carrier strike group from the Indian Ocean into the Arabian Sea. Dialogue is already under way with Jordan to stage conventional assets in preparation for war, and I've given authorization to JSOC commanders to deploy Special Operations contingents along the Iranian borders in Afghanistan and Iraq to begin operations to prep the battlefield. Instead of worrying about Ember, Ms. Morgan, you should be working closely with the Pentagon on conflict scenarios and the aftermath, because if you're not scared shitless, you should be. The number crunchers tell me that conflict scenarios with Iran where the US allies with Israel are likely to escalate into a nuclear world war. Whatever Ember is doing, rest assured it's serving America's best interests. I promise you that."

"Yes, sir."

The President stood and walked back to his desk, a signal her audience with him had come to an end.

She stood and turned to leave.

"I recognize, however, that not everyone's brain works like mine," he added, as if in afterthought. "So my parting advice to you is this: if Ember's operational autonomy is making you feel out of control, Catherine, then take fucking control." He pushed a button on the black phone beside him on the desk and said, "Get Peter and Claire back in here."

The President grunted and opened a folder on his desk. A beat later, the door to the Oval Office opened, and Warner's staffers hurried back in. She left through the same door without a backward glance.

"Have a nice day, Ms. Morgan," the woman at the oak desk said as she walked out of the most powerful office in the world.

Was this woman mocking her? Was it obvious she'd just had her ass handed to her by the President of the United States? Morgan said nothing in reply and headed down the hall, her mind raging. Jarvis was probably in Israel. In fact, she was certain of it. He was definitely up to something, undoubtedly working with the Mossad on some covert action against Tehran. God, she hated the fucking Israelis. *So self-righteous. So impetuous.*

She exhaled through her nose.

Take fucking control . . . That is what the President had said.

The people of the United States deserved transparency. They deserved accountability . . . and that is exactly what she intended to give them. Kelso Jarvis would bow to her will, whether he wanted to or not.

CHAPTER 20

This was it.

The Head Shed was finally going to man up and give them their tasking.

Thank God, Dempsey thought, because the waiting was making them all neurotic. Across the table, Grimes was chewing her nails, which she'd gnawed down to the quick on both hands. Adamo must have pushed his glasses up on his nose ten times in the past five minutes. Smith was on his fourth cup of coffee for the morning. Wang was bobbing his head to the beat of some song only he could hear. And Munn, well, Munn had shaved this morning.

Yes, it was time.

"I'm ready for game on," Munn said beside him, with a definitive tap of his index finger on the tabletop.

Dempsey looked over and smiled, happy to see that Munn's eyes had fully regained the fire he remembered from their days together in the Teams. For Munn, this operation would be cathartic—a much-needed return to the saddle as an operator. "Me, too. Enough with the foreplay," he agreed in a hushed whisper. "It's time to get it on."

The door pushed open, and Jarvis strode in with Elinor in tow. The Ember Director was wearing his game face today and instantly commanded the room.

Thank God, Dempsey thought, *the old Jarvis is back.*

Gripping the sides of the podium, Jarvis said, "For those of you who have been living in a hole, not reading the message traffic, or having entirely too much fun at the range, then it might come as a surprise that over the past forty-eight hours, both Israel and Iran have been busy preparing for war. Also, I think all of you should know that Prime Minister Shamone has authorized the IDF to conduct a retaliatory strike on Persia for the attack perpetrated at the DNI's estate."

"Sir, if I may," Adamo interjected. "The evidence we've connected linking VEVAK to the attack is hardly substantive enough to justify a military strike. The media will have a feeding frenzy with this."

"This is Israel, Mr. Adamo, not America," Elinor said, stepping in, "and Prime Minister Shamone is of the mind that we do not need the media's permission to protect our sovereignty. Rostami's body is not the only evidence we have. Mossad has HUMINT collected from sources inside Iran, we have our own signal intelligence program, and we have reconstructed signals intelligence still coming in from your own Ian Baldwin as we speak. The assassination of Rami Sharott is but one of hundreds of operations perpetuated by VEVAK against the state of Israel. Taken together, it's all the justification we need."

Adamo nodded, but Dempsey could see that Elinor had failed to change his opinion, and he understood why. Adamo's CIA career had been derailed because he'd been unable to produce sufficient hard evidence for the existence of an Iranian sleeper-cell program in the United

States. Adamo had been convinced of the Suren Circle's existence, but after spending millions of agency dollars and burning man-years of agency time, he had not been able to build a case strong enough to convince his superiors. As part of Ember, Adamo was vindicated and proven to have been right all along, but his career at Langley had been sidelined. Adamo wasn't debating the merits of an Israeli first strike; what he was debating was the paper trail. Whether Shamone liked it or not, history always judges the acts of men, and without substantive, irrefutable proof, the people of Israel would pay for the verdict.

"So when is this going to go down, and what does the IDF plan to hit?" Munn asked, getting straight to the point.

"Neither myself nor Elinor has been read into the IDF's plans," Jarvis said. "We don't know when the attack is going to happen. We don't know the targets. We don't know the scope. But what we do know is that regardless of the specifics, there *will* be an attack, and there *will* be significant geopolitical repercussions."

Munn kicked Dempsey's boot under the table and whispered, "Told you there was gonna be a war."

Dempsey grunted in acknowledgment but kept his gaze locked on Jarvis.

"Which brings us to the question of the hour: Why are we here?" Jarvis continued. "To answer that question, I will begin by telling you why we are *not* here. We are not here to collect intelligence in preparation for war. We are not here to conduct covert actions to facilitate war. We are not here to aid our brothers and sisters in arms in fighting a war. We are here, in fact, to prevent a war."

Eyebrows arched and incredulous dialogue erupted around the table.

With a tight grin, Jarvis waved them to be quiet.

"Now, I know what you're thinking: the old man must have hit his head, but I assure you my wits are fully intact. Regardless of whether retaliation is justified, war between Israel and Iran is not a path we want to go down. If Israel and Iran go to war, US participation is inevitable. Moscow has yet to release an official statement, but Petrov is shifting assets south and flying air patrols on the Syrian side of the Iranian border, signaling an intention to support Iran. We're all big boys and girls around this table; we all know that a full-scale Persian-Israeli conflict could quickly escalate into World War Three. I won't let that happen. No, strike that. *We* won't let that happen."

"While I appreciate the unbridled confidence you have in our capabilities, I'm not sure I understand how anything *we* can do stops this war," Grimes said with her characteristic contradictory flair. "You just said that the decision has been made; the IDF is going to hit Iran. What can we possibly do to derail the train?"

"Thank you, Elizabeth, for the perfect segue," he said. "To stop this war, someone needs to be held accountable. And when I say someone, I don't simply mean Iran as a nation. As primitive and dubious as this might sound, the only way to stave off this war is with a blood debt. Eye for an eye. For killing the DNI and the Mossad Director, the Persian responsible must be punished and punished on the world stage. Only by giving Iran a scapegoat do the Supreme Leader and President Esfahani have an opportunity to save face. Only by giving the United States and Israel possession of one of Iran's most powerful and dangerous men do we achieve both justice and the ability to harvest vital intelligence otherwise inaccessible. It is a long shot, but in my mind, it's our only shot." He turned to Elinor. "I'll let you do the honors."

The Seventh Order's acting Director traded places with Jarvis at the podium. She clicked a button and a Persian face—a face known to all of them—appeared on the screen behind her. "Amir Modiri," she said simply. "This is our target."

Dempsey leaned forward on his elbows, his eyes laser beams locked on to the face on the screen. Amir Modiri. This was his white whale. Like Captain Ahab's quest for revenge, hunting down Modiri had become Dempsey's obsession. There was nothing he wouldn't sacrifice to kill the beast. *Hell, I've got nothing left to give,* he thought, *except the heart beating in my chest.*

"Modiri has single-handedly done more to destabilize the region than any other foreign intelligence adversary since the creation of the Jewish state. One of the greatest challenges we've faced is penetrating his inner circle, an inner circle that he keeps incredibly tight. His recruiting practices are—in a word—intimate. He has a history of luring trusted friends and colleagues from his university days and even family members into service: the ultimate example being his brother, the former Iranian Ambassador who he employed to help facilitate the attack on the UN in New York last year."

"Hold on a minute," Grimes interrupted, sitting up straight in her chair. Her eyes went from Elinor to Jarvis, who shook his head with an admonishing *don't go there* look that Dempsey knew by heart. But that only seemed to add gas to the redhead's fire. "How did you know that? Did we provide you with after-action intelligence?"

Elinor met Grimes's gaze, but she didn't answer.

"That's what I thought—we didn't," Lizzie continued. "And as I recall, you guys bowed out after Frankfurt . . . We didn't connect the dots between Amir and the Ambassador until the eleventh hour and fifty-ninth minute." Red-faced, she turned to Dempsey, looking for backup.

"She's right," he said. "It came down to the wire. We were working the connection in real time as the players were already in motion."

"That intelligence would have been invaluable for us," Grimes said. "We could have intercepted the Ambassador before he cleared security and put the UN on lockdown. We could have foiled the attack before it started. Nobody had to die that day."

"I understand your frustration, Elizabeth, and it is warranted. But please understand, and I mean no disrespect when I say that Ember and the Seventh Order are separate, autonomous clandestine activities, serving different masters with different sovereign agendas. We have assets inside of Iran, longitudinally developed assets with long histories of providing us critical data. These individuals are irreplaceable—people whose identities and reputations we must safeguard at all cost. With respect to the specific case of Ambassador Modiri and his role in the UN attack, I was not privileged to this information at the time, nor do I know the source inside Tehran who provided this intelligence. All I can promise you is that the decision not to share this information with you was not made lightly, and it would have been a decision made only by the Director himself at that time."

Grimes opened her mouth to speak, but Jarvis beat her to the punch. "Hindsight is painful in our business, but now is not the time for divisiveness. When it comes to *this* operation, Ember and the Seventh Order are joined at the hip. There are no secrets being kept between us on this matter. So let's move on."

Grimes and Elinor both nodded in agreement, although Dempsey could see Lizzie's jaw muscles ripple as she clenched her teeth.

"As I was saying," Elinor continued, "the objective of this mission is to take Modiri."

"Take him?" Adamo interrupted, his eyebrows raised. "You can't be serious."

"Dead serious," Elinor replied.

"And just how do you propose we do that? Do you have reliable intel on Modiri's movements? Is he planning a trip outside of Iran to a location favorable to such an operation?"

Elinor shook her head. "This will be a capture/kill mission inside Iran."

A stunned silence enveloped the room.

"Inside Iran?" Munn whispered, both to himself and everyone.

"Inside Tehran, in fact."

"Are you insane?" Adamo said, pushing his glasses up onto the bridge of his nose. "What you're proposing is impossible. Infiltration will be hard enough, but kidnapping VEVAK's functional number two and exfiltrating the country with him is nothing short of a suicide mission. And that's a cold fact."

Dempsey leaned back in his seat. A capture/kill operation inside Iran? Adamo was right: it was insane. Even with his old Tier One unit, with everyone in perfect mental and physical condition and with unlimited resources and support, he never would have dreamed of running such an operation. It was, quite simply, the most dangerous mission imaginable for a special operator. And yet despite the sirens going off inside his head, and despite the big bright-yellow sign depicting a road going off a cliff, he wanted this. This was why he had joined Ember in the first place. He hadn't known it at the time—bandaged and broken in the belly of a C-130—but this was the opportunity he had traded his life for. He had traded Jake and Kate for Amir Modiri. Completing this operation wasn't just Ember's charter; it was his.

This was the mission Jack Kemper had died for.

This was the mission John Dempsey was born to complete.

". . . impossible alone, but with the support of Ember and her assets, it can be done."

Dempsey shook his head, snapping his attention back to the present. "I'm sorry," he said. "Say that last part again."

Elinor nodded and then said, "I was simply saying that this type of covert operation is what the Seventh Order was born for, but this particular mission would be impossible without Ember's support."

"What do you mean support?" Dempsey said, sitting up in his chair. *I didn't come all this way, and sacrifice so much, to be support.*

She didn't answer immediately but instead began clicking through a series of slides—which Dempsey recognized first as Irbil in northern Iraq, and then the rugged terrain of the northwest corner of the country, north of Soran, where the Iraqi border converged with Turkey to the north and Iran to the east.

"The United States has a robust Special Forces presence in northern Iraq. Although the bulk of your operations are to the west and south against ISIS forces, we know that your Special Forces also support covert operations along the Iranian border. Israel does not, for obvious reasons, have a strong military presence in the Iraqi conflict. The one thing that even warring radical Islamic factions can agree on is that Jews need to be exterminated. We do, however, have mature assets on the other side. In addition to a developed network in Tehran, we run a variety of assets in other Iranian cities. We've had past success facilitating border crossings from the inside. The trouble now is getting there. The recent Persian military activity and the massing of conventional forces along the borders will greatly curtail our ability to move in and out of Iran for this operation."

She paused and looked out across the room, locking eyes with Dempsey again. She continued, as if now speaking directly to him.

"This is where we need your help. By coordinating with your partner agencies and Special Operations contingent inside Iraq, you can ensure our assets make it to the border and into Iran. Once inside, our assets on the other side will handle the rest."

"Okay, just to be clear, our only job is to assist with security and transportation to the border? Infiltration . . . that's it?" asked Munn.

"And if everything goes according to plan, exfiltration, too," she said with a wan smile. "God willing."

"How big is the crossing party?" the doc continued.

"The plan is to insert a single agent—the smaller the footprint the better." She folded her arms across her chest as she let the words sink in.

"A single agent," Dempsey parroted back. "And just who the hell is this superman?"

On that cue, Jarvis stood and walked to the podium next to Elinor.

"Elinor has the necessary language skills, experience, and network of assets inside Iran to make this mission a success," he said, looking directly at Dempsey.

Unable to control himself, Dempsey popped to his feet, his neck hot. "With all due respect—"

Jarvis held up his hand, cutting him off. "Any sentence beginning 'With all due respect' never includes the respect it implies," he said. "This mission has been planned at the highest levels, John. We're confident this approach lends the highest chance of success."

Dempsey balked. *No, no, this is unacceptable.* He understood what Jarvis was saying—and on a purely intellectual level he agreed—but the answer was no. Fuck hierarchy. This was his mission. Fate had made this decision long ago. It *had* to be him.

"I am not questioning Elinor's abilities, or the capabilities of the Seventh Order. But taking Amir Modiri is not a solo job. A two-person team would increase the likelihood of success many times over—a second set of eyes, a second set of ears, a second gun, a second set of ideas. She needs someone to watch her back, and if things go to shit—a second operator means a second chance at turning things around."

Elinor flashed him a peculiar smile. Then, she turned to Jarvis and said, "Okay."

Jarvis rubbed his chin and after a beat said, "Am I to assume this outburst means you are volunteering your service, John?"

"Yes, sir. I am," Dempsey said, his eyes darting back and forth between Jarvis and Elinor for signs the wind had just shifted.

Jarvis nodded. "A two-person team is a scenario we contemplated. However, this is not a mission that I can, in good conscience, make compulsory. Quite frankly, I'm inclined to agree with Adamo's assessment. In all likelihood, this is a suicide mission. Ember is not the Teams, John. I needed you to volunteer."

"Does that mean I'm going?" Dempsey said, fighting back a victory grin.

Jarvis nodded and looked back and forth between him and Elinor. "Godspeed to you both."

"Wait, wait, wait," the Israeli called Rouvin said, getting to his feet now. "How can a man who speaks no Farsi, no Hebrew, and not even passable Arabic be allowed to go? It is absurd! If there is to be a second agent, it should be me or Daniel. We have trained for this very scenario. The idea that *he* could pose as Persian, or even as an Arab, is categorically absurd."

"Hey, my Arabic is pretty damn good. And I also speak some Pashto, which is very similar to Farsi," Dempsey fired back. "I've logged hundreds of missions in this region. Hell, I've practically lived half my adult life in the Middle East."

"As an American operator, yes, but that doesn't mean you can pass for an Iranian," Daniel chimed in now, clearly angry. "Look at you. You might as well be wearing a Navy SEAL T-shirt and ball cap. The very idea of *you* accompanying Elinor is madness. You will blow the cover before you make it ten kilometers."

"Enough," Elinor snapped. "This is not a democracy. We are sending one volunteer from each team. That is the decision."

"Then let me go," Rouvin said. "You are the acting Director of the Seventh Order. Harel put you in charge, which means your place is here, in Tel Aviv, running the show."

"The decision has been made. Agent Dempsey will be accompanying me; you and Daniel will work closely with the rest of the Ember team to plan the mission. Without all of you, we have zero chance of success. The mission, and our lives, will depend on you."

Dempsey nodded at Elinor and then Jarvis and then forced himself back into his seat. The Skipper didn't reciprocate the gesture, but his eyes told Dempsey everything he needed to know. This was the outcome Jarvis had wanted, but the Skipper couldn't advertise as much. To do so would be disrespectful to Rouvin and Daniel.

He felt a hand on his forearm. "You sure you wanna do this, bro?" Munn whispered.

He considered his friend's question and all its implications: Was he sure that Amir Modiri was one of America's greatest clandestine threats? *Yes.* Was he sure that somebody needed to take the bastard out? *Yes.* Was he sure that justice needed to be meted out for the murder of his entire

Tier One unit? *Yes.* Was he the most experienced and capable operator available for the mission? *Yes.* And most importantly, was he willing to die to see it done? *Yes* . . . In a fiery explosion in Djibouti one year ago, he had been spared for a purpose and one purpose alone . . . This was his destiny. This was the mission Jarvis had remade him for. He would bring back Amir Modiri, or he would die trying.

He looked at Munn, finally ready to answer his friend's question. "Yeah, Dan, I'm sure." Then, feeling Grimes's eyes on him, he looked at her. The fiery look he got back from her required no words: *You're a fucking idiot, JD, and if you make it back alive, I promise I'm gonna kill you.*

"When?" Smith asked the command duo at the podium, shaking Dempsey back to the brief. "When do they go?"

"There are a lot of variables in play here. Seventh Order needs to get word to their embedded assets in Iran and start prepping safe houses and movements. Elinor and Dempsey's NOCs need to be solidified. Ember needs to start coordinating with American Special Forces in Iraq to support the INFIL. We need to collect intelligence on Modiri's schedule and routine and then plan the grab. Exfiltration scenarios and backup contingency plans in the event of capture need to be worked out. Once all of that is done, then Seventh Order can request the green light from the PM."

"And what about the President?" Smith asked.

Jarvis narrowed his eyes at Smith. "That's a discussion you and I can have offline."

Smith nodded, taking the hint.

"Any more questions from Ember?" Jarvis asked. Dempsey had a hundred questions flying around in his head, as undoubtedly did all his teammates, but no one dared speak. "Very well," he said. "I have some calls to make, so if you'll excuse me, I'm going to leave the rest of the brief to Elinor." With that, he turned and left the briefing theater. But for a split second, Dempsey could have sworn he saw the

Skipper's right hand trembling, an instant before the legendary SEAL commander balled his fingers into a tight fist.

Strange, he'd never seen Jarvis suffer from nerves before.

Elinor picked up the presentation remote and resumed indexing through the slides—the current sequence displaying aerial views of truck convoys carrying surface-to-air missiles. "The redistribution of Iranian military forces and the changing threat level will dramatically impact our plans. As the tactical picture evolves, so must our operation. It is imperative that we closely monitor all observable Artesh and IRGC activity in the coming days . . ."

Dempsey leaned right and whispered around Munn to Smith. "We need to find out if Lieutenant Redman is in Irbil right now. With this buildup, I wouldn't be surprised if his team is here."

Smith smiled and nodded. "Good idea. Chunk and his SEALs are perfect for this. I'll get on it."

While he stared at the latest Israeli satellite imagery, Dempsey couldn't help but wonder if Chunk, aka Lieutenant Redman, would be glad to see him. Most likely, the junior SEAL officer would run the other way. They'd worked hand in glove together on two missions six months ago, but both had been a real kick to the balls. He wouldn't blame the SEAL for bugging out when he heard that John Dempsey was dropping by the neighborhood. He smiled to himself and hoped that wasn't the case. It sure would be nice to share a big fat lipper of wintergreen snuff with his brother SEAL . . .

One last time.

CHAPTER 21

"So, uh, we're supposed to be married?" Dempsey said, looking at Elinor but shoving his hands in his pockets.

Elinor smiled demurely and stepped into him, pressing her chest against his and bringing her lips within inches of his. "We're newly-weds," she said, with a coy smile. "There's a difference."

He took an awkward step backward, reclaiming his personal space. He glanced out the conference room–door window to see if anyone was watching them. The Seventh Order TOC was buzzing with activity like a war room. The sheer volume of logistical preparations necessary for their INFIL into Iran was mind-numbing. He should be out there right now, helping, not cooped up in some conference room playing Truth or Dare with Elinor.

The yearning in her eyes suddenly evaporated. "This isn't working for you?"

"No, it's . . . it's fine," he stammered. "It's just, this isn't normally what I do . . . I'm more of a—"

"Door kicker," she said, cutting him off. "I know. And that's okay." She sighed and made a show of surveying their surroundings. "I think it's this place. Too many distractions. Let's go for a walk."

"All right," he said and stared at her hand, wondering if he was supposed to take it.

"Not yet," she said, reading his mind. "When it's time, it will feel right."

Dempsey exhaled with relief and let her lead him through the conference room and out the vault door that secured the Seventh Order facility. He followed her quietly through the acquisitions and research lab and then up the concrete stairs and into the exhibit area of the Nechushtan Pavilion. A moment later they pushed through the glass doors and he caught up, walking beside her as they strode out onto the museum grounds. He squinted into the bright, sunny Tel Aviv afternoon.

"Why here?" he asked. "Why locate the Seventh Order at a museum?"

"Why not?" she replied.

"I don't know," he said. "For a NOC, it's all right, I guess, but you've got tourists and kids running around all over this place. Seems like a pain in the ass to operate out of here."

"I think you just summed up the difference between the American and the Israeli psyches," she said. "Levi was very intentional about selecting this location."

"I don't understand?"

"Walk with me," she said. "There's something I want to show you."

"Okay," he said and walked beside her to what looked like an active excavation site—brown earthen pits subdivided by rectangular stacked-stone walls.

"This place is called Tell Qasile," she said, stopping to look at it, fists pressed against her hips, the same way Kate liked to stand.

"What is it?"

"It is an excavation of an ancient port city, built in the twelfth century BC by the Philistines. The layout is indicative of thoughtful city planning, with intersecting streets, living quarters, a city temple, and a market," she explained. "Can you feel the energy?"

Dempsey chuckled. "Not really. Just looks like a bunch of rocks."

She smiled at this and then said, "Close your eyes . . . Now imagine the hustle and bustle of city life . . . people haggling in the market over prices; children laughing and playing in the streets; livestock braying, squawking, and grunting; and the salty Mediterranean breeze blowing and flapping fabric awnings overhead. This place, built over three thousand years ago and unearthed in the heart of Tel Aviv, is so much more than just a bunch of rocks. It's like looking at a baby picture. Do you know what I mean?"

He stared at her with wonderment. The metaphor was powerful and beautiful and something he could *never* have thought of. He wasn't creative and lyrical that way, but that didn't mean he couldn't appreciate artistic expression.

"We operate here *because* of the cultural exhibits, because of Tell Qasile, and yes, even because of the tourists and children running around. This place," she said, gesturing to the grounds, "reminds us of our charge. We do our jobs not in spite of these things, but rather because of them. If we stop, or if we fail, then the Tel Aviv that nearly a half-million people call home will disappear." Elinor looked around slowly, shifting her gaze from the excavation to the skyline in the background. "She has grown up and has become so lovely. We can't let anything happen to her."

"I understand," he said, staring at her in profile. *My God, this woman is so beautiful,* he thought and then immediately chastised himself for thinking it.

"Come on," she said cheerfully, snapping him out of the moment.

"Where to?" he asked. "Another exhibit?"

"No, now we go get some lunch. I want to take you to one of my favorite places. It's only a short cab ride; then we can walk around for the rest of the afternoon."

"The rest of the afternoon?" he said, cocking an eyebrow at her. "You do realize we have a lot of work to do to prepare for this mission."

"Believe me, I know," she said and looked up to heaven as if asking God to give her patience to manage the obdurately untrainable man-child she'd been saddled with.

It took him a beat, but her innuendo finally registered.

"No need to get melodramatic on me," he said.

"You need to trust your team with the preparations for the INFIL. That's not your job anymore. *I'm* your job. We are about to attempt the most dangerous covert operation that either of us will ever know. We cannot afford to be undone by sloppy tradecraft before we complete our objective. Do you know what they will do to us if they catch us?"

"I have a pretty good idea."

"Unimaginable horrors," she said, fixing him with her hazel-green eyes. "I know this from experience. Mossad does not have a perfect track record. Operating in Iran is incredibly difficult. I already don't like the idea of operating with a partner who doesn't speak Farsi. But I refuse to work with a man who either won't or is unable to embrace his NOC with everything in his being. Do you understand me?"

He nodded. "Don't worry. I'll get a handle on this whole newlywed thing. I promise."

"First we practice, then we promise," she said.

"Okay, then let's practice."

Fifteen minutes later, they were walking down tree-lined Dizengoff Street in the Old North district of Tel Aviv. They had a simple lunch at a sidewalk café, where she coaxed childhood stories out of him. He used real-life instances, just like he'd been taught to do at the Farm during one of Jarvis's many off-site training days, while working them into the framework of his NOC—an Irish Catholic named Corbin Odell. Her energy and enthusiasm helped him knock the rust off his role-playing skills, and then without even being aware of it, he slipped into character.

After lunch came shopping. Jack Kemper—the SEAL he had been before Ember—had abhorred shopping, even shopping with Kate and Jake. At the mall, his MO had always been to simply agree with whatever Kate said so as not to prolong the torture. *Leopard-print yoga pants? Sure, honey, absolutely. Noooo, they're not too much. Of course they'll look great. No, you don't need to try them on. They're stretch pants, so size is irrelevant; you can count on them fitting like a glove.* John Dempsey—the man he was now, the man Jarvis had created at Ember—was another matter altogether. Without a wife to goad him, he simply didn't shop. Period. All the clothes he owned had been provided to him by Ember. Shit just showed up in his locker from time to time in the right size. Hell, this was the first time he'd even contemplated the fact that, since moving from Tampa to Virginia a year ago, he could not recall shopping for anything other than food.

Strange.

According to his young bride, Corbin Odell loved shopping. And according to that same young bride, Corbin was generous with his wallet. She led him in and out of various shops, just window-shopping at first. But after spending real Ember expense-account dollars on imaginary apartment wares, his irritation began to spike.

She sensed this, put an arm around his waist, and whispered in his ear, "Relax. This is supposed to be fun. It's okay to let yourself have fun once in a while."

"I don't like shopping," he grumbled, trying on Corbin Odell's Belfast accent. "It's boring."

"In that case," she said, her lips curling up at the corners, "let's spice things up a bit."

Her next stop was a lingerie store.

"I'll wait outside," he said, planting his feet at the threshold.

"You said shopping was boring," she said. "Well, I promise this won't be."

He screwed up his face and narrowed his eyes at her. "You can't be serious."

"It's just a body," she said, gesturing at herself with coy nonchalance. But when he didn't budge, she laughed and acquiesced. "All right, fine, we'll skip the lingerie store, but I'm not letting you off the hook that easily."

He was about to ask her what the hell that comment was supposed to mean when she leaned in and kissed him. Not aggressively, but not tentatively, either. It was a hopeful kiss, a loving kiss, a beautiful kiss—and despite not wanting to, he liked it. He let himself kiss her back. No, he let Corbin Odell kiss his hopeful, loving, and beautiful young bride back.

When it was over, she looked almost apologetic. "Now see?" she whispered. "That wasn't so bad, was it?"

"No, I don't suppose it was."

She led him south on Dizengoff Street. As he began to relax and slip into his role, he couldn't help stealing glances at her when he thought she wouldn't notice. Once, she caught him staring at her, and this seemed to please her. As they walked, conversation came easier. She told a story. He told a joke. She shared a fact about Tel Aviv. He asked her about tensions in the West Bank. They talked and laughed, and eventually a silence lingered between them, but without the awkwardness from before. A block later, he spied a gelato stand, took her by the arm, and executed a detour. He let her pick the flavor, and they shared a scoop of gianduia in a cone. When they reached the intersection of Ester ha-Malka Street and Dizengoff, she stopped.

"What is it?" he asked, noting the abrupt change in her demeanor.

"This is one of the places I wanted to show you," she said. She led him to an angular metal memorial next to a tree on the sidewalk inscribed with a series of names in Hebrew. "On October 19, 1994, a Hamas suicide bomber wearing a land mine and twenty kilos of TNT blew himself up on the Number Five bus. Saleh Abdel Rahim al-Souwi killed twenty-two people and wounded fifty more. All civilians. It was horrendous."

As they shared a moment of solemn silence, his thoughts drifted to the TOC in Djibouti, where he'd watched his Tier One brothers get incinerated by suicide bombers. The American death toll from Crusader was about the same, more when you included the lives lost in Djibouti from the second suicide bomber. He felt his jaw tighten and the old familiar knot return to his stomach. Elinor's eyes were on him, and he wondered if she could read his thoughts. She had implied she knew his story, but just how much had Jarvis allowed Seventh Order to know?

"I don't want to talk about it," was all he said.

"I'm not asking you to," she replied.

They left the place side by side, but both very much alone. A half a block later, their hands found each other, and a curious something washed over him. Her long fingers felt delicate but warm in his hand. He felt something with this woman he'd not felt with Kate or Grimes, or any other woman for that matter. There seemed to be no single English word to describe it. With Kate, he'd felt a powerful, almost magnetic attraction. Like positive and negative poles drawn together by an invisible force, yearning to join and be complete. Soul mates in the truest sense. But in the joining there was also a nullification, and therein lay the problem. As opposite spirits, there were parts of him that Kate recognized but could never truly understand. Just like there were needs and desires in Kate that he recognized but could never satisfy while still being true to his operator self.

With Grimes he shared an intimate connection from their time working together at Ember, and that bond drew him to her. Yet he was reluctant to explore the possibility of physical romance. While she was technically not a blood relative, she was Spaz's sister, and a part of him felt obligated to step into his former SEAL teammate's shoes and fulfill that big-brother role. On top of that, if they attempted a romance only to fail, it could rip Ember apart. And then there was Shane . . . Even a door kicker like Dempsey was observant enough to see that Smith had an unspoken thing for Ember's fiery redhead. He shook his head. *With Grimes, it's just too damn complicated.*

Elinor, however, was one step removed from "the family." She was an operator but came from outside his world. Elinor was an amalgam of Kate and Grimes, which made her allure even more powerful. And yet, he couldn't help but wonder if any of the emotions he was feeling were even real. This was all a grand charade—two spooks playing newlyweds for the sake of the mission. No matter what happened between them, to lose sight of that truth would be a painful mistake, and he didn't know if his heart could take another scar.

"There's something on your mind," she said with a sideways glance. "Tell me."

"I was just wondering . . . What is the significance behind the name of your organization? Seventh Order—what does it mean?"

"Have you ever heard of the Mishnah?"

"No," he said simply.

"The Mishnah is the written compilation of what is commonly known as the Oral Torah. It was recorded over two millennia ago to document rabbinic oral traditions and Jewish cultural knowledge during a period of Jewish persecution. The Mishnah consists of six orders, each order outlining a series of laws and practices. Zeraim, which concerns prayers; Moed, which pertains to the Sabbath and festivals; Nashim, which deals with marriage vows; Nezikin, which explores criminal and civil law; Kodashim, which outlines death and burial rites; and finally, Tohorot, which codifies the laws of cleanliness and food safety."

"So let me guess," Dempsey said, nodding. "The Seventh Order is the missing order, something the rabbis could not have possibly imagined thousands of years ago to safeguard the Jewish people—clandestine defense."

"I couldn't have said it better myself."

They walked hand in hand to Goocha, a foodie favorite on Dizengoff Street where they dined on seafood. She ordered mussels in garlic butter, Mediterranean snapper, and white wine. While they ate, she told him about Corbin Odell, his cover identity, a NOC that he did not realize until that moment she had authored. Odell, she explained, was born in Belfast, but his mother and father hailed from Derry. His father had been a protestor in the Bloody Sunday massacre and had been running alongside William McKinney when McKinney was shot in the back by British paratroopers while fleeing through the Glenfada Park courtyard. Young Corbin was raised and socialized by his working-class parents to have a strong distrust and animosity for the British government. Although not IRA members, his parents were fervent nationalists, sympathizing with the IRA's agenda and regularly participating in Republican protests and marches. They believed in a free and independent Ireland where Catholics were not second-class citizens.

As she spoke, he could not help but notice the passion in her eyes, and he was struck by an epiphany.

"Did you construct my Irish NOC as a Palestinian metaphor?"

She nodded. "In Ireland, the IRA perceived violence and terrorism as the tools of last resort for political activism, just as the Palestinian Liberation Organization once did and Hamas still does today. Faith and religion are so deeply entwined in the culture here that any attempt to secularize 'right to exist' negotiations always fails miserably. In my opinion, that's the root of all the trouble—using scriptural rhetoric to both incite and justify violence. After all, you can argue with me, but who are you to argue with my God?"

He pursed his lips. Getting inside Corbin's head was important, but going twelve rounds with her on Middle Eastern politics and religion was simply not something he had the energy for right now. He raised his wine glass to her.

"A toast?" she said, lifting an eyebrow and then her glass.

"To my bride, Mrs. Odell," he said in an Irish brogue.

"To my groom," she said and clinked her glass gently against his.

Despite his glass being over a third full, he drained it. Then, he looked at her. Maybe it was the sleep deprivation, maybe the lighting, or maybe the alcohol, but Elinor looked more radiant now than the first time he'd laid eyes on her. His mind went to the kiss outside the lingerie boutique.

Get your head together, John, he chastised himself. *It's all an act. This isn't real. None of it is real.*

She smiled at him.

"Don't," he said, suddenly too weary to worry about his Irish accent anymore.

"Don't what?" She laughed. "I didn't do anything."

"You smiled at me . . ."

"It's just a smile," she said with the same coy, flirtatious tone she'd used before.

Just a smile . . . yeah, right.

"C'mon," he said after a beat, laying down sufficient cash to cover the tab. "Let's go."

"Oh, so you're in charge now, huh?"

"That's right," he said.

"So where are we going?"

"Back," he said. "I need to get some sleep."

"By 'back' you mean back to our hotel room, I hope," she said, taking his hand in hers.

"I don't think I'm ready for that," he whispered in her ear.

"To be honest, neither am I," she whispered back, and then with a mischievous smile she added, "You can sleep on the sofa."

Dempsey breathed a sigh of relief.

"Tomorrow is a busy day," she said, still in a hushed voice. "We travel to Jerusalem."

"Jerusalem? Why Jerusalem?"

"To put our NOCs to the test with observers and conduct a dry run of our mission with the Midrachov standing in for the Grand Bazaar."

"Who's the lucky target we get to rough up?" he asked.

She shrugged.

"I thought you were the boss?" he said, eying her with playful suspicion.

"Yeah, well, even the boss needs a good surprise . . . from time to time."

CHAPTER 22

"We're going the wrong way," Jarvis said to the driver, a heavily muscled Mossad operative who had introduced himself simply as Beck. "The restaurant is south."

"The Director picked a different location for your lunch meeting," Beck replied, intent on trying to maintain the ruse that Jarvis had already seen through.

As they drove north through Tel Aviv on Namir Road, Jarvis deduced that he was being driven to Mossad headquarters. This change in plans was not necessarily a good sign. He wondered if something had gone wrong. Had the operation to capture Modiri been scrubbed? Or was it something even more ominous? Was an attack on Tel Aviv imminent and Harel was bringing him in before the rockets started to fall? He angled his head to look at the driver's face in profile, checking for physical clues indicating anxiety, fear, or nervousness, but Beck was a statue.

They took the Glilot Ma'arav Interchange and looped around what appeared to be a regular office park, but Jarvis knew otherwise. They proceeded to the rear of the complex and then through two heavy automated gates that opened on approach without any apparent action on Beck's part. An armed security detail stopped them partway into a funnel-shaped concrete tunnel that, on cursory inspection, looked like it was designed to survive a sizable blast by directing all the explosive energy back out the flume. Beck turned over his ID card while a second guard walked around to the passenger side; Jarvis fetched his passport from the inside flap pocket of his sport coat, lowered the window, and handed it to him. Three minutes later, they were inside. Before being delivered to Harel, Jarvis had to be scanned at a formal checkpoint and loiter in a lobby while Mossad security ran the requisite background checks. Just when his patience was finally beginning to wane, Beck led him to an elevator bank that descended seven stories beneath the lobby level. When the doors opened, Harel was standing in the hallway tapping his foot.

"What the hell took so long?" the Mossad Director said to Jarvis's companion, his voice ripe with irritation.

"Everyone is being extra careful today, Chief," Beck replied.

"Okay, okay, thanks for playing chauffeur, Beck. That will be all," Harel said with clipped impatience, turned, and waved for Jarvis to follow him. With the handoff complete, the Israeli spymaster led him down the underground hallway to a security door flanked by two guards kitted up for battle. Beside the door was a sign in Hebrew that Jarvis translated to *Combat Operations Center*. The senior-ranking guard nodded at Harel and greeted him with a simple "Chief."

"How are the kids?" Harel said, pausing at the threshold.

"Good, sir," came the guard's reply.

"And Greta?"

"She's as busy as ever."

"Mothers of three usually are. Make sure you head straight home after your shift," Harel said, putting a hand on the young man's shoulder. "It could be a crazy night."

"Yes, sir," the guard said with a nod. "And thank you, sir."

Harel led Jarvis into a facility not unlike the dozens of TOCs Jarvis had worked in over the years, but this was at the high end of the spectrum, like the CTC nerve center in McLean. The dimly lit room was expansive, with a two-story ceiling in the center and a modern industrial design aesthetic—metal staircases with gleaming railings, graphite-colored workstations, exposed ducts painted black, and a tile floor the color of fog. A curved "jumbotron"-style monitor served as the entire north wall and was subdivided into a myriad of different-size windows displaying live feeds from various video streaming sources—satellite, drone, and aircraft, as well as a few ground-based feeds Jarvis presumed were hidden cameras set up by Mossad assets inside Iran. Instead of heading for the frenetic main floor—packed with analysts, programmers, and operators—Harel took a set of stairs leading to a second-story office with floor-to-ceiling windows and an elevated view of everything below. He held the door open for Jarvis.

"If I had known we were lunching in a skybox, I would have worn a suit," Jarvis quipped as the heavy glass door shut behind him.

Harel's mouth curled up into an amused grin as he tapped a Noblest from a pack sitting on a desk.

"*This* is your office?"

"It is now," Harel said, pleased with himself. "It used to be the COC Director's office, but I kicked him out. This is where the action is; why would I want to be above ground like some bureaucrat?"

Jarvis looked up and surveyed the ventilation system. "And it has nothing to do with the recirculating HEPA filtration equipment?"

"All right, you got me, Kelso," he said, lighting his cigarette and taking a long pull. "Apparently, this is now the only place I can smoke in the entire fucking building," he growled. "This new generation—they're so healthy and sensitive. As soon as they start asking for softer toilet paper, I'm going to quit."

"You already quit," Jarvis said with a laugh.

"Well, I'm going to quit and not come back next time."

After a beat, Jarvis said, "So, why am I here?"

Harel waved him over to the wall of windows and said, "I thought you might like a front-row seat for the show."

Jarvis felt the blood drain from his face. "It's today?"

"It's going to start any minute."

"Did Shamone notify the President?"

"Of course not," Harel said. "Unlike America, we don't announce our plans before we launch a surprise attack. It is self-defeating."

"Does that mean I'm the first American to know?"

Harel nodded solemnly. "As far as we're concerned, the White House can find out from CNN like the rest of the world."

Jarvis folded his arms across his chest. He respected the hell out of Israel for having the balls and the discipline to operate like they did, but Jarvis didn't work for the Israeli PM. He worked for the Commander in Chief of the United States. If there was a way to get a message to the White House, then he was duty bound to try.

"I know what you're thinking." Harel laughed. "Impossible. Your phone is a brick in here. That's why we let you keep it."

Jarvis smiled. "That's not what I was thinking."

"No?"

"No."

The Israeli spymaster nodded, but the grin never left his face.

"So what's the plan?" Jarvis asked, scanning the jumbotron tactical display on the far wall.

"I could tell you," Harel said, "but what fun would that be? Tell me, if you were in charge, what would you do?"

Jarvis flipped a switch and the whiteboard in his mind began to populate with color-coded information. He spoke as his mind's eye surveyed one of the very conflict scenarios he'd considered earlier: "Lead with a cyber offensive, Unit 8200 crippling Persian comms and the kids in Beersheba take down their networks. Next you hit Khatam al-Anbia Air Defense Base with Popeye SLCMs fired from Dolphins positioned in the Persian Gulf, and you follow up with an air sortie, your new F-35s in first to assess the kinetic environment, take out their S-300 batteries, and mop up at Khatam. Once you have control of the battle space, you're free to run sorties with your 15s and 16s and bring your 707s in for aerial refueling. You'll hit Emad intermediate-range ballistic missile sites and probably their Shahab-3 MRBM sites, too, eliminating a counter–missile strike. Next, you'll hit their nuclear sites—Fordow and Natanz—with HTMs and drop conventional ordnance on Parchin, Arak, and Isfahan. Simultaneously, IAF southern command will launch sorties into Gaza and southern Lebanon to take out known Hamas and Hezbollah rocket caches, mobile missile launchers, and command-and-control nodes to greatly diminish the severity of Iranian proxy retaliatory strikes in the aftermath. You could stop there, or if you're slitting throats today, you might also take out Mehrabad Tactical Air Base in Tehran and the submarine base in Bandar Abbas."

Harel took a final drag from his Noblest and then mashed it out in an ashtray.

"How'd I do?" Jarvis asked when Harel said nothing.

"The cyber barrage is under way," the Mossad Director said. "What happens next, you'll just have to wait and see."

Jarvis watched and waited while Harel fielded a flurry of phone calls as the IDF operation kicked into high gear. The attack unfolded almost exactly as Jarvis had foreseen, and as it did, an unfamiliar sensation washed over him. As a Tier One Navy SEAL, he had either participated in or overseen from the TOC dozens and dozens of covert action missions, but this was something different. How he felt now was probably similar to how his grandfather had felt when World War Two began in Europe—that a seemingly uncrossable geopolitical chasm had just been crossed. Think tanks and policy wonks had contemplated and debated the implications and aftermath of an Israeli preemptive strike on Iran for over a decade, but now it was actually happening. There was no going back, and for the first time in his career, Jarvis did not like the imagery the crystal ball in his mind was showing him. Israel, and the rest of the world for that matter, was about to find out what Persia was made of. Yes, Iran had publicly flaunted its acquisition of the advanced Russian S-300 surface-to-air missile system, but what other weapons technology had Esfahani brokered from Moscow in the dark? And what about Iran's other disturbing military trading partner in the East? With China cutting off coal from cash-strapped North Korea, had the lunatic in Pyongyang sold nuclear-warhead technology to Tehran? Did Iran have the atomic bomb, and if so, would a badly antagonized Supreme Leader order Esfahani to wipe Israel off the map once and for all?

A cheer in the analyst mosh pit down below snapped Jarvis back to the present. Satellite footage showed Khatam al-Anbia Air Defense Base being hit by the first wave of Popeye Turbo submarine-launched cruise missiles. Rocket trails zipped skyward as Iran's S-300 surface-to-air missile batteries came to life, attempting to intercept the incoming Israeli ordnance. The S-300s knocked down multiple Israeli cruise missiles, but the IDF commanders had clearly decided to err on the side of "shock and awe" because the first submarine salvo still packed a hell of a punch. Multiple buildings and ground structures flashed with fire in rapid succession as the missiles hit their targets. Plumes of smoke, dust, and debris mushroomed upward. With the Iranian air defense command and control crippled, the next wave began.

Six new icons appeared on a tactical topographical map of the battle space—six green triangles crossing the Iraqi border into Iranian air space. An operator selected and clicked on one of the green triangles, and two new windows appeared. The first was a fighter pilot's heads-up display, full of tactical theater information that could only be from one aircraft. The second was a camera feed streaming from the same aircraft. The corner of Jarvis's mouth curled up. The F-35 was Israel's first manned war machine to cross the border and the first time the multirole stealth aircraft would face live-fire surface-to-air missile defenses. Although the newest generation fighter jet, manufactured by Lockheed, had been much beleaguered in the media, the DNI had told him in confidence that the smear campaign was working out to be an invaluable strategic advantage. *The more the enemy underestimates this plane, Kelso, the more ass we'll kick when it's time to take the gloves off.* If only Director Philips were alive and beside him right now, because the gloves had just come off.

"Last I heard, Israel only had taken delivery of four aircraft. General Boaz was quoted as saying they would not be ready for fleet service until the end of the year," Jarvis said, glancing at Harel.

"Funny," Harel said with a sly grin. "I'd heard the same thing. Looks like that information was erroneous."

He watched the F-35s travel in pairs toward their respective targets: four angling northeast toward Fordow, Natanz, and Parchin and two toward Isfahan in central Iran. To his and everyone else's relief, the stealthy multipurpose fighters navigated Persian airspace without detection by the Russian-made S-300 batteries or the indigenous Persian SAM sites. The southern pair of F-35s reached Isfahan first, dropping conventional precision-guided munitions on SAM batteries protecting Persia's uranium-enrichment and specialty-materials facility and on Khatami Air Base. It wasn't until after the strike that four F-14 Tomcats were scrambled from Khatami Air Base to intercept, validating the effectiveness of the Israeli F-35s' stealth approach. Jarvis watched and waited, wondering how the F-35s would handle these once formidable but now obsolete fighter aircraft.

He didn't have to wait long.

The F-35s' superior radar and real-time link to the IDF's battle-space data stream allowed the pilots to target the Tomcats over the horizon. Four Python-5 air-to-air missiles were launched, and all four missiles hit their marks. Cheers erupted in the TOC below. Twenty minutes later, similar scenarios unfolded at Fordow and Parchin. What happened next, however, surprised even Jarvis.

Over the next forty-five minutes, the Israeli Air Force launched a protracted air campaign the likes of which he'd not seen since Operation Desert Storm. With the Persian ground-based radars and SAM batteries either decimated or disabled, the F-15 and F-16 attack runs could begin in earnest. Sorties out of Ramat David and Tel Nof commenced in rapid and synchronized fashion. And instead of bugging out and heading home, the F-35s stayed in orbit and were refueled by Boeing 707 aerial refuelers dispatched from Nevatim Air Force Base. Persian counteroffensive sorties with Soviet-sourced Sukhoi Su-24 and MiG-29 planes, as well as American-sourced F-4s, F-5s, and F-14s, were quickly squelched by the more proficient and capable IAF fighters. Within three hours, the IAF categorically owned the Persian skies.

"Would you like something to drink?" Harel asked, shaking Jarvis from his trance watching the Mossad's tactical jumbotron below.

"Water, thank you," Jarvis said and realized that over an hour had passed with neither man speaking a word.

The Mossad Chief walked over to a minifridge against the back wall and pulled out two bottles of water. Then he stood beside Jarvis at the plate-glass window.

"Do you know the story of David and Goliath?" Harel said, handing Jarvis his water.

"Of course," Jarvis said.

"What do you know?" Harel said, tipping a cigarette out of his pack.

"Do you mind?" Jarvis said before Harel could light it. "I could use a break from the smoke."

The corner of Harel's mouth curled up. "Okay, for you, my friend, I'll deny my cravings. I know how you hate these things."

"Thank you."

"So," Harel said, stuffing the cigarette back into the pack, "what do you think you know about David and Goliath?"

Although not a student of scripture, Jarvis was a student of history, especially military history, and he knew the legendary underdog story well. He uncapped his water, took a sip, and said, "Three thousand years ago, the Philistines marched across Israel, intent on splitting the kingdom in two, but King Saul rallied his army and met them head-on in the Valley of Elah. Both armies dug in, and eventually a stalemate was reached. As was common in that day, the Philistine commander proposed settling the standoff via single combat—where one warrior's death would decide the victory rather than tens of thousands'. King Saul agreed, and the Philistines promptly marched their greatest warrior, a monster of a man named Goliath, onto the battle plain. Seeing Goliath, not a single warrior in King Saul's army volunteered to fight. Ultimately, Israel's fate fell upon the shoulders of a young shepherd boy, David, who was the lone volunteer brave enough to fight. After that, I think pretty much everyone knows what happened . . ."

"No, no, please, continue."

"All right," Jarvis said. "Goliath is fully kitted up in bronze armor, with a breastplate, helmet, javelin, and sword, while David has only his shepherd's staff and a sling. Goliath proceeds to taunt David, but before Goliath even makes a single move, David loads a stone in his sling and hits Goliath square between the eyes—felling the giant and winning the battle for Israel."

"That's right," Harel said, nodding. "That's the underdog story everyone knows. But it's not the real story."

"Well, sure. I always assumed it was an allegory, just like so many stories in the Bible," Jarvis said.

"No, no, that's not it. The battle of David and Goliath was real, but the mythos is pure propaganda. Would you like to know the real story?"

Jarvis shrugged. "Sure."

"Like you, I knew the myth. Like you, I thought the story was a gross exaggeration . . . the Jewish equivalent of a 'tall tale,' but it turns out that the truth is much more interesting than the fiction. A couple of years ago, I heard a talk by an American Jewish author named Gladwell, who told a different story. It turns out that researchers now suspect Goliath suffered from acromegaly—a rare condition in which the pituitary gland produces excess growth hormone resulting in gigantism. But gigantism comes at a cost, including pronounced nearsightedness, double vision, headaches, arthritis, and a host of other physical ailments. In the scripture, Goliath taunts David, 'Come to me so I can feed your flesh to the birds of the heavens and the beasts of the field.' But there's subtext beneath the giant's words—by beckoning David to him instead of charging aggressively, Goliath reveals he is not as nimble and ambulatory as one would imagine an invincible warrior to be. As David draws closer, Goliath betrays himself again, saying, 'Am I a dog that you would come to me with sticks?' But David was not carrying sticks, only a single staff—this statement is evidence that Goliath was nearsighted and suffering from double vision."

"Interesting," Jarvis said, nodding.

"Indeed," Harel said. "And what of the preconception that David—marching into battle without armor, carrying only a sling and a staff—was outmatched by Goliath, who was fully *kitted up*, as you said. Here we find another misconception. In the hands of an experienced slinger, a pebble is a formidable weapon: deadly accurate inside one hundred and fifty meters, with the equivalent stopping power of a forty-five-caliber slug. So I ask you, now knowing this and Goliath's physical liabilities . . . Was David truly an underdog?"

Jarvis looked at Harel. How the man loved his riddles and his stories. "It would appear not."

Harel smiled and shifted his gaze out at the TOC below. "Which David is Israel? The misperceived underdog, or the formidable warrior who intimately understands both his own and his enemy's skills and liabilities?"

Jarvis considered the question and after a beat said, "Both."

"That's right, both. For the world, we must cultivate and project the notion that Israel is the underdog fighting for survival against overwhelming odds. But inside these borders, we must arm ourselves with the weapons and knowledge that give us an unperceived advantage over our adversaries."

Jarvis nodded and turned back to the big screen. Presently, the camera feed from an Israeli F-15E was on display as it dropped precision-guided bunker-busting ordnance on the heavily fortified Fordow site. As he watched the bombs fall one after another, he thought about Dempsey and his upcoming mission into Iran. Reframing it in the context of Harel's modern reinterpretation of the Bible's most famous underdog story, Jarvis couldn't help but wonder—in a face-off between Dempsey and Modiri, who would play David and who would play Goliath?

CHAPTER 23

Ben Yehuda Street
West Jerusalem, Israel
May 11
1430 Local Time

Dempsey held Elinor's hand and tried his best to look casual.

And happy.

Casual and happy, he told himself, despite the fact that Israel had just bombed the shit out of Iran and the world was on the verge of turning upside down. The irony of the situation was that here, in the heart of Jerusalem, life was carrying on as if nothing had happened at all. Rimon Café, the trendy restaurant at the western end of Ben Yehuda where they'd eaten lunch, had been packed. The sprawling outdoor market, known simply as the Midrachov, was alive and buzzing with a healthy afternoon crowd of locals and tourists alike. Clothing boutiques, souvenir shops, vegetable stands, sidewalk cafés, and a variety of artisan stores lined the avenue. Street musicians played while beggars sat and begged, both groups vying for the pocket change of passersby.

A gaggle of teens in ironic T-shirts and tight jeans cavorted by, and Dempsey immediately thought of Jake.

Elinor leaned in and gave him an unexpected peck on the cheek.

"What was that for?" he asked, not liking the authenticity of his Irish accent he was using today.

"Because I love you," she said, smiling at him with her eyes.

God, it felt real. She was so good at this . . . too good.

He squeezed her hand. "I love you, too."

Sorry, Kate, he thought to himself, feeling a pang of guilt. But she had divorced him—and he had since widowed her—and anyway, Kate was with Steve now . . . so what did it matter if he played lovebirds with Elinor?

"This is surprising to me," he said quietly to her.

"What is?"

"This," he said, gesturing to the hustle and bustle around them. "It's like yesterday never happened."

"This is Israel. War can happen anytime, any day. Life goes on."

"Makes sense for those who serve, but for civilians . . . It's just strange."

She leaned in close and whispered. "Focus. Your accent is slipping, and now is not the time for this discussion."

"Sorry," he said with a guilty smile. She was right. He was off his game today. He'd received language training at the Farm, but his performance had underwhelmed all his instructors. Eventually, they just laughed at him and said that an Irish accent was probably the only one outside his native speech he could hope to pull off. Today, he couldn't even execute that one.

"Don't make me take you lingerie shopping again," she teased.

"Oh God, no," he said and laughed. "Anything but that."

He felt his shoulders instantly relax. Her comedic timing was impeccable. He looked at her and marveled at her craft; she was so consistent, so "sealed inside" her NOC. She made it look easy, turning her legend on and off like a light switch.

"I have the package," Daniel said over the comms channel, snapping Dempsey's mind back to the mission. "He's east of HaHistadrut but appears to be on schedule."

Today's operation was a live-capture mission, meant to simulate and prepare for the kidnapping of Amir Modiri in Tehran. He went over the details quickly in his head. The plan was to disappear the target in broad daylight by herding him into an alley where an SUV was waiting. Grabbing someone and forcing them into a car wasn't difficult for someone with Dempsey's build, but pulling it off in broad daylight without being noticed in a crowded public place—well, that was something altogether different.

He was a door kicker, not an illusionist.

Still walking hand in hand, they passed a group of Korean girls singing and wearing matching green T-shirts bearing a large Christian cross across the chest.

"I have eyes on our tango," Grimes's voice said in his right ear, where the micro-Bluetooth earpiece sat invisible in his ear canal. He spied the Tutti Frutti gelato shop next to the alley fifty meters to the east. They'd arrived early by nearly a minute.

He stopped and pulled his new "bride" close, looking down into her eyes and smiling. Having the curves of her body pressed against him was distracting, and he immediately felt a stirring. "How are you enjoying the afternoon, love?" he asked, much more pleased with the easy Irish lilt he heard rolling from his mouth this time.

"It's been wonderful, but suddenly I'm wishing we were back at the hotel," she said with a seductive grin, pressing her pelvis firmly against his.

"Package is fifteen seconds out," Grimes said with a hard edge to her voice. Was that jealousy he detected? No, no way. That stupid kiss in Annapolis had him overanalyzing everything with women now. He shook it off.

"Since we're here and I know how much you love gelato," he said to Elinor, "perhaps we share a cone of gianduia and then head back to the hotel for the real dessert."

"I almost want to skip the ice cream," she said and bit her lip as if deciding. "Almost."

"Why choose? I promise you can have both."

He took her hand and moved toward the gelato shop, just as the "package" rounded the corner. In reality, Agent Rouvin was playing their target today. They hadn't made it three paces toward Rouvin when sirens began to wail. The sound immediately sent a shiver down Dempsey's spine, reminding him of air-raid sirens in iconic, old British World War Two movies. Elinor tugged his hand, deviating immediately from their previous trajectory. The crowd around them began to morph, tourists and locals becoming immediately and obviously distinguishable—with the locals moving briskly for cover while the tourists gawked and mulled about in clusters like lost sheep.

"Incoming rocket attack. Positive confirmation," came Daniel's voice over the wireless.

Elinor looked skyward, and Dempsey did the same. Streaks of white smoke raced up across the sky, originating in clusters to the north and east—only a handful at first, but then the handful became dozens, and the dozens became hundreds.

"Oh my God," Elinor breathed, and then yelled, "Mission abort. Move to cover." She jerked Dempsey toward the other side of the street.

"You've seen this before?" Dempsey shouted as they ran.

"Not like this. Never so many."

"Are those incoming rockets, or is that the Iron Dome we're seeing?"

"The Dome," she said, referring to the IDF's defensive missile-interceptor system. She was moving toward a shop with a blue-and-yellow sign beside the door, clearly designating it as a bomb shelter.

"But to see so many Tamir missiles going up—it means hundreds of rockets are incoming. Pray it performs as advertised."

Dempsey had heard whispers about Israel's new high-energy laser system, but last he knew, the Iron Beam and David's Sling were both still under development. When he'd questioned her about it earlier, she'd explained that the Israelis were building a "layered" defense system that covered the complete spectrum of enemy missile threats. The Arrow II and III were designed to shoot down high-altitude ballistic missiles; David's Sling was built to intercept cruise missiles; the Iron Dome targeted short-range missiles and rockets; and lastly, the Iron Beam—a directed energy weapon—was intended for small rockets and mortar shells. The battle management center at the heart of the system was very sophisticated, capable of analyzing the trajectories of hundreds or even thousands of incoming rockets simultaneously and projecting impact points. The system automatically prioritized each threat and only engaged incoming projectiles with the highest probability of hitting populated areas.

"How much incoming ordnance can the system handle?" he yelled.

"Don't know, but looks like our enemies are hitting us with everything they've got."

"Could they overwhelm the system?"

Before she could answer, the earth shook, and he felt and heard the *whump* of a large explosion nearby. A fireball erupted skyward in the background over Elinor's left shoulder.

The crowd panicked en masse, and people began running chaotically in every direction. Someone let out a bloodcurdling scream. Someone else another. And then, he heard someone shout, "Allahu Akbar!"

He released Elinor's hand and the SEAL inside him took control. All the noise and chaos fell away, and he scanned the street with laser focus, his mind assessing the battle space for threats. To the west, toward King George Street, he noted a man in a white tunic. The man was screaming like an animal, bent at the waist, bringing down what could only be a meat cleaver again and again on a crumpled figure. The crumpled figure was a man in a suit, covered in blood. Dempsey watched the businessman raise his arm and the cleaver take it off. The next blow landed square in the middle of the man's face, and a geyser of bright-red blood painted the terrorist's tunic. With rabid eyes, the jihadi zeroed in on his next target—a group of women this time. He ran toward them, the knife dripping blood in his right hand, while they fled in hysterics. One of the women stumbled, fell, and screamed.

A heartbeat later the maniac was upon her.

Dempsey took off in a sprint toward the jihadi, but Elinor was already in motion, her head down like a rugby player, barreling toward the man with the cleaver. The jihadi screamed something and raised the cleaver. Dempsey followed behind Elinor. The killer saw Elinor, but too late. She drove her shoulder into the side of his ribcage and knocked him to the ground. The man's head whiplashed against the pavement and the cleaver popped out of his grip. Elinor rolled out of the fall and was up straddling the man's chest in a split second. Her hands flew to the sides of the man's head, and gripping him by the hair and ears, she smashed his head repeatedly into the pavement beneath them. A dark puddle of blood grew underneath his head.

After the fifth blow, Dempsey grabbed her shoulders and pulled her off. She whirled toward him, her face contorted with homicidal rage.

"He's done," Dempsey barked.

"Sleeper agents," she growled, scanning the street. "There could be many."

Dempsey nodded and helped pull a fallen woman to her feet. "Get indoors," he commanded, having to peel the woman's fingers from where her nails dug into his forearm.

A gunshot rang out, and then more followed in rapid succession.

The shooter was close.

Dempsey dropped into a crouch and pulled his Sig Sauer from the holster at the small of his back. Someone was shooting at pedestrians in the fleeing crowd. He triangulated where the gunshots were coming from and saw a muzzle flare in the doorway of a nearby souvenir shop. He took aim, but the store's brick facade blocked him from getting a clear shot. Another muzzle flash, another pop, and in his peripheral vision Dempsey saw a teenage girl drop to the ground and shriek. He sprinted toward the souvenir shop, ducking and weaving through the manic crowd. He stopped short of the doorway, hugging the wall and sliding toward the shooter's outstretched hand, which was clutching a semiautomatic pistol. As the shooter's pistol burped fire, sending another round into the crowd, Dempsey slipped his own pistol into his waistband. Then, with lightning speed, he brought his left palm down on top of the shooter's wrist, grabbing and driving the hand down simultaneously. The shooter stumbled forward and squeezed the trigger, sending a round into the sidewalk. Clutching the shooter's wrist, Dempsey drew the arm toward him and into a deft arm lock. In a single fluid motion, he hyperextended the shooter's elbow with a sickening crack. Despite the wail of agony, despite the impossible angle of the man's arm, the gun remained somehow in the assailant's grip.

With a scowl, Dempsey flexed the arm and repeated the maneuver, this time completely shredding the elbow joint, turning the man's arm into a useless, dangling hunk of flesh. As the gun clattered to the ground, the shooter howled with rage and lunged forward. Teeth bared, the terrorist tried to bite Dempsey's face, but Dempsey drove his right elbow into the side of his foe's eye socket with a crunch. Dempsey finished him off by wrapping the man's neck into a headlock and dropping to a knee, breaking the shooter's neck.

He let the lifeless body drop to the ground and his fingers found his Sig. Dempsey scanned left and right from his kneeling position, sweeping for threats and looking for Elinor. He spied her twenty feet away, sparring with a woman in a long black dress. He launched himself from the doorway, sprinting to help.

"IDF is en route with a QRF," Rouvin said in his ear. "We need to reassemble our team."

"Copy. I'm with Munn," Grimes said, her voice clinical. "We're engaging two shooters with assault rifles firing from a second-story window. Wang and Adamo are moving back toward the rally point."

Dempsey assumed she meant the alley beside the gelato shop, but he didn't have time to ask. The scene unfolding before him sent a sickening surge of dread through his entire body. Elinor was engaged in a tactical dance with the woman in the black dress, circling and talking with intense focus while at the same time waving for him to back off. The woman, who Dempsey could now see was actually a girl no more than seventeen, was wearing a suicide vest. Her dark eyes were wild, darting this way and that with fear and doubt. The bulge beneath the torso of her dress made the rest of her rail-thin body seem frail and out of proportion.

Shit, she's wired to blow.

Elinor had both hands in the air like an orchestra conductor now, and she was pleading with the girl in Arabic. Dempsey gripped his pistol but kept it lowered at half-mast, not wanting to encourage the girl to detonate early. Something exploded a half block away, and he turned to see bodies flying before the scene was enshrouded in smoke and dust. Seeing this, the suicide bomber screamed and dropped to her knees.

She's going to do it. We gotta go, Elinor.

The girl raised her arms to heaven, and Dempsey saw that both hands were empty. No trigger, no dead man's switch. Was the vest on a timer? Detonated remotely? The girl was crying now, but instead of backing up, Elinor cautiously approached her. A commotion erupted to Dempsey's left. A crowd of people, mostly teens, came sprinting toward them, fleeing the detonation and carnage that had just happened down the block.

"Stay back," he shouted, but the frantic crowd kept coming.

The suicide bomber saw the crowd, too, and jumped to her feet. Dempsey could see it in her eyes: she'd made her decision. This was her target. She stepped first toward Elinor, shouted something anti-Semitic in Arabic, but then abruptly spun on a heel and sprinted toward the group of converging teenagers. Her dress flowing behind her like a trail of black smoke, she screamed, "Allahu Akbar!"

Dempsey aimed and fired.

The suicide girl pitched face forward and hit the pavement with a thud. The panicked teens split into two groups, parting like the Red Sea and diverging around the girl.

"Run," Dempsey yelled, and he and Elinor sprinted for cover.

Seconds later the girl exploded, consumed in a cloud of fire, smoke, blood, and flesh. The heat and shock wave knocked him to a knee, but he caught himself and kept moving while attempting to shield Elinor with his body. Debris rained down on him, and he wondered how many had died. He pulled Elinor to her feet, lifting her under the armpit. Blood streamed down her forehead, arced over her right eye, soaking her eyebrow and then continuing down her cheek.

"You're injured," Dempsey said, cocking his head to get a better look at the wound.

Elinor wiped the blood from her eyebrow. "Just a scratch," she said. Then, louder and to the rest of the team, she said, "We've got suicide bombers in the crowd. Inform the QRF the bombs appear to be remotely detonated, but control is within line of sight—probably an upper-story apartment within a one-block radius of my position."

"Copy," Daniel said. "IDF tac teams are on-site and moving into position. Stand by to evacuate."

Dempsey had Elinor by the elbow, pulling her with him onto the sidewalk while he scanned the crowd for threats. Sporadic gunfire began to echo in the distance; he hoped that it was the arriving IDF forces beginning to engage. The scene before him was the stuff of nightmares.

The lovely, lively Jerusalem of ten minutes ago was now replaced with destruction, death, and chaos. In the middle of the street, a thin middle-aged man in expensive slacks and a white dress shirt was waving a club over his head, blood running down the handle and soaking his right sleeve to the elbow. The jihadi ran toward an older couple huddling behind an upended food kiosk. From their dress, Dempsey pegged them as American tourists, no doubt separated from their tour group in the pandemonium. Dempsey led the target and fired. The bullet hit the club-wielding terrorist in the side of the head and dropped him straight down, like a marionette suddenly cut loose from its strings.

A familiar voice crackled in Dempsey's ear: "We have an urgent surgical. We need a CASEVAC right fucking now."

It was Munn.

Shit.

In all the years working with Munn, Dempsey had never heard the doc's voice more desperate. The casualty was bad, and it was one of theirs.

"Give me your position," Dempsey barked, sweeping left, pistol still up and at the ready.

"We pulled her inside a bakery. Southeast corner of the intersection. Second door down."

Her . . . Grimes is hit.

Dempsey's throat tightened, and he turned and locked eyes with Elinor, whose face was now a mess of smeared blood.

"On our way to you," Dempsey said.

"Hurry," Munn barked.

He turned to Elinor and said, "We need to reposition the SUV."

She nodded and gave the order to Daniel.

Behind Elinor, Dempsey saw a man's face peer out from behind a nearby doorway. They locked eyes, and then the face jerked back. In that split-second glance, Dempsey saw wild bloodlust—a jihadi consumed with rage and intent on murder.

Dempsey sidestepped right, training his Sig at the doorway. "Get behind me," he said to Elinor, releasing her arm and bringing both hands up to grip his weapon. He advanced, his weapon floating perfectly level and still while his legs churned beneath. A flash of white in the doorway was all it took. He fired twice and two dark-red holes appeared in the bearded jihadi's chest. The terrorist looked down, his eyes wide with surprise at the bloodstain growing on the front of his tunic. Then he pulled his lips back in a snarl and ran at Dempsey holding a long curved knife and screaming, "Allahu—"

Dempsey's third bullet silenced the jihadist's war cry as it split the top of the man's head practically in half. Dempsey's eyes were back forward before the body hit the ground. He kept moving, his entire focus on getting to Lizzie.

Seven rounds left, a voice inside his head reminded him.

Elinor shifted into the lead, crossing the street and heading toward the southeast corner. Seconds later, they were in front of the bakery— the name in Hebrew he could not read, but the picture of a croissant on the window removed any doubt. The bottom pane of glass in the two-panel front door was blown out, but the top was still in place. Dempsey jerked the door open, and the top plate of glass crashed to the ground and crunched underfoot as he entered. Power must have been out on the block because the bakery was dim inside. Grimes was lying supine on the floor with Munn kneeling on her right side, leaning over her chest. Adamo was opposite Munn, squeezing an IV bag against his chest, forcing fluids into her through a large needle in her arm.

Behind them, Wang paced back and forth, hands wringing. "It's really fucking bad, John," the young cyber expert said.

"We gotta get her out of here," Munn said, his arms soaked in blood to his elbows. "We don't have much time."

"Daniel went for the truck," said Rouvin, who was sighting over his rifle, keeping an eye on the street. "He's going to pick us up at the corner."

Dempsey nodded then and bent over for a better look at Elizabeth.

Her eyes were glazed and darted back and forth, not seeming to see him. Her face was paler than he'd ever seen it—gray, in fact—and fresh, wet blood glistened on her lips and chin. She lay in an enormous puddle of blood, and her long-sleeve tactical top had been cut open as well as her sports bra. Dempsey saw that she had a foot-long section of plastic tubing as wide as his thumb sticking out of a hole beneath her right armpit. A few inches below, along the outside curve of her right breast, a ragged bullet hole dribbled purple while bloody, pink bubbles formed and popped one after another.

"How?" Dempsey asked, not even sure what he was asking.

"AK-47," Munn said. "She took a 7.62 round through the lung."

Dempsey looked up, and his expression communicated the next question for him because Rouvin nodded and said, "I killed the bastard myself."

Dempsey knelt and stroked Grimes's cold forehead with the back of his hand and felt his throat tighten up.

"I put a chest tube in," Munn said, his expression grave. "She had a tension pneumothorax and too much blood in her chest and couldn't breathe. I relieved the pressure and then clamped the tube so she wouldn't bleed out, but she is still filling up with blood in there. We have to get her out of here ASAP."

"Jerusalem Medical Center is minutes away, once we're in the truck," Elinor said softly, but her expression suggested to Dempsey that she thought the trip would be futile.

The sound of screaming erupted outside, followed by a terrible crash.

"Is that our truck pulling up?" Munn asked.

"I don't think so," Rouvin said.

"Go. I've got her," Munn said and passed Dempsey his short-barreled SOPMOD M4 rifle.

Dempsey followed Rouvin out the glassless door and turned to his right, toward the screaming. He watched in horror as the semitractor, without trailer in tow, tore down the street, weaving back and forth and plowing through the crowd. Dempsey immediately realized that the truck was not trying to avoid the pedestrians, but to hit them. An elderly woman, one stocking down at her ankle and her purse still on her shoulder, jogged ahead of the truck and then disappeared under its left front wheel with a crunch he could hear over the roar of the engine.

He stepped out beside Rouvin and they both sighted in. Dempsey placed the floating red dot of the holographic sight on the windshield, just above the steering wheel, knowing that a shot through the glass would deflect upward. He squeezed off two rounds in tandem with his Israeli teammate. The truck lurched suddenly to the left, smashing into the wall of a souvenir shop. After impact, the tractor drifted slowly backward into the street, the rear wheel coming to rest on the bloody lump of the old woman the terrorist had plowed down seconds earlier.

"We've gotta go," Dempsey said to Rouvin. "Now."

When he turned back to the bakery, the team was already coming through the door. Munn had Grimes under her shoulders while Adamo and Wang had locked arms beneath her hips and knees. Dempsey fell in next to Munn, who repositioned so that Dempsey could share the load. Their four-man litter followed Rouvin east on Ben Yehuda with Elinor bringing up the rear, covering their flank with Adamo's rifle. Dempsey held Munn's rifle at the ready with his free hand in the event Rouvin needed additional fire support.

Grimes's head rolled from side to side as they ran, gurgling and coughing red blood from the mouth. The short but awkward twenty-meter sprint took them to the intersection at the end of the block where Daniel was waiting with an SUV, the tailgate open and the third-row seat folded down. They slid Grimes's limp body in feet first, Rouvin grabbing her legs through the open passenger-side rear door to help. Munn crawled in next, hunched over his patient in the cramped space. Dempsey squeezed in across from the doc and cradled Grimes's head on one outstretched leg. As the tailgate came down, Adamo, Wang, and

Elinor piled in the second row with Rouvin taking shotgun. Daniel whipped the big SUV expertly around and accelerated.

"Gotta be the pulmonary artery," Munn grumbled, looking down at her.

Dempsey didn't know exactly what that meant, but the pain and worry in Munn's face spoke volumes.

A bump and jolt knocked the side of Dempsey's head against the window as Daniel piloted their vehicle through the chaos in the streets. But Dempsey never looked out the window, even when he knew the Israeli operator was driving over sidewalks and crashing into street kiosks. No, he kept his eyes glued to Grimes's ever-graying face and blue lips. He stroked her forehead and her cheeks; her skin had gone cold and rubbery. He'd been here before, peering into the black human abyss, but not like this.

Never like this.

"It's okay, Lizzie," he said, his voice cracking. "We've gotcha, girl. We're almost there."

Grimes arched her back and gasped, the muscles in her neck straining bands.

"Shit," Munn said and grabbed the tube in her side. "Watch out."

Dempsey wasn't sure what he meant until the surgeon unsnapped the metal surgical clamp fixed to the end of the chest tube. A slug of blood shot out of the tube with so much pressure that it spattered the ceiling and wall, followed by an audible hiss like a car tire deflating after being punctured. When the hiss was gone and red blood started to flow, Munn replaced the clamp, and her body relaxed. She immediately sucked in a long, gurgling breath.

Dempsey shot Munn a *what the hell was that?* look.

"She's got two problems I'm dealing with here, JD," Munn said. "Air leaking into the chest cavity, which is compressing her lung, and the pulmonary artery dumping blood inside the lung. I'm trying to manage both problems and keep her from bleeding out, but also able to breathe."

"I trust you, Dan," Dempsey said. "More than any other."

At that, Grimes's eyelids began fluttering and she mumbled something. Dempsey squeezed her hand and then leaned over and kissed her cool forehead and whispered, "Hang in there, kid."

Elinor turned in her seat.

"One minute out," she said. "I called them and they have trauma blood and an OR ready, but there are tons of casualties."

"She can't wait," Munn said.

"And she won't," Elinor said. "I told you I called ahead. We have an *arrangement*."

"I'm operating on her," Munn said.

Elinor paused. "That . . . I can't promise."

"Munn is the most qualified doc to operate on her," Dempsey said without looking up from Grimes's face. "He's done more field surgery than any doc in the group. If he can save a mortally wounded SEAL in a dirty basement of a bombed-out school in Ethiopia, he can sure as hell take care of this."

"Okay," Elinor said. "I'll make it happen."

The SUV jerked to a halt, and the tailgate opened slowly—too slowly—under electric power. Munn rolled out of the growing gap and forced the tailgate up all the way with his hand. He grabbed Grimes under the shoulders while Dempsey jumped out and lifted her lower body. A gurney smashed into his hip, and the driver spun parallel to them.

"Bravo-two-seven?" a stern, fit woman dressed in scrubs asked.

Dempsey shrugged, clueless what the hell that meant, but Elinor was already beside him. "Yes," she said. "Bravo-two-seven. Authenticate Alpha-one-one-eight."

"Okay, let's go," the female doc said.

Dempsey wondered what it was like to live in a city where even access to trauma care required this level of security. Elinor read his mind.

"This is a civilian hospital," she said as they wheeled Grimes toward the glass doors of the emergency room entrance. "But we always have a secure suite with military surgeons who provide care for operators from Aman, as well as Mossad and Shin Bet. That's where we're taking her."

Dempsey nodded, clutching the handrail of the gurney with a grip like his own life depended on it. He wasn't read in on Aman, but he assumed it was the Hebrew slang for the Directorate of Military Intelligence under which the Seventh Order loosely resided—sorta like Ember's dotted-line connection to the rest of the US intelligence community.

They made a sharp left turn as they passed through the second set of glass doors. The next hallway was short, dead-ending at an oversize elevator door just fifteen paces away. The stern-looking doctor—at least he assumed the woman was a doctor—entered a code on a panel beside the door, and the light turned from red to yellow.

She then turned to Elinor and said something in Hebrew.

"Excuse me," Elinor said, squeezing past Dempsey.

Elinor punched in a second code and the doors slid open. They rolled Grimes into the elevator, and then the Israeli doctor departed with nothing more than a curt nod. Dempsey looked down and his heart sank. Grimes's head was lolled to the side, her eyes now lifeless and her pupils wide and dark.

"Oh shit," he said as the elevator stopped and the doors opened. "Dan . . ."

Munn tore his hand from the gurney. "Let go, JD. I got this."

Dempsey's voice cracked. "I think she's dead."

Munn shoved the gurney into a large circular space containing four operating suites and eight recovery beds. He was sprinting now—pushing the gurney ahead of him and then crashing through double doors into the nearest OR, where a surgical team was waiting to receive Grimes. As the doors swung shut, he looked over his shoulder at Dempsey and growled, "She's dead when I say she's dead."

Dempsey stood at the large window, palms pressed on the cold glass, watching as they moved Grimes's corpse onto the operating table in the center of the room and attendants repositioned rolling tables with instruments spread out on them.

"Two more large IVs and get me a thoracotomy tray stat," Munn commanded. The SEAL doc quickly sprayed brown liquid from a plastic bottle onto Grimes's torso around the chest tube he'd already inserted. Munn snapped on sterile gloves but made no move to change his clothes, put on a gown, or even a mask. Dempsey had seen Munn operate in the back of a Ryder truck on his knees once, so Dempsey wasn't surprised. The only thing that mattered now was speed.

"Four units of trauma blood."

Munn draped her chest with blue towels, picture framing a square of sterilized flesh where he was going to operate.

"Close those curtains," Munn snapped.

Dempsey expected his friend to look over, give him a nod—give him something. But it didn't happen. The last thing Dempsey saw as the curtains pulled closed was a flash of metal under the surgical lights as Munn plunged a scalpel deep into Lizzie's chest, just below her right breast, and sliced downward toward her back before thrusting his hand into her chest cavity up to his midforearm.

"I need a large vascular clamp," he heard Munn bark from behind the closed curtain.

Dempsey felt a hand on his back but didn't turn to see who it was. He knew without looking. He closed his eyes, pressed his forehead against the cool glass, and did something he hadn't done in a very, very long time . . .

He prayed.

CHAPTER 24

Secret Seventh Order Jerusalem Annex
Sub-basement, Bronfman Archaeology Wing
Israel Museum Jerusalem
11 Ruppin Boulevard, Hakyria, Jerusalem
May 11
1930 Local Time

Dempsey stared at his hands, certain he could still see traces of Elizabeth's blood, despite having scrubbed them raw. He ignored the quiet, hushed conversations happening around the conference table in this TOC annex used by the Seventh Order for operations in Jerusalem. Access and security had been more discreet here, and the TOC was smaller than in the Tel Aviv facility. All the monitors were dark except for two news feeds, i24 News and CNN International, which were both muted at present.

A hand patted his back. He looked up and saw Smith. The Ember Ops O looked tired, or older, or something. It was the eyes.

"You hanging in there, JD?" Smith asked, though the tightness in his voice told him Smith was far from okay himself.

Dempsey nodded. "Yeah . . . easy day."

Smith pulled out the chair beside Dempsey and collapsed into it. He sighed and rubbed his face. "You should have seen her, dude," he said, throwing his head back in the oversized chair and staring at the ceiling. "She was a real fucking operator out there today. I'm talking badass. She saved a lot of people and sent lots of those sleeper-cell jihadi motherfuckers straight to hell."

"Stop it," Dempsey said, slamming a fist down on the table.

Smith looked at him, his face clouded and confused. "Stop what?"

"Stop talking about her like she's dead," he said, his voice cracking.

Smith nodded, his lips tight. "You're right," he said. "I'm sorry."

"She's in good hands," Adamo said, the first indication he had been listening and the first thing he'd said since they'd relocated here nearly an hour and a half ago.

"I know," Dempsey mumbled. "I know."

They all sat in silence, even Wang the motormouth, each man staring blankly into empty space. Time passed, until the door opened and Jarvis stepped in. All eyes turned to the Ember Director.

"I don't know anything," he said. "Munn was still operating last I heard. He had the best chest surgeon in Jerusalem helping him—a former Sayeret Matkal guy, I'm told. Everything that can be done to save her is being done."

Elinor appeared behind Jarvis, and she met Dempsey's gaze, her mouth tight but her eyes kind. Jarvis nodded at her, a wordless handoff of the floor.

"You've all seen the news, and you know the attack we suffered was massive," she said simply. "The retaliation for our strike on Iran was exactly what you would expect. Whereas the IDF targeted Iranian military and nuclear sites, our enemies targeted civilians exclusively, including . . ."—she looked down at her note card—" . . . the brutal and savage murder of one hundred and eighty women and children, many of whom were neither Israeli nor Jewish. But conflict reveals the true nature of us all, does it not?"

Dempsey nodded solemnly; he was beginning to feel sick to his stomach.

"We expected sleeper-cell terrorists would play a role, but we never imagined anything on the scale we witnessed here today. Reports from Tel Aviv and Haifa tell similar stories—sapper bombers, knife attacks, vehicular manslaughter, and opportunistic snipers wreaking havoc in markets and city centers. But where we were, at the Midrachov, was the worst."

"Typical," Dempsey grumbled to himself. *The suck follows me wherever I go . . .*

"Similarly, the rocket barrage we experienced was on a scale not previously seen and involved every munition in our enemies' arsenals. The attack by Iran's proxies was highly coordinated, requiring a level of command and control that IDF thought would not be possible after our air strikes crippled critical components of the Persian military communication network. Which means that all elements of the proxy attack were preplanned and designed to be executed without Persian real-time oversight. IDF is launching a counteroffensive as we speak, targeting Gaza and the West Bank."

Elinor paused and rubbed her temples. She sighed heavily and continued.

"I think it is safe to assume that despite the massive amount of ordnance fired at us, our enemies' arsenals are not empty. We should expect and plan for follow-on attacks—"

The door opened and Munn came in, escorted by Rouvin and Daniel. He was in new clothes—cargo pants and a black T-shirt, but with his own now-bloodstained boots. He looked exhausted.

"Sorry to interrupt," he mumbled, standing by the door, his hands folded in front of him.

"No, please," Elinor said. "We are all desperate to know about Elizabeth."

Dempsey's stomach tightened and he tasted bile.

Oh God . . . She's dead. He couldn't save her.

Munn took a deep breath and then said, "She's alive but in critical condition. The bullet tore her pulmonary artery—the artery from the heart that delivers deoxygenated blood back to the lungs for renewal. I was able to repair it with the help of an amazing Israeli surgeon." He turned to Elinor. "Thank you so much for securing Dr. Epstein to assist. I could not have done it without him."

Elinor nodded.

"She lost her total body blood volume like two times over," Munn said, shaking his head with a tired smile, "but the team just kept filling her up and somehow managed to keep her stable throughout the operation. We were able to save her lung, and the artery is repaired. The bullet tore through the dome of her diaphragm also, but that was an easy repair. It ended up lodged in her back just beside her spine. I know it sounds trite, but an inch to the left . . ."

"Did you get it out?" Wang asked.

"We don't hunt for bullets. That's just in the movies. Unless they pose an immediate danger, we fix the damage left in the wake and leave them be. In my experience, you do more damage cutting and rooting around than just leaving well enough alone."

Wang nodded.

"How is she?" Smith asked. "Is she awake?"

Munn shook his head. "She's stable for now. It'll be a tough few days. Whenever you replace that much blood, patients experience coagulopathy—you know, their clotting mechanisms don't work—so they tend to ooze and bleed. A lot. She still might need another transfusion. The other complication is that changing out someone's entire blood volume weakens their immune system, putting her at higher risk for infection. On top of that, her right lung is hamburger meat, so it could be a few days before we get her off the ventilator and she's able to breathe on her own. She'll have to keep the chest tube in for a day or two at least to keep the lung inflated, and the tube and ventilator both increase the probability of getting pneumonia."

"Christ, Dan, you make it sound like she's fucked," Dempsey said. Munn shook his head and smiled at him.

"No, not at all. She's young and strong as hell, which is the only reason we were able to bring her back. She'll get through this, but it will be a tough slog."

"Full recovery?" Jarvis asked, his voice more clinical than concerned.

Munn hesitated. "Yeah, I would expect so. Physically, anyway."

Jarvis nodded and said, "Thanks for the update, Dan. Great work."

Wang was already handing Munn a cup of coffee from the station at the back of the room. Munn clapped the cyber whiz on the back and followed him to a seat at the table across from Dempsey.

Dempsey held Munn's eyes—*Thank you.*

"We were just briefing on the attack," Elinor said, taking the floor back. She turned to the flat screen behind her and clicked on a map of Israel, which began to populate with the color-coordinated dots signifying, according to the legend at the bottom, the sites of various sleeper-cell attacks broken out by type. "This is the slide we are using to brief the PM and the Knesset, our parliament. We are still updating it as intel comes in, so the number of dots will continue to multiply . . ." She paused, closed her eyes for a beat, and took a deep breath before continuing. "It's unfortunate that we weren't able to conduct our operation before this attack, and I know that most of you are undoubtedly thinking that we've lost the window of opportunity to act, but Captain Jarvis and I are of a different opinion. We believe there is still value to taking Amir Modiri. This man is more than a nuisance; he is a clear and present danger to both our nations' clandestine operations, citizenry, and way of life."

She advanced the slide, and a map of the Iranian and Iraqi border appeared on the screen.

On that cue, Jarvis said, "If it isn't obvious by now, what Ms. Jordan is telling you is that our operation is a go. She and Dempsey will execute the mission we've been prepping these last several days. The rest of you will support their INFIL and border crossing. A US Navy SEAL contingent is standing by in Iraq to support us. The Seventh Order will coordinate with Mossad to leverage embedded assets for cover and transport on the other side. The plan is to execute a night crossing in Iraqi Kurdistan from the village of Tawella, which is about twenty clicks east of Halabja. From there, it's a three-mile hump to Route 15, depicted here, running north to south on the map. We'll have a vehicle staged and ready to drive to a safe house in Sanandaj. If everything looks good, they'll shelter until morning, make a vehicle change, and travel to a second safe house in Tehran."

"Crossing at Tawella is quite a haul from a crossing at the usual areas east of Irbil," Adamo said, tapping his index finger on the table as he spoke.

"Yes, it is," Jarvis agreed. "But, based on the latest intelligence and satellite imagery confirming the deployment of Persian military forces, we believe this is the safest location."

"Have you considered a covert entry through Turkey? I have an extensive network of well-developed assets that could smuggle them into Tabriz," Adamo pressed.

"Let me ask you a question," Elinor said, her face contorting as if she'd just sucked on a lemon. "Would you trust these Turkish assets of yours to babysit your children?"

Adamo smiled wryly at this but held his tongue.

"That's what I thought," she said.

"At this stage in the game," Jarvis said, jumping in, "we're going to stick with the plan we've developed. We have the SEALs ready to support, and Seventh Order has already begun moving the chess pieces inside Iran to support."

"If memory serves, isn't there a border crossing east of Penjwen a few clicks to the north, boss?" Smith chimed in. "I would imagine that crossing probably has an IRGC contingent now. How the hell is this supposed to work, crossing right under their noses?"

"That's the reason we cross there. The plan is to initiate an engagement with Persian forces massing at Outpost Bashmaq. We'll begin with an artillery exchange and then escalate, which will serve as a diversion while our people slip across to the south. We cross in the heat of battle."

"So we're inviting the bad guys to gather and engage us right where we cross? How the hell does that work?" Dempsey asked.

"The Bashmaq outpost is thirty miles north of Tawella. And in case you've forgotten, we're not talking thirty miles on Interstate I-70. This is rough, desolate mountain terrain. Without air assets, there's no easy way to prosecute. And don't forget, the Artesh is in disarray right now due to the crippling blow to their comms in the wake of the cyber and air attacks from the IDF. Which leads me to the other reason we've selected this location. The city of Marivan—which is just south of the Bashmaq crossing—is in chaos. The IDF hit the Iranian nuclear facility there, and the city's largely Sunni Kurd population, which has always been at odds with their Shi'ite masters in Tehran, has seized upon this opportunity to take control of the city. To steal an expression from social media, this particular little corner of Iran is a hot mess. We've got aid workers rushing into Marivan while citizens are fleeing, giving Elinor and JD an opportunity to get lost in the traffic between Marivan and Sanandaj."

"I'm on board with the plan," Dempsey said, feeling that old familiar pre-op anticipation building in his gut. "What's next, Skipper?"

"The only thing left, I suppose, is to name this op," Jarvis said, meeting his gaze. "I thought we'd give you the honors . . ."

"Crusader," Dempsey said without hesitation, clenching his right fist. "Operation Crusader."

"Beautifully politically incorrect, which I love of course," Rouvin said, "but it fails to represent the Jewish contribution to the team, don't you think?"

"It's not about politics," Dempsey said, his jaw set and his thoughts on all the men—friends, teammates, SEALs—who died one year ago because of Amir Modiri's diabolical handiwork. "It's about payback."

"Crusader it is," Jarvis said with a tight approving grin, "which, I believe, makes you . . . Crusader One."

CHAPTER 25

Sa'dabad Palace
Shemiran, Greater Tehran, Iran
May 14
1130 Local Time

"The President will see you now," Esfahani's aide said and gestured to the door.

Modiri stood and wordlessly accepted the invitation. His summons to Sa'dabad, the Persian equivalent of the American White House, while not entirely unexpected, was not a meeting he was looking forward to. That Esfahani had called him here instead of traveling to the Ministry's offices, as would be customary, was noteworthy. It was also telling that Modiri's boss had not been summoned. As he entered Esfahani's office alone and for the very first time, Modiri wondered if it would also be his last.

The President stood at the window, behind his desk, his back to them.

"Director Modiri, sir," the aide announced.

"Leave us," Esfahani said, without turning.

With a wordless bow, the aide—a man who looked more like a cage fighter in a suit than an administrative type—departed and shut the door behind him. The room smelled of tea and cigarettes, but with a subtle floral undertone. *Lavender? Lilac?* Whatever it was, he liked it, and it seemed familiar—

"The last time we met," the President said, "I told you that the party responsible for the bombing in America must be found and revealed to the world. I said, 'Succeed, and Iran will continue to flourish. Fail, and the Persian caliphate will go up in flames, along with our cities and our bases.' Do you remember that, Amir?"

"Yes, Mr. President."

"And now, our cities and our bases are burning, and our nuclear sites are destroyed. *Who* should I blame for this?" Esfahani said.

Modiri hesitated. How much did Esfahani know? Without being able to see the man's face, there was no way to know if this question was meant to be rhetorical or a death sentence. "If you are looking to assign blame," he said at last, "then blame the party responsible for all this death and destruction—blame the Zionists. If memory serves, you also said that if Persia burns you would raze Israel to the ground."

Esfahani turned to face him and looked as though he had aged ten years since their last meeting. "Did you do it? Did you kill the American DNI and Mossad Chief on American soil?"

"I did not," Modiri said with conviction, before adding, "but, I've recently come to fear that one of my operators may have acted unilaterally and carried out the attack."

The corners of Esfahani's mouth turned up in an angry smile. "Unilaterally?"

"Yes, Mr. President."

"I assume you're referring to Behrouz Rostami?"

"That's correct," he said without hesitation or a hint of trepidation in his voice. He'd already played this conversation out in his head a hundred times, rehearsing both his and Esfahani's lines. So far, the script he'd imagined had unfolded almost verbatim in real life. Unlike Safavid, Amir's myopic boss, Esfahani was a ruthless tactician hewn from the same stuff as Modiri. To prepare for this encounter, all Amir had had to do was imagine sparring with himself—himself with incomplete information. But incomplete information was not the same thing as zero information. Modiri knew that Esfahani's lapdogs had been digging and sniffing, sniffing and digging, all around VEVAK and beyond. How did he know this? Because Maheen had told him so. Just as Esfahani had his dogs, Maheen had her little bees, always buzzing and listening, listening and buzzing. Rostami's absence had gone unnoticed by most, but not all, and word had apparently gotten back to the President. And so Modiri's only play left was to pin the blame squarely on Rostami and hope that some part of Esfahani secretly both admired and recognized the magnitude of the operation he'd pulled off. VEVAK had successfully managed to wipe out the intelligence Chiefs of their two greatest enemies on American soil. Despite the tremendous cost, it was still an accomplishment worthy of being lauded, one that maybe only another former VEVAK Director could appreciate.

"Go on," Esfahani said.

"As you know, I've been pushing my department very hard these past eighteen months. We've been recruiting and developing assets all over the globe. We've been aggressively taking on the Americans and the Zionists inside clandestine circles—collecting intelligence, rooting out their spies, and hitting them where it hurts. All the while, I've worked diligently to conduct my operations in such a manner that I provide you and the Supreme Leader with plausible deniability. This is the model that you pioneered while you were Minister. I'm merely a humble servant of Allah continuing the work you began."

"Cut the shit; it doesn't work with me," Esfahani said, his expression darkening.

"Nevertheless, it's true," Modiri said. "I have been working my people to the bone. Especially Rostami. I don't imagine you've seen his psychological profile, but if you had, you'd know that Rostami was flagged for having sociopathic predispositions."

"That's not uncommon in that line of work."

"True, but couple this with his grandiose aspirations and a god complex, and you get an agent who—if pushed too hard—might crack and go over the edge, which is what I believe happened in this case. I believe Rostami went rogue and decided to execute one of the Red Sabre operations we've been developing."

"So this was your operation after all?" the President said, narrowing his eyes.

"The operation was one of mine, yes," Modiri said. "But I never gave the order to execute it. I never gave the green light."

"What are Red Sabre operations?" Esfahani asked.

Modiri resisted the urge to smile. It was working; he was slowly easing the bull's-eye off his back and onto his dead scapegoat. "High-risk/high-reward missions involving only my most senior analysts and operators. The missions are all scenario based. Some are crazy, some are impossible, but some have gone on to become our greatest triumphs. The operation to hit the DNI's private estate was a Red Sabre operation, although in its original incarnation, only the DNI and his wife are in residence at the time of the attack. I suspect that learning the new Mossad Chief would be visiting the mansion with his staff simply was too much for Rostami to resist."

"He was already in the US?"

"Yes, collecting intelligence and meeting with the Suren Circle DC residents, which, despite the beliefs of the Americans, is still very much intact and fully operational."

"I don't know whether to embrace you or hang you," Esfahani said, suddenly deflating.

I've won, Modiri realized. *It's over . . . Now only to finish without making a mistake.*

"I would prefer the former," Modiri said with a cautious smile. "Sir."

The President took a seat in the chair behind his desk and gestured for Modiri to sit in the chair opposite. Then, scratching his beard, he said, "Maybe there is still a chance this catastrophe can be salvaged. American forces in Iraq are repositioning along our borders. The Fifth Fleet is in the Arabian Sea, and I'm told a second aircraft carrier is steaming to the Mediterranean. If the Americans form an alliance with Israel and declare war on us, it will lead to our destruction. And if they come, they won't stop until regime change is effected. We can't let it come to that. Do your job, Amir. Give me something or someone I can trade to the Americans to satisfy their President and stop the escalation. Either find me Rostami or manufacture evidence that someone else is responsible. Boko Haram, Al-Shabaab, ISIS—I don't give a shit—just get me a sacrificial lamb."

"I don't have Rostami. He's in the wind," he said. "Or maybe he's dead."

"Do you think the Americans already have him?"

"No," Modiri said. "If they had him we would know. They would have publicized his capture to paint us the villain to the world."

"Maybe they are just waiting for the right time."

"I think that time has passed, but let's say for argument's sake they kept it from the media; they certainly would have informed the Zionists," Modiri said. "But if they'd informed the Zionists, I would know because I have a highly placed source in their intelligence community."

"Ah yes, the fabled Broken Mirror . . . but why did we hear nothing from your source two days ago? Hmmm? Where was your loyal Zionist double agent when we needed him most before the Israeli attack?"

"I don't know, sir. I assume my asset could not get word to us because of the elevated security. An attempt to do so could have proven disastrous."

"The attack was disastrous!" Esfahani shouted, slamming his fist down on the desk.

"With all due respect, sir, would it have changed anything? We anticipated an attack was coming; it would have been confirming intelligence only. The outcome would have remained the same. The capabilities of the Artesh are what they are. We are outgunned. It is the simple truth."

"You're right, of course. I know . . ." Esfahani's words trailed off.

"On the positive side," Modiri said, filling the silence, "reports are coming in about our counterattack. The sleeper cells activated, and our brothers in Hezbollah and Hamas continue to hammer Israeli cities. Civilian casualties are climbing."

"Yes, but their damn missile defense system is performing better than expected. It's all over the news."

"The media is controlled by the Zionists; these reports are lies and propaganda."

"Is that what your spies tell you?"

"My assets are saying that the damage exceeds what the media is reporting."

Esfahani nodded, but his gaze was off into space.

"When will we attack the Zionists directly?" Modiri asked, fully expecting to be lied to.

"As of this moment, we will not launch an overt attack. To do so would all but ensure American intervention. I intend to maintain our innocence as long as possible. We paint the Zionists as the aggressors while maintaining plausible deniability. We cannot win a war with the Americans in our current state."

"What about Russian intervention?"

"Petrov will not commit."

"So what, then . . . We do nothing?"

Esfahani had no reply.

"What happened to 'razing Israel to the ground'?"

A pained look washed over Esfahani's face. He sighed, rubbed his temples, and was quiet for a long beat. When he finally spoke, he said, "If we attempted this—and the odds are staggeringly low that our military would prevail—the Americans would intervene, and the outcome would be devastating. Our cities would be left in ruins. The regime would be toppled. Sunni factions would unite inside our borders and incite civil war . . . I cannot . . . I *will not* let Persia become the next Syria."

From his first day on the job as Director of Foreign Operations, Modiri had understood his charter to be to antagonize, foil, and injure the giant on the other side of the world in ways that did not breach the threshold of triggering a full-scale retaliation. Until now, he had been incredibly successful at fulfilling that charter, perpetrating real harm to American assets, interests, and security. The victories in Yemen and Djibouti that decimated the Navy Tier One units had been a tremendous blow that US Special Forces was still trying to recover from. The terror attacks he facilitated at the New York United Nations and later in Atlanta, Omaha, and Seattle—while not full-blown successes—had achieved the psychological objective of demonstrating to the world that America was not invincible. In none of these operations had the Americans gathered sufficient evidence to hold Iran accountable. He did not believe his bold assassination of the DNI to be any different, whether they recovered Rostami's body or not. What made this case different from the others were the Zionists. They did not have the same threshold as the Americans, and their brazen strike on Persia was proof of this.

By attacking Iran, Israel had changed the game. It was never Modiri's intention that Iran be put in this position, but now that it was, Iran had no choice but to act with strength. The President had it backward. By yielding to the Zionists, Persian credibility would be lost. Their Sunni adversaries in the region would become emboldened and challenge Persian sovereignty. It was his duty to convince Esfahani of as much.

"By doing nothing, the world will know us as cowards. Our adversaries will unite and take our homeland from us. We cannot roll over before the Zionists. We must show our adversaries that any attack on Persia will be revisited with tenfold the destructive power," Modiri said, meeting the President's gaze. "We have parity in our pocket. It is only a matter of having the courage to use it."

"Are you talking about a nuclear strike?" Esfahani said, his eyes widening behind his silver-rimmed glasses.

Modiri nodded. "We have the capability. I can covertly shuttle one of our twenty-kiloton warheads to Hezbollah. They have nine operational SCUD missiles. We load the warhead on one and fire all of them at Tel Aviv in the middle of a second-wave rocket attack. The Iron Dome is vulnerable. We proved that in the first attack."

"No, Amir," Esfahani said, shaking his head. "I will not do this. I will not be the architect of Persia's demise. I will not be the man who starts World War Three."

Modiri met the President's gaze.

"Then what will you have me do?" Modiri asked.

"Find me a scapegoat's head to offer the Americans and the Zionists on a platter so we can get on to the business of rebuilding, before we don't have anything left to rebuild!"

Modiri swallowed down his vitriol and pride and bowed his head in deference. "I will see it done," he said and then turned to leave.

Spineless fool, he seethed. *If you don't have the courage to act, then once again you leave me no choice.*

PART III

We share enemies, my friend. Enemies everywhere.

—*Levi Harel*

CHAPTER 26

JSOTF—Iraq Compound
Irbil, Iraq
May 31
1630 Local Time

Dempsey had no time for nostalgia.

No time for déjà vu.

On his last visit to this American Special Forces compound, the young SEAL officer whom everybody called Chunk had accompanied him on a capture/kill mission into the Wild West of Iraq. Last time, everything had gone to hell, and they'd had to fight their way to freedom, taking turns saving each other's lives in the process. This time, all that mattered was getting in; everything else was just noise. This was the reason the universe had spared him, and him alone, from the attack in Djibouti. This was the mission Jarvis had recruited and trained him to fulfill.

This was his purpose.

This was his destiny.

"You good?" said Munn, his face drawn with anxiety.

"Yeah, just thinking about Lizzie," he lied and returned to the task of cleaning and oiling his assault rifle. He'd been thinking about vengeance, not his friend, and suddenly a wave of guilt washed over him.

"Yeah, me, too." Munn sighed, snapping the lower receiver of his own rifle back in place and pushing the pin back in. He cycled the charging handle and locked the bolt back, inspecting his rifle closely. "Thank God we had the Seventh Order medical assets so close." Munn inserted a magazine into his rifle. He tapped the bottom of the magazine and released the bolt. Then, he leaned the weapon against the bench beside him.

"I can't stop thinking about our last conversation," Dempsey said, shaking his head. "It wasn't a conversation."

"What do you mean?"

"I mean we were quarreling. She was really upset with me, and as usual, I didn't understand why."

"You guys seemed okay during the workup."

"No, that was just us trying to stay out of each other's way. We were going through the motions, but ever since that night at the bar in Annapolis, things have been off. If something happens and she doesn't make it . . . I don't know what I'll do."

"She's gonna make it, bro."

"You sure?"

"It was touch and go there for a while, but she's a fighter. The last status report they sent me was solid. She's turned the corner. I'm not worried, JD, which means you don't have to, either."

Dempsey searched his friend's eyes for any modicum of insincerity and found none. If Munn hadn't been there—if he hadn't recruited the doc onto the team—then Grimes would be dead. She would have died before they got anywhere near the hospital. He felt like he should say something, somehow give Munn the credit he deserved, but the right words didn't come to him, so they sat in silence. With anyone but another blooded operator and former teammate, this might have been awkward, but not with Munn.

Dempsey boxed up his worry and anxiety over Grimes and locked them in a vault in his mind. Now wasn't the time. He needed to be thinking about his target. If this were a standard SEAL Team capture/kill mission, he'd be completely relaxed. But a two-person team infiltrating the Islamic Republic of Iran during wartime was a whole new beast. This was real-life cloak-and-dagger spy shit—a mission that fell outside his wheelhouse. Of course, that was why he was going in with Elinor . . .

On cue, a shapely pair of hips stepped into his field of vision.

"When do we meet these superhero friends of yours?" Elinor asked.

He looked up and she smiled at him. She was dressed in BDU pants and a snug coyote-brown T-shirt; she wore a pistol in a drop holster on her right thigh and had a rifle slung combat style across her chest. In her left hand, she casually carried a combat vest, which the red-blooded part of him was grateful she had yet to put on. He grinned at her and wondered if she knew that he found her even sexier now than he had outside that lingerie shop in Tel Aviv. The whole scene reminded him of the time these OGA guys were selling T-shirts in Iraq printed with "Chicks Dig Guys in Body Armor" on the front and "Guys Dig Chicks with Guns" on the back. He'd bought two—in his and her sizes—but he'd never been able to convince Kate to wear hers out in public. Elinor, he surmised, would have no such hang-ups.

"They should be along in a few minutes," he said, taking a mental snapshot of her. If the mission went to shit, this memory would be a good one to hold on to in an Iranian torture cell.

"Why are we meeting here?" she asked. "Shouldn't we be briefing in their TOC?"

Instead of setting up shop in the JSOTF TOC, they'd been instructed to camp out in a private section of the "diplomatic" building on the ever-growing compound. This facility, originally built to function as an actual diplomatic mission, had since evolved into a counterinsurgency operations base focused on ISIS. Along with the SEALs, the compound housed a whole host of OGA folks, as well as friends from other three-letter agencies.

"Lieutenant Redman wants to meet here first. That way we can brief him separately before he briefs the rest of his platoon . . . if you catch my drift."

"And you've worked with him before?" Elinor asked, her eyebrows pinching together with concern.

Dempsey got it. The two of them were putting their lives in Chunk's hands, and she wanted Dempsey's personal assurance Chunk and his team warranted that kind of trust. "Yes," he said, checking the batteries for his holosite and the PEQ-4 IR target designator on his rifle. "He's good. We've fought side by side—staged out of this very compound for a capture/kill operation. He saved my life on that op. After that, I pulled him and some of his guys to support some Ember black ops work. He is my number one choice for this INFIL. Trust me, we're lucky to have him."

Elinor nodded, his assurance seemingly satisfactory to her.

Munn stood and found a spot on the wall. He leaned back, folded his arms across the butt of his rifle slung over his kit, and looked very much the same eager SEAL that Dempsey had first met nearly two decades ago. "So, when do we meet the tadpole?" Munn asked with a sly grin, slinging a little jab at Chunk.

"I'm right here, old man," came a voice from the door as it swung open. "Feel free to sit and rest, that is, if your hips will let you." Chunk winked at Dempsey and then flashed Munn a toothy, tobacco-stained grin.

"Dan Munn," Munn said, extending a hand.

"Lieutenant Redman," the SEAL officer said, shaking Munn's hand. "But you can call me Chunk."

"I don't usually trust Dempsey's judgment when it comes to important things like tactics and people, but in this case your reputation precedes you . . ."

Chunk laughed. "Ahh, I see you've been in the suck with Dempsey before, too. Now I get it."

"Oh yeah, nobody knows how to get himself into a jam like JD."

"Now that explains why he's so good at getting out of them. He's one Rambo, death-dealing motherfucker when he wants to be. I ain't never seen anyone in action like him before."

"All right, all right, it's clear you're both jealous," Dempsey said as the younger and older SEAL officers were sizing each other up. "Chunk, Dan is the SEAL doc I was telling you about earlier."

"That's right; I've heard of you, bro," Chunk said to Munn. "You're quite the legend back at SEAL Team Four, especially with the eighteen-Deltas. Any operator who can kick ass and then has the smarts to become a surgeon is solid in my book."

Munn smiled and nodded but said nothing. Nothing else needed to be said. Ritual complete.

Chunk turned to Dempsey, and they gripped forearms and pulled each other in—slapping each other hard on the back—for a Team-issue man-hug.

"Good to see you, man."

"You, too, Chunk. They keeping you busy?"

"Always," he said, pulling out a can of Skoal. After quickly and expertly packing his lower lip with snuff, he said, "Hey, I don't know if you heard, but they've just about got the Tier One stood back up. I've thrown my name in the hat, and I'm hoping to screen."

Dempsey nodded. "I mighta heard something about that."

"You know, I'd ask you for a letter, but I guess you'd have to write it in invisible ink or some shit, so they'd probably just throw it in the shit can."

"It is true that I don't exist," Dempsey said, looking Chunk in the eyes now. "But I happen to know a particular retired O-6 and former Tier One skipper who I hear can make shit happen."

"Well, ain't that a thing," Chunk said and then held a plastic water bottle up to his lips and dribbled a stream of brown saliva down the inside. "Thanks, bro."

Dempsey gave Chunk's shoulder a squeeze. "It's the least I can do for a steely-eyed frogman who shoots better than me."

Then, as if seeing her for the first time, Chunk looked Elinor up and down, his smile broadening. "Damn, you Ember guys love your hot chicks with guns . . . Hi, I'm Chunk," he said, extending his hand to her.

"Elinor," she said, seemingly unfazed by the SEAL's misogynistic bullshit. She was, no doubt, accustomed to being tested.

"Speaking of beautiful operators," Chunk said, looking around, "where's Grimes?"

The room fell quiet. Dempsey and Munn traded glances.

"She is"—Dempsey said, hesitating—"temporarily out of commission."

"Elizabeth was wounded during the rocket and sleeper-cell attacks," Munn said. "She took a high-velocity round to the chest. She's in the surgical ICU in Jerusalem—stable and improving. We hope to have her chest tube out in another couple of days."

"Jeez," Chunk breathed. "I'm sorry, guys. That sucks." He nodded to Dempsey and then was all business, the mission at hand now maybe a bit more personal. "Before we get started, I need to tell you that you guys have definitely pissed off someone important back home."

Dempsey looked at Chunk, confused. "What are you talking about?"

"We received a memorandum at the Joint Task Force to be on alert for a possible unauthorized spook mission that might come through for our support. Anything out of the ordinary, we're supposed to route through the chain back to the DNI." Chunk spit another mouthful of tobacco juice into his bottle. "I figured it was you guys even before Shane Smith reached out for our help."

"And?" Munn asked softly. "Was our request routed back through the DNI?"

"What request?" Chunk said, the corners of his mouth curling up. "I know Director Philips supported you guys one hundred percent. Not sure what kind of turf pissing war is going on right now in DC, but until all the political bullshit gets sorted out, we're standing by to support you."

"Thanks, man. I can't tell you how much that means to us."

"No worries," Chunk said. "But it would be nice if you read me into the basics of your op so we can provide some cover for you. If I'm gonna be your shit screen, I need to know where to hold the umbrella— you know what I'm saying?"

"Yeah, of course," Dempsey said. "It's pretty straightforward. We need you to help get me and Elinor into Iran."

"Shouldn't be a problem," Chunk said, unfazed. "We've been running daily cross-border missions for a while—probes, intel gathering, shuttling the spooks over for asset building, prepping the battlefield . . . that sort of stuff. I've locked in a number of good crossing points. The Activity and Group Ten are working the border as well. Depending on where you need to go, and how long you need to stay, we might beg, borrow, or steal some help if need be."

"Good," Dempsey said, nodding. "Very good."

"So, where you trying to get to?"

"Tehran."

Chunk adjusted the Team Four ball cap on his head, spit more tobacco in his bottle, and then folded his muscular forearms across his "Bars of Virginia Beach" T-shirt. "Tehran! You know damn well I can't get you to Tehran, JD," he said and started to laugh.

"Don't worry; we don't expect you to."

"What in the hell are you guys up to?" Chunk asked. Then, seeing Dempsey's expression, he added, "I know, I know. You can't tell me, and I'm pretty sure I don't want to know anyway."

"You don't," Elinor said, her voice hard and serious. "And you can't."

"Our actual mission is SCIF-level stuff," Dempsey added, "but I thought it was important for you to understand what the stakes are for this op."

"All we need you to do is get us across the border safely and unde-tected to our meet location. I have assets embedded in Iran who will help us manage the rest," Elinor said, signaling to Dempsey with a cold stare that she was *not* okay with how much information he'd shared with a SEAL she'd just met two minutes ago.

"Yeah, well, like I said, I don't want to know. But I do want to help," Chunk said.

Dempsey pulled a map from his cargo pocket and unfolded it on the table between them. He pointed to the area commonly known as Iraqi Kurdistan.

"We want to stage in Halabja and then drive the back roads to Tawella, here on the border. That's where we'll cross. Tawella is set down in a valley and we can cross on foot. It's only two clicks to Route 15, which is where we'll rendezvous with local assets who'll be waiting in a vehicle to pick us up. We'll ditch our gear, change, and head north until we intersect Route 46. From there we head east to Sanandaj."

Elinor shook her head, beseeching him to shut up, but he met her gaze and just kept talking.

"I want you to know this, because if our asset is a no-show, we'll need help getting to Sanandaj."

Chunk stared at the map and then repositioned his ball cap. "Well, that's a frigging haul, guys," the SEAL said, tapping his finger on the map. "And this is some rugged-ass terrain, JD. We gotta hope you make the meet on 15, because I don't think we can get you across this mountain range running north–south in a single night. We can't travel on the road like your spooks can. If your asset doesn't show, the cross-country trek to Sanandaj is gonna be a real bitch. We better hope it doesn't come to that."

"It won't," Elinor interrupted. "The asset will be there."

Chunk shot her his best cool-guy smile, probably more effective in the Virginia Beach bar scene than here. "I love your confidence, but in my experience, something always goes wrong in these types of operations. What's your backup plan to get to Sanandaj?"

"We don't have one."

Chunk put his palms on the table and bent over the map again. "Got a satellite image, JD?"

Dempsey opened another folded topographical map, this one generated from satellite imagery, which better illustrated the tortuous mountain terrain. Chunk traced his finger along a dirt road that intersected 15 and then zigzagged six miles to where it intersected a river that cut between the mountains, serpentining back and forth while creeping northeast.

Dempsey knew exactly what he was thinking. "Up the river?"

"Maybe," Chunk said. "Wouldn't be easy, and there could be a shitload of places we could get jammed up."

"But possible?" Munn asked.

"Yeah, definitely possible. The idea here would be to avoid Route 15 altogether and intersect Route 46 fifteen clicks south of where it intersects 15. That way you keep as far away from Marivan as possible. It's getting pretty hot there with the Kurdish riots and IDF strike on the nuclear facility. If I were the IRGC, I'd set up a checkpoint at that intersection because it's a choke point for all the north–south traffic along the western border."

"So we would need a second vehicle?" Elinor asked.

"Yes, you would need your assets to stage a vehicle here . . ." Chunk said and tapped the map at the bottom of the southern dogleg on 46. "For when we run out of water. Otherwise it would be a two-day op to get you to Sanandaj, and even that would be pushing it. We'd have to get small during daylight hours here"—Chunk tapped a finger on the north side of a mountain just west of Sanandaj—"and then finish the INFIL on foot by next dark. My EXFIL would be two days in reverse," the SEAL said, leaning back and stroking the thin beard on his chin. He sighed. "It would be hard to keep off the radar. We'd need a ton of support . . . Shit, Dempsey, this is a lot of asset to keep quiet. It's gonna raise some eyebrows."

"Yeah, but remember this is the backup INFIL plan. Hopefully it doesn't come to that," he said.

"And what about supporting their EXFIL?" Munn asked, shooting Dempsey a *hey, dummy, aren't you forgetting something?* look.

"You mean, like, waiting in place?"

Munn nodded and tapped a spot on the map.

"We could dig in for twenty-four, maybe forty-eight hours tops. But that will require running this much farther up my chain. You've got me and my guys in Indian country for like four or five days at least. When a squad disappears for that long, trust me, people notice."

Munn pursed his lips and nodded. "Just an idea."

"I already have a plan for getting out," Elinor interjected. "One that does not require nighttime border crossings and SEAL team support."

"I know," Dempsey said, resisting the compulsion to roll his eyes. The Seventh Order's Cold War–era plan was to drive out of Iran to Armenia and then work their way home from there. In theory, it sounded feasible, and Elinor had assured them it was a mature system that was time tested. But Iran was on the brink of war with the West. If they actually succeeded in taking Modiri, the nationwide manhunt for them would be on a scale never seen before. He'd rather retrace than try to go north. "Just plan the INFIL primary and backup, Chunk, and let us know what's feasible. Okay?"

"I'll work up something to get you up to Route 46 West. It's still thirty clicks west of Sanandaj, but it saves you thirty miles of driving and avoids that northern intersection near Marivan. What do you think?"

Dempsey looked at Elinor. "Can you get a request to your assets to stage a secondary vehicle along 46?"

"I'll try, but no guarantees."

"I'm sure that unlike us Americans, Israelis never need a backup plan because your missions unfold seamlessly. But since your partner happens to be an American, my hands are tied on this one. I gotta cover my bases," Chunk said to Elinor and then flashed her a disarming smile.

She shook her head but relented with a smile of her own.

"The more I think about this," Chunk continued, shifting his gaze to Dempsey, "the more I'm convinced we should use DPVs."

"That could definitely work," Dempsey agreed with a nod.

"We have an advanced team make a hard crossing with the DPVs and we monitor the Persian response. If things go bad, they haul ass back and we reevaluate. But if everything goes well, the DPVs are pre-staged if we need them. Then, we make the soft crossing on foot to the rendezvous. If your asset doesn't show or things go to shit, we can either retreat back to Tawella or proceed with the backup plan," he said, then, looking at Elinor, added with cordial, dry sarcasm, "again, in the very *unlikely* scenario something goes wrong."

"What are DPVs?" she asked.

"They're like badass dune buggies," Dempsey told her. "They can do eighty miles an hour on flat open ground and are equipped with a fifty-caliber machine gun and grenade launchers on their rails. These things were conceived for ops like this."

"Well, don't expect speed like that over terrain this shitty," Chunk said, "but it would sure beat humping another six miles on foot to the boats if the primary falls apart on us. And yes, the extra firepower will come in very handy in case we run into an Iranian patrol."

"Okay, fine," Elinor said, her tone suggesting she was still dubious about the whole plan but knew that arguing with this crew was pointless.

"Then it's settled; we use DPVs," Dempsey said.

"All right, I need to jump on the requisition, and I'll need tonight to pre-position both the equipment and some manpower. Can your timeline allow for a twenty-four-hour hold? Dropping boats along that river is going to take some work."

Dempsey looked at Elinor.

"I've already set assets in motion. A hold now would put my people in danger."

"If dropping boats is going to be a problem, then I might have another option. But I'll need to call Jarvis to help with the logistics," Dempsey said, rubbing his chin. When he was with the Tier One, they'd played around with a prototype inflatable water asset. The field tests had been a success, and he was pretty sure the tech had found its way into the service. The question was, where was the closest one, and could Jarvis get it here in time? "If I can solve the boat problem, the particular water asset I want to use can be loaded onto the DPVs."

Chunk nodded. "That would be way better. I wouldn't want to risk an air insert with all the activity along the border. We could still use an air drop to position gear or transportation at the end of the river INFIL here . . ." He tapped a spot at the end of the winding river valley on the northeast side of the mountain range.

Dempsey smiled; it was coming together.

"I assume you have a NOC in place that will give you safe passage if you get stopped without your assets?" Chunk asked.

"Yes," Elinor said and then shot Dempsey a hard look: *Don't you dare say a thing.*

"Okay," Chunk said and stood. "This is enough for my planners to get started." He looked at his watch. "Meet me in our TOC at 1830? We can go over what my planners gin up and then fine-tune it for a briefing with new intel at 2000."

"Mission brief at 2200?" Dempsey asked.

"Assuming you're wanting to go tonight?"

"Yes," Elinor said. "We need to make it to Sanandaj before sunrise . . . one way or another."

The SEAL officer nodded. "Okay. Well, I should have you guys an answer by 1830 on what we can do."

"And you can keep the operation off the radar until then?" Dempsey asked.

"What operation?" Chunk said with a huge grin, turning to leave. At the door, he paused and looked back. "Great getting to have my ass kicked beside you guys again. I love it when the spooks show up."

And with that, he was gone.

Dempsey looked at Elinor and cut her off before she could lecture him.

"You've gotta chill out about the OPSEC. These guys will get us there no matter what, or die trying, but you gotta show some trust."

Elinor opened her mouth, ready to argue, but then apparently thought better of it.

"It's a sign of respect, and that respect might be the difference between us getting out of Iran intact or in body bags," Dempsey added.

"Okay," she said. And then, as if a light switch was thrown, her face transformed into his sexy, adoring wife from their NOC. "I trust you, baby."

CHAPTER 27

"What the hell do you mean you've got nothing?" Catherine Morgan said with exasperation. She was surrounded by technicians and equipment capable of reading a VIN number off a car windshield at night from outer-fucking-space, and yet they couldn't find an entire American covert operations team and their Boeing 787 jet.

"I'm sorry, ma'am," the boy—yes, a boy—at the console in front of her said. "I'm in contact with our Special Operations forces in Iraq, scanning all the OPORDS, checking satellite feeds and message traffic, and there's absolutely nothing unusual to speak of. SOF teams are engaged in approved missions along the Iranian border for intelligence gathering and shuttling some of the clandestine services missions into place. Group Ten is also moving assets, but it's all expected stuff."

Before she could fire back, CTC Director Brad Johnson—whom she didn't particularly like—stuck his nose into the conversation. "We have word out to the JSOTF teams at all three border-operations sites as well as in Irbil to watch out for them. We've done what we can, but with all due respect, Ms. Morgan," he said with a voice that implied rather little of it, "the workload here at present is insane. Not only are we trying to support our usual counterterror operations; we've got an exponential jump in requests to support the Persian conflict. I'm having trouble justifying using JCAT resources to hunt down one of our own task forces."

She turned on him, eyes blazing. "Director Johnson, this unit has gone rogue. They are off the reservation and engaged in activities that could easily escalate the tenuous standoff into a war that no one wants. It is my assessment that Task Force Ember represents a clear and present danger to the security of the United States. I am ordering you to find them."

"We did find them," the CTC Director said softly. "In Israel."

"They *were* in Israel, but now you've lost them. I want to know where they went, and what they're doing. This is a priority for the office of the DNI, do you understand?"

"I do," Johnson said. "Keep in mind, ma'am, they could have been killed in the attacks, or wounded and hospitalized. Certainly they're using NOCs, solidly constructed NOCs, that is, which means finding Ember is like finding a needle in a haystack. And on top of that, I'd go so far as to say the Israelis are actively running interference for them. Mossad has been borderline obstructive since we started fishing."

"Why does that not surprise me," she mumbled, holding the eyes that held absolutely no "all due respect" for her.

"But I promise you, if they try to utilize any of our resources, we'll hear about it," he said, a backhanded assurance that there was little more he could—or *would*—do.

"Find them," she said again and turned and stormed off.

The whole damn intelligence and Special Operations network was like some kind of fraternity—and Jarvis seemed to know just the right fraternity brothers he could trust to turn down the volume. She decided to head back to her office; Philips must have kept compartmentalized records on Ember and its operations. Ember was black, but she knew with confidence that they begged, borrowed, and stole from both the intelligence community and Department of Defense. As a former Tier One unit commander, Jarvis would be partial to tapping old relationships and leveraging trusted and familiar personnel pools and logistics chains. If she could identify which Special Forces assets they had utilized over the past year, she might be able to narrow her search.

She would find them, and stop them. She would cut off their access to resources and asphyxiate their entire operation if she had to. She had no tolerance for cowboys and megalomaniacs. No one operated outside the chain of command. To do this—the job she was born to do—she needed complete control over all of America's intelligence assets.

CHAPTER 28

One Mile East of Route 15, Iran
The Islamic Republic of Iran
June 1
0115 Local Time

Dempsey was a SEAL again, if only for a moment, and it felt good. He was number two in the diamond formation, moving quietly through the brush in the green-gray world of night vision, scanning his sector over a SOPMOD M4 with a comfortable familiarity. He listened to the regular *boom boom* of the artillery barrages meant to distract the enemy away from their track. It reminded him of another war, in another lifetime, in this very area. Elinor was behind him, to his left, fully kitted up—including helmet and NVGs—looking just like a SEAL, albeit a little on the small side. Chunk was lead, and his senior NCO was number three, off to Dempsey's right. Munn was advancing parallel to Elinor in the formation, and three other SEALs completed the diamond behind them. Chunk raised a closed fist and they all stopped, taking a knee; they scanned their sectors while Chunk took time to deconflict whatever it was that had him worried.

The terrain was brutal on the north side of the valley, so Chunk had elected to travel along the southern slope, where the hike was manageable. Taking this route was a double-edged sword. Agreeable terrain meant better speed over ground but also meant the odds of being spotted were greater.

"The drone has a vehicle on Route 15," came Chunk's voice over the comms circuit. "Hold here."

"Can you describe it?" Elinor asked softly in his ear.

Chunk didn't answer immediately, and Dempsey knew the LT was talking with the Reaper pilot back at the TOC on another channel. After a beat, Chunk came back: "Old-model sedan, south of our position, headed north. Lights are off. We've had a few vehicles on 15, but none without lights."

"That's the signal, but I expected them coming from the north," she said. "I guess it's possible they left Marivan early and drove past the rendezvous to scout the pickup."

"Not a bad idea . . . but if that's your people, they're gonna be fifteen minutes early."

"They won't want to loiter long. Should we move toward the rendezvous?"

"Negative," Chunk said. "We hold here until we confirm."

A few minutes passed and then Chunk reported, "I don't think it's them. The vehicle passed the pickup and kept heading north."

Dempsey sighed and scanned the opposite ridgeline for threats while they waited.

"The same car just pulled off the road and stopped about a click north as the crow flies," Chunk reported a beat later.

"Show me on the map," Elinor said.

Chunk pulled out the satellite image and pointed to a section of road north of the rendezvous.

"I see what happened. They got confused. The valley bifurcates on the Iranian side of the border at Dezavar village. We went east, keeping south of the village," she said, tracing her finger due east from Tawella until it intersected Route 15. "But they must have thought we'd take the northern spur. Both points are equidistant from Tawella, so it is a coin flip."

"I could see that," Dempsey said, nodding. "But to get up there we'll either have to walk the road or backtrack and hike north, which ends up being two legs of the triangle. That's at least three miles."

Chunk held up a finger, silencing them, and pressed his hand to his right ear. "The driver is getting out . . . male . . . He just raised the hood."

"That's the signal," Elinor said. "Is there a woman?"

Chunk called in the question, paused, and then said, "Yes, the passenger is female. She just got out of the car."

"Okay, that's them," Elinor said. "We need to go."

"What do you think—skirt the road or backtrack through the valley and north?" Dempsey asked Chunk.

"We're three hundred yards from the DPVs, and I don't like the idea of following the road," Chunk said, rubbing his chin. "I think stick to the valleys, but we drive."

"Roger that," Dempsey said.

Chunk rose and the formation rose behind him. The SEAL officer led the team across the dangerously flat and open ground. After a few minutes, a flashing green strobe appeared ahead of them, an IR signal visible only in night vision that marked the position of the DPVs. As they closed the last seventy-five yards, their diamond collapsed on itself until the team formed up around the vehicles. The SEALs set up a perimeter as Dempsey, Chunk, and Elinor joined the four SEAL drivers who were waiting with the four DPVs.

"'Sup, boss?" said the short SEAL beside the closest of the tactical dune buggies, which were circled like wagons in the Old West.

"Hey, Buddha," Chunk said in a low voice, shaking the man's hand. The SEAL was not Asian and was definitely not shaped like anything resembling a Buddha, which suggested a great story behind the nickname. "Meet my buddy, JD."

"Any buddy of Chunk's," the SEAL whispered with a grin, "is someone with questionable judgment."

Dempsey smiled and shook the man's hand.

"So, eight pax and we leave four of my guys here, right?" Buddha asked.

"Nah," Chunk said. "I think we all go. I want SEAL gunners—the fifty is tricky in a bouncing DPV if you ain't trained on it," he said with a glance at Elinor and then back at Dempsey. "Cool?"

"Cool, boss," Buddha said.

"JD, myself, and Mr. and Mrs. Jones back there will split up and ride shotgun," Chunk said, pointing to Elinor and Munn as he spoke.

"The Joneses, huh," the SEAL said with a chuckle. "You spooks are a fucking trip."

Dempsey smiled at the dig that a year ago would have been coming from his lips.

"I'll ride in the lead vehicle and JD will be in the rear."

"Check," the SEAL said.

"All right, let's load up," Chunk said. "Their ride is waiting, so we gotta move."

"Hey, just want to make sure you loaded the packages we sent?" Dempsey asked, catching Buddha by the shoulder. He wanted positive confirmation that the two gray, bulky packages—like oversize folded blow-up beds—strapped under cargo netting on the rear stands of two of the DPVs were indeed his boats.

"Yeah," the SEAL said. "That's them on three and four. I'd love to see them in action. Looks like pretty slick tech."

Moments later, they were strapped in to the DPVs and bouncing their way through the valley in a diamond formation. From the rear vehicle, Dempsey scanned the terrain through his NVGs, alternately looking left and right. Behind him on the raised gun platform, he knew the SEAL machine gunner was scanning their six o'clock position. He'd forgotten how quiet the DPVs were. In the Tier One, he'd rarely had occasion to use them, with most of their INFILs being via helicopter. He was happy to reacquaint himself with the remarkably effective four-wheel independent shock absorber system and "floating" suspension under each seat. The world *should* have been careening wildly around him, but as the vehicle's chassis bobbed and rolled, his seat practically hovered over the ground. Thank God, too, because Dempsey wasn't sure that the metal implants stitching his lower spine back together could have survived the pounding otherwise.

They covered the distance quickly, and the next thing Dempsey knew, Chunk was halting the convoy at what Dempsey estimated was a quarter of a mile from the road. Although they were in separate DPVs, Dempsey could picture Chunk getting a report from their eyes in the sky. As they waited, an unfamiliar feeling suddenly washed over him. *Nerves.* The idea of stripping off his kit, helmet, and NVGs and then ditching his assault rifle and fellow SEALs to hop in a car with Elinor's assets and drive off into the Persian night was horrifying. The only protection he'd have, *the only protection at all*, were a set of questionable papers identifying him as a foreign humanitarian medical worker and his fists—both of which were useless against a trigger-happy, AK-47-toting Iranian trooper. The little sedan was certain to be stopped at least once en route to Sanandaj, and if his NOC didn't hold up—or Elinor's assets sold his ass out—he would either be taken into custody or shot dead on the spot. He had always harbored a secret fear of being beheaded by an Islamic terrorist and broadcast on the Internet, but the thought of having his rotting body hanging for a week in a public square in Tehran was no less disturbing.

"Shit, we have a problem," Chunk said, pressing his fingers to his ear.

Dempsey tightened the grip on his SOPMOD M4, the thought of forfeiting it now almost nauseating.

"Drone's got an Iranian patrol coming down from the north," Chunk said. "It ain't some local militia bullshit, either. They're in a high-end armored personnel carrier . . . My eyes guy thinks it's a Sarir with a twin-barrel KPV heavy machine gun on the turret up top."

"Most of the Sarirs are owned by IRGC," Dempsey said. "They use them for border patrol and counternarcotics operations."

"Yeah, but it could also be Quds Force."

"That's impossible," Elinor snapped, but the tenor of her voice betrayed uncertainty.

"Well, it's happening," Chunk said tightly. "And they're hauling ass toward your assets. We don't have enough time to drop you and bug out before they get there."

"Well, shit," Munn said. "What do we do?"

"We're a quarter mile out. We can bug out now, back to the valley for cover, but then we lose line of sight. If we stay here, we're exposed. We should assume they have night vision, especially if they're Quds," Chunk said, his tone making it clear he thought this op was quickly going to hell.

"But if we back out and Elinor's assets need our help, there's no way we can intervene from down in the valley," Munn said.

"If the patrol interrogates the assets, we cannot intervene without jeopardizing the operation. They understand the risk. They're on their own," Elinor said, her voice making it clear that she owned the decisions on this aspect of the operation.

"That's some coldhearted shit, lady," said one of the other SEALs.

"The mission can recover from two burned escorts," she said, her voice hard. "But if we get burned, it's over."

"Hold on," Chunk said. "We've got a troop truck coming up from the south now. Gonna arrive on scene a few minutes after the APC. Any chance this is a setup?" Chunk asked, his voice grim.

"None," Elinor said. "No one knows about this operation except our task force. Tell him, John." Her voice was sharp and accusing.

"She's right," Dempsey said. "This was planned completely in the black. The circle is tight."

"Well, I don't like it. I could see this happening near Marivan, but down here in the middle of nowhere . . . seems like one helluva coincidence," Chunk said. "I guess we'll see what happens."

"Better to validate your assets' NOCs now than when JD and Elinor are in the car," Munn said. "If things go bad, we can intervene."

"Range here isn't good for the grenade launchers," Dempsey pointed out.

"But we can tag their asses with the fifties," Chunk countered.

"Stop—no matter what happens, we cannot intervene," Elinor said, her voice ripe with irritation that the SEALs didn't seem to get it. "You're not listening. Intervention signals that these people are something worth protecting, which burns their NOCs and makes them useless to us. But if they check papers and let them go, we can wait until the soldiers leave and see if the assets reposition for another rendezvous."

Chunk thought a moment.

"Yeah, maybe, but only if that APC clears the hell out of here."

Elinor nodded.

Chunk climbed out of the DPV and walked just north of their DPV circle. He lifted a pair of high-powered night vision binoculars to sight in on the assets.

"Got another pair of those?" Dempsey asked the driver of his DPV.

"Use these," the SEAL said and handed Dempsey a pair from a box behind his seat. Dempsey stepped out of the vehicle and walked over to Chunk. He raised the binos to his eyes and zoomed in: a woman dressed in pants, a loose-fitting shirt, and a hijab leaned casually against the car while a man bent over the engine under the raised hood. Dempsey could see the spotlights growing brighter as the armored troop carrier approached. Soon, two blinding spotlights lit up the car from the front, washing out Dempsey's night vision and forcing him to turn it off.

The female asset waved her arms at the Iranian APC as if summoning help—glad that someone had stumbled across them. Dempsey wondered what she was really feeling inside. Pure terror? The man came out from under the hood and joined her. As the APC braked to a halt, both the assets raised a hand in front of their faces to shield their eyes from the blinding lights.

Dempsey watched two soldiers exit the APC, rifles up and ready. Both assets immediately raised their arms over their heads in surrender. Two more soldiers then jumped out and sprinted around the shooters to grab and force the couple to their knees in the dirt. Dempsey could see the larger of these men shouting at the female asset. The woman was saying something back, her hands trembling in the air. Then another pair of soldiers exited the APC. The first began walking a perimeter, while the other hung back and watched, his hands folded behind his back. Dempsey pegged this guy as the officer in charge.

After an uncomfortable pause, the male asset lowered a hand, undoubtedly in an attempt to retrieve his papers. The nearest soldier reacted immediately, raising his rifle as if to smash the man in the face, but then froze and looked back over his shoulder at the officer. The officer, his hands still behind his back, said something, and the kneeling couple seemed to relax. The officer then tasked two soldiers to search the vehicle, and Dempsey watched as they opened the doors and trunk and began tossing items out onto the dirt. One soldier emptied a cooler of bottled waters onto the ground while the other was buried waist-deep in the trunk pulling up the liners.

The officer began pacing slowly back and forth, talking as he did to the kneeling couple. They seemed reassured by whatever he was saying because they no longer had their hands up over their heads.

"The troop carrier is pulling up," Chunk said.

Dempsey looked to his right, where the lights of the approaching truck lit up the curving road. He got back on the binoculars just as a soldier jogged over from the car back to the officer. He said something, and then the officer nodded and gave an order, and the three soldiers hustled back to the APC.

"We may be okay," Elinor said. "It looks like they're leaving."

The couple were still on their knees, but Dempsey thought he made out what looked like a smile on the male asset's face. The Iranian officer continued talking but paced around them in a circle. When he was directly behind the man, his hands came from behind his back, and Dempsey saw the pistol. His gut tightened as the realization hit him. The officer fired point-blank into the back of the man's head, the asset's face exploding outward in a gory spray and the body pitching forward. The woman screamed and raised her hands just as the man fired a shot into her temple. Her dead body crumpled to the ground.

"Oh shit," Chunk hissed.

A soldier climbed out from the passenger seat of the newly arrived multiaxle transport, which the driver had pulled in behind the "stalled" sedan. The new arrival and the murdering officer spoke for a moment and then shook hands. The officer walked back to the troop carrier, stepping over the woman's corpse while waving his hand in a circle over his head. The soldiers in his unit remained back by the APC, but they didn't climb inside the rear cabin.

Meanwhile, two soldiers ran from the newly arrived truck carrying gas cans, which they poured all over and inside the sedan as well as onto the dead bodies sprawled beside it. Dempsey watched the driver of the troop transport back up a few yards and then stop again, just as the car and bodies burst into flames.

"I think we have our answer," Chunk said, his voice grim from the executions. "We scrub the mission and I get you back across the border."

"No," Elinor said. "We have a backup plan."

Dempsey looked at the gray bags on the back of two of the DPVs. "Wait for these guys to clear out; then we haul ass over to the river."

"Are you two out of your minds?" Chunk said, looking back and forth between them. "Did you not just see what I saw? You are in hostile enemy territory. They are running patrols. They are executing civilians without provocation. Your assets' NOCs were irrelevant because that asshole didn't even look at their papers. Route 15 is closed for business. Period, end of story."

"Then we try Route 46," Dempsey said and looked at Elinor.

"Agreed," she said, turning to Chunk. "You get us to 46, and we'll get ourselves to Sanandaj."

"We don't even know if your people got your request and prestaged a backup vehicle."

"Yes, but we can check that with the drone," Dempsey said.

Chunk screwed up his face and scratched his beard. "You're serious?"

They both nodded, but Dempsey could see that it was going to take something else to convince Chunk of the merits of risking his life and the lives of his men. Something to convince him that John Dempsey had not lost his friggin' mind.

"You wanna know what the call sign is for this operation?" he asked.

Chunk shrugged. "Sure."

"Crusader," Dempsey said, putting a hand on his brother SEAL's shoulder. "Do you understand what that means? Do you understand who my target is?"

Epiphany washed over Chunk's face. "You're going after the bastard responsible for wiping out the Tier One in Yemen?"

Dempsey nodded. "And this is the best shot I'm ever gonna get."

Chunk met his gaze. "All right, we'll take a look with the drone. If a vehicle is parked where Elinor instructed it to be, we go. If not, we bug out. Deal?"

"Deal," Dempsey said before Elinor had a chance to answer.

"All right," Chunk said, raising his binoculars to look back at the scene alongside the road. "We just hang tight and wait for these assholes to . . . uh-oh."

Dempsey quickly raised his own binoculars and saw two men carrying a heavy black box between them. He zoomed in and watched as the soldiers set the box down and opened the lid. Next they unlatched the hinged lid and opened it, but he couldn't quite see what was inside.

"Something's not right," Chunk said. "I got a bad feeling about this, JD."

Dempsey watched as the two bent over the open box on the ground. "I agree. We need to go."

"We're too close," Chunk said, still watching. "They'll hear the DPVs."

A beat later, Dempsey's heart sank as one of the soldiers lifted a compact drone over his head while the other tapped on a handheld tablet.

"Shit. Shit," Chunk said. "Time to go."

Chunk, Dempsey, and Elinor hustled back to the DPVs, Chunk spinning his hand in a circle over his head. As they strapped in to the DPVs, Dempsey took one last look through the binoculars toward the road, and what he saw made his chest tighten. The drone was banking right toward them at about five hundred feet, freshly alerted, no doubt, by the sound of four engines coming to life. Behind the drone pilot, a mortar team was rushing to set up as two other soldiers passed shells out the side hatch of the APC.

"Go, go, go," Dempsey barked as he heard the *whump* of the mortar leaving its tube.

"Mortars incoming," Munn called as the four DPVs fishtailed in the dirt and broke out of formation.

The first mortar shell struck the ground by the front right corner of the DPV with the team LCPO. The explosion lifted the front of the dune buggy off the ground and rolled it onto its left side, where it spun in a half circle before coming to a stop.

Dempsey heard another *whump*.

"Fuckin' light them up," Chunk hollered.

The SEAL gunners of the three upright DPVs responded, and the roar of the fifty-caliber machine guns filled the air, the smell of sulfur comforting and familiar. Dempsey watched the stream of tracers rip through the night toward the road. The mortar team retreated behind the protection of their armored vehicle as the first volley pounded the earth and the side of the APC.

"Keep 'em pinned down," Chunk yelled. "Strafe the APC. Don't let them fire up the heavy gun."

Dempsey jumped out of his vehicle and was sprinting toward the overturned DPV when the second mortar exploded behind him. He felt the heat and the shock wave but no shrapnel; the trajectory was too short.

"You all right?" Dempsey asked the Senior Chief, who was just getting to his feet beside the overturned vehicle. The LCPO nodded and turned back to his crew. The SEAL gunner was unhurt. He jumped off the overturned chassis, dropped to the ground, and immediately fell into a prone firing position. The SEAL sighted in with his SOPMOD M4 and joined the firefight just as enemy bullets began pinging off the metal frame of the overturned dune buggy.

Dempsey skirted to the other side to check on the driver. "Are you hit?"

"No," the frustrated SEAL grunted, "but my left arm is pinned."

"I need help," Dempsey hollered. In a flash Munn, Chunk, and two other SEALs were beside him.

The five men squatted and grabbed the aluminum rails of the DPV.

"One . . . two . . . three," Dempsey barked, and they all lifted with everything they had, raising the DPV a full foot off the ground. For a moment, Dempsey thought they might be able to actually flip it upright, but once the driver slithered out from under the roof rail, the vehicle became instantly and immensely heavy again—the adrenaline of the rescue ebbing. In unison, they all let go and it crashed back to the ground. A bullet ricocheted off the frame near Dempsey's face, and he reflexively crouched and found cover behind the vehicle. A heartbeat later, he had NVGs on, rifle up, and was searching for targets. Unfortunately, there were many and they were closing fast.

He squeezed the button on the forward grip, activating the IR targeting system, and placed a green dot on the forehead of a sprinting soldier. He pulled the trigger and the Persian assaulter pitched forward and fell face-first in the dirt.

"How many fucking Iranians can you fit in one truck?" someone shouted as enemy soldiers poured out of the troop transport like angry bees from a hive.

"It's like a damn clown car up there," Munn shouted back.

Enemy fighters were converging everywhere, but the SEALs were dropping targets left and right with headshots. In the corner of his eye, Dempsey saw Elinor drop prone beside him and start shooting with the battle-hardened calm of a blooded SEAL. She dropped an IRGC soldier and he took down two more. But then, to his dismay, the armored personnel carrier's headlights began to shift. It was turning straight toward them. He saw a torso pop up in the turret to man the KPV heavy machine gun. The Sarir APC was armor-plated to withstand .50-caliber rounds, but the dune buggies wouldn't last a second against the 14.5 mm rounds from the double-barreled beast on the top turret.

"We gotta go, Chunk, right now," Dempsey shouted as he sighted in on the gunner's head while the Iranian assault vehicle bounced across the rough terrain toward them. He squeezed the trigger and watched his round miss and ricochet off the turret. As if reading his mind, two SEAL gunners with .50 cals lit up the APC, shredding the gunner to ribbons as he tried to drop back down inside.

"Everyone to the vehicles," Chunk shouted as Buddha activated three satchel charges on the doomed DPV.

"Go, go, go . . . *now*!"

Dempsey strapped in to the DPV and then turned his rifle behind him, firing at the small army of advancing Persian troops. Because they were down one DPV, each vehicle had an extra man, with two SEALs crammed in and clinging to the one-man gunner turret in back.

"They can't catch us in that piece of shit," the SEAL driver said, spraying a rooster tail of dust behind them as the trio of DPVs sped off toward the valley below. A beat later, the sound of gunfire was drowned out by a thunderous explosion and blinding fireball as the scuttled DPV was practically reduced to molecular constituents by the satchel charges—thereby eliminating any hard proof the SEALs had ever been there.

"We're not out of the shit yet," Chunk said in his earpiece. "Even if they can't catch us, they still got that drone. If they have an air asset in orbit, we're fucked."

"It's less than three clicks to the border," the LCPO said. "We can make it."

"What about the river?" Elinor asked as the APC disappeared behind them and the Iranian troopers stopped firing as they moved out of range.

"Are you fucking kidding me?" Chunk said. "The entire Republican Guard will be hunting for us. This is an abort."

Dempsey looked behind him and saw he was riding in one of the two vehicles with the large gray bags. This could still be salvaged. The thought of missing Amir Modiri, of failing his dead brothers, was too much to bear. "Chunk," he said calmly into the microphone boom by his mouth, "we need you to drop us near Dezavar village with one of the boats before you cross back over. Elinor and I are gonna continue on alone."

Dempsey could actually hear Chunk laughing over the comms circuit. Then the SEAL officer said, "That bag of boat has to weigh close to two hundred pounds. How are you going to carry it? It's seven miles to the Daryan Dam. There's no fucking way, dude. Besides, they're hunting us."

"They're hunting a squad of SEALs on dune buggies. We just need to make it to the other side of Route 15. I'll steal a donkey in Dezavar if I have to."

A long, silent pause followed.

Finally, Chunk said, "All right, I just got confirmation from our eyes in the sky that there appears to be an abandoned vehicle parked a half mile off Route 46 and a hundred yards from the river. Looks like Elinor's asset came through . . . so, I need one suicidal volunteer to accompany me and our two insane spooks deeper into hell so they can float their boat on the River Styx."

"Count me in," Munn said without hesitation. "But we can't hump it on foot. We have to use a DPV."

"Then we have no choice but to take out that APC and their drone," Dempsey said. "Do you have ordnance on the Reaper?"

"Yeah, four Hellfire IIs," Chunk said, but his tone clearly indicated his displeasure with what Dempsey was suggesting. "But JD, if we do this, then yours truly just unilaterally declared war on Iran on behalf of the United States."

"Wrong," Dempsey said. "Amir Modiri declared war on the United States on behalf of Iran when he used VEVAK operatives to blow up the DNI at his home on American soil. We didn't start this fight, but we sure as hell are going to finish it."

Dempsey understood what he was demanding of Chunk. It was a potentially career-ending ask, but the courage to make decisions like this was what separated true leaders from lesser men. After an excruciatingly long silence, Chunk came back on the line.

"Okay, I called it in," the SEAL officer said, and as hellfire turned night into day behind them, he mumbled, "May God help us."

CHAPTER 29

Dempsey felt naked.

He'd shed his combat gear, slick BDUs, and the Under Armour top for blue jeans, a University of Limerick T-shirt, and a garish long-sleeve Patagonia travel shirt. He'd even traded his Oakley boots for a pair of Toms shoes that Elinor insisted he wear. But most gut-wrenching of all, he'd forfeited his weapons. All of them. Elinor forbade him from even carrying a compact 9 mm in the small of his back. He could not remember the last time he'd gone anywhere unarmed. High school, he reckoned. It felt like he'd stepped into the phone booth as Superman and stepped out as Clark Kent.

Good-bye, John Dempsey, lethal operator.

Say hello to Corbin Odell, craven civilian.

Sure, he had his NOC credentials in the weathered, gray Trakke backpack, including an ambulance driver's license from Cork and his identification as a medical aid worker with the Universal Care for All NGO. He also had an Irish passport. His visa was dated two months earlier, and his passport showed he had traveled as an aid worker extensively in the Middle East and Africa. The documents were all perfect, but what had happened to Elinor's assets hours earlier proved that paperwork was worthless against an armed patrol. He slung the pack over his shoulder and, for the first time since crossing the border, wondered if maybe this operation was a mistake.

"Well, bro, I can't believe we actually made it," Chunk said as he finished packing Dempsey and Elinor's gear tightly into the high-tech inflatable boat. "These things sure are slick."

The two inflatables, with their integrated, quiet drive motors, had made the trek upriver without incident. They were so silent, the only sound they'd made was the *swoosh* of the dirty water along the nylon hull.

"You got enough power to make it back?" Dempsey asked.

"Yeah, should be more than enough," Munn said, checking the reserve-power indicator. "Plus, we've got the current helping this time."

"Well," Chunk said, turning to Dempsey with a wan smile, "as much as I'd love to camp out and roast marshmallows with you kids, we better get moving before my guys eat my food, steal my Skoal, and ship all my shit back home."

The SEAL officer's voice sounded confident, but the trip had burned enough night that making it back across the border before sunrise was going to be impossible. Chunk and Munn would have to find a place to hole up in the mountains during the day and hope the DPV they'd camouflaged and left behind wasn't discovered. As a SEAL, Dempsey had always hated the missions where he had to lie low in enemy territory and pray some goat herder wasn't the end of him.

Dempsey stuck out his hand and the SEAL officer gripped it. "I owe you one, brother."

"Yeah, you do . . . Now go get that bastard Modiri, but when you're ready for someone to rescue your dumb ass from this hellhole, don't call me."

Dempsey laughed and turned to face Munn, who'd stepped up beside Chunk.

"I don't have the words, man," the doc said and pulled Dempsey in for a bear hug.

"Take care of Lizzie," Dempsey said, the words catching in his throat. "And, uh, Jarvis and Smith are going to need you in the coming days."

Munn released Dempsey and took a step back. "Dude, don't talk like that."

"Like what?"

"Like you're not coming back."

Dempsey gave his friend a tight smile but offered no rebuttal. There were a million things he wanted to say to Munn—to express his admiration and gratitude for everything this incredible human being had done for him over the years—but all he could manage was, "Hooyah, frogman."

"Hooyah," Munn and Chunk barked in unison.

With that, Dempsey turned his back on his friends and teammates for what, in all probability, would be the very last time. Elinor, her hair now covered by a silk headscarf in accordance with Persian norms, extended him her hand.

He took it and, in his best Irish accent, said, "Helluva way to spend the rest of our honeymoon, love. If only you liked drinking piña coladas on the beach like all the other lasses."

Elinor laughed and led him toward the beat-up Toyota sedan parked next to a tree. "Beaches are boring," she said in a Persian-flavored English accent, thick and sexy. "Besides, how was I to know there was a war brewing?"

"There's always a war brewing, love," he said. "Always."

When they reached the car, she let go of his hand and walked to the driver-side door. Finding it unlocked, she exhaled with relief. Dempsey meandered to the passenger side, fighting the urge to look back until he couldn't bear it any longer; he glanced over his shoulder and caught a fleeting glance of two of the finest SEALs he'd ever known silently disappearing around the bend in the river. He took a deep breath, steeled himself, and climbed into the car. Elinor checked for car keys: behind the sun visors, inside the center console, then the glove box, and at last found them tucked under the driver's seat. She inserted the key into the ignition but, before starting the engine, turned to him.

"You ready for this?" she asked.

He blew air through pursed lips. "Yeah. I'm ready."

"We're a team, you and me. Everything we do, we do together. It is our bond and our commitment to each other as a couple that validates our legends. Do you understand?"

He nodded.

"Deception has an odor," she continued, taking his hand in hers. "People can smell it. If we're stopped and questioned, our history is our shield." She pulled his hand over and pressed it to her heart. "This is what they will question; this is the only thing that can save us."

He felt her heart pounding, strong and certain beneath his palm. He looked into her bold hazel eyes and he saw adoration, and certainty, and yes, even love. He exhaled all his anxiety and tried to muster those same feelings for her. He tried pretending that she was Kate, that his ex-wife was the woman sitting across from him, but it had the opposite effect of what he wanted. Frustrated, he closed his eyes and thought back to the afternoon he and Elinor had spent together in Tel Aviv. Snapshots danced to the front of his mind—their kiss, the angst she felt at the 1994 bombing memorial on Dizengoff Street, then later her courage talking down the girl in a suicide vest during the rocket attack on Jerusalem, her competency under fire engaging the IRGC—and he felt a spark. Instead of substituting Kate's face on Elinor's body, he tried the reverse. He Photoshopped Elinor into all the most powerful memories he had from the early years of his marriage, when he and Kate's partnership had been healthy, and strong, and unbreakable. And as he revised history, he felt gravity shift beneath him. Elinor was a remarkable woman, and he found himself yearning for her.

He opened his eyes and told her all of this without uttering a single word.

"Very good," she said and smiled. "We're ready."

The drive into Sanandaj took almost an hour through the twisting mountain turns and switchbacks of Route 46. Dempsey's stomach tensed with anxiety every time a set of converging headlights appeared, but they reached the outskirts of the city without incident.

"Where exactly are we going?" he asked, eying an approaching car warily.

"A doctor's house."

"You mean a safe house?"

"No, no, you're thinking in the wrong paradigm. These people are not Persian. They're altruistic, liberal Westerners just like Corbin Odell. They're not spies operating under NOCs. They're real doctors working for a real NGO."

"Oh, I didn't realize," he said, suddenly thinking that maybe he hadn't studied up on this part of the mission as well as he should have. "What about our two dead escorts?"

"They *were* Persians and working as paid Mossad assets. That's not important. All you need to remember is that we're coming from Marivan. We were working there when the Israeli raid happened. Our facility was damaged in the attack, and we're angry and upset."

"Should I behave overtly anti-Semitic?"

"Absolutely not. These type of people don't discriminate based on race, religion, or gender, but they are committed humanitarians and strongly antiwar. You and I were critical of Israel and its foreign policy before the attack. Now, we are furious."

Dempsey nodded. "All right, fine. I can do that. But I'm concerned about their response when we show up alone. The other assets are supposed to be our escorts."

"It'll be fine," she said.

"They're dead, Elinor. How do we explain that?"

She glanced at him, not hiding her irritation. "First of all, these people don't know about the border INFIL. They think we're coming from Marivan as a group of four. All that matters is that we had to travel from Marivan by ourselves."

"You're right, you're right," he said, shaking his head. "I'm sorry, just tired."

"It's okay," she said, her face softening. "I'm going to be doing all the talking anyway. You don't speak Farsi . . . or did you forget that, too?"

She laughed at her own jab, and he couldn't help but laugh with her.

"I'm telling you, Elinor, screw Sanandaj; we should have gone to Sandals," he said.

"I know. Skinny-dipping in the surf is so much more fun than dodging mortars and evading murder squads in the desert," she added with a wistful smile.

They kept up a lighthearted banter for the rest of the drive, and before he knew it, they had arrived at the outskirts of the city. Sanandaj, it turned out, was bigger than Dempsey had expected, but it was nothing like a Western city. Elinor drove to the city center, looped around the central fountain, and then drove straight to their destination.

"That's it," she said, driving past the two-story row house, which despite the early hour was lit inside. Dempsey scanned the street and neighboring residences.

"You see any problems?" she asked, circling the block.

"No."

"Good, me neither."

On the second time around the block, she parked their Toyota on the street in front of the house. Carrying only their backpacks, they walked to the door and knocked. A thirtysomething Caucasian woman answered. Her tousled platinum-blonde hair was uncovered and accented by a long blue streak running down one side; she was dressed in cutoff shorts and wore a Dartmouth hoodie unzipped low enough to show a little cleavage. There was nothing in her presentation that remotely met the Sharia rules of female conduct, modified or otherwise. She surprised him, however, when she greeted them in Farsi, a broad smile on her face. Elinor answered in Farsi, and the woman ushered them inside.

"Do you speak English?" Elinor asked as the door shut behind her. "My husband is not fluent."

"Oh God, yes. As you can tell, I'm not Persian," the woman said in an Australian accent. She laughed. "My name is Barbara. I'm the doctor on the Sanandaj team—well, we used to be a team. Like you guys, they're pulling us out. Everyone has to evacuate except for people with surgical and trauma backgrounds."

"I know; it's so upsetting."

"Where are the others?" Barbara asked expectantly. "I thought there were four of you."

"They never showed up. We don't know what happened, but Corbin thinks they decided to stay behind," Elinor said. "They are both from Marivan. Maybe it was hard for them to leave."

Smooth, Dempsey thought. *Very smooth—always defaulting to the core human emotions.*

"Well, hopefully they're okay," Barbara said. "We're glad you're here safe."

"Thank you. I'm Ameneh by the way—a critical-care nurse—and this is my husband, Corbin. He's a paramedic," Elinor said.

"Great to meet you, Barbara. And wonderful to meet another English-speaking transplant like myself. I'm from Ireland, and we Irish struggle with foreign languages, including English," Dempsey said with a self-deprecating smile, shaking the Aussie doctor's hand.

"I love Ireland. I spent a summer there during my university days," Barbara said, leading them into a living room where three others, a woman and two men, all Caucasian, sat conversing.

"I miss it, yeah, especially now with this war brewing," Dempsey said, smiling cordially at the others, who were dressed similarly to Barbara in sweatshirts and athletic shorts. Then, he saw another figure, a Persian male, leaning against the door frame to what looked like a kitchen beyond. Dempsey nodded, and the man nodded back, but the Persian's dark eyes seemed to drill into him.

"Where are you two headed next?" Barbara asked.

"We were thinking a Sandals Resort," Elinor added wistfully. "You?"

This garnered an ice-breaking chuckle from the group, and Dempsey felt the tension melt away.

"Actually, we're traveling north, to Gorgon," Elinor said.

"There's an opportunity to backfill the mission there," Dempsey added. "It seems the beach vacation will have to wait."

"That's very brave," said a long-haired young man with a thick German accent. "Especially now, with the Americans preparing for war."

"I think it's foolish," the other seated male said in an accent Dempsey pegged as Croatian. "You'll have to drive through Tehran."

"My love is nothing if not committed," Dempsey said, taking Elinor's hand and patting it. "We're not Israeli; we're not American. I think we will be okay."

The Croatian responded with a *good luck with your death wish* shrug.

Dempsey glanced at the Persian in the doorway. His spidey sense was tingling. Something was off about this guy, and he didn't like the vibe.

"Come; have some coffee," the other, heavier-set woman said with a distinctly London accent. "Unless you prefer to nap? We have a bed made up."

"Coffee sounds great," Elinor said and followed their hosts into the small kitchen where unwashed dishes lay piled in the sink and half-full coffee mugs lingered on the table.

"This is Farvad," Barbara said as they reached the doorway.

"Corbin," Dempsey said, holding out his hand and studying the man's dark eyes. "Pleasure to meet you, mate."

"The pleasure is mine," Farvad said, gripping Dempsey's hand with strong, calloused fingers. "I'm the interpreter assigned to the medical mission from the UN. Not everyone speaks Farsi like Barbara."

"Omigosh," said the heavyset woman. "Farvad is much more than an interpreter. He does it all. We couldn't get from A to B or even figure out how to get food and water, much less replenish supplies, without him. On top of all of that, he interfaces with the Iranian government to keep us out of trouble."

"I do what I can, when I can," Farvad said, releasing Dempsey's hand but holding his gaze.

"Glad you're on our side," Dempsey said, searching the other man's dark eyes for duplicity.

"I most definitely am," Farvad replied with a confident smile. "On your side."

Dempsey took a seat at the small kitchen table, positioning himself between the rear door of the house and Farvad, who went back to his post at the doorway, only this time facing into the kitchen. As Barbara poured them coffees, Dempsey eyed the Persian. Either Farvad was a VEVAK agent sent to murder them in their sleep, or he was a Mossad asset assigned to facilitate the next leg of their journey into Tehran. Odd that Elinor had not mentioned him in any of their conversations. He watched her talking and laughing with Barbara, completely unperturbed by Farvad's presence. She was so relaxed—too relaxed, in fact—and he didn't like it.

He didn't like it at all.

CHAPTER 30

Mossad TOC
Tel Aviv, Israel

Jarvis balled the fingers of his right hand into a fist and squeezed. The weakness was back, and it was not doing anything to help his already sour mood. Munn and Chunk were trying to make it back across the border at this very moment, and he was blind . . .

Blind because of bureaucracy.

"You need to get this shit deconflicted now, Smith, and I mean right now," Jarvis said, leaning over Smith's shoulder and staring at the blank terminal where their live satellite feed had been before going black on them without warning.

His Operations Officer held up a finger and then spoke into the microphone boom attached to his earbud: "I understand . . . No, believe me, Ian, I know exactly what you're dealing with . . . Yeah, we're standing by." Smith swiveled in his chair, looked up at Jarvis, and then cupping his right hand around the microphone said, "Don't worry. Baldwin's got this, boss."

Jarvis folded his arms across his chest and tapped his foot with agitation.

After two excruciating minutes, the monitor flickered and then refreshed with satellite imagery—first showing the mountains of western Iran from altitude, then repositioning and rapidly zooming to focus on a single DPV. The tactical dune buggy was moving fast and dragging dust behind it as Chunk and Munn—the last of the INFIL team—screamed west to safety in Iraq.

Smith shook his fists with victory as the vehicles crossed the magenta line overlay depicting the Iraq-Iran border. "Yes! They made it. Great work, Ian . . . Roger that, let's keep eyes on them all the way back to the rally point."

Jarvis tapped Smith on the shoulder. "I want to know how the hell we lost our eyes in the middle of the op."

"There was a stop-task order from the Office of the DNI floating out there, and NSA didn't know what to do, so they retasked our satellite. You know how it is over there. They're afraid of their own shadow if they think political fallout is involved, but Baldwin took care of it."

"I want to know how. How did he take care of it? You might think we're deconflicted now, but what about going forward? What happens when it's time for Dempsey and Elinor to EXFIL? We're in the middle of coordinating Ember's charter mission, the most dangerous operation of Dempsey's career, and we have some jackass at Fort Meade playing rice-bowl games. If that satellite gets retasked again—"

"It won't," Smith interjected. "Baldwin is well connected, sir, especially at Meade. It's been deconflicted on the inside at the deputy level."

Jarvis gritted his teeth and was about to lay into his Operations Officer for not getting "by name" confirmation when he saw Smith's gaze shift at the same time he heard footsteps behind him. Jarvis turned to see Harel smiling at them.

"If you have a moment, Director?" Harel asked and gestured to the metal staircase that led up to the glass cage he used for an office. Jarvis unclenched his right hand, and the sensation of pins and needles dissipated. He followed Harel into the office and closed the heavy metal door behind him.

"What are you doing?" Harel said, turning to face him.

"I'm trying to deconflict the clusterfuck known as satellite retasking," he growled.

"No, you weren't."

"Excuse me?"

"Smith was doing that; you were micromanaging."

Jarvis sighed, loudly. "I'm not in the mood for mentoring today. So, if you don't mind, I'd like to get back to where I'm needed."

"That is exactly my point. What are you doing here?"

"My job, of course."

"No, you're trying to do Smith's job. You're functioning here," Harel said, putting his hand at chest level, "when you should be functioning here," he continued, lifting his hand to his forehead. "You want to help your team? Let them deconflict at their level, and you deconflict at yours. You should be in Washington greasing skids, solidifying alliances, and trading favors. Don't get me wrong; you needed to come to Tel Aviv to negotiate this operation with me, but once we had the green light, you should have been on the first plane back to DC."

Jarvis took a deep breath and exhaled through pursed lips.

"You have a fine Operations Officer," Harel continued. "So let him run the operation."

"You're right," Jarvis said at last. "I let myself get lost in the weeds."

Harel reached inside his sport coat and pulled out a folded piece of paper.

"What is it?" Jarvis asked, accepting the document.

"It's a plane ticket home. The flight leaves in two hours. I have a driver standing by to take you to the airport."

"That's very generous of you, but I can take the Boeing."

"Leave your jet here. From what you have told me, your acting DNI is doing everything she can to put obstacles in your way. Take a commercial flight under a NOC. Don't give Catherine Morgan an opportunity to impound your asset in a power grab. And speaking of Morgan, you have to determine her motives, Kelso. Once you understand her endgame, the two of you either need to kiss and make up, or you need to bury her."

Jarvis nodded.

"It's time, my old friend," Harel said, putting a hand on Jarvis's shoulder. "Time to make good on that alliance we promised to forge on the beach two decades ago."

CHAPTER 31

Cyrus leveled his pistol at the paper target, fixing the iron sights on the head of the silhouette. He exhaled and then squeezed the trigger. The first round found its mark, and after a brief pause, he put a second round a centimeter above it. He fired double-taps after that in a tight cluster, hollowing out the target until the final two rounds passed through the hole, not even moving the paper. He was a born marksman, Arkady had said, one of the best young shooters the Russian had ever seen. The key, Arkady had instructed him, was to find a weapon and become intimate with it. He'd chosen the Arsenal Strizh 9 mm pistol, the new favorite of the Russian Spetsnaz. Its short recoil and in-line barrel operation meant improved accuracy over weapons employing Browning tilting barrels. The grip fit his hand, the weapon was well balanced, and at seven hundred grams, it felt substantial without the heft of a Sig Sauer. On top of all the technical reasons, he just liked the look of the thing. It was a formidable piece of hardware, and when he carried the Strizh, he felt like a killer.

He was about to recall the target when he felt a presence behind him. He set his weapon down on the counter in front of him and turned to find his uncle standing there.

"A nice cluster, Cyrus," Amir said. "I'm impressed."

"That was warm-up. Next target I move back to ten meters. Then fifteen. We'll see what you think then."

Amir cocked his head to look around Cyrus at the pistol. "Can I see it?"

"Sure, I guess," Cyrus said with a shrug and handed the weapon with its spent magazine to his uncle.

"The Strike One," Modiri said, using the English name for the pistol. "I hear it was conceived by an Italian and a Russian. An intriguing partnership—no one knows how to design beautiful things better than the Italians, and no one knows how to kill things better than the Russians. Can you imagine a joint venture between Ferrari and RAC MiG to produce a fighter aircraft? It would win every engagement because the enemy would find it just too beautiful to shoot down."

Cyrus couldn't help but smile. "I'd like to see that aircraft."

Amir released the slide and then proceeded to examine the pistol as if it were a fine diamond. "Polymer shell, ambidextrous design, good weight . . . very nice," he said and handed the weapon back to Cyrus.

Cyrus took the weapon and studied his uncle's face. This was the first time he'd seen Amir since the Israeli attack. Given his uncle's position at VEVAK, this did not come as a surprise, but he'd not even heard him come home the last two nights to sleep. The man was so haggard, he looked like he had one foot in the grave. It was insulting to ask after his uncle's condition, so instead he simply said, "I presume you're here because you have tasking for me?"

The Director of Foreign Operations nodded at him and said, "He's here."

Cyrus felt an immediate surge of adrenaline. "The American operator you've been hunting?"

"Yes," Amir said.

"In Iran?"

"Yes."

"Tell me where he is, and I will find him and put a bullet in his head."

"That is not the plan anymore, Nephew," Modiri said, the corners of his mouth curling up into a malevolent grin.

"But you said—"

"I've changed my mind. This man is much more valuable to me alive than he is dead. We're going to take him, and once he's in my possession, I will break his body, his mind, and his soul. Only after he has betrayed his country, his friends, and his principles will I permit him to die. And I promise, that honor I will gift to you."

Cyrus cringed; he didn't like what he was hearing. The American was a highly trained operator and assassin. Men like this needed to be dispatched as soon as the opportunity presented itself. *When you're hunting a lion, better to take the shot from a distance while the beast is unaware than when it's charging straight for you.* He smiled tightly at Arkady's voice in his head, trying to remember if his teacher had actually spoken these words or if his mind had forfeited his internal monologue to the Russian.

"What is the venue?" Cyrus asked.

"I don't understand the question."

"The venue for the operation to trap the American?"

"The Grand Bazaar."

"And how are you going to lure him there?"

"I'm going to tempt him with something he can't resist . . . me."

Cyrus made his face a blank slate, not wanting to anger his uncle with the skepticism he felt inside.

"Why are you asking all these questions?"

"I'm concerned, Uncle. This American is crafty. How is this information going to be communicated to the American without betraying the plan?"

"I have an agent inside the enemy ranks close to the situation."

Cyrus perked up at this. "Who?"

Amir scowled. "You know better than to ask such things."

"I apologize, Uncle," Cyrus said, seeing the pronounced displeasure on Amir's face. "It was presumptuous of me to ask, but I would feel much better if you permitted me to be part of the capture team. Let me help, please."

Amir shook his head. "You will get your moment with the American, I promise, but for right now I need you to lead a mission critical to Persian national security. Make no mistake, Nephew; history will judge this as the moment when Persia triumphed over Israel or begged surrender at the Zionists' feet. We have the means to turn the tide and win this war, but only VEVAK can deliver the victory, and I trust only you to see it done. The brief is in two hours in the SCIF. Don't be late."

"Yes, Uncle," he said, nodding his head deferentially.

"Oh, and one more thing," Amir said before he turned to take his leave. "Maheen says you expressed interest in resuming your university studies. Is that true?"

Cyrus squeezed the grip of the Strizh 9 mm he still clutched in his hand while forcing a smile. She was actually doing it—trying to force him out of VEVAK and back into civilian life. *Unbelievable.*

"I might have mentioned that I enjoyed my time at Moscow State University, but I never meant to imply—"

"You don't have to apologize. You're young and, well, I remember being young. I also remember what it was like at university," Amir said with a wan smile. "It's nothing to be ashamed of. Your profession and your education need not be mutually exclusive. I will look for an opportunity for you to become a student resident abroad in a place where I can put all your skills to work."

"Thank you, Uncle. That is very generous of you."

"Two hours. Don't be late," Amir said and then spun on a heel and left.

Cyrus turned back to the range. He retrieved the paper target, hung a new one, and sent it down range to the ten-meter mark. He reloaded his Strizh, chambered a round, and stepped into his firing stance. Then, as he leveled the weapon at the target, a very strange thing happened— instead of imagining he was taking aim at the American agent, his subconscious superimposed his aunt's face on the target. He hesitated a beat . . .

Then, he squeezed the trigger.

CHAPTER 32

Sheykh Hadi Neighborhood
Tehran, Iran
June 1
2345 Local Time

Dempsey's head bobbed with microsleep in the passenger seat of their little Toyota sedan as Farvad piloted the car through the city streets of Tehran. He was exhausted, both physically and emotionally. His brain knew that technically they weren't out of the woods yet, but his body apparently hadn't gotten the memo. Now that they were minutes from their destination, all his willpower and adrenaline spent, he was losing the war to remain conscious.

The drive from Sanandaj had been long and nerve-racking. They'd been stopped twice, but both times Farvad—who had filled the role of driver and escort—had expertly talked them out of the jam. Most surprising of all was that Elinor had kept quiet during both encounters. Maybe this was because of Persian gender norms, or maybe Farvad was just that good. Dempsey's pitiful grasp of Farsi was insufficient for him to do anything but guess the reason. It didn't matter now, he supposed; they'd made it.

"This is it," Elinor said, tapping Farvad on the shoulder and pointing to an apartment complex off to the right.

"Okay," Farvad said and pulled the Toyota along the curb.

Dempsey groggily turned to look at Elinor.

She looked nervous, more nervous than she'd been anytime in Tel Aviv or Jerusalem, more nervous than when everything went to hell on their INFIL across the border. He noted her respiration rate was elevated and she was fidgeting—something he'd never seen her do before.

"What's wrong?" he said, her nerves sending a fresh shot of adrenaline into his veins, perking him up. "Do we have a tail?"

"No," she said, shutting him down. She looked at Farvad. "Thank you, Farvad. Your performance today was excellent."

"You're welcome," the Persian said with a nod. "Now both of you need to get some sleep. I will pick you up tomorrow at the scheduled time."

"Were you able to procure the weapons and communication gear I requested?" she asked.

"Of course," Farvad said, flashing her a weary and placating smile. "Besides, without them, what would be the point of any of this?"

Farvad turned and nodded at Dempsey, who climbed out of the car and then opened the door for Elinor. They stood on the sidewalk, backpacks hanging from their shoulders, and watched Farvad pull away.

When the Toyota was gone, Dempsey turned to her. "Is there a problem I need to know about?"

"No."

"Then what's going on with you?"

"It's nothing," she said, scanning the street and sidewalk in front of the apartment building.

"Hey, look at me," he said, grabbing her wrist. "Look at me . . . We're partners, remember? My life is in your hands, and vice versa. If something has your antennae up, you need to tell me."

She exhaled and met his gaze. "I'm nervous. That's all."

"I thought you said this place was solid."

"It is . . ."

"Then what?"

"Trust me. You'll understand soon enough." She leaned in toward him. "Kiss me."

"Excuse me?"

"Kiss me," she breathed, "like you mean it."

"I don't think anyone's watching. There's nobody—"

Before he could finish his protest, her lips were on his. He tensed and tried to pull away, but she leaned into him, not taking no for an answer. The kiss, for all its awkward beginnings, quickly turned passionate. In the embrace, he felt a complex mixture of emotions from her—yearning and desperation, lust and apology. Before long, the tide had shifted, and when she broke for air, he was the one who chased her lips, hungry for more. They kissed until their chests were heaving and kissing was no longer enough.

Twenty years in the Teams, surviving countless impossible missions, gunshots, explosions, even a helicopter crash, and in the end, it's my dick that's going to get me killed, the voice inside his head scolded . . . and that was when he got angry.

"What are we doing?" he said, suddenly clutching her by the shoulders. "We're on a mission, for Christ's sake. This sort of bullshit is going to get us killed."

"No," she said, shaking her head. "We're newlyweds. It's a critical part of our legends for this operation."

"Then stop keeping me in the dark. Who are we meeting now? More doctors? Another Persian asset like Farvad? I don't like being surprised, so tell me, who are we trying to convince this time? Who?"

"The man in this house," she said, imploring him to trust her with her eyes.

"Fine. Be that way." He sighed. "But I'm only playing your little game for one more night."

"Thank you." She gave him a quick peck on the lips. "Are you ready to go?" she said with an impish grin, glancing down at the pronounced bulge in his pants. "Or do you need a minute?"

"You did this to me," he growled, readjusting himself. "And it's not funny."

"It's a little funny," she said. "It is."

Three minutes later, they were standing in front of a second-story apartment door. She took a deep breath and blew it out through pursed lips. Then, she knocked. With her free hand she quickly found and clutched his. Her nerves were making him anxious, and he instinctively slipped his right hand to the small of his back to search for the grip of the subcompact pistol that wasn't there.

A beat later he heard footsteps inside and then the door lock being unlatched.

"Smile," she whispered.

Grudgingly, he managed to force a smile as the door swung open.

The man standing in the doorway was in his midsixties, and gaunt. He stood about six feet tall, was balding with salt-and-pepper hair and a full beard—both neatly kempt. Behind wire-rimmed glasses, his eyes ticked from Elinor to Dempsey then back to Elinor, and his expression went from suspicion to elation in a heartbeat.

"Adina?" he said. "Is it really you?"

"Yes, Papa," she said, releasing Dempsey's hand and throwing her arms around the man. "It's me, Papa, it's really me."

CHAPTER 33

Sheykh Hadi Neighborhood
Tehran, Iran

The emotion Dempsey witnessed in the tearful father-daughter embrace at the threshold was not something that could be faked. Nor were the unbridled joy and adoration he saw in the man's eyes every time he looked at Elinor. And as Dempsey studied their host's features, he saw reflections of Elinor only possible by paternity. This man was indeed Elinor's father.

She'd brought him home . . . home to meet her father in Iran.

"Papa, I'd like you to meet someone very special," she said, wiping her eyes with the back of her sleeve and then taking Dempsey by the hand. "This is my husband, Corbin. He's from Ireland."

Thank God she'd added the Ireland prompt at the end, or he would have completely blanked on his accent. "It's an honor to meet you, sir. Even though we've never met, I feel like I practically know you. El . . . I mean Adina is always talking about you."

"This is quite a surprise, but a good surprise," the man said in accented English, extending his hand. "It's a pleasure to meet you, young man. And you don't need to call me sir. Ciamek will do nicely."

Elinor squeezed his hand, but he wasn't sure whether it was meant to compliment or chastise his performance.

"Come in, come in, please," Ciamek said and ushered them inside the modest but tastefully maintained apartment. He directed them to a sofa in the living room and then scurried into the adjoining kitchenette. "Can I offer you refreshments? Tea and cakes? Fruit? Water?"

"Whatever you have. Thank you, Papa," she said as they took a seat on her father's sofa. She sat snug up against him and rested her hand on his left knee.

When her father's back was turned, Dempsey glared at her for subjecting him to this incomprehensible blindside. She responded with the happiest, most painful smile he'd ever seen. In that moment, he saw her differently, and the profundity of what had just transpired hit him. Puzzle pieces clicked together in his brain. Their newlywed legend had been wholly Elinor's idea. From the day of Ember's arrival in Tel Aviv, Dempsey guessed it had been Elinor who had primed Jarvis that this mission needed to be a two-person operation. She'd planned to visit her father from the beginning. How long had it been since their last father-daughter reunion? Years? A decade? For the two of them to see each other would be nearly impossible. After all, she was an Israeli and he was a Persian . . .

His stomach suddenly went sour as the paradigm of what he thought he knew shattered like a glass temple and came crashing down all around him. Elinor wasn't an Israeli Jew; she was a Persian Jew, just like her father. Elinor Jordan, acting Director of the Seventh Order, was Iranian.

"Were you born here?" he whispered.

She swallowed and smiled. "Yes."

"Does Harel know?"

She turned to him, her dark eyes both piercing and pained.

"Of course."

A surge of anger welled up inside him, just as Ciamek returned with a tray holding three teacups and a plate of what looked like walnut cookies. Dempsey forced a smile.

"So, tell me," Ciamek said, setting the tray on the coffee table and taking a seat opposite them, "how did you meet, and why have you kept this big secret from your papa, Adina?"

"We met six months ago in Dublin," she said, rubbing Dempsey's knee. "I was there on business for the firm, and he was the project lead for our client."

"So was it love at first sight?"

"For her, most definitely," Dempsey said with Irish bravado. "I made her work to win me over."

"Oh, that's not how I remember it." She laughed, playing it up. "He practically begged me to go out to dinner with him."

"It's true. In Ireland it's proper custom to get down on one knee and beg when you ask a girl out on the first date."

"Is it really?" Ciamek asked, chuckling.

"No," she said, playfully slapping his knee. "This is how he always is, Papa. I think sarcasm was invented by the Irish."

Ciamek nodded at this and took a sip of tea. "Well, I'm very happy for both of you. I just wish you would have told me. I am sure the Zionists are watching everything you do; they spy on everyone. And now with them launching this war against Persia . . . Well, don't get me started."

"Papa," she said, her gaze imploring, "I want you to know we eloped. There was no wedding ceremony. I wouldn't do that to you."

Dempsey saw tears rim Ciamek's eyes. "Maybe we can have it here. How long can you stay?"

"Not long," she said, her voice cracking. "They don't know we're here. No one knows."

Upon hearing that statement, Dempsey actually began to feel nauseous. *What the fuck is going on here?*

Ciamek nodded, but his already pale face managed to somehow grow paler. "This is a very dangerous time. You should not have come here."

"I had to, Papa," she said. "I had to see you."

Ciamek looked at Dempsey. "I can see from your face she hasn't told you."

Whatever expression he was wearing, Dempsey erased it and made his face a blank slate. "Told me what?"

Ciamek smiled wanly. "That I'm dying." He shifted his gaze back to Elinor. "That's why you came, I presume. You got my last letter?"

She nodded and then turned to Dempsey. "My father has stage-four liver cancer. He announced this out of the blue in his last letter to me. He also told me he had two months to live. I'm sorry I didn't tell you."

Dempsey's mind was racing now, working out the only lie that could possibly salvage this ruse these two strangers were depending on him to tell.

"I always suspected as much," Dempsey said, wrapping his arm around her shoulders. "Why else do you think I agreed to make this crazy trip in the middle of a war?"

She leaned in and kissed him on the cheek.

"There's something I don't understand," Dempsey said. "And please know that I mean no offense in asking . . ."

"By all means," Ciamek replied. "Ask."

"How can you, an openly Jewish man, live here in Tehran?"

Ciamek laughed. "There are ten thousand Jews living in Iran, maybe more. Many of us live in Tehran."

"But you aren't afraid of persecution?"

"No, no. As a foreigner, you don't understand. The world doesn't understand. Persian Jews are a protected minority in the Islamic Republic of Iran. This was officially proclaimed by the Supreme Leader himself."

"But this is the same man who also has publicly decried Israel as a scourge that must be wiped off the face of the earth."

"It is a paradox, I know, but the Iranian government makes a clear distinction between Israeli and Persian Jews. The Israeli Jews are Zionists—champions of a Jewish state—and seen as a threat to Islamic hegemony. Persian Jews are a law-abiding minority, an important community in Iran contributing to the country's diversity and commerce. Persian Jews are business owners and taxpayers. We even have a representative in the Iranian parliament. There are five Jewish schools and thirteen synagogues in Tehran. The doors are open; people are free to come and go without need for security. In fact, I would argue that my synagogue is one of the safest places in the city . . . Of course, with this Zionist attack, that could change. I would not be surprised to see an upwelling of anti-Semitism in the coming days. And this is the problem for Persian Jews and something you need to understand—the greatest threat to our community is not persecution from the Persian regime; it is Zionist aggression."

Dempsey nodded, not sure what to say. He glanced at Elinor, certain that she must have a strong opinion on the subject, but she kept her silence, legs crossed and holding his hand. Everything Ciamek explained made perfect sense to Dempsey and confirmed the age-old adage that "all politics is local." Nonetheless, he had trouble swallowing the duplicity of the Iranian regime. Wasn't compartmentalized anti-Semitism still anti-Semitism?

With the soul baring complete and political-religious banter stalled, at least for the moment, Ciamek made a joke to break the ice. After that, he worked hard to turn the conversation toward the upbeat and make the most of what would—in all likelihood—be his final visit with his little girl. Dempsey let daughter and father do most of the talking, only jumping in to provide levity and tender imagined anecdotes from time to time. Eventually, Ciamek's eyelids began to grow heavy; he apologized but said exhaustion was forcing him to bed. He showed them to the guest room, gave his daughter a hug and kiss good night, and retired for the night.

Dempsey followed Elinor into the guest bedroom, and she shut and locked the door behind her. When she turned to face him, tears were streaming down her cheeks. She tried to speak, but the words caught in her throat, and all she was able to do was stand there, looking at him with her bottom lip quivering.

He was so angry with her. He felt duped and betrayed and used. He wanted to seize her by the shoulders and yell at her, but he couldn't. He just couldn't . . .

"Thank you," she finally managed with a tight smile. "I know this was not what you were expecting. I know you feel betrayed, but I had to . . . I had to do it for him. Now, he can die in peace, having passed the mantle of responsibility for my care to you. "

Dempsey screwed up his face at this last statement.

"Don't look at me that way," she said. "He is from a different generation. A different culture than you. It's a father's responsibility to protect and provide for his daughter. Marriage lifts this yoke from his shoulders. You gave my father the ultimate gift tonight. Please don't ruin it now."

His mind immediately went to Jake. He might not be a father to a daughter, but he was a father. He understood what parental obligation felt like. And he also understood the guilt and self-flagellation that came with believing one had failed to adequately shoulder that responsibility. "I understand," he said at last, completely abandoning his Irish accent.

She looked at him, vulnerable and with all her secrets laid out before him. "Do you hate me?"

He shook his head. "I don't hate you. I just feel foolish . . ."

"For what?"

"For wanting to believe the lie."

"You mean the lie that I could love you?"

He nodded but immediately picked up on the nuance in her words.

"It's not a lie," she said and took a tentative step toward him. "I'm already halfway there."

"You are?"

She nodded.

"In that case, I need to know—our day in Tel Aviv together, was any of that the real you, or was that just the woman you thought I wanted you to be?"

"That was the real me, just the real me rushing things along at light speed," she said.

"So all of it, our NOCs, you and me as a couple, it had nothing to do with the op. It was all for this moment?"

She nodded. "The op we probably could have executed as strangers. But not this. No way. This had to be real—for both of us. Otherwise my father would have seen it for a sham, and instead of making things better, I would have only made them worse."

"Why me? Why not pick Rouvin or Daniel?"

"No, it had to be you."

"Because I'm a dumb, gullible American, is that it?"

She took another step toward him and pressed her hand on his chest over his heart. "No, because we're kindred spirits, you and me. Soldiers who've sacrificed everyone and everything we've ever loved to fight for a world where people don't have to live under the shadow of tyranny. I saw it in your eyes the first time we met in Brussels. You've given everything for your country and asked for nothing in return. No one can appreciate John Dempsey better than I can. And the same is true in reverse."

Maybe her words were true; maybe they were bullshit, but he didn't care. With this woman, all of his guilt and regret and pain served as a bridge rather than a wall. She had entrusted him with the most intimate and important responsibility imaginable, granting her father's dying wish. He looked into her eyes and he longed for her.

She took a step back, dropped her headscarf to the floor, and lifted her shirt up and over her head. Next, she unbuttoned her pants, pushed them down over her hips, and let them fall to the floor. She paused a beat, meeting his gaze as if reconsidering, before she undid her bra and stepped out of her bikini briefs. Then, she stood in front of him, naked, vulnerable, and beautiful.

"My real name is Adina," she said, her shapely breasts rising and falling as her respiration rate began to pick up with anticipation. "This is all of me . . . Is it enough for you?"

"Yes, it is," he whispered, gazing at her and battling the hurricane of emotions he felt. He repeated the ritual and undressed in front of her.

She extended her hand.

He took it, and she led him to the bed . . .

Later, he lay on his side gazing at the exquisite naked woman beside him.

"What?" she asked, with sultry half-closed eyes.

"I've never been with a woman who looks like, well, you before."

"It's just a body," she said coyly.

"Just a body," he said, rolling his eyes and laughing. "Yeah, right."

They lay in afterglow for a long while, not talking, just touching. Eventually, he started to get sleepy. "Now what?" he asked, although not sure what answer he was hoping to hear from her.

"Now, we sleep," she said. "And tomorrow, we try not to die."

CHAPTER 34

The Grand Bazaar
Tehran, Iran
June 2
0935 Local Time

In principle, the plan was simple enough. Grab Amir Modiri, shove him in the back of a delivery van, and drive away. But like all simple plans, the devil was in the details. The first problem immediately apparent to Dempsey was that the Grand Bazaar was nothing like the Midrachov in Jerusalem where they had trained. Yes, both were shopping markets and had merchants peddling their wares, but the similarities ended there. With two hundred thousand vendors spread across twenty square kilometers, the Grand Bazaar was the largest market on the planet. The sheer enormity of it, coupled with the hustle and bustle of the crowd, was enough to make anyone's head spin, let alone a field agent trying to pull off a kidnapping in broad daylight.

Dempsey glanced up. Intricately painted Persian vaults, with pointed arches and intersecting arrases, lined the ceiling in this corridor. In the middle of each vault was a round opening, creating the impression you were standing beneath a giant iris looking skyward. He lowered his gaze and inhaled, taking a primal measure of this place. The air carried a mélange of odors: the sweet tang of brewed tea, the miasma of stale cigarette smoke, the zest of fruits and vegetables, the aroma of cooking spices, and the musk of woolen blankets and carpets. Everywhere around him people bartered and bickered, laughed and lolled. Dempsey felt like he had been transported back in time. This was how commerce had been conducted for 99 percent of human history—before the days of mobile phones, online shopping at Amazon, and twenty-four-hour global delivery compliments of FedEx. Here, shoppers had to rely on their five senses to assess quality and value, and to suss truth from mercantile chicanery. Here, commerce was a tactile experience, where relationships and shrewd bartering ruled the day.

"Have you ever seen anything like it?" Elinor asked as they walked across a particularly busy intersection.

"Never," he replied, remembering to use his Irish accent. "It just goes on and on and on."

As they made their way through the crowd, Elinor casually picked over this and that, moving from booth to boutique and so on. If he didn't know better, he'd have thought she was actually shopping; that's how relaxed and expertly she was playing her role. She moved as if she were gliding, her tall, lithe frame as graceful as a figure skater on ice. The turquoise headscarf she wore was tied loosely about her head and neck—a subtle cultural recalcitrance from a modern woman dressing in compliance without the desire to do so. She must have felt his eyes on her because she turned and met his gaze with a smile—a lover's smile—and it made his heart skip a beat. He smiled back, and then the SEAL in him woke up.

What the fuck are you doing, dude? This is not fucking vacation— you're on an op, Dempsey. Get your shit together.

He ran his tongue between his lower lip and his teeth and suddenly, desperately, craved a pinch of wintergreen snuff. The SEAL was irritated. The SEAL wanted to be kitted up and clutching a SOPMOD M4. The SEAL wanted embedded snipers covering their six, a second team moving invisibly among the crowd, and QRF with help in hot standby fifteen mikes out. But the SEAL didn't plan this op. The SEAL had been dragged on this mission without his team by the spook named John Dempsey who'd forfeited control to another spook whom he'd just met three days ago.

What the hell had he been thinking?

He hadn't, and that was the problem. The thirst for vengeance had degraded his judgment. The thirst for sexual and emotional intimacy had snuck up on him—some dormant, forgotten part of his psyche that he'd gravely underestimated—and degraded what had been left.

I shouldn't have slept with her last night. That was fucking stupid. Stupid, stupid, stupid . . .

The wireless earbud buried in his right ear canal crackled to life.

"Crusader, this is Rome," said Farvad, who was tasked as the primary driver. "In position."

A beat later, a second report came in: "Crusader, this is Tripoli," said the voice of their decoy driver. "In position."

Elinor uttered a coded response in Farsi, acknowledging the reports.

An Iranian security guard dressed in a light-green uniform shirt and black pants walked by Dempsey, eyeing him with suspicion. Dempsey pretended not to notice and just kept trailing after Elinor. This was the third security guard he'd seen since they began walking the Bazaar not ten minutes ago. Given the recent Israeli strikes, he was not surprised to see heightened security in public spaces such as this, but the extra scrutiny was going to make their job all the more difficult. The multiple diversions Elinor had planned to draw security away from their position would be all the more critical for their mission to succeed. Every member of their five-man support team was a Seventh Order asset, which meant he was placing his fate entirely in Elinor's hands. The pre-op brief had been conducted entirely in cyberspace on Elinor's computer, with all members logged in remotely to a dark-web chat room.

This was a nerve-racking first for him. He'd run plenty of operations with strangers before, but in all of these cases, any concern he might have had about tactical competence was backstopped by the reputation of the training pipelines his teammates had matriculated from—be that the Teams, Delta, MARSOC, AFSOC, FBI HRT, CIA SAD, et cetera. Any concern he had about individual motive and loyalty was also backstopped by the operator's affiliation with his command. Anyone with an American spec ops pedigree, even former operators now working as contractors, he knew he could depend on as a brother. But this was different. Everyone on his team was an unknown variable.

In addition to Farvad—whom quite frankly he didn't trust—and the other driver, they had three roving spotter assets moving in the crowd, none of whom he could identify by sight. Besides providing visual surveillance and tracking, the spotters were also responsible for executing the diversions with remotely detonated nonlethal charges designed to create chaos and draw Iranian security guards away from the objective.

How do we know Modiri will show? Dempsey had asked during the drive over.

Trust me; he'll show, was all Elinor had said.

Suddenly, that answer wasn't good enough for him, and he didn't know why. Something felt off about this whole thing, but he couldn't put his finger on it. He stepped up next to Elinor and took her right hand in his left. She gave his palm a little squeeze and then quickly released it. Elinor was right-handed, and that was her shooting hand, so he understood why holding hands was disadvantageous. But when she didn't even look at him, he casually asked, "Are you sure your *cousin* is coming?" using the code word they had selected for Modiri.

"Yes," she said, picking through a pile of woven leather bracelets decorated with beads, silver trimmings, and semiprecious stones.

"How do you know?"

She didn't answer.

He waited until the shopkeeper struck up a conversation with another patron to say, "Why here? It's a security nightmare."

At this she whispered, "Because it's noisy and crowded. The Grand Bazaar is his preferred venue to meet deep-cover assets face-to-face."

Something in the timbre of her voice was off. A sudden wave of nausea washed over him. "You? You're the asset?" he murmured.

She looked at him with a tight-lipped smile that morphed into an apologetic frown . . .

It seemed, to his great dismay, he had his answer.

CHAPTER 35

The Grand Bazaar

Cyrus wasn't supposed to be here.

He was supposed to be en route to intercept a convoy carrying a twenty-kiloton nuclear warhead, one of six warheads that Iran had managed to hide from the world despite the nuclear treaty and IAEA inspections. But sometimes disobedience was obligatory. His uncle's life was in danger, and only Cyrus could see it. Amir had already arranged a dedicated standby helicopter for his travel to intercept the convoy. By crashing this party, he'd simply elected to delay his departure by a few hours. If things went smoothly, no one would ever know he'd been here. If not, his uncle would be grateful for his intervention. The only other VEVAK operative with the skills to match the American was Rostami, and Rostami was dead. Cyrus was the last line of defense for his uncle. Amir would see that.

On the outside, he appeared calm and collected as he moved through the crowd, but on the inside his nerves were on fire. Something insidious was afoot; he could feel it in his bones. The American operator was here. This he knew with certainty because they had received confirmation from the mole. Cyrus had successfully linked in to the capture team's comm circuit on his arrival at the Bazaar; he knew VEVAK protocols and had his own transceiver, so it hadn't been difficult. Comms had been smooth and professional from the outset, and he'd been feeling good about the operation, until one of the spotters reported that Amir and Maheen were not at the rally point and he'd not been able to make visual contact. A beat later, someone's microphone transceiver started transmitting an ear-piercing squeal, rendering their comms useless. He couldn't even call the others to change the channel. The only good sign was that everything in the market was subdued—no gunshots, no screaming, no stampede of civilians fleeing an attack.

He was confident that his aunt and uncle had not slipped past him. Maheen would be difficult to miss with her brightly colored turquoise hijab. Cyrus wondered if the selection of the Grand Bazaar as the capture venue was Maheen's idea. It was too big, too crowded, and too tangled a labyrinth to pull off an operation like this without complication and collaterals. He didn't like it. Maheen had somehow managed to insert herself into the operation, but to what end he did not know. She was not a field operator, and her very presence jeopardized the mission. Someone who was not expecting to die would meet their end here today; the only mystery was who.

His heart rate picked up.

The mission clock in his mind was ticking down. He had to find his aunt and uncle before the American assassin did. He resisted the urge to pull the Strizh 9 mm pistol from the holster he wore under his shirt.

Patience, he told himself. *Patience.*

The passageway he was walking soon intersected a corridor, forming an atrium of sorts where the ceiling was decorated with intricately painted tiles and carved wooden arch supports. Round skylights punctuated each vault, creating a line of blue-sky circles providing light and ventilation. He pulled his gaze down from the Persian architecture and looked left, scanning the crowd for his aunt and uncle. Not seeing them, he looked right. He let his gaze meander along and over hundreds of heads moving this way and that.

Nothing.

He scanned left . . .

He scanned right . . .

Just as he was about to look the other way, he glimpsed a flash of turquoise in the crowd. He stepped into the river of foot traffic, his gaze fixed on a turquoise hijab playing peekaboo with him thirty meters away. Was this Maheen? As he bobbed and weaved through the crush of people, he strained to spot his uncle—Amir would be easy to recognize . . .

He sidestepped a merchant carrying a stack of boxes and a broad-shouldered figure came into view, standing beside the woman in the turquoise hijab. A shot of adrenaline dumped into his bloodstream.

Not his uncle.

This was the American.

At last, he finally had acquired his target.

CHAPTER 36

The Grand Bazaar

Dempsey stood frozen, his jaw clenched and his gaze fixed on Elinor. She was avoiding eye contact, still picking through the displays of handmade jewelry. No, this was not a dream. No, he had not misheard her. Elinor had just admitted that she was a double agent—the only remaining question was, where did her loyalties lie? Was she working for Israel or for Persia? That she had broken cover to reveal this to him now, of all times, was perplexing. Or had last night been the revelation and he'd been too dumb to connect *all* the dots, choosing instead to believe what she wanted him to believe?

She can't be VEVAK, he told himself. *Harel and the Mossad would have sniffed her out years ago . . . unless she's just that good.*

"Elinor," he said softly, slipping his left arm around her narrow waist.

"Yes?" she said, still not meeting his gaze.

"Look at me."

She hesitated a beat, and when she finally turned to look at him, he saw her eyes were rimmed with tears. There was no point in mincing words; he had to know the truth, and he had to know it right fucking now.

"Elinor, whose side are you on?" he asked, his voice low, calm, and steady.

A strange detached expression washed over her face. Then she started to laugh with a bizarre manic quality he'd never seen from her before. "I don't know," she said. "I don't even know who I am anymore."

He was no headshrinker. Hell, he was probably about as far from a psychologist as a guy could be, but he knew a thing or two about wrestling demons. He knew about the corrosive impact of managing the stress, guilt, and anxiety that came with this line of work. And he'd seen guys crack from the pressure . . . not many, but enough. Elinor was cracking, and the timing could not be worse.

He swallowed and then carefully, gently reached up and wiped a tear from her cheek with his thumb. "Last night, you said we were kindred spirits. Do you remember that?"

"Yes," she said, sniffling.

"Do you believe in destiny?"

"I don't know. I never did before, but now . . . maybe."

"Well, I do," he said, looking deep into her eyes, trying to coax her back from the emotional hell her mind was drowning inside. "We found each other for a reason. You said it yourself: you needed me for last night. To give your father peace before he died. Now I need you to fulfill your end of the bargain. I need you to help me execute this mission for the same reason. Can you do that?"

"I think so."

"Are we still a team?"

She nodded.

"Good," he said and pulled her in for a hug. As he held her, he looked over her shoulder, scanning the crowd. Amir Modiri stepped into his line of sight, not ten meters away. Time slowed to a crawl. Their eyes met. A chill chased down Dempsey's spine.

Then, the bombs went off.

Chaos erupted. People started screaming and running in all directions. It took Dempsey's mind only milliseconds to register that the explosions were the nonlethal concussion-grenade packages that his three roving accomplices had been tasked with detonating when "the package"—Modiri—moved inside the target zone.

He released Elinor and vectored straight toward Modiri. As he started to run, he couldn't help but wonder if the next thing he felt would be a bullet slamming into his back, fired from his partner's gun.

"Rome, Tripoli—Crusader One has eyes on the package. Stand by."

"Copy, One," came Farvad's voice in his ear.

His right hand found the grip of the pistol he had been given that morning and pulled it from the holster concealed under his untucked shirt. He sighted Modiri fleeing and holding hands with a woman in a turquoise headscarf and clothes matching those Elinor was wearing. He glanced over his shoulder to see if Elinor was with him and, to his relief, saw her sprinting at his side, lagging behind by only the length of a stride. Modiri darted down a narrow passage that intersected the main corridor. To Dempsey's amazement, this action was exactly what they had hoped he would do, as this passage eventually bisected an alley used by vendors to park delivery vehicles and unload goods for transport into the Bazaar. This alley was where Farvad was loitering with the delivery van. Modiri and his female companion, however, were not the only ones fleeing to the alley. Dozens and dozens of people, both patrons and vendors, were stampeding that direction as well. People were screaming behind him. A middle-aged man running beside him tripped, smashed into Dempsey's right shoulder, and then tumbled to the ground. Dempsey's reflexes took over; he maintained his balance, hurdled the tumbling pedestrian, and kept on running. He heard Elinor grunt to his left. He glanced over his shoulder just in time to see her falling, her legs having gotten swept out from underneath her by the tumbling man.

"Go," she shouted. "I'll catch up."

He looked forward and kept sprinting. His gaze swept the scene ahead until he spied the turquoise headscarf of Modiri's companion. He was closing, and a surge of anticipation gripped him. After everything he'd suffered, Amir Modiri was finally within his reach. Someone was shouting in Farsi behind him, a deep baritone voice, but he ignored it. A beat later, the shrill staccato pulse of a police whistle being blown in successive bursts overpowered all the other noise. He glanced back over his shoulder and saw he was being pursued by a green-shirted security guard, blowing a whistle and waving a pistol at Dempsey's back. This guy was a problem, and if he kept blowing that damn whistle, Dempsey would soon have an army of green-shirts converging on him.

Dempsey whipped his head back around to reacquire Modiri and caught a fleeting glimpse of the turquoise headscarf disappearing around a corner to the left, twenty feet *before* the alley.

Shit! Where are they going?

A gunshot rang out, and a bullet whizzed past Dempsey's head.

Dumb move. Very dumb . . .

He veered left, spun on his left foot, and put a single round in the forehead of the guard, spraying the crowd behind the man with blood and brains. A second later, his legs were churning again at full speed back on course. He quickly reached the passage where Modiri had turned and skidded to a halt. As he took a knee at the corner, Elinor pulled up beside him clutching her Jericho 941 PSL. Dempsey popped his head out low for a split second to sight around the corner and then pulled it back.

"Clear," he barked.

They rounded the corner in unison, him hugging the wall to the left, her sweeping to the right. The passage was oriented parallel to the alley where Farvad was parked, but it was shorter, coming to a dead end twenty meters ahead. A metal door slammed somewhere in front of them. He pointed two fingers at his eyes and then gestured to the second-story windows lining the building on the right side. She nodded and shifted her gaze upward to watch for snipers as he remained focused on the passage ahead.

Crowd noise from the corridor behind them was beginning to fade as they advanced farther down the narrow passage. He slowed as they approached a doorway on the right. The door was shut, and the doorway was too shallow to conceal a shooter. He tried the knob and found it locked. He glanced over his shoulder to check their six o'clock and, finding it clear, chopped a hand forward. They advanced to the next and final doorway five meters away, also on the right. He halted them at the threshold, but unlike the last door, this one was unlocked and slightly ajar. With hand signals, he instructed Elinor to clear right and he'd go left. Then, he whispered, "Three . . . two . . . one . . . go."

He pushed the door open with his left hand and crossed the threshold, leading with the pistol in his right. Instead of opening into a room, the door swung open onto a landing at the top of a flight of stairs. A steady plume of smoke billowed up from below, and a red neon sign glowed at the bottom of the otherwise dark stairwell, creating a strange otherworldly vibe. His mind christened this the "stairway to hell" as he sighted down into the gloom. A sweet, fruity smoke filled Dempsey's nostrils as he began the descent.

"What is this place?" he whispered.

"A *hookah* bar," she whispered back.

Although he'd never partaken, Dempsey was familiar with Middle Eastern water pipes from his time in Afghanistan, where some of the village elders he'd met relaxed by smoking shisha tobacco. The thought of infiltrating a dark, smoky lounge where a posse of armed undesirables and Persian mafia could be hanging out did not sit well with him. He wasn't kitted up, he had no team, no assault rifle, and his only backup was a double agent on the verge of a mental breakdown.

Fucking wonderful.

At the bottom of the stairs, they stepped onto another landing and were met by another metal door. He paused and gestured for Elinor to open the door. For this breach, it was imperative that he was unencumbered and could lead with both hands on his weapon. There was absolutely no telling what was waiting for them on the other side, no telling how many shooters had guns trained on this door.

He took a deep breath and nodded at her in cadence to his internal countdown.

Three . . . two . . . one . . . go!

Elinor pushed the door open, and Dempsey charged into the room sighting over his Sig Sauer. Instead of gunfire, he was met by a room full of wide-eyed stares. A beat later, fear and confusion spread like electricity through the lounge as he swept the muzzle of his weapon systematically across the room searching for threats. A middle-aged Persian man sitting on a stool behind a counter said something to them in Farsi. Elinor barked a reply, and the man pointed to the far side of the room.

"They went through there," she said to Dempsey, nodding at the darkened doorway on the opposite wall.

"I'll breach, but you'll have to cover our six. I don't trust any of these guys," he said, his gaze fixed on a young, burly Persian in the far left corner with hate burning in his eyes.

"Roger," she said.

Dempsey moved with purpose across the dim smoking lounge toward the doorway, scanning right and left. Elinor fell in behind him, turned, and backpedaled to keep pace, allowing her to keep an eye on the room. When he reached the doorway, he found a black curtain instead of a door. He took a tactical knee, shielding as much of his body as possible behind the door frame, and drew the curtain aside. Standing inside this back room, shoulder to shoulder, he saw a man and a woman, both pointing semiautomatic pistols at him. The man was Amir Modiri, and he could now see that the woman was Modiri's wife. From their body language, demeanor, and firing stances, he knew that both of them had field experience and had fired weapons under duress.

Two decades of experience as a Tier One SEAL—hard earned from conducting hundreds of compound raids, capture/kill operations, and hostage rescue missions—meant Dempsey knew immediately how this standoff was going to play out. The capture option was off the table. There was no time for deliberation. No time for second-guessing. No time for marveling that Amir Modiri—the villain responsible for taking away everything and everyone he'd ever loved—was finally standing in front of him. Only one man was walking out of this room alive, and that man was going to be John Dempsey. And so without a second's hesitation, he sighted and squeezed the trigger—dropping the VEVAK Foreign Operations Director with a round to the forehead.

At the same time, Modiri's wife fired two rounds at Elinor, hitting her in the back and sending her pitching face forward onto the floor.

"You have thirty seconds to escape, Mr. Dempsey," Modiri's wife said, lowering her weapon. "After that, I cannot save you."

He narrowed his eyes at her, then looked down at Elinor, who was lying in a growing puddle of blood.

"She's a spy. She works for my husband," the woman said. "You have twenty-five seconds before my husband's capture team figures out what happened and finds us."

"If she works for VEVAK, then why did you shoot her?"

"Because today, VEVAK needs to lose."

Dempsey slowly rose to his feet, keeping the muzzle of his Sig Sauer trained on the woman's chest and using every ounce of willpower not to look down at Elinor. In this moment, his feelings for Elinor were irrelevant. She was a conflicted, compromised double agent, and no amount of self-debate was going to solve the mystery of where her loyalties truly lay in the next five seconds. He forfeited absolute control of his mind to the operator inside. The operator would complete the mission. The operator would do what needed to be done. John Dempsey could sort out his feelings in the aftermath.

"The door behind me leads to the alley where your driver is waiting. Go now or you die."

"Your husband was my mission. Nothing else matters now," he said, walking toward her.

"That's not true," she said, all the color having completely drained from her face. "My husband has tasked VEVAK operatives to deliver a tactical nuclear warhead to Hezbollah. They are going to blow up Tel Aviv. You are the only one who can stop it, because you are the only one I can tell . . . Twenty seconds."

He looked into her eyes, and he knew with certainty she was telling him the truth.

"How do I find it?"

She squatted next to Amir and retrieved a tablet the size of a mobile phone. "There's a convoy transporting the weapon somewhere east of Tehran. The warhead will be transferred to a less conspicuous courier somewhere prior to reaching the Syrian border, and from there it will be driven to Lebanon. Each warhead has a tracking transceiver. I don't know how it works or if it is even still pinging. Take this and go," she said and handed him the device, tears streaming down her cheeks. "Fifteen seconds."

Dempsey glanced back at Elinor, who was still writhing on the floor.

Soldier up, barked the voice inside his head. *She's a traitor, and you—you can die another day.*

"Why are you doing this?" he asked, turning back to face the woman.

"Because the time has come for the vendettas of a few angry men to no longer determine the fate of millions of innocents. Now go—stop World War Three."

Dempsey's legs were already moving before he'd made the conscious decision about what he should do. He ran past Amir Modiri's dead body and the sobbing widow to the back stairwell leading up to the alley. He took the stairs two at a time, sprinting toward the top. He reached the top landing and barreled out the door into the blinding light of day. Squinting, he scanned the alley and saw Farvad waving frantically at him from the driver's seat of a white delivery van. The sliding side door of the van was open.

Gunfire popped behind him, reverberating up the stairwell.

Dempsey charged toward the van and dove headfirst into the rear cargo compartment as the van was already pulling away. He rolled and spun around, then slammed the slider door shut. He wanted desperately to look out the back window, but he resisted the compulsion, rolling onto his back to lie on the floor as they sped away.

"What happened?" Farvad yelled over his shoulder.

"It went bad," Dempsey said, dropping the Irish accent and clutching his head with both hands. His heart burned with angst at his having abandoned Elinor bleeding to death on the floor. SEALs didn't leave anyone behind. But spies and assassins—like the operator he had now become—did whatever the mission required. "They're dead, Farvad . . . They're all dead."

CHAPTER 37

The Grand Bazaar

Cyrus stared down at the young woman in the turquoise hijab bleeding on the floor of the *hookah* bar.

"Help me," she gasped, her eyes pleading.

He'd never seen this woman before. She might have been Persian, but also looked vaguely Jewish. It didn't matter who she was; she'd be dead soon enough. He kicked what he assumed was her pistol well out of her reach and then stepped past her into the back room. Inside, he found his aunt Maheen standing over the fallen body of her husband, clutching a pistol with tears streaming down her face.

"Was it you? Did you kill Amir?" Cyrus asked.

"No. Despite everything, I loved him too much to pull the trigger," she said.

"The American did this?"

She nodded.

"But you let him?"

She nodded.

"Why? I don't understand."

"Do you know why we never had children?" she asked, her voice catching in her throat.

"Because you were too busy with your careers."

"No," she said, laughing and crying at the same time. "It was my fault. Due to a genetic defect, my body was not able to conceive and carry children. But standing here, looking at you, the last Modiri, I'm grateful for my curse."

Cyrus shook his head, staring perplexed at the woman he'd secretly adored his entire life and now felt nothing for but contempt. "What are you talking about, woman?"

"You and your brother were my surrogate children. Your mother was like a sister, your father like a brother, and I loved all of you. But Amir drafted every Modiri male into service—service of an agenda of hate, murder, and revenge. Amir destroyed your family . . . *our* family. If we'd had children of our own, he would have conscripted them and I would have lost them, too. I tried to stop him with you, but he wouldn't listen. I tried to give you a way out before it was too late, but you're just as stubborn and deluded as he is."

She raised her pistol and leveled it at his chest.

He narrowed his eyes at her and then reciprocated. "You won't shoot me . . . just like you couldn't shoot your own husband."

She was crying now, her shooting hand bobbing with each sob.

He heard the sound of tires squealing and an engine roaring to life. That's when he noticed the staircase behind her. This entire conversation had been a ruse, a delay tactic to give the American time to escape.

Tricky, tricky bitch.

He squeezed the trigger twice and dropped her with a double-tap to the head. He walked over to her body, spat on her corpse, and said, "You're a traitor. You're not a Modiri in death, and you never were in life."

He charged up the back staircase and burst through a door into a brightly lit alley, but the American was nowhere in sight. He lowered his head in defeat. Thanks to Maheen, the American had won, and there was nothing he could do now to settle the score.

Then he remembered his mission, the mission he was supposed to be executing right now.

If I can't make the American devil pay for his crimes, at least I can make certain that his friends and brothers pay the debt for him. They will all die. Persia will be served, and the Modiri blood debt will be satisfied.

He tapped his breast pocket where he kept the orders with his uncle's signature. This was the final dagger, and he would plunge it into his enemy's heart.

CHAPTER 38

190 km East of Tehran
June 2
1135 Local Time

Cyrus's palms were sweating, and not because this was his first time in a helicopter. He scanned the skies from the copilot seat, fully expecting to see an Israeli F-16 materialize on the horizon and blow them out of the sky with an air-to-air missile. No matter how much it pained him to admit it, the Israelis owned the Persian skies. If his aunt had said anything to the American operator about the nuke before she let him escape, then he would have certainly warned the Zionists, and all suspected Persian convoys would be targeted. The sooner he took control of the warhead the better, because he had no intention of letting the warhead disappear or even find its way to Hezbollah. He had his own plans for the weapon now. One that would inflict pain directly on the American devils who had decimated his family.

The Artesh was utilizing a strategy similar to what the Pakistani military used to protect its nuclear warheads—subterfuge and mobility.

This particular convoy was carrying a Shahab-3C medium-range ballistic missile, which, if fired from western Iran, was capable of striking Tel Aviv. The Artesh had over two hundred Shahab-3 missiles in inventory and three dozen mobile launchers. This was one of three designed to be fitted with a nuclear warhead.

"There it is," the pilot said, pointing to three vehicles traveling in a line and kicking up dust on the road below. The convoy was organized in a sandwich configuration, with the mobile missile–carrier vehicle in the middle flanked by a Rakhsh APC up front and a KrAZ off-road 6x6 heavy truck in back. "What do you want me to do?"

"Call them, authenticate, then direct them to stop," Cyrus said. "Then set the helicopter down and let me out."

The pilot did as instructed; once the convoy braked to a halt in the middle of the road, he landed the helicopter fifty meters away, kicking up a tremendous dust cloud in the process.

With the rotors still spinning, Cyrus stripped off his headset, opened the passenger-side door, and climbed out. Ducking, he ran from the helo to the lead vehicle, where an Army officer and his First Sergeant stood waiting, their expressions tight with anxiety and irritation at this strange breach of protocol.

"What is the meaning of this?" the officer demanded.

Cyrus wasted no time with small talk and simply handed the man his papers and recited the ten-digit top-secret authorization code he had committed to memory. The officer read the signed orders and grumbled, "This is highly unconventional."

"I know," Cyrus said, taking the papers back. "But recent intelligence suggests that the Zionists have designated this convoy as an HVT priority. We're obligated to separate the payload from the missile."

The Army officer's face went pale at the implication of Cyrus's words: Cyrus would be taking the warhead while he would be forced to continue on with the missile—a doomed asset targeted for destruction by the next Israeli Air Force strike.

Cyrus shifted his gaze to the nosecone of the missile on the carrier. "Is the warhead installed?"

"No," the Sergeant said, answering for his superior. "That is a dummy nosecone. Authorization to mount the nuclear payload has not been given."

"Good," Cyrus said, glancing at the KrAZ truck in back. "It's in there, I assume?"

The Sergeant nodded.

"What about the technician responsible for mounting it? Is one traveling with you?"

"Yes, the technician rides with the warhead at all times."

"Good," Cyrus said with a malevolent smile. "Here's what's going to happen. The APC and the missile will continue on together. I am taking command of the KrAZ and custody of the warhead. I will need a driver, two soldiers, and the warhead technician. Understood?"

The officer and Sergeant looked at each other, their expressions both grim at the prospect of turning a twenty-kiloton atomic warhead over to a boy.

Cyrus picked up on the cue and said, "I understand your reluctance. After all, you have one of Persia's most valuable and secret possessions in your care, and you look at me and think I'm barely old enough to grow a beard. But I am Cyrus Modiri, nephew of Director Amir Modiri and a VEVAK operative with official orders approved at the highest level. It doesn't matter that I'm VEVAK and you're Artesh; we are on the same team. We have the same goal—to safeguard Persia and defend her from the Zionists who are trying to destroy us. What we do now, we do to protect the only weapon in our arsenal that can tip the balance of power. So, you call your superiors if you want, but they have already been informed of this operation. Every second we delay is a second longer we give the IDF to observe what we're doing and jeopardize the likelihood of our subterfuge going unnoticed."

"Very well," the Artesh officer said. "The warhead is now in your custody. I will have my Sergeant accompany you. Good luck, and may the grace of the Mahdi be with you."

CHAPTER 39

Route 48
Twenty-Five Miles South of Azadshahr, Approximately Two
Hundred Miles Southwest of Tehran
June 2
1445 Local Time

Dempsey looked at Farvad, the young man at the wheel who had risked everything to make the mission a success. Had things gone according to plan, he would be risking his life to smuggle Modiri out of Iran. As it was, he was still risking his life to drive Dempsey where he needed to be. He doubted there were many who would not have just disappeared when the operation went south. He had misjudged Farvad badly. But there were still questions that needed answers.

"Did you know?" Dempsey asked Farvad from where he sat cross-legged in the back of the van. "Did you know Elinor was a double agent?"

"Yes, but I had it backward," Farvad said. "She recruited me for Mossad. She confided she was a double, but I thought her loyalties lay with Israel."

Dempsey shook his head. "I still can't believe it."

"I know," said the Persian. "It doesn't make sense."

"I left her," Dempsey said, his stomach an acid bath of guilt and anger. "Bleeding to death on the floor . . . I left her."

"What else could you do? She was turning you over to them. It's clear."

"Is it? I don't know," he said, hearing himself echo Elinor. "I don't know anything anymore."

What was really going on? Who were his allies? Who were his enemies? How had they escaped Tehran so easily in this white panel van after a massive attack in the Grand Bazaar? Who was helping them now? Was it Modiri's wife? Had she tricked her husband and walked him into a trap in that hookah bar? Where had his security personnel been? Nothing made sense.

"Listen to me," Farvad said. "I know you're upset and so am I, but you need to tell me what to do. I was not trained for situations like this. How do we stop this nuclear weapon? We are only two."

Dempsey ran his fingers through his hair and did two rounds of four-count tactical breathing to center himself and clear his head. When he was finished, he said, "First and foremost, I need a phone. There are people I can call to help if you can find me a fucking phone that works."

"I have a mobile phone, but there is no coverage here. The network has been weak and unreliable since the Israeli attack."

"Then we need to find a satellite phone."

"I d-d-don't know where," Farvad stammered, his nerves finally starting to get the better of him.

"There must be more people like you we can contact—assets that can help us get word to my people."

"Okay, okay, let me think . . ."

"And we need firepower," Dempsey added, pulling the one weapon he had—the subcompact Sig Sauer—from where he'd tucked it in his waistband. "Real firepower. Something we can actually use to assault an armored convoy."

"Okay," Farvad mumbled, as if Dempsey were asking him to turn water into wine.

"And fighters," Dempsey continued. "Real fighters who can help assault an armored convoy."

Farvad seemed to deflate in the driver seat at this, and then suddenly he sat up straight. "I know what to do! I know where to get all of these things."

"Where?"

"There is a man who lives in Iranian Kurdistan, not too far from here. He was a leader in the PJAK as recently as a few months ago. He will have a satellite phone, he will have guns, and he will know fighters who can help us," Farvad said, his bravado back in earnest.

Dempsey knew little about the PJAK—aka the Kurdistan Free Life Party—only that they were a resistance group dedicated to Kurdish self-determination. The PJAK employed both political and militant tactics in dealing with Tehran and was officially labeled as a terrorist organization by Iran, Turkey, and, oddly, the United States.

"Do you really think he'll help us?" Dempsey asked.

"Yes, his daughter fought under Gulistan Doganin, the PJAK Women's Defense Forces, but she was killed by an IRGC counteroffensive in 2011. Believe me; he will help us."

"Okay, let's do it. How far?"

"Forty kilometers, plus or minus," Farvad said.

Dempsey nodded, and the two men rode in silence for ten minutes until Farvad began to slow.

"What is it?" Dempsey asked, popping his head up.

"Look," Farvad said, the tenor of his voice suddenly crisp and urgent.

Through the dusty windshield, Dempsey saw two armored pickup trucks blocking the road ahead.

"What should I do?" Farvad asked. "Should I turn around?"

"No," he barked. "Then we look guilty. They'll pursue us for sure."

"Then what do I do?"

"Go to the checkpoint, stop, and try to act normal," he said, ducking down in the back and pulling the black curtain across behind Farvad's seat to hide the cargo area.

"Normal?" Farvad said.

"You have papers for the van, right?"

"Yes."

"Okay, then get out your papers and have them ready. Be cooperative. Be polite."

And let fate decide, he thought, keeping the macabre sentiment to himself.

"All right, I'll try."

As Farvad braked, Dempsey pulled out his pistol, checking that a round was chambered. He had used two rounds in the Grand Bazaar—that left thirteen rounds in the weapon. "How many soldiers do you see?" he asked Farvad through the curtain.

"There are two soldiers in front of the trucks," Farvad said. "And . . . there are two other soldiers behind the trucks. I see nobody in the driver's seats. The truck on the right has a big machine gun."

"Is the machine gun manned?"

"No."

"Okay, listen carefully," Dempsey said, taking a knee in the center of the empty cargo area of the van. "If soldiers demand to check the cargo area, cough. Then, cough one time for each soldier walking back. If they man the machine gun, you say *inshallah*. Understood?"

"Yes."

"Is your weapon accessible?"

"Yes. It's under my shirt."

Dempsey felt the van slow and then settle to a gentle stop. He tensed but took two four-count tactical breaths and felt his pulse slow.

Next, he heard the squeak of the window coming down and then Farvad speaking in Farsi. If a security alert on a white panel van had been issued, they were dead. If not, they probably had a coin-flip chance of surviving. Even if they opened the cargo doors, so long as nobody manned the machine gun and Farvad managed to take out one guard, they could probably pull it off. Death had been his dancing partner for years and always let him go when the music stopped. He smiled wryly.

Two more dances, he mouthed silently. *This and one more. That's all I ask.*

He listened carefully to the exchange happening at the driver's window—the Farsi words meant little, but the tone, the inflection . . . That spoke volumes. The interrogating soldier's voice was stern and commanding, but not full of stress. He detected arrogant belligerence, maybe, but nothing to suggest the soldier believed he'd apprehended the getaway vehicle housing the assassins who had just killed a high-ranking VEVAK official.

Farvad coughed—once.

He said something in Farsi, then coughed twice more in rapid succession. More talking, then another cough, but Dempsey couldn't tell if it was from Farvad or the soldier at the door. He gritted his teeth. Shit, was it two or three? He readied himself, leveling the muzzle of his Sig at the vertical seam between the two windowless back doors. He tried to recall if he'd seen the rear of the van from the outside. Which door opened first? It made a difference.

He dropped his gaze and saw that the left-hand door had a paddle handle and a toggle lock. His mind projected the most likely scenario: one soldier standing slightly offset behind the left door, the other standing a pace behind and centered, sighting over a rifle pointed into the cargo hold. Dempsey exhaled slowly and moved his index finger onto the trigger.

The door handle clicked.

The left door opened, but after a few inches it stopped. One of the soldiers said something to the other. Dempsey's pulse was pounding in his ears like a bass drum, and he couldn't make out if the other answered.

He gritted his teeth.

Open the fucking door . . .

The door moved a fraction of an inch . . .

His index finger twitched . . .

Then the door swung open.

In a millisecond, his eyes confirmed what his mind had previsioned: two men, one with a rifle at combat ready dead center, the other offset with his hand on the door. Dempsey fired twice, felling the ready shooter with two headshots. He shifted his aim left, targeting center of mass on the second soldier, who was backpedaling and trying to raise his rifle. Dempsey's first round caught the man in the left chest as he ducked behind the door and out of the line of fire.

Behind Dempsey, at the front of the van, two pistol shots rang out. Dempsey prayed this was Farvad firing, but he didn't dare look back. Instead, he leaped from the back of the van, twisting in midair to get eyes on the second soldier he'd wounded. The man was on his hands and knees, crawling away. Dempsey landed in a crouch and fired once, the bullet hitting the crawling soldier in the back of the head. He spun around, dropped flat, and sighted under the van. A soldier lay crumpled against the side of the van along the driver-side doorsill.

Hooyah, Farvad.

Three down, one to go.

An instant later, Dempsey was back on his feet, scanning over his pistol and trying not to cough from the dust. He moved in a combat crouch along the passenger side of the van, fully expecting the fourth guard to be making a beeline toward the pickup with the machine gun. No matter what, Dempsey had to make the shot before that happened. As he cleared the front of the van, he spotted the fourth soldier. But instead of running toward the heavy gun, this guy was running away down the dusty road. Dempsey sprinted after him, closing the distance while veering right for a better angle. When he reached the armored pickup trucks, he skidded to a halt, dropped to a knee, and sighted. Steadying his shooting hand with his left, he squeezed the trigger twice. The soldier jerked midstride, stumbled, and fell. After a moment, the wounded soldier struggled to his knees and tried to get back to his feet, but Dempsey fired again—this time a headshot pitching the man forward.

Dempsey ran his tongue across his teeth, coughed up what felt like an entire lungful of moondust, and spat until he cleared his mouth of gritty desert.

"When they stopped us, I was sure we were dead," Farvad said, running up to him.

"If you hadn't handled the guy at your window, we probably would be," he said, realizing that this might have been the first time Farvad had killed. "You did well."

"Now what do we do?" the Persian said.

"We take that," Dempsey said with a crooked smile, fixing his gaze on the six-barrel, Gatling-type Muharram machine gun in the back of the armored pickup, "and we haul ass to meet your PJAK friend."

CHAPTER 40

National Counterterrorism Center
McLean, Virginia
June 2
0630 Local Time

For the first time in days, Jarvis smiled.

Somehow, they'd done it. They had confirmation from Harel's assets in Tehran that an event had occurred at the Grand Bazaar. Despite missing the last check-in, the white van Dempsey and Elinor were using for egress was confirmed via satellite as heading west out of Tehran. While the tactical picture was far from definitive, it would appear that despite the odds, John Dempsey had actually managed to kidnap the most dangerous man on the planet. With Amir Modiri in their custody, he would be able to hand President Warner the perfect scapegoat he could use to broker a de-escalation between Tehran and Tel Aviv that would allow both nations to save face and stop the angular momentum of war.

Despite not having comms with Dempsey and Elinor, Jarvis wasn't nervous. He'd taken Harel's advice to heart and delegated the supervision of Dempsey's EXFIL to Smith in Tel Aviv. He'd resisted the compulsion to plant himself in the Ember TOC and take control. Smith could do this without his help. And besides, this was John Dempsey they were talking about . . . God help anyone who tried to get in his way.

There was a knock at the door.

"Come," he barked.

The door opened, and a young woman, dressed in the modern-day counterterrorism uniform of blue jeans and a Pink Floyd world tour T-shirt under a denim jacket, stepped only partway in. The staff at the CTC was not sure what to think of Jarvis taking over an office here—though an order from the President of the United States to accommodate him squelched any complaining.

"Sir," the woman said sheepishly, reluctant to break the plane of the threshold with any part of her body.

"Yes, what is it, Abby?" he asked. At least the cerebral portion of his nervous system was still functioning normally, he thought, flexing his tingling left hand.

"I have a call for you. Is it okay to forward it?"

Jarvis smiled and swallowed his impatience. Of course it was, and he wondered who at CTC had conditioned her to fear expediency.

"Who is it?"

"A Mr. Smith," she said, her sarcastic tone telling him she suspected otherwise.

"Put it through," he said, and then before she closed the door, "Oh, and Abby?"

"Sir?"

"Luck or skill?"

She gave him a deer-in-the-headlights look at the non sequitur.

"If you could only have one, which would you choose—luck or skill?"

"Skill," she said without hesitation.

He nodded at her. "Thank you; that will be all."

Skill. He chuckled to himself. *When I was her age I would have answered the same. Now, I'm not so sure.*

The desk phone chirped and he picked up the receiver. He cursed again the fact his encrypted cell phone wouldn't work inside the NCTC nerve center, scrambled by the same energy waves that disrupted any unvetted signals going in or out.

"Jarvis."

"Hey, boss, it's Shane. We've got issues. Are you watching the satellite feed?"

"No," he said, afraid he was about to regret his decision to delegate.

"Harel's guys found the van we think Dempsey's in. We've been following it since the outskirts of Tehran."

"And?" Jarvis asked, not liking where this was going.

"And he's going the wrong way, and they're about to run into a checkpoint. You need to pull this up, sir."

"Wait one," he said, sprung from his chair, and threw open the office door. "Abby, I need you," he snapped, but the young analyst was already heading his way. He put Smith on speaker, and the two of them worked together to get the Israeli satellite feed patched to CTC and streaming on his desktop monitor.

"Shit," Smith said as they watched the scene begin to unfold in ultra-high-resolution detail in real time.

"Oh my God," Abby mumbled as they watched Dempsey defy the odds and kill three Persian soldiers in less than a minute. Dempsey and his Persian driver then proceeded to gather the assault rifles and spare magazines from the dead Iranian soldiers and load the weapons into the back of one of the armored assault trucks.

"Is that a Gatling gun in the back of that pickup?" Smith said.

"What the fuck is he doing?" Jarvis growled as Dempsey climbed into the passenger seat. "Where is Modiri?"

"I don't know, sir," Smith said. "Hopefully still in the back of that panel van and the asset is going back to get him."

But when the Persian driver got into the pickup truck with Dempsey and the two of them sped away into the desert, Jarvis's heart sank. "I didn't see Agent Jordan. Has Elinor checked in?"

"No, sir."

"Goddamn it!" Jarvis barked and slammed his fist on the desk, making Abby jump. "If Modiri is not with them, then it means he got away, or he's dead."

"I fear you may be right," Smith said.

"And what the hell is Dempsey doing?"

"I think he's just trying to survive, sir. The Artesh has these checkpoints set up all over the country. It didn't matter which direction they went; it was inevitable that they'd get stopped. I don't think he had a choice, and now he's just trying to get enough firepower to fight his way out."

"Then what the hell are you waiting for? Stand up an operation to get him out of there."

"Yes, sir, but that's the other thing I needed to talk to you about. Our friend sitting in the DNI chair is fucking that up," Smith said. "There's a stand-down order for the EXFIL mission I was prepping to get Dempsey out."

"What?" Jarvis roared. "And you traced it to the acting DNI?"

"Yes, sir," Smith said. "Baldwin actually has the order in hand—he snagged it off the OGA server. It went out to all theater assets."

Jarvis tamped down his rage and let the analytical part of his brain take control. There was absolutely no way that Morgan knew details of this operation. All she knew was that Ember was in Israel and Iraq, and she was doing everything in her power to fuck them, with no thought to what her actions would have on living, breathing operators in harm's way.

What a bitch.

"Where are we?" Jarvis asked.

"I have Chunk on board, but the stand-down order is curtailing our access to other assets. We could use drones, air, and satellite support. If it wasn't for the Israelis we'd be blind. We're about to lose the feed we're using now in just a few minutes. We won't be able to see him at all if I don't get some support. I'm struggling to even get—"

"I'll handle it," he said, cutting Smith off. "Give me ten minutes and you'll have everything you need."

"Yes, sir."

"If you don't hear from the JSOTF commander by then," Jarvis said, "call me back. And Shane?"

"Sir?"

"From what I just saw, Dempsey's about to have the entire Iranian Army hunting his ass down. He's not going to make it to Iraq. We're going to have to go get him."

"Understood, sir. Smith out."

He hung up the phone with a look that told Abby he needed the room.

"I'll be right outside if you need me," she said.

He nodded at her and then dialed a five-digit number. The phone clicked live in half a ring.

"Century," a crisp, calm voice said.

"I need to speak with the President," he said. There was no need to identify himself. That he had the number was enough.

"Yes?" said President Warner two minutes later.

"Mr. President, it's Kelso Jarvis. Sir, I need your help to shut down Catherine Morgan before she gets my people killed."

The President sighed. "I thought I told you two you needed to work together."

"Yes, sir, Mr. President, and that's a work in progress, but right now I'm out of time."

"What exactly are you asking for, Captain Jarvis? And be precise."

"Respectfully, sir, I need her offline for the next four hours. I need unhindered JSOTF cooperation in Iraq to organize a rescue operation. Can you help me?"

There was a short pause and then, "I'll take care of it, Kelso, and in exchange, I expect you'll deliver good news—the kind of news that will save many, many lives."

"Yes, sir," Jarvis said.

The President clicked off.

Jarvis tapped the receiver again and then dialed 2 on his keypad.

"Yes, sir?"

"Abby, I need to speak with Tom McCaffery, the JSOC commander, immediately."

"Right away, sir. Do you have a message you want me to pass?"

"Tell him Kelso Jarvis needs a favor and that it's urgent."

"Understood," she said in a flash.

Jarvis placed the phone back in its cradle and massaged the palm of his left hand with his right thumb. McCaffery was a good man. The General and Green Beret always put the mission ahead of politics. He'd free up whatever theater assets Jarvis needed.

Besides, Jarvis had been holding a favor chit with Tom for over twenty years. As young officers in JSOC, Jarvis had bailed the Green Beret out of a situation during a joint op that had nearly cost McCaffery his life.

Time to finally cash that chit in.

CHAPTER 41

Route 17
Southwest Iran, 250 Miles from Tehran and 40 Miles from the
Iraq Border
June 2
1615 Local Time

Dempsey glanced at the driver-side mirror and the massive cloud of dust billowing skyward in the distance behind them. From the looks of it, the entire Iranian Army was after them. Despite being barely able to maintain control of the truck on the pitted and pocked desert road, he pressed the accelerator down just a bit more. The machine gun mounted in the bed of the truck was formidable, but it alone was no match for the force coming after them.

"We have a problem," Farvad said, his voice tight.

"You think so?" Dempsey said with all the fatalistic sarcasm he could muster. Then he saw the new threat that Farvad had been referring to through the windshield—an armored troop carrier racing up from the south on an intercept course.

"Oh shit," Dempsey said, but at this point did it really make any difference? They were fucked. Totally and completely fucked. And it felt surreal. And it felt like nothing. Or maybe, it just felt like destiny . . .

"Slow down; we're almost at the turn," Farvad said, grabbing his shoulder.

"Where?"

"Right there," he hollered. "That dirt road!"

Dempsey slammed the brakes and jerked the wheel hard to the right. Farvad flew across the bench seat and nearly into Dempsey's lap as the truck careened around the corner. Because of the machine gun, the vehicle's center of gravity was higher than Dempsey anticipated, and the right wheels lifted off the ground. The truck yawed, and his gut tightened in preparation for the inevitable roll. But his reflexes took over, cutting the wheel left and reversing the moment of inertia. The right tires slammed back down onto the earth, and Dempsey flashed Farvad a victory smile. He guided the heavy pickup through the rest of the turn and avoided skidding off the road into a deep, rocky ditch by no more than six inches.

"We have one last hope," Farvad said. The young Persian's face was pale with fear, but his eyes were on fire with the will to live. "If PJAK is here, they'll fight with us."

Dempsey grunted acknowledgment as he bounced violently, unable to keep his ass planted on the seat as they raced over the rock-strewn road. As abysmal as this road was, the fields on either side were categorically impassable, with deep gullies and boulders the size of Volkswagens. Dempsey glanced in his mirror. The troop carrier had reached the turn, but there it had stopped, probably calling in for instructions on what to do next. Given he'd just killed Amir Modiri, Dempsey suspected that Iranian higher authority would prefer to take him alive. They'd want to interrogate him and then make an example of him to the world. There was no way in hell he would let that happen.

Farvad leaned forward, squinting through the dirt-covered windshield at a brown, two-story house, which appeared to be practically carved into the side of the rocky hill that rose behind it.

"This is the place," Farvad said.

"The number one priority is getting that sat phone. You understand?"

"Yes."

"If I can't call my friends, we're dead, Farvad."

"I know, I know," the Persian said. "But will your friends make an incursion this far over the border?"

Dempsey exhaled loudly through his nose and said, "Yeah—that's what they do."

They have to, he thought to himself, *because we have a nuclear bomb to stop.*

Dempsey braked and pulled the truck along a low rock wall in front of the house; then he backed it into position so it blocked the entrance to the short driveway. Farvad was out the passenger door in a flash, sprinting toward the house.

"I'll hold them here as long as I can," Dempsey hollered after him and then turned to look out at the approach. Then he had a thought and said, "Set a fire by the house to mark our position!" Farvad gave a thumbs-up over his shoulder.

The Iranian trucks and the troop carrier were now formed up in a semicircle at the entrance to the dirt road, maybe three-quarters of a mile away. He could see soldiers climbing out of the vehicles and fanning out, taking positions in the ditches along the road and behind the scattered rocks. Dempsey climbed out of the driver's seat and into the bed of the truck. They'd acquired four KH-2002 Khaybar assault rifles from the soldiers they'd killed at the checkpoint, and three of those weapons were in the bed; the fourth was with Farvad. He picked up one and checked that it was ready. He was happy to see two extra magazines of 5.56 in a pouch on the stock. Assuming all the Khaybars were fully loaded, they had roughly 350 rounds of ammunition. That sounded like a lot, but it would go very quickly.

Next, he checked the Muharram heavy machine gun and verified it was loaded and ready for combat. The Muharram was a modern Gatling gun, similar to the US military's M134 Minigun that utilized six rotating barrels to help prevent overheating. But unlike the Minigun, which fired 7.62×51 mm NATO rounds, the Muharram used 12.7 mm ammunition—making it arguably the most badass .50-caliber machine gun on the planet. Dempsey checked to see that the two wooden ammo boxes sitting on the truck bed were full and was relieved to see that he hadn't lost his ammo on the wild ride up the dirt road. He had no idea the maximum effective range of this weapon, but if it was like other .50 cals, fifteen hundred to two thousand meters would not be a problem. That meant he could not only reach the entrance to the dirt road, but he'd be able to strafe approaching vehicles coming in from either the north or south along Route 17.

He had the range. What he needed was time.

He watched as dozens and dozens of Iranian troops scattered in the fields, taking up positions behind rocks and boulders on both sides of the dirt road. If they wanted him dead, this battle would not last long. He was hopelessly outnumbered and outgunned. But if they hoped to take him alive, and he could get Chunk on a sat phone, he might just have a chance.

But if the Iranians had air assets en route, then it was game over.

Dempsey shook his head and smiled. This situation reminded him of his father's favorite movie—*Butch Cassidy and the Sundance Kid*—a film they'd watched together countless times when Dempsey was a kid. This standoff was shaping up to be a real-life reenactment of the final scene of the Hollywood classic, all except for the nuke, of course.

He heard commotion behind him, turned, and saw Farvad sprinting toward him, Khaybar rifle in his right hand, a Russian made AK-47 slung over his shoulder, and a satellite phone held out in his left hand.

Dempsey looked back toward the battlefield, scanning for new developments, and saw two clusters of soldiers on either side of an APC setting up mortars.

Great . . . Not this again.

"It's for you," Farvad said, panting as he jumped up into the truck bed beside him.

"How did you—" Dempsey asked, staring wide-eyed at his Persian accomplice.

"I called my Mossad contact, who called the Chief, who called a man named Smith, who called somebody called Chunky," Farvad said, handing him the sat phone.

"Chunk," Dempsey corrected, smiling broadly as he took the phone, pressed it to his ear, and said, "Crusader."

"I thought I told you if your ass needed a rescue not to call me," Chunk's voice came back, along with the distinctive sound of MH-60s spinning up in the background.

"In case you haven't noticed, I have a problem following directions."

"I'm spinning up two birds right now. We got you on satellite, and I'm in the air in two mikes. We're coming to get you, bro."

"Bring lots of friends, cuz it's going to be a party."

"How bad is it?"

"Remember that time when we crashed that Russian bird in the Wild West and we were completely surrounded by bad guys with machine guns and rocket launchers?"

"Yeah."

"This is way worse."

"In that case, you just do that Rambo shit you do, and hang on as long as possible. The cavalry is coming."

"Roger that. I'll give you smoke just west of our position. We are the heavy pickup in front of the fire near the house, and everything east of us is the enemy."

"Copy," Chunk said. "Before I go, Eagle has a question. Do you have the package?"

"Negative," he said. "We are two. I repeat, we are two."

"Copy."

"There's more, Chunk. We have another problem—"

But before he could tell the SEAL about the nuke, white smoke streaked skyward from a mortar tube beside the Persian troop carrier.

"Oh shit," he exclaimed. "Gotta go."

Dempsey dropped the phone and dove into the bed of the truck, taking cover inside the armored bedrails. The rocket exploded harmlessly well right and at least sixty yards short.

Dempsey scrambled to his feet, taking position behind the Muharram and turning to Farvad as he did. "Great job with the phone," he said. "And I see you got yourself an AK. So, how many PJAK fighters are here? Are they going to help us?"

Farvad shook his head. "I'm afraid I have bad news. The only one here is the old man. All the others are off conducting raids."

Dempsey nodded. "Okay, then what are we waiting for?" he said. "Let's get this party started."

He pressed his torso into the weapon's shoulder braces, grabbed the gunner handles, and squeezed the trigger. The heavy gun whirred to life, and the truck rocked backward as a dragon's tongue of fire and red tracers erupted from the ends of spinning barrels. A cloud of dust kicked up along the ground in front of the southern mortar team. Dempsey walked the fiery death onto his target, letting the stream of 12.7 mm rounds cut one man in half and then explode the neatly stacked cache of mortar shells into a giant fireball. He released the trigger and the six barrels stopped spinning. He swept right and sighted in on the northern mortar squad, on the other side of the APC. These guys—having just witnessed what happened to their comrades—were already running, but Dempsey cut them all to ribbons.

He released the trigger and the Muharram coasted to a stop.

"They're advancing," Farvad yelled, pointing to the Iranian troopers in the field who sure enough were slowly but steadily closing in on the house.

Farvad knelt beside the front of the truck to Dempsey's right, sighting over his assault rifle. In his peripheral vision, Dempsey saw a figure walking toward them from the house. He glanced back over his shoulder and locked eyes with an old Kurdish fighter sporting a thick pepper-gray beard and clutching an AK-47. The proud, battle-hardened PJAK warrior smiled at him. Dempsey smelled smoke and burning kerosene and saw that the entire house was on fire. Tendrils of black smoke snaked skyward from the windows.

Good, Dempsey thought. *Pilots can't miss us now.*

The old man leaned against the armor-plated side of the truck, sighted over his weapon, and fired two rounds—dropping an Iranian soldier who was sprinting in a low crouch between two rocks.

From behind the Muharram, Dempsey scanned the scene in front of him. The noose was tightening; the first wave of Iranian soldiers was already within two hundred meters. Behind them, another wave of soldiers was advancing at five hundred meters, except they were moving laterally to the wings, undoubtedly directed to conduct a pincer-style flanking maneuver. Back at the end of the dirt road, another two fire teams were already setting up new mortars on either side of the trucks.

The old man barked something in what sounded like Sorani Kurdish, and Farvad translated, "He says there are more soldiers coming," and pointed to the northern ridgeline. Dempsey could make out three distinct plumes of dust rising over the ridge—which meant three more APCs or troop trucks. Then he looked south and saw two more heavy trucks advancing.

Shit.

Dempsey gritted his teeth, sighted in, and sawed the two new mortar teams to pieces with the Muharram. He slid a box of 12.7 mm ammo toward him with his foot as he let go of the twin grips and raised his rifle. The trucks approaching from the south were still out of range, and whatever was coming from the north was still behind the rising ridgeline. As much as he'd prefer to use the Muharram to mow down everyone and everything in sight, he simply didn't have the ammunition for that. He picked up the Khaybar, sighted on a soldier peering from behind a rock just beside the road, and fired. The bullet impacted the rock, but the shrapnel must have sprayed the man's eyes because the fighter pressed both hands to his face and fell backward behind the rock, out of the fight.

"RPG!" Farvad yelled, and Dempsey glanced right to see a streak of smoke and an enemy soldier dive behind a rock after firing a rocket. The RPG impacted fifty yards short, but the track had been perfect. Any closer and the guy would have put the rocket square in the bed of the truck. Dempsey slung his Khaybar and settled back in behind the heavy gun. When the smoke and dust had settled, he squeezed the trigger. The volley of bullets walked up the side of the rock and cut the RPG gunner to pieces in a horrific explosion of red-and-gray gore.

With his peripheral vision, Dempsey noted that the trucks moving from the south were in range now. He swung the Muharram left, sighted in, and squeezed. The first volley was short and left, but he walked the maelstrom of bullets up the lead truck's front left fender and across the windshield. The truck's entire left front wheel flew off, and the lumbering beast ground to a halt. The truck following behind slammed into the lead truck, and several soldiers spilled out the back of the first truck and onto the hood of the second. Dempsey resighted and squeezed, pulling the tracer stream across the engine, the cab, and then the side-mounted fuel tanks of the second truck. A puff of smoke burped from the undercarriage, and then the second truck erupted in a brilliant fireball. Like a giant, fiery serpent, the flame leaped to the lead truck and devoured the canvas-covered rear compartment. Soldiers dove and tumbled out of both trucks, most of them on fire. He raked a stream of bullets and tracers waist-high over the ground, cutting down anything that was moving.

Noting a change in the tenor of the big gun, Dempsey released the handles and picked up his assault rifle, giving the Persian Gatling gun a moment to cool.

"You're about to run out of ammo for the Muharram," Farvad said, sighting over his rifle and firing, and then dropping the magazine out of the weapon and slamming a fresh one in place. Dempsey looked down and saw the first ammo box empty, only a short strand of the ammo belt left hanging from the gun. He was about to reach for a new belt from the second box when a bullet skipped off the edge of the truck bed, ricocheted off the machine gun, and buried itself in his right thigh.

"Owww . . . Shit, that hurts," he muttered. He picked up the Khaybar and scanned for targets, his right thigh screaming with pain, but not enough to indicate his femur could be fractured.

He scanned right and left and saw that they had a triple line of Persian soldiers advancing—scurrying between rocks and ditches—and the enemy had closed in much more than he expected. He dropped to his knees, taking cover behind the armored side panels of the truck bed, and began firing at targets.

But there were simply too many.

Bullets pinged regularly off the pickup truck now, but he ignored them, firing over and over—emptying his magazine and dropping it with a clatter to the bed, slamming his last fresh one in place, and releasing the bolt. Without missing a beat, he returned to picking targets and dropping soldiers one headshot after another as they peeked from behind rocks. But for every fighter he killed, four more seemed to materialize, popping up even closer than before. It was like a murderous game of whack-a-mole, and he was losing badly. The nearest soldiers were less than sixty meters from the truck. There were simply too many damn rocks to hide behind. As a three-man team, it was impossible for Dempsey and his companions to keep the advancing horde pinned down. He heard the whistle of an incoming rifle round and then the familiar fleshy thud as it found a target.

The old man to Dempsey's left grunted and then pitched forward onto the ground.

At first Dempsey thought he was dead, but a moment later the PJAK fighter struggled to both his knees, pulled his rifle up again, and began firing before a new volley of incoming rounds tore through his face and throat, sealing his fate.

Dempsey picked another target, fired, and felt the bolt of his rifle lock back.

Empty again.

"I need ammo or another rifle," he hollered to Farvad.

"Here," Farvad yelled, and a rifle clattered in the bed behind him. He belly crawled around the machine gun mount as enemy bullets pinged off the truck's armor plating. He grabbed the third—and last—Khaybar and checked it. The magazine pouch on the stock held a single spare magazine, which meant he was down to his last sixty rounds of assault rifle ammunition. If he and Farvad could push the front line of soldiers back, then maybe he could get back up on the heavy gun without getting cut to pieces.

Dempsey scanned over the edge of the side panel and saw two soldiers sprinting toward him only ten yards away. He dropped them both with single shots, conserving his ammo as best he could. Four more soldiers were closing aggressively, sprinting from rock to rock, maybe twenty yards away. With five rounds, he killed three of them, the last one making it to another large boulder. He kept shooting, and they kept coming, and soon he was slamming home his final magazine.

The armor plating on the left side of the pickup reverberated with a barrage of enemy gunfire—suppressing fire intended to keep him pinned down and permit more soldiers to advance on them. But instead of dropping prone, Dempsey popped to a tactical knee, unloaded on anything moving—which turned out to be a half-dozen soldiers sprinting toward the truck from the south. He slowed his breathing and time seemed to grind to a halt. His vision was as sharp as he could ever remember, and his aim was as true as if he were using a target designator and not iron sights. He locked his targets one by one and squeezed the trigger: *pop pop . . . pop pop pop . . . pop pop . . . pop pop pop pop.* He dropped them all while a torrent of enemy rounds whistled past his head and ricocheted off the sides of the truck.

I should be dead . . . which means they want me alive.

He fired three rounds at the boulders behind the fallen soldiers—suppressing the suppressing fire—but, in his peripheral vision, saw a plume of gray smoke and then heard a familiar whistle.

"Mortar," he yelled and dropped to his belly in the bed of the truck.

The shell exploded somewhere by the front right quarter panel, rocking the truck up on its suspension and sending dust and debris raining down on him from above. He shifted in the cramped space between the Muharram mount and the bed rail—executing the best version of fire-and-move his circumstances would permit—and popped up at the rear of the bed to unload a volley.

In that split second, he saw at least a dozen soldiers advancing inside twenty meters toward the north side where Farvad was sheltering.

"I'm hit," Farvad cried in a wet, muffled voice. "It's bad, I think."

Dempsey popped up, shot a man not five yards from the front of the truck, and dropped down.

"Can you fight?" he yelled over the rail.

"I'll try," Farvad said after a beat, his voice stronger but still full of cotton.

Dempsey had less than ten rounds left in his Khaybar, and there were more men than that advancing. Rock by rock, meter by meter, their position would be overrun. He thought about calling Chunk on Farvad's sat phone—he needed desperately to tell him about the nuke, maybe even pass the coordinates from the tablet device Modiri's wife had given him—but it was simply too late. He was out of options. It was over. He refused to let them take him alive, and he would take as many of them down with him as he could.

Dempsey stood, heard an animal scream, and, realizing it was him, fired into the line of Persian soldiers as he pedaled backward toward the Muharram. Bullets pinged off the armor siding all around him as he grabbed the twin handles and squeezed. He dragged the line of tracers across the field of men, cutting them down, but there were more behind them. Then the heavy gun abruptly went quiet, and he realized he'd never reloaded. He ducked, grabbed the loose end of a fresh belt of ammo from his last and final ammo box, and fed it into the receiver. Holding the belt with his left hand, he squeezed the trigger with his right, and the machine gun roared back to life. He popped to his feet and unleashed hell, sweeping the barrel in a 120-degree arc across the desert. Advancing soldiers dove and took cover anywhere they could, and those who weren't able to in time were cut down. He focused fire on a large boulder, watched the stream of .50-caliber rounds chew the rock apart until the two men cowering behind were exposed and then evaporated in a cloud of blood, guts, and bone.

To the west, he saw a newly arrived Sarir APC with a turret-mounted KPV heavy machine gun rolling toward him. The armored vehicle had advanced nearly halfway down the dirt road and was shielding three trucks behind it. But that wasn't even his biggest problem. A Karrar battle tank advancing across the rocky field—a line of soldiers falling in and ducking behind as it rolled by—would be his final undoing. There was nothing funny about his situation, but Dempsey started to laugh. If they wanted him dead, then the 125 mm gun on the tank's turret would have evaporated him already. No matter how many Persians died in the process, it appeared they were going to take him alive.

Dempsey turned the gun toward the tank and fired, knowing even the 12.7 mm rounds would bounce off the tank's thick armor, which they did, like tiny hailstones bouncing off a windshield. He didn't care. He just held it there, howling a primal scream as fire and metal pummeled the front of the tank. Then the machine gun seized—either overheated or out of ammo—and it was over.

Dempsey dropped to his knees in the bed of the truck, and his fingers found the grip of his Sig Sauer pistol.

I won't let them take me.

He put the muzzle under his chin, closed his eyes, and . . .

The sound of salvation filled his ears.

He laughed, lowered his Sig, and opened his eyes. A Persian soldier, not five yards in front of him, yelled something at him in Farsi. Dempsey leveled his pistol at the man, squeezed the trigger, and blew a hole in the center of his forehead just as two MH-60M Special Operations Blackhawk helicopters screamed overhead at impossibly low altitude. Fire and smoke streaked out from both sides of the lead helo, and two Hellfire II missiles slammed into the tank. The first hit low and exploded, separating the right track from the chassis. The second hit and disappeared. A muffled explosion followed as the armor-piercing ordnance penetrated the tank and killed everyone inside. Then black smoke poured from every part of the tank. The soldiers behind the tank turned, scattering and scurrying behind rocks for cover.

The second Blackhawk similarly dispatched the Sarir APC with missiles before the turret gunner was able to engage the helo with his KPV heavy gun. With the Sarir now a burning hulk of wreckage, the pilot looped the bird around, and the door gunner began hosing down the semicircular formations of enemy soldiers surrounding the truck. Dempsey picked up his assault rifle and emptied what was left in the magazine into the crowd of fleeing soldiers—out of bloodlust more than necessity—until the trigger went dead. The lead helicopter banked sharply and executed a second pass overhead before flaring and setting down between the pickup truck and the burning house behind him.

Dempsey vaulted out of the truck, leaping over the side rail despite his right thigh screaming in protest, and landed in the dirt beside Farvad. The young Persian's face was streaked with blood, and there was a large gash in his forehead, just below his hairline, that extended back into his hair, which was matted with wet blood. But it was the dark hole in his right side, just below his armpit, that had Dempsey worried.

"I think I got shot, Corbin," Farvad said.

"Corbin is my NOC. You can call me Dempsey," Dempsey said, "and I think it's shrapnel from the mortar. But don't worry; we're going to get you help. You'll be all right. The best combat surgeon in the world is waiting for you just a short hop away."

"Thank God you're on our side," a familiar voice said behind him, gesturing to the field of carnage with a sweeping hand.

Dempsey turned to face Chunk. "You're late."

"Nah, right on time," Chunk said, clutching Dempsey's shoulder. Then, dropping his gaze to Farvad, he said, "Looks like your friend needs a CASEVAC."

Dempsey grabbed Chunk by the shoulders.

"We've got a problem, Chunk. There's a nuke in play," he said. "It's headed toward the border. I think it's Modiri's last play."

"Modiri has a nuke?" Chunk said, confused.

Dempsey shook his head.

"Modiri is dead," he said. "And so is Elinor. But we have to stop that truck." He reached into his cargo pocket and pulled out the small tablet Maheen Modiri had given him. He touched the screen and it flickered to life.

Thank God it wasn't damaged.

"The warhead is here," he said, pointing at the blue dot.

"Understood, but what about your teammate? He needs surgical care," Chunk said. "Can we stop this nuke with only one bird?"

Dempsey looked at the Blackhawk and its ordnance then back at Farvad. "Yeah," he said. "We can do it."

"All right," Chunk said. "The other bird will CASEVAC your asset. You're with me, JD."

Dempsey took a knee beside his Persian ally and put a hand on the man's shoulder. "Thank you, Farvad, for everything."

Farvad gave him a thumbs-up and then closed his eyes and laid his head back down in the dirt.

"Let's go," Dempsey said, getting to his feet. "I hope you have extra gear for me. It seems I'm all out of bullets."

They were airborne seconds later, looping around so the door gunner could strafe the remaining enemy fighters as the other helicopter swooped in and landed. Dempsey watched them load Farvad into the second bird. Once the second Blackhawk was airborne, the helos parted company. Dempsey shuffled forward to the cockpit and grabbed the aircraft commander by the shoulder. The Army Major looked up, and Dempsey handed him the satellite tracking transceiver showing the position of the nuke. Next, he grabbed a headset hanging from a hook on the bulkhead and pulled it on. "This is our target," he said.

"What is it?" the pilot asked.

"A nuclear warhead."

The aviator pursed his lips and raised a sarcastic thumb. "Awesome."

"I don't know if it's an armored convoy or strapped to the back of a pickup," Dempsey said. "All I know is that it's real and the bastards intend to use it."

"Roger that. Whatever it takes, brother, I'll do it."

"Hooyah."

Dempsey settled back into the rear. Chunk handed him a SOPMOD M4 and tactical vest with a plate carrier. "Thanks," Dempsey said, slipping into the vest, but Chunk just stared at him. "What?" Dempsey growled.

"It's just always so cool working with you, Dempsey," Chunk said with a crooked grin. "Helicopter crashes, jungle ops with poisonous fucking everything, suicide bombers with heart-rate monitors, wartime INFILS into Iran, and now this. Tactical nukes. It's a party every day with you."

"Don't pretend you don't love it," Dempsey said, securing his Velcro panels.

"By the way, did you know you're shot?" Chunk asked, pointing to a circle of dark blood on Dempsey's right thigh. "I mean, I know you're, like, immortal and shit, but just thought you should know."

"Just a flesh wound," Dempsey said with a sarcastic smile. "And I don't suppose I'll give a shit about it or anything else if a mushroom cloud goes up."

Chunk shook his head and then proceeded to pack a giant wad of snuff into his lower lip.

"Five minutes," the pilot said, holding up a hand with his fingers and thumb spread wide.

"Want some?" Chunk asked, holding out the Skoal.

"Hell yes," Dempsey said, taking the tin. "You only live once."

CHAPTER 42

Approaching Route 46
Twenty-Five Miles Due East of Zrebar Lake, Western Iran
Mountains
Twenty Miles South of the Iraqi Border
June 2
1705 Local Time

Dempsey stared at the serpentine scar that wrapped his left forearm. It was an old wound, pearly white and smooth, all the pink and tenderness bleached away by sun and sea and time. He traced his fingertip along the ridge of the imperfectly healed flesh but felt nothing. Jack Kemper's compulsion was gone; the tether was severed. This was another man's scar, from another man's life . . . a life he was tired of trying to hang on to.

He stopped and used his right hand to do something more useful, tracing over the SOPMOD M4 rifle in his lap and then inventorying the magazine pouches on his vest.

"Still only the single truck," came Baldwin's calm voice in his headset from the Ember TOC on the other side of the world. Dempsey had requested Smith bring Ember's resident genius regarding all things technical on the line. But was that the real reason he'd wanted Baldwin in his ear? Or was it because—despite his propensity to pontificate at the worst possible times—the man had been there, like some kind of a guardian angel in his ear, during the most stressful and dangerous moments of his life over the past year? Dempsey snorted a laugh through his nose. He might as well admit it: Baldwin had become his damn lucky rabbit's foot, and if there was ever a time he needed luck, it was now.

"Any converging vehicles or hostile aircraft within twenty-five clicks?" Dempsey asked, wanting to make sure that the Persian Army wasn't sending another assault their way.

He waited while Baldwin correlated images from satellites with those from whatever drones he had working the theater now. "Keep in mind, John, that the target is only 32.3 miles from the western border, and there is considerable activity along the border, particularly around the Bashmaq outpost west of Marivan, but you already knew that. So, if you could be a trifle more specific?"

"Okay, let me rephrase," Dempsey said. "Do you see a Persian QRF on an intercept course with the truck?"

"No," came the reply.

Dempsey looked over at Chunk, who gave him a thumbs-up at that news, but the SEAL officer's face was completely devoid of its normal humor and nonchalance. Dempsey reckoned that Chunk was feeling the same "door kicker's anxiety" that he was feeling. Taking on bad guys with guns, even when the odds were overwhelming, was one thing. But tangling with a nuke was an entirely different proposition. With a nuke, their combat experience, their superior training, and their M4s with laser target designators were irrelevant. With a nuke, there was no duck-and-cover. No headshot to win the day.

"How many in the truck?" Dempsey asked.

"Thermals show five. Two in the front and three in the back," Baldwin replied, his voice entirely too cheerful. "Undoubtedly babysitting the device."

"Two minutes," Chunk said.

Dempsey nodded and realized at that moment that this had become a SEAL team assault. Technically, he'd been EXFIL'd, meaning this had gone from his deep-cover covert operation to Chunk's mission to lead.

"All right, listen up, here's the brief," the young SEAL officer said. "We loop in ahead of the truck and the gunner puts enough fifties into the engine block to stop them dead. Gunner, hold on the target for support, but don't engage unless ordered. If possible, our spooky friends would like us to take at least one bad guy alive for intel, but the priority is to gain control of the nuke."

"Check," came the voice of the 160th Special Operations Air Regiment door gunner.

"We are a four-man team, so two per side from a low hover to get us down quickly. Two advance and two hold back."

"I'll advance," Dempsey said, leaving no room for doubt.

"Of course you will," Chunk said with a tight grin. "Dempsey and I advance on the truck. Sonny and Psyche, you hold the road behind us, air offset hover for fire support. Easy day."

"Hooyah," said Sonny, his voice relaxed. He was a SEAL, fearless and young. For him this wasn't a life-and-death, brink-of-war, possibility-of-nuclear-holocaust event—it was just another op.

"We're Crusader," Dempsey said. "I'm Crusader One."

"Okay," Chunk said, ignoring the shift in leadership that implied. "I'm Two. Sonny—Three. Psyche—Four."

"One minute," the pilot said.

Dempsey closed his eyes. The low, red sun shone warm on his face through the open door of the helo. The wind buffeted his leg as it dangled out the open door, snapping the fabric of his pants rhythmically against the inside of his calf. He inhaled deeply and savored the aromatic mélange of oil and propane, sweat, and sulfur. The radio static in his ears connected him to every element of the operation, and every element to him. The SOPMOD M4 he clutched in his right hand was not a separate thing; rather, it seemed to be an extension of him.

He was a machine of war, and the machine of war was him.

He opened his eyes.

He felt the nose lift as the helicopter flared on approach. Then, the pilot swung the bird around, perpendicular to the road. Fast ropes were kicked out, and a short burst from the door gunner on the opposite side of the helicopter set off the assault. He repositioned his rifle along his right flank and gripped the rope in both hands, twisting it tight. Then, he stepped out of the helicopter, his feet doing the lion's share of the work controlling and guiding his descent to the ground.

The .50 roared again, above him now, for suppression as he slid to the earth in under two seconds flat. He stepped off the rope and advanced on the Iranian cargo truck, pulling his rifle up to the ready and positioning the floating red reticle of his holosite in space as he scanned for targets. White steam and black smoke rose from the engine compartment the Blackhawk gunner had torn to pieces as liberated water and oil vaporized against the red-hot engine block.

He was aware of Chunk moving parallel to him off to his left, but he felt another presence accompanying him, too. Ghosts of his fallen teammates—his Tier One brothers lost in the original Operation Crusader—were advancing with him. On his right were Thiel, Pablo, Helo, and Gabe. On his left, Rousche, Gator, and Spaz. They were all here. And so were their wives, and their children. Everyone had come to help him, the entire Tier One extended family he'd lost. Normally, he chased his ghosts away, but not this time. Not today. He let his teammates and their families advance on the truck with him. This was their mission, too. Hell, they *were* the mission.

Through the windshield, he made eye contact with a soldier in the driver's seat. The driver's hands were up, but he was gripping a pistol in his right hand and the door was hanging wide open. Dempsey put the red floating reticle on the center of the man's face and squeezed the trigger. Then, he sensed movement to his right and shifted his aim. His brain recognized the Artesh uniform in a tenth of a second, and he put a bullet in the man's forehead.

Chunk, who had drifted to the passenger side of the vehicle, was hollering something in broken Arabic at the soldier sitting in the passenger seat of the cab. Dempsey, who was now even with the cab, glanced left through the open driver-side door and saw that the passenger was holding a rifle low and pointing through the door at Chunk. Dempsey placed his dot, squeezed, and shot that man dead as well.

No more games. No more distractions.

As he approached the canvas-covered trailer section of the truck, it took all his willpower not to empty his magazine along the entire length of the compartment. But instead of doing that, he ducked low and sprinted toward the back of the truck, his shoulder hugging the trailer chassis. When he reached the back corner, he had a decision to make. There were two men inside. One must certainly have been Modiri's VEVAK agent. The other was either a bomb technician or another shooter. Kill the wrong guy, and the outcome could be disastrous. Hesitate, and he'd probably get shot in the face.

The little voice inside his head told him he should wait for Chunk. But . . . Fuck it. Today was his day to die.

He stepped around the back of the truck, sighting into the open rear compartment over his rifle, and as expected there were two Persian men: one old, one young. The old man was shaking with terror and had his hands raised over his head. The young man had a pistol leveled at Dempsey's forehead. Between them was a nuclear warhead.

In his peripheral vision, he saw Chunk step up beside him, rifle raised.

"Get out of here, Chunk," he ordered. "And pull the bird back, too."

Chunk said nothing and didn't move.

"Do it, Lieutenant," he barked.

"Stalker, drift west a hundred yards," Chunk said, but he didn't move a muscle.

Dempsey heard the pitch change of the Blackhawk's rotors as it repositioned—*at least somebody listened.* He locked eyes with the young shooter and saw the hate, malice, and rage of a man bent on revenge.

"You are him," the young man said in clipped English. "You are the one. The one responsible for the death of my father, of my brother, of my mother, and now my uncle as well."

Dempsey studied the face in his gunsight and realization crashed in on him. The resemblance was unmistakable. "You're Masoud Modiri's son," Dempsey said, his own voice now filling with rage. This young man was Amir Modiri's final weapon. This young man was the missing assassin. He had killed Rostami. He had killed the DNI, and now he was going to use a nuke to kill God only knew how many more.

Dempsey saw the Persian's jaw tense. "This is for my—"

Dempsey's bullet struck Modiri in the face just above the bridge of his nose, and the young man tumbled backward. His body hit the truck bed with a thud.

"Jesus, dude," he heard Chunk exclaim, but Dempsey's focus never wavered from the objective.

In a flash, he was up in the back of the truck, his rifle trained on the old man as he advanced toward the warhead. He was no munitions expert, but he immediately knew something was wrong. Instead of being locked inside a case, or installed inside a nosecone ready for mounting, the device was laid out in front of him. He scanned the old man up and down for a weapon, then looked back at the bomb. After a second, his heart sank. There was a detonator, and it was active.

"Turn it off," Dempsey barked at the gray-haired technician.

The man, who was shaking now, started babbling in Farsi and waving his hands.

"English! Talk in English!" Dempsey shouted, wishing desperately that Farvad was with him.

"Dude, he doesn't speak English," Chunk said from his right shoulder, staring down at the unholy mess in front of them.

Dempsey fumbled for the Arabic, but then a switch flipped in his mind and the words came to him. "Turn it off."

"I can't turn it off," the technician answered in Arabic. "He made me disable the fail-safe."

"Then what the hell do we do?" Dempsey asked.

"That's what I've been telling you," he shouted. "We need to go!"

Dempsey looked at the numerical timer, counting backward from three minutes fifty-nine seconds, and he began to laugh. This was the way it was supposed to be. He was the last one left on either side. Everyone in this blood feud was now dead, everyone except for him. He lowered his weapon and smiled at the ghosts of his brothers standing beside him. And as the tears of vindication, joy, and irony rolled down his cheeks, he tilted his gaze up to heaven.

I'm ready, he said in silent prayer. *Take me home to my brothers.*

A strong hand jerked the straps on his plate carrier toward the back of the truck, almost pulling him over.

"What the fuck is wrong with you?" Chunk barked. "We gotta go, bro."

Wind buffeted the canvas cover of the trailer as the Blackhawk repositioned behind the vehicle. Chunk jerked Dempsey toward the back of the truck, and they both jumped out, landing on the dirt in unison. Then, Chunk turned back to the technician. "Well, c'mon, you, too," he shouted.

Dempsey felt himself being dragged toward the open door of the helo. He looked over at the SEAL officer but couldn't understand why Chunk was doing this. His brothers were waiting. This was his destiny.

"Come on, Dempsey," Chunk hollered, pushing him into the chopper. "You got people who need you."

Suddenly Dempsey's mind filled with new images . . . Lizzie in the ICU in Jerusalem, her chest tube draining blood; Munn at the FARP performing emergency surgery on Farvad; Smith staring at satellite feeds; Jarvis meeting with President Warner; Baldwin putting on a headset in the Ember TOC; and that smartass Wang typing on three laptops at the same damn time. What the hell was wrong with him? Yes, some of his brothers were dead, but not all of them . . .

Not all.

Chunk's SEALs pulled the Iranian technician into the helo behind them as the rotors beat the air into submission and the great metal beast rose into the air.

"What kind of bomb is that?" Dempsey asked the technician in Arabic, his wits returning.

"Twenty-kiloton atomic bomb," the man answered.

"How far do we need to go to be safe?" he asked.

"I can answer that question, John," Baldwin said, piping up. "Your warhead is equivalent in size to the bombs dropped on Hiroshima and Nagasaki in World War Two. From the hypocenter, everything inside a one-mile radius will be instantly vaporized by a nuclear fireball. You can expect moderate to severe damage inside two miles from the kinetic shock wave and thermal radiation. Outside two miles—"

"Haul ass, pilot. We need to fucking go, go, go!" Chunk shouted at the pilot, drowning out Baldwin.

The helicopter's engines screamed in protest as the pilot accelerated like Dempsey had never felt in a Blackhawk before. For an instant, he wondered if they might not just die in the explosion of the overtaxed twin turbines above them.

"How long do I have?" the pilot shouted.

"Three minutes," Chunk shouted.

"Actually, you have two minutes and forty-three seconds," Baldwin said.

"What do we need to do to live, Ian?" Dempsey said, his voice surprisingly calm.

"At your current speed, you will be outside five miles in two minutes. That gets you out of the kill zone and also means you will likely not suffer anything other than first-degree burns, but the kinetic-energy shock wave could down the helicopter, and you may be exposed to a lethal dose of ionizing radiation—"

"Damn it, Baldwin, you didn't answer the question. Help us!"

"Listen very carefully, John," Baldwin said. "Radiation intensity diminishes quickly with distance because it follows the inverse square law. Distance and shielding are the key."

"What do you mean shielding?"

"Metal, water, concrete, earth—all these things absorb and attenuate ionizing radiation."

Dempsey looked out the door at the mountains rising on either side of them. To the south, a formidable-looking mountain towered over a valley pass.

"Can you get around the mountain?" he asked the pilot. "Put all that rock between us and that bomb?"

The pilot didn't reply, but then the helicopter banked steeply to the left, answering his question, and Dempsey slid toward Chunk, grabbing the frame of the door to steady himself.

"Hang on, people," the pilot said. "I'm gonna shoot the valley and try to stay below that shock wave. It's gonna be close."

Dempsey slid to the rear of the helicopter and pressed his back against the rear bulkhead. He secured himself to the aluminum tubes of the bench with his safety line and carabiner. Then he pulled his knees up to his chest and closed his eyes. The hull shuddered, the engines roared, and Dempsey was sure that, despite the banking and rolling, the pilot was setting a new overland speed record. His stomach floated up as the helicopter twisted to the right and then dropped. Dempsey opened his eyes and saw Chunk watching him. The SEAL shot him a toothy, tobacco-stained smile.

"I'm not worried," Chunk said. "I'm with you—*if* you were kill-able, you'd be dead already. You're one death-cheating, bullet-dodging, good-luck-charm son of a bitch."

Dempsey laughed. If only the young SEAL officer knew how true that had been the last twenty years. But maybe now the streak was finally over. He looked left and saw the rock face of the mountain ravine impossibly close to the door. Why weren't the rotors shattering against the rocks?

"Any second now," came Baldwin's reassuring voice.

The helicopter pushed over forward and then banked hard left.

The world went silent, but the air turned electric and a wave of heat swallowed them. A bright light flashed behind them, illuminating the mountains beyond with the brightness of a hundred lightning strikes.

The helicopter shook violently.

But then stopped and kept on flying.

And just when he thought it was over, the entire Blackhawk began to rattle and shake as it was buffeted by wind shear so violent he was sure the rivets holding it together were going to fail and it would be ripped apart in midair. But somehow the pilot maintained control. They continued to weave through the mountain pass, and Dempsey looked up and noticed the ridgeline above them. But something was wrong: the ridgeline was moving. A cascade of rock and debris was falling toward them—but the pilot dipped the nose and dove. This time, gravity was their ally as they raced to escape the maelstrom of the mountain. He heard pings of falling rock and debris hitting them—striking the rotors above. A dark choking cloud of dust enveloped them and the engines growled in protest, but then it was light again and suddenly they were out, on the south side of the mountain, emerging from dust and smoke and falling rock, and still descending fast enough to pull Dempsey's stomach up into his chest.

A moment later the whine of the engines dropped into a more comfortable, familiar pitch, and the pilot leveled them out. They'd made it. They'd survived.

"Crossing the border in two kilometers," the pilot said, his voice almost a whisper. "I can have us on the ground at Irbil in forty-five mikes or so."

"Hit the FARP first," Chunk said, referring to the forward air refueling point—which was serving as their staging point for CASEVAC and additional air support on Special Operations missions like this one. "We should probably check this bird out, don't you think?"

The pilot only laughed.

"On the ground in about four minutes then," he said.

"We have a FARP set up just north of Halabja, on the Iraq side of the border. That's where Munn is, probably operating on your guy Farvad," Chunk explained. "I suspect he will want to check you over personally. After that . . ."

Dempsey's eyes must have asked the question on his mind, because Chunk shook his head.

"What happens in Vegas, stays in Vegas," the SEAL said, his cocky, crooked grin apparently back to stay. "Besides, I have a terrible memory for details."

Dempsey held his eyes and gave him a grateful nod.

"So, what's next for John Dempsey?" Chunk said, a rare seriousness creeping into his voice.

Dempsey looked out the window at the mushroom cloud blooming skyward behind them. "I honestly don't know, Chunk. Tell you what, how about you ask me that question tomorrow?"

CHAPTER 43

West Wing of the White House
June 4
0740 Local Time

Jarvis rolled a quarter back and forth across the knuckles of his right hand while he waited for a meeting with the President. He'd taught himself this nifty little trick in middle school after watching a sleight-of-hand magician perform the flourish and then disappear the coin to the delight of the class. He'd mastered the technique in two days and had been able to do the party trick ever since without even thinking about it . . . until now.

Not dropping the quarter took pretty much all his concentration.

There was something awry with his nervous system—no point in lying to himself anymore. His symptoms were indicative of early-stage ALS or multiple sclerosis. Other possibilities included Parkinson's or Huntington's, both degenerative nerve diseases without cures. A simple gene test could confirm or rule out Huntington's; the others would require more extensive evaluation.

"That's a pretty neat trick," the woman behind the oak desk said to him. "I bet that was hard to learn."

The quarter slipped between his middle and ring fingers and dropped to the floor.

"Oops," she said and flashed him an awkward smile.

If you only knew the half of it, he thought to himself and smiled politely back at her.

Just then, the door to the Oval Office swung open and out stepped Catherine Morgan. Her eyes ticked to meet his. "Kelso," she said in curt acknowledgment.

"Catherine," he replied with a nod.

She tugged on the waist of her suit coat, straightening it, and then strode away down the hall without another word.

The President appeared in the doorway. He was wearing an ironic grin, looking very much the victor after a playground scuffle. He looked at Jarvis and beckoned him inside with a double-curl of his index finger.

"The President will see you now," the woman behind the desk said.

"That much I gathered," Jarvis said, getting to his feet. He followed the President into the Oval Office and shut the door behind him.

Warner walked over to the pair of beige sofas facing each other in the middle of the room and gestured for Jarvis to take a seat. This was Jarvis's first time in the famous room, and he permitted himself the simple pleasure of living in the moment. Being invited to a conference in the Oval Office was like climbing behind the wheel of a Ferrari for the first time—one helluva joyride.

"Would you like some iced tea?" the President asked.

"No, thank you, sir."

Warner's fondness for iced tea was storied and well known.

"I used to drink sweet tea," Warner said, taking a seat opposite Jarvis and picking up a half-full glass from the coffee table. "But the docs said my blood sugar was getting too damn high, so now I drink half and half."

"Half and half?" Jarvis asked.

"Half tea, half lemonade," Warner said. "You know, an Arnold Palmer."

Jarvis nodded, his mind immediately contemplating the oxymoronic nature of this dietary adjustment; lemonade contained as much sugar—if not more than, he imagined—as sweet tea.

"Ahh, I know what you're thinking. I can see it in your eyes. You're thinking, *Warner's a bigger moron than I thought. Lemonade is packed with sugar, so all the dumb bastard is doing is just trading one devil for another.* Am I right?"

Jarvis shrugged. "The thought did cross my mind."

The President took a sip of his Arnold Palmer and then said, "Well, when you get to be my age, Kelso, that's the thing you realize . . ."

"What's that, sir?" Kelso said, thinking this was another funny comment from a man who was only seven years his senior.

"*Every* decision is trading one devil for another." Warner leaned back on the sofa and propped his left ankle up on his right knee. "Take, for example, Ms. Morgan, who was sitting in that same spot not two minutes ago. Hell, I bet you can feel her lingering presence with your ass cheeks right now. That cushion should still be warm."

Jarvis couldn't help but laugh at this. "Yes, sir. It most definitely is."

Warner smiled and nodded with approval that he'd gotten the reaction he was hoping for. "So here's the thing . . . Catherine Morgan is sweet tea. Do you know what that makes you?"

"Arnold Palmer."

Warner slapped his knee. "See, I knew that giant brain Philips talked so much about meant you were a quick study."

"In that case, sir, I accept."

"I haven't even offered you the job yet," Warner said.

"Yes, you did," Jarvis said with a sly grin of his own. "When you invited me here."

"I can see this is going to be fun," Warner said, uncrossing his legs to lean forward and extend his right hand. "Congratulations, Director Jarvis. You are now the second most powerful man in the world."

Jarvis shook Warner's hand, silently grateful that his own hand cooperated by reciprocating a firm, solid countersqueeze.

"You'll still have to be confirmed by the Senate, of course," Warner said, getting to his feet. "But I don't expect any trouble there."

"Thank you, sir," Jarvis said, cueing off the President and standing.

"What about Ember? You planning to keep it operational?"

"That was my intention, yes, Mr. President."

"You do realize you're not gonna have time to be the DNI and run Ember at the same time—I hope you don't have any illusions about that. Is your number two in command—Smith, if I recall—is he up for the job?"

"Yes, sir. He is."

Warner picked up his Arnold Palmer and headed back to his desk. "Who are you thinking about for your Deputy?"

"I have a short list, sir."

"Well, throw it away," the President said and took a swig from his glass.

"Excuse me, sir?"

"Yeah, throw it away, because I just told Catherine she could have her old job back, so the two of you better figure out how to work together real quick."

All the satisfaction he'd just been feeling evaporated, and now he felt like a guy who'd just had the rug pulled out from underneath him.

Warner flashed him a fox's grin. "No one knows how to navigate clandestine bureaucracy better than that woman. She's a pit bull—tenacious and with a bite as big as her bark. Trust me; you need someone like Catherine Morgan to keep you out of trouble. And I need her to shoot me straight when you don't."

"Yes, Mr. President," Jarvis said through clenched teeth.

"Oh, don't be angry with me, Kelso. It's not personal; this is simply how the game is played. Checks and balances. Strengths and weaknesses. You didn't think I was gonna let you run the entire intelligence community the way you ran Ember, did you?"

Something the President's former Chief of Staff, Robert Kittinger, said to him suddenly replayed in his mind: *The President is not a moron, Captain Jarvis, but sometimes he plays one on TV. That's how it works. That's how the game is played.* Warner was a chameleon . . . just like Jarvis. Everything the President did and said was purposeful. Warner's demeanor was designed to make people underestimate him; Jarvis could not let himself fall into the same trap.

"Your country owes you a debt of gratitude," the President continued. "Hell, the whole world does for that matter. If it wasn't for you, Amir Modiri not only would have gotten away with murdering Admiral Philips and the Israeli Mossad Chief, but he would have unleashed a nuclear weapon that would have killed hundreds of thousands of Israelis and started World War Three."

"Thank you, sir, but I can't take credit for that. It was my team—they're the ones who deserve the credit."

"Well, tell them not to bask in the glory of their success for too long because we still have one hell of a mess on our hands. Despite President Esfahani admitting to the existence of a rogue element in the Persian government, and despite de-escalation of Israeli and Iranian military forces, the world now knows that Iran was lying all along. Iran has the bomb, and that means the region will never be the same. Thank God this device was detonated in the middle of nowhere with no casualties except the maniac who set it off. But the Saudis and Jordanians are furious and afraid nonetheless. Soon they'll be demanding the bomb for parity. This thing isn't over; it's just the beginning. I'm going to move our carrier battle group out of the Med as a sign of confidence in the peace process, but I'm keeping the USS *Florida* in theater just in case things heat back up again."

Jarvis nodded. "Prudent thinking, sir."

"Prime Minister Shamone overstepped and almost got Israel nuked in the process. He and I already had words this morning, but make sure you tell your Mossad friend Director Harel that the next time his boss decides to act unilaterally, Israel is on its own. You understand? Make sure you tell him that."

Jarvis thought about those five words—*Israel is on its own*—and he imagined Harel's response were he standing in the Oval Office beside him.

This is nothing new, my friend. Israel has always been, and always will be, on its own.

"Yes, sir, I'll pass along the message."

"All right, Crystal Light, we're done here. Time for you to get the hell out of my office. We've both got work to do."

Jarvis cocked an eyebrow. *"Crystal Light?"*

"The kitchen uses Crystal Light lemonade in my Arnold Palmers. It's sugar free. At first, it left a bad aftertaste in my mouth I didn't much care for, but I gave it a chance and eventually I got used to it."

The metaphor wasn't lost on him; Jarvis gave the President a tight smile. "I won't let you down, Mr. President."

The President picked up his pen and started to write something in a notebook on his desk. Without looking up, he said, "See you at tomorrow's Security Council meeting. Better get yourself a good secretary, Kelso. You're about to become a very busy man."

Jarvis walked out of the Oval Office to find a line of people waiting outside for their turn with the leader of the free world. Some he recognized; others he didn't. As he passed the reception attendant's desk, she stopped him. "Director Jarvis?"

"Yes."

"Don't forget your lucky quarter," she said, holding out the coin he'd dropped earlier. "I thought it might be something you wanted to keep, as a memento from today."

He took it from her, placed it on the back side of his index finger, and rolled it expertly down and back again across his knuckles, vanishing it down his sleeve with a flourish. With a genuine smile, he said, "Thank you. I think I will."

She smiled back at him and then turned her attention to the next person in line: "Senator Fulton, the President will see you now . . ."

As he walked the halls of the West Wing, he pulled out his encrypted mobile phone and dialed a number from memory. The call picked up on the second ring.

"You're not still mad at me for kicking your ass out of Israel, are you?" Levi Harel said with a hoarse laugh.

Jarvis chuckled. "Hell no. That's what I like about you, Levi. You told me what I needed to hear, not what I wanted to hear."

"You can always count on me for that."

"I have some good news and some bad news. Which do you want first?"

"Bad news, always the bad news first. That's the Jewish way."

"Confirm the line is secure."

"It is."

"There's no easy way to tell you this, old friend, so I'm just going to say it. Elinor Jordan was compromised. She was a VEVAK double agent."

After a painfully long, silent pause, Harel said, "I know."

Jarvis stopped in his tracks. There was something in Harel's voice he didn't like. "Wait a second. Do you mean that you *know*, or that you *knew*? There's a big difference."

"The latter . . . I've known for some time."

Jarvis felt a surge of anger. "For how long?"

"Two years."

"Two *years*?"

"Yes, my friend."

"And you orchestrated a mission for her to lead my best asset into Iran? Why would you do that?"

"Because it was the only chance we would ever have to get Modiri . . . the only chance."

Jarvis took a deep breath. "You lied to me."

"No," Harel said. "I've never lied to you."

"A lie of omission is still a lie, Levi."

"I told you she was my best operative, and that was the truth. I told you that she was the only person who could possibly get Dempsey into position in Tehran to execute the mission, and that also was the truth. And as far as Dempsey's fate was concerned, I left that entirely up to you and John. He volunteered for the mission, remember? He knew the risks."

"If I had known the truth about her, I never would have let him go."

"Are you sure about that?"

"Damn straight, I'm sure."

"Pity, because from what I understand, there might be half a million dead Jews right now if you'd made that call."

Jarvis was the one who was silent now, his mind running a retrospective assessment of his decision based on the new information. Finally he said, "But she was the enemy."

"Do you remember the day we first met on that beach at Atlit Naval Base?"

In the background, Jarvis could hear Harel lighting a cigarette. "Of course, like it was yesterday."

"Do you remember what I said to you at the end of our conversation?"

"Yeah, you said beers were on you, a promise which I believe you've yet to make good on."

"Now you're just being a smartass."

"You deserved it."

"You're probably right," Harel said with a sigh.

"No, I remember," Jarvis said at last. "I've thought about it many, many times over the years. You said, *We share enemies . . . Enemies everywhere.*"

"When I first met Elinor she was the enemy. But I influenced her. I molded her into something else. She was a Persian Jew, brainwashed by VEVAK into believing that we were monsters. But over the years, she came to see us as people. I became the surrogate father for the one she had left behind in Tehran. She worked for Modiri, but she worked harder for me. She did more to undermine VEVAK with the Seventh Order than she did to undermine us."

A lump formed in Jarvis's throat as he contemplated a thought too dark to possibly be true. And yet he had to ask the question. "If what you're saying is true, then what about the hit on the Philips estate. Please tell me you didn't know about that?"

"I swear to God, Kelso, there are no possible scenarios where I would have let that knowingly play out. I didn't know. Elinor didn't know, either. I kept her on a very tight leash. I had people watching and listening to her twenty-four-seven. Modiri worked the DNI op extremely close to the vest. Even my top source in Tehran didn't know about it. You have to believe me."

"I believe you . . . Who's your top source in Tehran?"

Harel laughed, and this sent him into a coughing fit that took him nearly a minute to work himself out of. When he finally spoke, he said, "You said you had bad news and good news. What's the good news?"

"You tell me the name of your asset in Tehran, and I'll tell you the good news."

"That's a terrible trade. Five minutes ago you were going to tell me the good news for free."

"That was five minutes ago, before I knew you lied to me."

"I didn't lie to you," Harel insisted.

"All right, all right." Jarvis laughed. "The good news is that the President just offered me the DNI job."

"Congratulations, my friend. Perhaps your President isn't as stupid as Shamone says."

"Thank you. I thought you'd be pleased."

"Yes and no. You've just made it very hard for me to quit again. The PM asked me to stay on as Chief. I was going to say no, but now this . . ."

"I guess the day finally came where we both desperately need a friend on the other side," Jarvis said with a wry smile.

"I couldn't have said it better myself."

"Who's your source?"

Harel took a deep breath and then exhaled. "Next time I'm in Washington, I'll tell you in person. Can you live with that?"

"I can live with that," Jarvis said. "And don't think I'm letting you off the hook. The beer is still on you, old friend."

CHAPTER 44

Acquisitions and Research Center
Nechushtan Pavilion, Eretz Israel Museum
Ramat Aviv Neighborhood, Tel Aviv, Israel
June 5
0930 Local Time

Sitting at a terminal in the Seventh Order TOC, Dempsey massaged the hypersensitive tissue around the ricochet injury in his right thigh and thought about Elinor. The pain he was feeling had nothing to do with the hole in his leg; it was his guilty heart that ached.

It was all an act, he told himself. *She was a character in a play—a sick, twisted play where politics and power superseded love and loyalty. She was a traitor, a conflicted traitor but a traitor nonetheless. You need to forget about her, dude . . .*

He closed his eyes, rubbed his temples, and began to second-guess himself.

Had she actually betrayed him? The final seconds had happened so fast—a blur of adrenaline and emotion—and now he wasn't sure what had really happened. Had she delivered him to Amir Modiri, or had she delivered Amir Modiri to him? The way it all unfolded almost suggested the latter, but if that were the case, then he had abandoned Elinor to her death. Which meant he'd committed the ultimate of all SEAL transgressions. He'd left a teammate behind.

Oh God, his head was spinning.

He hadn't shared any of this with Jarvis, beyond telling him that Elinor was a double agent. At the moment, he considered his judgment to be compromised. He didn't trust himself to be objective when it came to her, and so he'd simply debriefed the facts of the operation in the Grand Bazaar and left the onus of interpretation and extrapolation to his boss. He *would* have the uncomfortable soul-baring conversation when the time was right, but that conversation would be with one person and one person only—Levi Harel.

He blinked and the BBC website on the computer monitor in front of him came back into focus. The press was having a field day, and the talking heads were like sharks in the throes of a feeding frenzy, devouring one another and any so-called expert brave and foolish enough to be interviewed on the Iran-Israeli conflict that was dominating all the channels. Despite failing to capture and disappear Amir Modiri, Jarvis's plan had achieved its geopolitical objective of de-escalation. Tehran had released a statement that a rogue element within the Iranian Foreign Ministry had been uncovered, just about the time that the President released information that they had killed the mastermind from the same rogue element near the border of Iraq. It didn't matter that Modiri had actually been killed in the Grand Bazaar in Tehran, or that it was his nephew who had been killed near the border. These were details Dempsey suspected Jarvis had advised the President to keep secret in an effort to let Iran maintain a modicum of self-respect. Tehran went on to claim that their security forces had covertly killed an operator from the rogue element within the Pakistani embassy in Washington, DC—a "poke in the eye" that the White House categorically denied. Regarding the nuke, Tehran's official position was that the explosion in the desert had been caused by a collision between a fuel truck and a munitions convoy. Iran did not possess nuclear weapons; this was all simply a big misunderstanding. But despite the rhetoric and despite the obfuscation, the genie was out of the bottle. Iran had the bomb, and the world would never be the same again.

Dempsey sighed and clicked the mouse to close the web page. Nuclear politics was above his pay grade. He'd done his part to safeguard the world, and when called on to do it again, he would step up to the challenge. But until that day came, he just wanted to put it all out of his mind. He was about to get up when a nagging, familiar compulsion nudged at him. He opened a new browser window and typed in the URL address for Kate's Facebook page. The social media site loaded, and pinned to the top of her wall was an image that made his heart skip a beat: Kate smiling and holding up her left hand to the camera while her new boyfriend, Steve, kissed her cheek. The sparkle from the diamond engagement ring on her finger paled compared to the sparkle he saw in her eyes. Steve, in his golf shirt and khaki slacks, was about as far from an operator as a man could get . . . but maybe that was a good thing.

Why am I not angry? Why am I not cursing, stomping around, and punching walls right now?

Instead of feeling jealous, hurt, or betrayed, he felt . . .

Relieved.

Kate was happy. Finally, happy. The look on her face melted his heart, and the strange thing was, he was happy for her, too. What else was there for him to feel for Kate but happiness? She had finally moved on. US Navy SEAL Senior Chief and Tier One operator Jack Kemper had been a year in the grave, and it was time for his ghost to stop haunting her. Maybe it was time, Dempsey realized, for Jack Kemper's ghost to stop haunting him, too.

He scrolled down, looking at the happy pictures, until he got to one with Jake. He paused, and the contentment he'd been feeling faded a little. Jake was smiling, but his eyes were distant. He'd seen that look before. Unlike Kate, Jake had not let go. And the truth was, Dempsey was not ready to let go of his son yet, either. But if he was dead to Kate, then shouldn't he be gone from Jake's life forever as well? He couldn't play by two sets of rules—one for Kate and one for Jake.

So he had to let go of both of them, and it hurt.

It hurt bad.

"You coming?" a familiar voice said behind him.

He closed the browser and swiveled in his chair to face Smith. "Yep, right behind you," he said, rising slowly, painfully, from his chair.

He felt old.

"You all right?" Smith asked with an unsure smile.

"Yeah, I'm just raw . . . really fucking raw."

Smith was one of the handful of people alive who could say they had seen him get emotional, but not today. He didn't have anything left. The past year—hell, the past twenty-four hours—had sucked him dry. There wasn't any warm blood left in his veins to give.

"This will cheer you up, I can promise," Smith said, wrapping an arm around his shoulders.

He followed Smith into the conference room, and he immediately saw what had him smiling so big.

"Hi, John," Grimes said, seated in the chair at the far end of the table. "Dude, you look like shit."

He tried to think of a barb, a bantering insult, something to fire back at her, but nothing came to him. Instead, he simply strode over to her and wrapped his arms gently around her. She hugged him back, squeezing tighter than she probably should. It felt good, like maybe the tension from the past weeks was gone. Near-death experience had a way of doing that to people. He realized he loved her—more than the love for a teammate, but what kind of love it was he couldn't say.

He felt Smith's eyes on him and looked over. Smith was looking at him, both friendship and envy in his eyes. Dempsey smiled at him in a way he hoped his friend understood. Then he closed his eyes and hugged Grimes more tightly.

"I'm sorry," he whispered in her ear.

"You've got nothing to apologize for," she said, but when he didn't let go, she whispered in his ear, "You okay, JD?"

"I am now," he said, breaking the embrace and smiling at her. She looked thin, and pale, and her eyes were a little glazed—pain medicine, he was sure—but she was more beautiful in that moment than ever before. "I thought I'd lost you there," he said, blinking just to make sure this wasn't a dream.

"Yeah, well, bad penny and all of that," she said, her cheeks flushing. Then, after an awkward beat, she added, "I'm sorry about Elinor. I heard what happened. I know the two of you had gotten, um, close."

His stomach tensed at the sound of her name. "Things didn't go down in Tehran like I thought they would. It got . . . complicated." This, of course, was the understatement of the century, but what else was there to say? A part of him desperately wanted to tell Elizabeth the truth—unload every decision, detail, and doubt—but another part of him worried that would be a mistake. It wasn't about trust; it was about jeopardizing this tenuous reconciliation he was feeling between them.

"If you ever need to talk about it, I'm here for you."

"Thanks. And maybe someday . . ."

Munn emerged from the break room carrying two cups of black brew and a smile plastered ear to ear across his face. He set the coffees on the table, walked straight over to Dempsey, and said, "See, I told you you'd be back."

Dempsey extended his hand with a wry smile.

Munn scoffed at this and yanked him into a manly SEAL embrace. "We're family now, bro."

After Munn's bear hug, the impromptu homecoming continued with Dempsey talking with Adamo, Rouvin, and Daniel—and a round of shadow boxing with Wang. When the handshakes, hugs, and high-fives had run their course, Smith cleared his throat and said, "All right, all right, now that we've got the band back together, the boss has something he'd like to say." The Ember Ops officer pressed a button on the podium, and the oversize flat-screen monitor on the wall flickered to life—streaming Kelso Jarvis dressed in a suit, sitting in an unfamiliar office, and smiling.

"Where is he?" Dempsey whispered to Munn, who shrugged.

"First, let me begin by saying that I'm sorry I can't be there with you today in person. It's been a difficult and emotional week, and I'm proud of each and every one of you for your courage, commitment, and sacrifice. And to our friends at the Seventh Order, we're sorry for your loss, and we owe you both our gratitude and our thanks for everything you did to support this joint operation."

Jarvis paused, and Dempsey saw a strange look wash over the Skipper's face. After a beat, he cleared his throat and said, "We've got changes coming down the pipe, both policy and personnel, but I'll leave Director Smith to brief you on that and your new roles. I'll see you when you're back in the States. That will be all."

Jarvis signaled with a hand, and someone on his side ended the transmission.

Smith stared at the screen for a beat, then turned to look at Dempsey, his face all kinds of screwed up.

"What the hell was that about?" Dempsey said.

"I have no friggin' idea," Smith said. "We're all hearing this at the same time."

"Well, it sounds like you just got promoted, dude," Munn said, grinning. "I know I'm the new guy, but I think the Skipper made a fine choice for his successor." Munn started a slow clap, and the rest of the team—Daniel and Rouvin included—joined in.

Smith waved his hand, still in a daze. "Okay, okay. Let's everybody take five and give me a second to process what just happened."

"And then what, boss?" Dempsey said, grinning at Ember's new Director in Chief. "What's next on the Ember agenda?"

He felt Grimes slip her fingers around his. "We go home," she said, giving his hand a squeeze. "We go home and we start over, again."

EPILOGUE

Hoza Restaurant
Hoza 25A
Warsaw, Poland
June 17
2130 Local Time

Catherine Morgan rotated the stem of her wine glass in her fingers as she waited. The red wine she was sipping, a fine Spanish Rioja from a vineyard she'd never heard of, was helping knock the edge off her nerves. But she needed to be careful. She rarely drank, and wine went straight to her head.

She checked the time on her phone. He was late . . .

Some things never change.

Next, she used the front-facing camera on her phone to check her makeup. The face looking back at her on the screen did nothing to improve her mood.

So old . . . so hideous.

She had once been beautiful. Many men had told her as much. It was one of the reasons she'd been selected for the program. She closed the camera app and then powered down her phone. Then she slipped it into a special little sleeve with technology that supposedly rendered the device impotent.

She took a sip of wine.

And then another.

The ambience and decor were masculine and tasteful—an indoor brick facade, burgundy-colored carpet, and dark stained-wood cabinetry. Wine bottles were prominently displayed in wooden racks and shelves throughout, serving double duty as convenient storage and decoration. The decor set the mood and, along with the wine, kind of made her horny. It had been so very, very long . . . Hopefully tonight they could find a way to make love, despite the risk.

The waiter checked on her and made an attempt to refill her glass. She stopped him and said she would be fine until her guest arrived. Her Polish was passable enough for benign interactions like this. Someone on the staff turned up the volume of the music in the restaurant. A beat later, someone turned it back down to where it had been.

A metaphor for my life.

She became aware of his arrival a moment later—a beat before he stepped foot inside the restaurant. They'd always had a strong connection. The moment their eyes met, her heart skipped a beat. How long had it been since they'd seen each other? *Eleven? No, twelve years,* she thought. He'd aged, yes, but not as much as she had. Time was kinder to his gender. She smiled at him and stood to greet him.

He kissed her on the cheek and said, "Ahhh, my little *Maschenka.* I've missed you so."

"I've missed you, too," she answered, her voice a desperate whisper.

The table he'd reserved was in the corner. She'd taken the seat with her back to the wall, giving her a view of the entire restaurant. She switched chairs with him as a courtesy. And as a statement of trust.

"So, how are you, Catherine?" he asked, waving off the approaching waiter and pouring his own glass of wine.

After a moment's hesitation, she said, "I failed you. I'm sorry."

"No, no, Maschenka, you have not failed me. Quite the contrary, I could not be more proud of what you've accomplished."

"But the President chose another," she said. "There won't be a second chance. I've plateaued."

He smiled warmly at her. "The rules of advancement break down when you reach the top. The stars must align perfectly, and none of us controls the stars."

She studied his face for tells of insincerity but found none, and this made her relax . . . but only a little. It had been difficult, her assignment, so very, very difficult. And she'd had to do it alone.

He reached across the table and squeezed her hand. "There's no need for shame. No need for embarrassment. Your career, your performance"—he laughed with genuine mirth and tribute—"has exceeded all expectations. We are so proud of you."

"Really?" she said, switching to Russian. "You're not just saying that because you know it's what I want to hear?"

"You know me better than anyone. I could never lie to you. And even if I could, what would be the point? We're both at the apogee of this rocket ride called life, you and I, and it's not like we can change our trajectory now. Wouldn't you agree?"

"I would . . . I do," she said and smiled at him warmly.

"So," he said, taking a sip of wine, "tell me about the new DNI—Kelso Jarvis."

She didn't answer immediately, choosing to collect her thoughts on the matter first. "What would you like to know?" she said at last.

"Your personal assessment of the man."

"Stalwart, overconfident, observant, mildly misogynistic, and clever . . . The two of you would probably get on like brothers."

Arkady laughed. "I like him already. He is a former SEAL, yes?"

She nodded. "A Tier One unit commander who stepped out of the shadows and into the dark to run a black ops counterterrorism unit called Ember."

The Russian spymaster nodded and then rubbed his nose. "Okay, so in your opinion, how big of a problem is Director Jarvis going to be for us?"

"I don't know. Until now, all he's focused on is the terrorist threat. He eats, sleeps, and breathes hunting down crazy Muslims, and he's quite good at it. He's spent his entire career either planning, running, or overseeing covert counterterrorism operations in the Middle East and Africa."

"Good," Arkady said, taking a sip of wine. "He sounds like a man locked inside a paradigm. We can take advantage of that."

"Yes . . . Except now as DNI, he has been forced to open his eyes. That's why he sent me here, to meet with the Poles and discuss Russian aggression in Eastern Europe and the Baltics."

"Well, that is unfortunate, but I still would rather have Jarvis as DNI than someone like Evans, who used to sit on the Moscow desk and knows Russians."

"Can we talk about something else?" she said, reaching over and squeezing his hand.

"One more thing. Can you get close to Jarvis?"

She sighed. "I don't know."

"Is he married?"

"No."

"Good. Then you have an opening."

She rolled her eyes. "Put on your glasses, you old charmer, and take a good look at the woman across the table. My skin has gone to shit, my hair's turned silver, and the body under these clothes is not the one you remember."

"I'll be the judge of that," he said with a mischievous smile.

She felt her cheeks flush and looked down at her hands.

"You are a beautiful woman, Catherine, no matter at what age," he went on. "And I like your hair—short and silver. You look sophisticated. Powerful."

"Enough," she said. "I'm tiring of this game."

"It's not a game," he said, his expression darkening ever so slightly. "You need to try; it's what we do."

"Men like Kelso Jarvis don't generally want to sleep with old ladies who tried to submarine their careers."

"Don't be ridiculous. You're the same age as him."

She shooed the comment away with the wave of her hand.

"Has it been so long you've forgotten your own motto?"

"What motto is that?" she asked.

"You said, and I quote, 'You'd be surprised what a woman can get a man to do by telling him everything he wants to hear while maintaining an illusion of being unobtainable.'"

"I said that?"

He nodded.

She smiled wanly. "I don't remember that. Was I right?"

"It worked with me," he said.

"*Pffffit* . . . You seduced me," she said. "When I was young and naive."

"Are you saying if we met today, Maschenka, my charms would have fallen flat?"

She smiled and took a sip of wine. "I could lie to you, but what would be the point?"

He laughed like a Russian at this and then raised his glass in a toast. "To our next conquest, Kelso Jarvis."

"To our next conquest," she echoed, clinking glasses. "Now, let's eat because I'm horny and I don't know how much longer I can wait."

He snapped his fingers at a waiter walking by and asked for the check. Then, turning back to her, he said, "Forget the entrees; I'm ready for dessert."

ACKNOWLEDGMENTS

There are a lot of dedicated and talented people that go into taking our stories and making them novels. We would like to thank our entire team at Thomas & Mercer for their endless support and tireless work in keeping the Tier One series moving forward. We owe special thanks to Caitlin Alexander, our developmental editor and the very best in the business. As always, we thank Gina, our agent, who never rests until everything is right.

Thank you to our brothers and sisters in arms who are always there, at the pointy tip of the spear, keeping us safe, often from the shadows.

And more than anything we thank our families, who continue to put up with our devotion to this crazy business of storytelling. None of it happens without the support of our amazing wives and children. We love you.

GLOSSARY

- AFSOC—Air Force Special Operations Command
- AQ—Al Qaeda
- BDU—Battle Dress Uniform
- BUD/S—Basic Underwater Demolition School
- BZ—Bravo Zulu (military accolade)
- CASEVAC—Casualty Evacuation
- CENTCOM—Central Command
- CIA—Central Intelligence Agency
- CO—Commanding Officer
- CONUS—Continental United States
- CSO—Chief Staff Officer
- DNI—Director of National Intelligence
- DoD—Department of Defense
- Eighteen Delta—Special Forces medical technician and first responder
- Ember—American black-ops OGA unit led by Kelso Jarvis
- EMP—Electromagnetic pulse
- EXFIL—Exfiltrate
- FARP—Forward Area Refueling/Rearming Point
- FOB—Forward Operating Base
- HUMINT—Human Intelligence
- HVT—High Value Target

- IAEA—International Atomic Energy Agency
- IC—Intelligence Community
- IDF—Israeli Defense Forces
- INFIL—Infiltrate
- IRGC—Islamic Revolutionary Guard Corps. A branch of the Iranian Armed Forces
- IS—Islamic State
- ISIS—Islamic State of Iraq and al-Sham
- JCS—Joint Chiefs of Staff
- JO—Junior Officer
- JSOC—Joint Special Operations Command
- JSOTF—Joint Special Operations Task Force
- KIA—Killed in Action
- MARSOC—Marine Corps Special Operations Command
- MEDEVAC—Medical Evacuation
- MOIS—Iranian Ministry of Intelligence, aka VAJA / VEVAK
- Mossad—Israeli Institute for Intelligence and Special Operations
- NCO—Noncommissioned Officer
- NETCOM—Network Enterprise Technology Command (Army)
- NOC—Non-official Cover
- NSA—National Security Administration
- NVGs—Night Vision Goggles
- OGA—Other Government Agency
- OPSEC—Operational Security
- OSTP—Office of Science and Technology Policy
- OTC—Officer in Tactical Command
- PJ—Parajumper/Air Force Rescue
- QRF—Quick Reaction Force
- RPG—Rocket Propelled Grenade
- SAD—Special Activities Division

- SAPI—Small Arms Protective Insert
- SCIF—Sensitive Compartmented Information Facility
- SEAL—Sea, Air, and Land Teams, Naval Special Warfare
- SECDEF—Secretary of Defense
- SIGINT—Signals Intelligence
- SITREP—Situation Report
- SOAR—Special Operations Aviation Regiment
- SOCOM—Special Operations Command
- SOG—Special Operations Group
- SOPMOD—Special Operations Modification
- SQT—Seal Qualification Training
- SSGN—Nuclear-powered cruise missile submarine
- TAD—Temporary Additional Duty
- TOC—Tactical Operations Center
- UAV—Unmanned Aerial Vehicle
- UN—United Nations
- UNO—University of Nebraska Omaha
- USN—US Navy
- VEVAK—Iranian Ministry of Intelligence, analogue of the CIA

ABOUT THE AUTHORS

Photo © 2012 Jennifer Hensley

Photo © 2015 Wendy Wilson

Brian Andrews is a US Navy veteran who served as an officer on a 688-class fast-attack submarine in the Pacific. He is a Park Leadership Fellow and holds a master's degree in business from Cornell University. He is the author of the Think Tank series of thrillers (*The Infiltration Game*, *The Calypso Directive*). Born and raised in the Midwest, Andrews lives in Tornado Alley with his wife and three daughters.

Jeffrey Wilson has worked as an actor, firefighter, paramedic, jet pilot, and diving instructor, as well as a vascular and trauma surgeon. He served in the US Navy for fourteen years and made multiple deployments as a combat surgeon. He is the author of three award-winning supernatural thrillers: *The Traiteur's Ring*, *The Donors*, and *Fade to Black*. He and his wife, Wendy, live in Southwest Florida with their four children.

Andrews and Wilson also coauthor the Nick Foley Thriller series (*Beijing Red, Hong Kong Black*) under the pen name Alex Ryan.